HONOR OF THE CLAN

JOHN RINGO & JULIE COCHRANE

HONOR OF THE CLAN

A Baen Books Original

Baen Publishing Enterprises
P.O. Box 1403
Riverdale, NY 10471
www.baen.com

ISBN 13: 978-1-4391-3335-4

Cover art by Kurt Miller

First Baen paperback printing, February 2010

Distributed by Simon & Schuster
1230 Avenue of the Americas
New York, NY 10020

Library of Congress Control Number: 2008045912

Pages by Joy Freeman (www.pagesbyjoy.com)
Printed in the United States of America

NEED TO KNOW

"I'm sending the ACS platoon and *you*," Lieutenant General Tam Wesley said. "This thing is the political hot-potato to end all political hot-potatoes. And it has to stay *totally* black. We need someone with experience on site."

Mike O'Neal put his face in his hands again and shook his head. "Problem being, as previously discussed, I'm not sure I disagree with their objectives," he pointed out.

"Which we've discussed," Tam said. "Bottom line, General. Are you willing to take this mission and carry it out to the best of your ability?"

"Define the mission clearly," Mike said.

"Locate and eliminate hostile insurgents at specified location and detain any Indowy there present pending charges of conspiracy, rebellion and treason against the Galactic Federation. Noting that the primary mission is the capture of the Indowy there present. Try not to kill the Indowy and, frankly, try to keep all casualties to a minimum."

"May have GalTech weaponry," Mike said. "Joy. What's the nature of this enemy base?"

"No real clue," Tam said. "It's all below ground. But there are one hell of a lot of people in there."

"Tam, how much are you *not* telling me?"

"I'm telling you everything you need to know, General," Tam said. "Hell, I'm telling you everything that *I* know. Do you accept this mission?"

"I wonder if this is how General Lee felt at Harper's Ferry?" Mike muttered. "Yes, I'll do it. At least it gets me out of these Goddamned meetings! Send word to whoever needs to know that *I* need to know. When I ask a question, I'm going to need a clear and honest answer."

"I'll . . . try," Tam said.

"Try," Mike said. "Try very hard."

For

Master Corporal Erin Melvin Doyle
KIA in the Panjwayi District, Kandahar Province,
Afghanistan, 8/11/2008.
http://www.ppcli.com/files/Last_Post_Inserts/
Serving_Patricias/MCpl%20Doyle.pdf

And

SPC Ray Joseph Hutchinson (Hutch)
KIA on patrol with Alpha Co 2/502 101st Airborne
in Mosul, Iraq, 12/7/2003.
http://www.rjhfoundation.org/bio.html

They do not grow old as we who are left grow old.

And, as always:
For Captain Tamara Long, USAF
Born: May 12, 1979
Died: March 23, 2003, Afghanistan
You fly with the angels now.

PROLOGUE

Saturday, December 19, 2054

The room was ornate in a way that put rococo to shame. On the walls, many of the sub-details in the gilded reliefs incorporated fractals, so that one could have examined the gilded scenes and abstract curlicues with a microscope and not run out of exquisite detail. The base for the gilding was a white substance similar to ivory, but with an opalescent sheen that no elephant tusk could ever boast.

All in all, the effect would have given a Himmit a heart attack, had one of those worthies tried to rest on that surface, and had it had a heart. The other surfaces were similarly ornate, reducing the Himmit on the carpet to a body surface of merely gothic levels of detail that shifted quiveringly. Every hour or so, the Himmit placed a forelimb against its head, as if it was in pain.

1

In the center of the room was a large table of stone. In the stone was a sword. From the sword emanated a voice that was heavily modulated to prevent identification.

"This situation disrupts the entire plan. It is grossly unacceptable. Curse the Epetar group for clag food! What were the rest of you thinking? Progress be damned, I'll be hard pressed to salvage something other than outright war over this," he fumed.

"Abject apologies, Master." The Indowy got no further.

"Don't bother. You, yourself, didn't do it, so your apologies are hardly sincere for all that you speak for others. Shut up and let me think."

The Indowy decided that it was more likely than not to be in the interests of his clan to volunteer some information. "Master, I have news that the O'Neal is traveling to Barwhon to approach the Tchpth on a diplomatic mission," it said.

The leader of the Bane Sidhe, whoever it was, was not known for its sense of humor. Indeed, so seldom was its humor triggered that its existence was largely regarded as mythical. The Indowy before it and the Himmit in the corner were, therefore, shocked senseless when a strange sound emanated from the blade of the sword.

"Stop . . . stop . . ." it rasped. "I'm not . . . it's just . . . O'Neal . . . diplo . . . too funny." The rasping crept into its voice. For just a moment it became normal enough to make out what sounded strangely like the mellifluous tones of a Darhel.

"The greater problem still exists," the sword hummed with a last chuckle. "Whether this drives the plan backwards or advances it must be considered. I will give you orders in time. You are dismissed."

If the Himmit was affronted, neither of the other species had the experience with its expressions to discern it. The crack at the edge where the ceiling met the wall widened around the body of the Himmit as it exited, sealing back to invisibility behind it.

"O'Neal. A diplomatic mission," the sword hummed once more. "Too funny. Oooo. *I* have an idea. . . ."

Then it vanished.

CHAPTER ONE

Covered in sweat and blood
Yet still our heads held high
Actions have consequences
When you live for foolish pride
—Atreyu, "Honor"

Sunday, December 20, 2054

Major General Mike O'Neal rolled his AID, then slapped it onto his wrist forming a band. Slapped it on hard.

"Hey," Shelly said. "Don't take this out on *me*!"

"Sorry," Mike said grumpily.

He was intensely bored. Bored of gaming, bored of reading newsfeeds, bored of reading, period. Bored of watching movies, TV and every other form of video broadcast. Porn just wasn't his style but he'd even watched some of that. And found it very boring indeed.

4

In part it was his own fault. When he'd been recalled to Earth and boarded his first Fleet vessel he had treated the Fleet officers with even more disdain than usual. Fleet had, year by year, sunk lower and lower in his opinion. The officers were slovenly and corrupt, the sailors were abysmal and the only reason the ships operated at all was that they were Indowy made and damned hard to break. He'd never been the diplomatic type and his dislike of Fleet was displayed by saying he'd be in his cabin. An orderly, or whatever you called it in the Fleet, brought his meals, he made trips to the tiny gym and that was that. For the last five months the only time he'd spoken to a living soul was at starports.

The rest of it wasn't on him. First of all there was the fact of *five months* on board ships. That was just *insane*. These weren't even the bulk transports they'd used in the first part of the war. These were *Fleet* vessels, the fastest in the *universe*. But between having to hunt from star system to star system and tween-jump transits, not to mention jump transits, it just took forever to get to Earth from out on the edge of the Blight.

Then there was the recall. It read damned near as relief. Just a simple order to turn over command of the First Division to his assistant division commander and return to Earth. No clue as to why, no incoming division commander. Nada.

So five months of not speaking to a living soul and worrying, any time he let it get past his iron self-control, about what the orders meant.

Probably it meant a staff job on Earth. He'd done them. It wasn't his favorite job by a long shot but he could do the deal. But that begged the question why there wasn't an incoming division commander. And if it was just a staff job they'd probably have said that in the orders along with "and General So-And-So will be along at some point to take over the Division."

It *could* be forcible retirement. But Fleet Strike didn't have an "up or out" policy. To avoid the cronyism that was destroying Fleet, positions were purely merit based. To get his division, some younger brigadier would have to show that he was better at running the division than Mike. They rotated potential commanders in from time to time, shuffling the commander off to a staff position or sideways. But most of the time the new commanders, after a reasonable time to learn the job, went back to a lower rank or wherever the hell they'd come from. Mike and Major General Adam Lee Michie had been running divisions of the ACS corps for nigh on thirty years. Some time in and out but mostly in command. Mongo Radabaugh was the junior, having beaten out Bob Tasswell about five years ago to take over one of the division commander's slots.

Mike probably could have taken Corps at some point if he wanted it. George Driver was an excellent corps commander, no question. But Mike figured he had the edge. Thing was, Corps wasn't his style. It was a thankless job since the divisions were spread across a sizeable chunk of the galaxy clearing Posleen worlds. Corps Command was based on Avauglin, a marginally habitable "recovered" world about sixty light-years, and a month transit, from Earth.

The divisions, though, moved as a unit, lived as a unit, dropped as a unit. Mike knew every guy in the division, more or less. Hell, with the way that the

ACS hadn't been restocking, First Division wasn't much larger than a brigade. *One* of the things he planned on bringing up whatever the reason that he'd been brought back to Earth. Surely they could get *some* ACS restock. It was getting as bad as back in the Siege . . .

And here he was stuck in the loop. Again!

"Shelly, time to Titan orbit?"

"One hour and twenty-three minutes, General," the AID said liltingly. "You did well, this time. Six minutes and seventeen seconds from the last time you asked. That's up from your mean of three."

"Iron self-control, Shelly," Mike said. "Iron self-control."

"Message from General Wesley's AID," Shelly said. "You're on another shuttle from Titan to Fredericksburg immediately after landing. Quote: Get some sleep on the shuttle; briefings immediately on landing so you can quit asking Shelly what's going on. The answer is good news and bad. Close quote."

"My iron self-control is clearly well known," Mike said.

To human eyes, the Ghin was an average-looking Darhel. To human eyes, Darhel fur looked metallic gold or metallic silver, with black traces threading through it, and the Galactic's eyes a vivid green in a white sclera, laced with purple veining.

There were no humans in the office. The Tchpth who was present saw the Ghin in a rather different light. The eyes, so vivid to humans, were rather dull; but the fur glinted brightly, like the color play across anodized titanium.

"I greet you, Phxtkl. Thank you for granting me the favor of a game," the Ghin said.

"It is always a pleasure to instruct, O merely expert student of aethal."

The Tchpth bounced rapidly upon its ten legs, tapping in a sequence that was either arhythmic or too complicated for the Darhel to decode. No one knew if the Tchpth meant to give offense or not when they used blunt descriptors in speaking to others. Since they were similarly descriptive with their own, more often than not, and still seemed to interact in a functional way, the other Galactics had decided that tact was absent from the Tchpth makeup.

It didn't matter. Tact was no part of the Ghin's purpose today. He made no further commentary, but merely moved to the aethal table in the center of the room. Pieces were positioned within a holographic display.

"I wished to start from this position and play out the problem, if you would."

"You are placing me in a position of much advantage, although you are allowing yourself much opportunity. Are you sure you wish to choose this starting configuration?"

"Yes. Very sure."

"This is quite likely to be in my critique at the end of the game."

"I understand. Perhaps better than you realize."

"Ah. So you have a purpose in your choice. You make the game interesting. And, of course, your problem draws from existing conditions, with much variation."

"Of course. Many problems and configurations may arise in the game," the Ghin offered.

"Within reason, O erring and insufficiently experienced student," the Tchpth said.

Their play proceeded at a dignified rate, Phxtkl withholding commentary for most of the game, as was his custom. He would wait until major crises in a problem emerged before lecturing on errors and the alternate options which a lower ranked opponent might have selected.

Merely rating high expert in the game, the Ghin was not ranked in the Galactic standings. Tchpth and Indowy masters played him on request out of deference to his position, but equally from what the humans would call the "waltzing bear" factor. Very few Darhel treated aethal with anything other than tolerant contempt, as a meaningless distraction from the realities of power and commerce. Intangible relationships had power only so long as they were honored. Darhel only honored relationships as stipulated by contract, rendering the alliances and intricacies of aethal meaningless from their point of view. Or, more accurately, irrelevant to their own lives.

The game drew to a crisis, a positioning almost certain to weaken the Ghin's position enormously and, by extension, grossly distort the interactions of Phxtkl's pieces in an unfavorable way.

"Now it is time for my comment, O arrogant slave to physical items." The master highlighted a section of the display in a red haze. "Observe this section and how it is now cut off from the influence of your web, held by only the tiniest of threads, the minimum connection that never ends. It may seem an insignificant set of resources, but look at the potential." The Tchpth pointed to various nexus pieces above the table. "Despite the loss of face here, here, and here, or the losses in several of your tertiary relationships, this was a critical play."

"I see that. I will set up an alternate problem for just a moment," the Ghin said. He had no worry of losing the current game which was, of course, saved in his AID. If Phxtkl was surprised that the referenced alternate problem was already crafted and saved, he gave no sign, bouncing and tapping upon his low stool as always.

"Here is a starting problem. You will see the relationship to a recent past current Galactic situation. Here is the current situation. You see, of course, the likely moves if no sacrifices are made to alter the web."

The alien creature was silent for a long few moments, looking at the three displays. "I disagree with a number of the particulars of the various patterns, but . . . your overall point is taken. Isolation is loss of influence. Avoiding that is worth much. Worth enough, in this case." Phxtkl was still for a few seconds, in his species' equivalent of a deep, martyred sigh. "This is one of the least enjoyable games of aethal I have ever played, O intriguing schemer of much age. Today, I have been the student; unpleasantly so. I must make some necessary social sacrifices to continue the movement you have begun just now. I wish you success, O annoying one, and I leave."

"Leave for Earth." The Ghin was uncharacteristically blunt. "You have something to repair."

Her silver-blond hair framed her face, drawing attention to the startlingly intense, cornflower-blue eyes. Other than a subconscious awareness of the soft brushing against her face and neck as she walked, her hair was the last thing on Cally O'Neal's mind as she rubbed sweaty palms on her jeans before entering Monsignor Nathan O'Reilly's secular sanctum sanctorum.

"Cally. Good, you're here. Can I get you some water or a soft drink?" the priest inquired gently.

Uh-oh. Whenever the leader of the O'Neal Bane Sidhe started out with the kind and gentle routine, you knew you were in for it. Not that it was her fault. At least, she didn't think there was anything serious going on that was her fault. She was a bit late on her expense report for the last mission, but she'd think he'd give her some slack for blowing it off over Christmas. She had had a feeling something was wrong, but this was obviously more serious than she had thought. She allowed a wrinkled forehead to show her worry as she started to get up. There was a cooler just outside.

"Just water, I'll get it," she said.

"Sit." The gentle tone carried the force of command; he pulled a pitcher from his small refrigerator and poured her a glass.

Her eyebrows lifted as Granpa came in, sitting across and facing her. They were both facing her. She instantly noticed that Papa O'Neal had no chew, and no cup. This was not good.

"Papa, can I get you anything?"

"Nothing, thanks."

"Can I ask?" the assassin asked.

"Cally, you have got to learn not to kill someone on a job just because he's a bad man and he's in your way," the monsignor said. "In this case, he wasn't even in your way."

"What in the world was wrong with killing Erick Winchon, and if you didn't want him dead, why the hell did you send *me*? Dead's what I do."

"The Aerfon Djigahr was your target, not Winchon," Papa pointed out. "Also, if you remember, *we* didn't pick you for this mission, your sister did. Not that we wouldn't have anyway. Personally, I think the little prick looked a lot better as a corpse, granddaughter, but there have been . . . complications."

"Michelle said she could deal with all that." She absently brushed her hair back, tucking the strands behind her ear.

"No, she said she'd *try*," O'Reilly said. "It didn't work. We've been disavowed."

"Disavowed by who and why? I thought violent mass-murderer scumbags like Winchon were persona non grata with *all* the races."

"The Tchpth, the Himmit, the Indowy with whom we still *had* a minimal backdoor relationship," the monsignor said with a sigh. "Thank God Aelool and Beilil felt too much personal responsibility to join the exodus. The whole reason the Crabs wanted Pardal dead was that plotting the death of one of only five emergent human mentats, the beginning of our species' enlightenment, was a far *worse* evil. Turns out, they viewed it as a problem on the scale of the Posleen war. That is the *only* reason they authorized the killing of Pardal, to protect Michelle. And then you have to go and kill one of the *other* four mentats!"

"He was a freaking psychopath," Cally said. "A powerful and dangerous one for that matter."

"They feel they could have managed that," O'Reilly

said, holding up his hand to forestall a reply. "The point is, I've tried to find words to describe to you how angry they are, and I can't come up with anything remotely adequate."

"Like a kicked hornet's nest?" Papa said.

"Angry like a supernova is hot?" Cally asked.

"Angry like I'll get if you two can't take this *seriously*!" O'Reilly shouted. "Cut off. NO support. None! *Totally* on our own!"

"We've got funding," Cally pointed out, shrugging. "A lot more funding than we did before this went down."

"Would you care to consider what we *don't* have?" O'Reilly asked sarcastically. "Just consider the following. No access to GalTech. No access to Galactic medicines. No access to Galactic injury care, not nannites, not even a tank much less a slab. We don't even have *human* medical support. The next time you get seriously injured, you'd better be able to do internal surgery, Cally, because otherwise you're going to *die* for real and for certain."

"Oh," Cally said.

"No access to GalTech weaponry," O'Reilly pointed out, turning to Papa. "No plasma weapons. No gravguns. No armor. No plasteel. No logistic support except what the Clan can provide. And entirely out of Clan funds instead of the trickle of continued support we got. We're entirely on our own for buying ammo for what weapons we've got or buy on the open market. Only our own access to black market."

"Stewart can help there," Cally said.

"Minimally," Papa pointed out. "Unless you want to get my son-in-law killed."

"Not . . . usually," Cally said.

"No access to Bane Sidhe intel," O'Reilly continued. "Or Himmit. No—"

"Okay," Cally said. "Okay. Got the picture. I fucked up. I was under a certain amount of pressure at the time."

"Not a good enough excuse for the mess you've created," O'Reilly said. "However, even though you were *intimately* involved in the unfolding of this mess, I can't figure out a way to help in the salvage operation."

"Yes, sir. No excuse, Father," she said.

"Cally, what were you thinking?" O'Reilly asked.

"I made a serious mission planning error, sir, and I was winging it."

"Quit sirring me, this isn't the army."

"Yes, sir—I mean, yes, Father." She watched him sigh and knew it wasn't the response he'd been looking for.

"In any case, you're not here for a dressing down. Or, more accurately, I'm done. What you're here for is a joint Clan/Organization planning meeting," the priest said, sitting down in a chair next to Papa's.

It wasn't what she'd expected to hear. Cally decided it was a very good opportunity to keep her mouth shut.

"My own mistakes in this debacle include not having pulled your grandfather behind a desk, doubtless kicking and screaming, ten or fifteen years ago. My reasons seemed good at the time." He sighed. "Hindsight is twenty-twenty." The young-looking old man rubbed his thumb and forefinger together, fingering rosary beads that weren't there.

"They say that infantry captain is the best job in the

army. Every generation, every new crop of captains, has to face the same fact—you can't be a captain forever. Operations is fun."

"You're pulling me from the field," she said woodenly.

"I certainly would if I could, but we don't have a good replacement. And we're down on support for training. Right now, with Direct Action Group no longer being trained by the Federation and both you and Papa in the field, we're effectively eating our seed-corn. Your DAG recruits aren't ready to do covert ops. So you're going to have to do the two-hat shuffle and train them."

"Can I ask what the other one is?"

"You just did. We cannot survive without Galactic allies. We need raw materials, transportation, tools, technology, information. These are all things they have, that we need. Papa here is going to have to put on his clan-head hat and go play diplomat for us."

"Granpa? Diplomat . . . ? Have you gone *bonkers*?"

"Why does everyone react that way?" Papa asked. "I'm a perfectly diplomatic person."

Nathan gave Cally a wry grin.

"He's the only one who can," the monsignor said, serious again. "As bad as things are, they'll only meet with a clan head—O'Neal's clan head. We're all going to be making some sacrifices and doing things we'd rather not. From the point of view of the Galactics, the *only* way to ensure that Clan O'Neal isn't going to go rogue, again, is to have agreements with the Clan Leader."

"If I promise you won't kill any more of the *nomenklatura* without authorization, they'll accept that as an unbreakable promise," Papa said. "Which it *will* be, granchile o' mine."

"Yes, O Great and Powerful Oz," Cally said flippantly.

"Which means that we're all going to have to be doing things we'd rather not," O'Reilly said. "I will be without my right arm, for example, since he'll have to go with Pàpa. His assistant will therefore have to speed up her learning curve, something that is good for her but not welcome. Which brings us to your second job. Although in normal line of succession your father would be clan head, that's not . . . appropriate at this time. You will, therefore, be acting clan head in your grandfather's absence."

"Which means you get all the headaches of running Clan O'Neal," Papa said with an evil grin. "Like herding Bengal tigers that is."

Cally felt the beginnings of a crushing sensation in her chest, her face automatically defaulting to an expressionless mask. Perversely, the first coherent thought to wander through her head was that this would ruin Christmas, and how was she going to tell Shari.

"Don't get used to that feeling," O'Reilly said. "You have *a lot* of material to cover, and then you can expect a lot of practical work. In an area that is about as far from your skill set as any I can imagine."

"Nailed that one," Cally said, trying not to grin.

"Hush," the monsignor said, suppressing a chuckle. It wasn't a moment for humor. "If you see less than a ten hour day the whole trip, praise God for the break."

Cally took the opportunity to grab her grandfather in a tight bear hug, loosening up when he grunted from the pressure of her Crab-upgraded muscles.

"Good luck in the lion's den," she said.

"Good luck to you in the hot seat. See you when I get back. If you get a chance, hug your sister for me."

In the hall, she watched him walk away, O'Reilly's

deputy at his elbow, until they turned and were out of sight.

The first thing Michelle noticed when she entered her construction bay an hour before Adenast's nominal start time was the unaccustomed emptiness of the bay. A lone employee sat at the far end of the bay, headset engaged, holding the existing products static. She recognized him as one of the Sohon masters. Below adept level, the masters were the middle managers whose coordination skills, paired with their technical competence, glued each project together by mutual communication and ensuring everybody knew his or her assigned tasks. Everything from starships to the enormous building control machines grew whole in a single tank, a massive endeavor requiring years of effort by a single family—"family" for Indowy could encompass generations of an older breeding group— and it all had to be coordinated by the masters. Mental visions of the project had to remain in tune, and across multiple work shifts. Apprentices had to feed the great tanks with needed raw materials on a precise schedule and at precise input loci to support local control of the necessary reactions. In the rare but inevitable case when one of the experts found an engineering issue in the design, it was the masters who coordinated with the adepts to design a fix and communicate the revised design image to every member of the production team.

In the current case, the Indowy Iltai Halaani sat on a stool at one end of the bay, headset connected to all the tanks with an absurd spaghetti tangle of wiring, holding all the tanks in a stable state. Work had stopped. Michelle walked to the center of the bay and turned full circle, absorbing the sight. She had expected the response, once word got back to Adenast that she had at last been compelled by circumstance to see her clan head. With that meeting ended the polite fiction that the estrangement of the human Clan O'Neal from the rest of the Indowy species did not reach to Adenast. Clan Aelool and Clan Beilil had remained aligned with O'Neal in the Bane Sidhe split of 2047. Aelool was minuscule, and had a paltry three breeding groups on Adenast, and those refugees lived completely on the other side of the world. Beilil was also quite small, one of the smaller groups reoccupying the most habitable portions of Dulain.

Despite growing up there, Michelle O'Neal had no pressing reason to live and work on Adenast rather than relocating to Dulain—no reason except for the contracted projects in the middle of construction in this very bay. Once again, she faced a life or death situation. If she could not complete her projects on time, within specified variations of delivery, theoretically she could be hauled into contract court and her debts called in. With the troubles the Darhel Epetar Group was having from their recently foiled plot to do just that, she doubted another group would court similar disaster. Also, one of her projects had been contracted by the Epetar Group. In the likely event of its default, she would have to write a new contract with a new buyer. A building main control system wouldn't lack for demand, and she could write its contract for delivery as late as she had to, effectively keeping the project in abeyance for years.

Her mind busily calculated the options. What was

that saying? *I expected this, but not so soon.* Her problem was that she would have to exquisitely coordinate schedules and new project deadlines to move her operations, picking up lower-return short-term work as the long-term projects completed. It would cost a great deal of FedCreds, and further her debt. It was possible but only if she had the workers to get those coordinated projects to completion. The Aelools had contracts. She might be able to find a couple of Beilil families who were between contracts and could help her wind up her operation in the interim, but her work was large. There was low probability that their help would be enough, and the scheduling delays while they traveled from Dulain to Adenast were going to be prohibitive.

It wouldn't be enough.

Her mind turned the problem over like a game of aethal laid out on the board. It was a losing board, but her highly skilled gamesmanship refused to stop gnawing away at the problem.

The Aelools were not blacklisted. It was possible she could get the Adenast families to swap out other-clan replacements for *their* current projects. If she could persuade them, she could have the Adenast Aelools relocated and working in any time between one and ten days. Three breeding groups could take on one eighth of her current projects, and she could make all but one of her immediate deadlines for the Group most likely to be hard cases about her "issues."

The problem there was that Beilil, while remaining friendly with O'Neal, did not owe much of a favor balance to the clan. She'd have to get the word to Dulain, get groups with the right skill mix re-tasked, get those groups to Adenast for even the most temporary of jobs. She calculated best and worst case estimates. It was an impossible task.

If Grandfather's diplomatic mission to Barwhon was a complete success, he might succeed in mending relations with at least one of the major clans on Adenast. The Koolanai Clan who raised her were, on the whole, quite fond of her. They, reasonably, felt that her high achievement reflected well on them and brought their own clan honor. Or, they had. If Clan O'Neal's reputation was restored, they stood to gain as much as anyone. They were also one fourth of her work force.

Clan Roolnai was her real problem. They had staked a lot of personal reputation on the collaboration with humans, albeit covertly through the Bane Sidhe, and were furious at the embarrassment caused by the now near-universal public opinion verdict of humanity's irredeemable mass insanity.

Since 2047 she'd held her Roolnai workers through force of personality, sheer will, and a very liberal hand with favors to the breeding groups contracted for her project. That same liberality with favors had prevented her from replacing Roolnai families with Koolanai families as several projects had completed and been replaced with new work.

The bottom line was that without some kind of give from the Indowy Roolnai, she was toast. Maybe not dead, but in so unenviable a debt position that her carefully nurtured ability to pick and choose her projects would be gone for life. She'd have to take whatever projects would give her the best short-term profit, like crumbs from the Darhel tables.

However, if Grandfather agreed it was useful to

the Clan, trickling in the credits she'd won for the O'Neals by "fencing" the level nine code keys would gradually pull her back up, but slowly, so slowly as to stretch even a mentat's long-term view.

First, try the obvious, she thought, resisting the temptation to smack herself on the forehead. She walked the length of the bay, using the transit belts to cover the vast distance, until she stood beside Iltai Halaani. "I will take over this task. Please convey my regards to the Indowy Roolnai and pass on to him my humble request that he agree to see me on a matter of importance to his clan."

"Indowy Roolnai, I see you," she said, rising effortlessly to her feet.

She had been honestly worried he wouldn't come. If he hadn't, it would have spelled ruin.

Iltai Haalani had accompanied the clan head back to the bay and, as they had come in at the end where she'd been keeping vigil over her work, he was able to immediately resume control of the tanks, freeing her for discourse with the clan head.

"Human Michelle O'Neal, I see you," Roolnai replied politely, his green-furred face blank of all expression.

"I appreciate your great kindness in coming to meet me personally," she said.

The Indowy inclined his head in acknowledgment, an expressive gesture common to both species. "Knowing you, I am sure you would not represent a matter as important to my clan if it was not."

A warning. He was prepared to hear her out, but not favorably inclined, and not disposed to spend any great time on the meeting. "I notice that the workers on these projects are absent today," Michelle got right to the core of the problem.

"Did you expect otherwise?" he asked.

"No. Not under the circumstances. I did, however, hope that they might remain while Clan O'Neal reorganized obligations with allied labor."

"Such action is not customary in the circumstances. The clans who formerly worked on these projects are at odds with Clan O'Neal. How can the estranged exchange favors?"

"I recognize that Clan Roolnai and Clan Halaani have already been more than kind."

"You had not yet communicated with your clan head. How could we decently proceed without allowing time for both sides to receive the news?"

She accepted the polite fiction for what it was—a recognition of her own history of proper loolnieth towards her clan.

"In my . . . news . . . from the O'Neal, he also communicated his intention to travel to Barwhon and attempt to restore relations with the Tchpth," she offered. Leaving out the chronology also preserved necessary fictions about the speed of communications and related matters for discretion.

"Interesting news," he said, ears twitching in surprise. "Still, the nature of the breach is of a delicate kind, possibly unmendable."

The Indowy deciding humanity was fundamentally insane qualified as unmendable if anything did. Her only hope lay in introducing doubt in that conclusion.

"Perhaps. You are aware that certain intriguers among my race massively altered their brain chemistry."

There. Frame the "insanity" as artificially induced by primitive medical practices.

"The Indowy Clans, as all civilized races, recognize consumption of flesh as a dangerously primitive trait." Roolnai shuddered at the word "flesh." "There are natural concerns about such a species from the very beginning."

"Of course. But the 'beginning,' as you say, goes back far beyond the present eye-blink. Your race has a great deal of experience of mine, and of your clans engaging with ours."

Again the clan head's ears twitched, surprised. "I suppose it is to be expected that you would be better informed than other humans. Your observation is true. It is also true that human clan structure has weakened, particularly in the survivors of the great slaughter, and many clans have judged that change not to be for the better. Including my own. Advancing medical care an infant's step is all very well, but if the fundamental cause lies elsewhere. . . ."

"Recent events, deplorable though they have been, should properly mitigate one of the causes for concern. However horrific the events, the O'Neal's judgment of the value to our very small clan of a particular member has in some measure been vindicated. Primitive skills, but a link in the chain not only to Clan O'Neal survival but to Path value that even the Tchpth acknowledged."

"You would speak to me of *that*?"

He was stiff with rage, as she had expected, given the bloody nature of her sister's skills—and actions. Still, her case largely rested on the proved truth that Grandfather's choice to rescue Cally, in violation of the will of a large chunk of the Bane Sidhe, was not mere sentiment, but rationally in the interests of Clan O'Neal and not adverse to its then-allies. She had no doubt that Grandfather's choice *was* based entirely on human two-way loyalty and his personal sense of honor, with sentiment to sweeten the pot, but the Indowy understanding of human xenopsychology was limited. The Indowy Roolnai was not, in the next five minutes, going to come to an understanding of why two-way loyalty was a survival advantage for human clans. She had to use the argument that would work—she hoped.

"Primitive. Abhorrent. But the action was not only arguably necessary to Clan O'Neal's vital interests, it also *appeared*," she strongly emphasized the word, "*appeared* so favorably tied to Galactic interests and the safety of the Path itself that even the Tchpth believed those abilities were strictly necessary. Outside precedent, but necessary. I concede that aspects of the outcome were overwhelmingly unfortunate—"

Roolnai's expression of complete revulsion told her she'd better win him over fast or she'd have lost her chance.

"The Tchpth are wiser than all of us. If their wisest, for a time, believed the *Path itself* was at stake, how can the Clans judge the same decision to be insane in a species all admit is underdeveloped and primitive? How can one judge a species, even a clan, on the action of one member who, under the greatest possible stresses and absent full information, took an action that the *Tchpth* contemplated?"

The Galactic turned away from her, breathing slowly and carefully, in an action reminiscent of the Darhel breathing exercises. Emotional control was not vital to his continued existence as it was for theirs. That did not negate his need to recover it. After a long moment he turned back to face her.

"We may have acted in excessive haste. *May*," he emphasized.

"When a breach is not sure, a small favor of keeping families on their current, well-paid contracts while the matter is under consideration is surely not unusual."

"When you were personally in danger, I saw no emotion for yourself—which is only proper. Now, with far more of your clan's interests at stake, emotion leaks through despite yourself. Knowing your professionalism and dedication to the Path, that is no small thing. This is what persuades me. Clan Roolnai will agree to continuing this exchange of favors with Clan O'Neal for the present. I feel confident that Clan Halaani, having an even closer personal tie in the matter, will take a similar view. And, as you say, the Tchpth are wiser than we, and farther along the Path. We will permit time for the reconsideration."

Oh my. Grandfather, I hope you do a very good job, she thought. *I cannot believe that my lapse in control was the deciding factor. Even for me, what my sister says holds true: alien minds are alien.*

Before he turned to go, Roolnai's face crinkled in amusement. "Some of your workers may not arrive back until tomorrow morning. I understand many have taken the opportunity to do something with their children. I believe *that* is something our species have in common."

CHAPTER TWO

"General O'Neal," the lieutenant colonel said, saluting as Mike stepped out of the aircar. "Welcome to Fredericksburg Base." The colonel was tall, slim, so racially mixed it was anyone's guess the inputs, and wearing the tabs of an aide to a lieutenant general. Mike vaguely recognized him but that could be said about most of the senior officers in Fleet Strike.

"Thank you," Mike replied, waving a hand at his head.

"General Wesley has you blocked out for an hour starting, well, now, General," the colonel said. "But he said if you're fatigued from your travels . . ."

"I've been sitting on ships for five months," Mike said, gesturing toward the front entrance. "It's not hard work."

"Yes, *sir*," the colonel said. "It's this—"

"I know where the Chief of Staff's office is, Colonel," Mike said, putting an edge on his tone. "Just *go*."

✧   ✧   ✧

"Lieutenant Colonel Timmons looked a bit put out," General Wesley said as Mike grabbed a chair.

"He's so perfectly polished I'm surprised you noticed," Mike said.

"I'm pushing eighty and he's been my aide for five years," Tam said. "I can read him like a book if not the other way around, no matter what he thinks."

"I guess he's used to generals being 'fatigued by their travels,'" Mike said. "Which I am but mostly I want to know why in the hell I was yanked out of command like I'd screwed the Tir Dol Ron's daughter or something. So, with all due respect, if you could get right to the point, whatever it is."

"You're promoted, Lieutenant General," Tam said. "You're getting Eleventh Corps. That's the basic. You need some expansion. Veritable teams of people will fully expand, but that's the basic."

"I don't *want* Corps," Mike said. "I really *really* don't want Corps. I don't want Corps, I don't want your job and I don't want FS command or I'd have worked to get any of the three and probably gotten them. We've *discussed* this."

"Corps is going to be division sized and move as one unit," Tam said. "I *said* it was only the basics."

Mike set down his AID, which had been displaying the provisional TOE for the new "unified" Eleventh Corps and shrugged.

"You know, you can give me the rank and you can *call* this a corps but it's more like a full division again," Mike said. "Putting a lieutenant general in charge of this, not to mention major generals in these 'divisions,' is just paying extra salaries. And what's General Michie going to do?"

"He's less than thrilled by the new TOE," Tam said. "And uninterested in roaming around the Blight digging out Posleen. So he'll retire shortly after you assume command. He *likes* his current job. I felt like a heel when I told him it was going away."

"So . . . why is it going away?" Mike asked. "There's work to be done out there. We need more bodies, not fewer."

"You and I both know that's not true," Tam said. "So don't try to play that line. I'd have kept the numbers up, anyway. I've been keeping them up as much as I can manage. But reality and politics, especially some really goofy stuff, is making it impossible. Some of this you're going to get in your briefings. Some of it's too closely held for those. You ready? Or are you 'fatigued by your travels'?"

"Go," Mike said, pulling out a can of dip and holding it up. "If you don't mind, General, sir?"

"I've known you for fifty years," Tam said, sighing. "If you don't dip, bad things happen. Okay, Item One, which will be covered in some of the briefings. Getting the funding for more suits out of the Darhel has become flat impossible. But not just because they're cheap, which is what the briefings will cover. There's other stuff."

"And the other stuff is . . . ?"

"Remember when General Stewart was killed in the shuttle accident?" Tam asked.

"Seven years or so ago," Mike said. "Time differentials are killer, but about that . . ."

"Well, let's back up a little from there," Tam said,

his jaw working. "The question is always what to leave in and what to leave out."

"Start at the beginning . . ." Mike said, frowning. "What does James have to do with not getting funding?"

"The beginning . . ." Tam said. "The problem is, we don't know the beginning."

"If you're talking about the Darhel," Mike said. "I'd go with first contact."

"Which was when?" Tam said, raising an eyebrow. "I'll start with that, though. When it became apparent that the Darhel knew a lot more about us than we knew about them, the U.S. military formed a small group to try to penetrate their information systems and figure out exactly what their background was in regards to humans. And, hell, just stuff about what the Darhel and the other Galactics were. They've always been less than forthcoming about their history and background."

"Hume," Mike said, frowning. "Why does that name stand out? Standard academic type one each. Crazy hair, head in the clouds. I was less than impressed."

"Which was the intent, from the information I've gotten," Tam said. "And it didn't work. He was assassinated along with his top xeno guy about the time you shipped out for Diess."

"Assassinated?" Mike said, frowning. "You sure?"

"There was a lot of that for a while," Tam said. "DoD ended up losing over six teams of investigators over the period of the war."

"To whom?" Mike asked angrily. "That's insane."

"The Darhel tried to pin it on another group, which I'll get to," Tam said. "But it was the Darhel. They really don't like us prying into their background. But then we sort of called a truce. Have you ever heard of the Protocol?"

"Plenty of protocols," Mike said. "But that has a capital on it, doesn't it?"

"Big one," Tam agreed. "I know you remember when General Taylor was assassinated."

"Clear as day," Mike said. "Despite the fact that I was in the middle of a murthering great battle. And I'm not much of a conspiracy theorist but I never bought that it was Free Earth. He told me he'd been investigating the hack during the battle of Daleville and then he's taken out. I put it on Cyber, frankly."

"Backwards, again," Tam said. "Here's the truth as far as anyone can determine without lie detectors. The Darhel arranged the hack. Taylor had come to the same conclusion. The Darhel assassinated him, or rather had him assassinated. Cyber, in retaliation, took out five major Darhel on Earth along with some of the Darhel assassin groups. Cyber was assisted by still another group called the Bane Sidhe. When it was all over the Darhel agreed to not attack human military personnel nor interfere in a direct fashion in military affairs. The Cybers and Bane Sidhe agreed to not assassinate any more Darhel. And we agreed to stop investigating the background of the Federation."

"That is insane!" Mike said.

"More like xenic," Tam said, frowning. "It actually made the Darhel rather happy. We were acting like Darhel."

"That's sort of what I mean," Mike said. "Why the hell are we dealing with these bastards?"

"Oh, it's worse than that," Wes said. "The Darhel

worked very hard to make sure we nearly lost the war. They're afraid of us, Mike. Very afraid. And they should be. They can't fight. So they have tried very hard to neuter us militarily just like they neutered the Indowy politically. They've completely coopted the Fleet. Fleet Strike is the only remaining really functional military unit. They can't get rid of us completely. The Posleen remain a threat, even if a much reduced one. They need us to keep making sure they don't reconstruct. But they don't want us to be a real power. Humans in general and Fleet Strike in particular."

"That's why they're cutting back on the ACS," Mike said. "Well, they'd better. Because if I had my druthers I'd wipe them the fuck out. For Daleville if nothing else."

"So would I," Wesley said. "But we can't and you know it. They're the nerve system of the Federation. Take them out and it would become total chaos. So we have to live with them. They don't assassinate our military personnel, including most particularly generals, and humans don't declare open war on the Darhel. At which point that group I mentioned, the Bane Sidhe, become of rather greater importance."

"So who are what are . . . is the Bane Sidhe?" Mike said, tilting his head as he tried to figure out the grammar.

"The Bane Sidhe is an underground group of rebels against the Darhel," Wes said. "That's the simple answer. They are mostly among the Indowy . . ."

"Wait," Mike said, giggling. "Indowy *rebels*? What do they do, send pointed memos?"

"They penetrate the Darhel for information," Wes said, his face blank. "Very, very thoroughly."

"Oh," Mike said, suddenly serious. "And they pass that information to . . . ?"

"Mostly they just seem to collect it like misers," Wes said with a sigh. "Look, we don't know a lot about the Bane Sidhe. They also have a very serious counterintelligence capability. But this is what we know and suspect. First of all, there's the name. Does it sound familiar?"

"It doesn't sound Indowy or Darhel," Mike said. "Or Crab for that matter."

"It's not, it's Gaelic," Wes said. "It translates as Killer of Elves. The Darhel Killers in other words."

"Why Gaelic?" Mike asked. "I take it that's the name for the human component."

"No," Wes said. "It is the name of the overall group, which existed prior to *this* contact."

"So there was prior contact," Mike said, nodding. "That was pretty evident but . . ."

"But now we get back around to why the Bane Sidhe matter to Fleet Strike," Tam said. "First of all, they're a rebel group against the Federation as it's currently constituted. As I pointed out, much as we may both hate the Darhel, taking them out is out of the question absent creating something to replace them and having it in place beforehand. Otherwise we're faced by a widespread civil war. Which would give the Posleen time to recover and then, depending on how long the war took and what replaced the Federation, we'd be back in a hole. Given the weapons that could be used in such a war, Earth might not survive. I don't want that sort of war. Not now. Not absent some way to make sure it doesn't go insane."

"And they do?" Mike asked.

"We're not sure what their goals and aims are except taking out the Darhel," Wesley said. "But recently there have been several developments. The first is that we finally turned a human Bane Sidhe and got some serious information about their internal structure. At least on the human side. We were . . . somewhat surprised to find that their main human component is called the Clan O'Neal," he added with a smile.

"O'Neal?" Mike said. "Why?"

"The agent never explained. Just that their main combat component, which was broken down into several teams, used that as its name. For that matter, there was a Team Papa, Team Cally, etc."

"Bastards," Mike said, his face hard. "How fucking *dare* they?"

In many ways the loss of his wife, father and daughter in the war was as fresh today as it had been sixty years ago.

"I believe it's intended as a compliment," Tam said, carefully.

"I don't give a shit," Mike said. "Pisses me off. I take it you're getting to why we care about these guys. Besides that they're pissing me off."

"General Stewart was the investigation commander . . ." General Wesley said.

"Did those bastards kill Stewart?" Mike asked angrily.

"We're told no," Tam said. "Can I get more than a half sentence out, please?"

"Go," Mike said.

"Yes, sir," Wesley said, smiling.

"Sorry, General," Mike said, nodding. "Please continue, sir."

"General Stewart was the commander of the investigation. But he wanted more than the mole who was fairly low level. So he set up a trap. He let information leak out that a) we had a mole and b) the information on who the mole was was in a particular Fleet Strike office. Then General Stewart took a position as an aide in the office and eventually caught the agent the Bane Sidhe sent in to try to find the information. Well, caught the agent just *after* they sent out the information."

"So we lost the mole," Mike said.

"We lost the mole," Wesley agreed. "But we'd captured one of their top agents with far more information. She was, in fact, the Team Leader for Team Cally."

"Bitch," Mike said, shaking his head.

"As you say," Wesley said. "Female, twenties . . . Maybe."

"Maybe?" Mike said.

"Maybe twenties, maybe older than us," Tam said. "Her level of bioengineering was just unreal. Most of the investigators couldn't figure out how her body could work. All of her surface genetics, right down to intestinal epithelials, were those of the Fleet Strike captain she'd replaced."

"What happened to the captain?" Mike asked.

"Turned up afterwards alive and unharmed," Tam said. "But about the agent. Never found out a real name. DNA was so screwed around it was impossible to tell what was originally hers. Muscular enhancements, neural enhancements including to the brain. Rejuv but not standard. Something different. Resistant to every interrogation drug, resistant to pretty much every drug up to and including alcohol, LSD, morphine . . ."

"Christ," Mike said, frowning. "Where did she get all those enhancements?"

"Wouldn't we like to know," Tam said, smiling thinly. "But Fleet took over the interrogation. And then they lost her."

"Killed trying to escape?" Mike asked, his face tight.

"More like escaped," Tam said, shaking his head. "Oh, first reported as having died during interrogation. One gets the impression the interrogation was rather hostile and physical. But then it was 'probable successful escape.' Shortly afterwards, General Stewart died in a shuttle accident."

"And you say it's not these Bane Sidhe bastards?" Mike asked with a snort.

"We were informed that they had nothing to do with it," Tam said. "After the incident with the agent we became *officially* aware of the Bane Sidhe. And with official awareness we could open up the sort of back-channels that always exist between intelligence groups. They are insistent that they had nothing to do with General Stewart's death. Then there's the other kicker."

"Don't leave me waiting," Mike said.

"From our perspective, prior to this incident, the Protocol is that we don't investigate pre-war contact between the Darhel and humans and the Darhel stop killing off our investigation teams. It wasn't until we established a back-channel to the Bane Sidhe that we found out about the other side, that if the Darhel kill military personnel the Bane Sidhe start killing Darhel again."

"So are they on our side or what?" Mike asked.

"You begin to understand the complexity," Tam said. "Thus on to the next level. A year ago there was a major shake-up among the Darhel. Among other things, the Epetar Group went out of business and the Clan Leader suffered lintatai."

"Hooray," Mike said with a grin.

"Yeah, great," Tam said. "The problem being, it wasn't just bad business practices. At least, not the normal sort. What, exactly, happened I'm not even too sure. But we *know* the following. There was an Epetar facility here on Earth conducting classified research having to do with 'neurological interfacing.'"

"I thought the Darhel were dead set against that," Mike said.

"Well, for one thing, their research wasn't anything to do with neurological interfacing," Tam said. "What, exactly, they were researching we're not too sure. What we're sure of is that SOCOM got a heads up that there might be a 'terrorist' attack on the facility. There was such an attack. DAG was sent in to secure the facility and arrest the terrorists. DAG, instead, switched sides."

"I'd heard they were going deep undercover or something," Mike said. "They went rogue?"

"They went rogue," General Wesley said. "Which should have been the end of it. But there was an additional . . . event, the nature of which we're still trying to figure out and the building is now essentially slagged. What slagged it, why it was slagged, how many of DAG escaped, why they went rogue . . . All unanswered questions. Except one. The 'terrorists' were Bane Sidhe."

"This 'Clan' that names themselves after my family," Mike said.

"Yes," Tam said. "And that apparently has SOCOM totally penetrated. Two of the members of DAG were long-service, back to before the war, veterans. Two members did not go rogue. They're the only people we've been able to question. Everything else about the event has been put under a gigantic tarp that is way above our pay level. Everyone that is anyone in the Federation hierarchy wants to pretend nothing ever happened. So then we get to Epetar. Epetar came apart shortly thereafter. The clan head died of lintatai apparently when he realized the entire clan was going out of business. But as a result of some recent actions, especially by Clan O'Neal, the Darhel have opened up about the Bane Sidhe to the level of admitting their existence and admitting that they, the Darhel, are now taking 'more aggressive' actions against them."

"And, again, I say 'Hooray!'" Mike said.

"And I repeat, do we really want to deal with a full-up civil war?" General Wesley said. "The Darhel are the ugly little glue that hold this whole shebang together. This isn't the Boston Tea Party. If there's a full-up civil war, the first thing the Darhel will do is use the Fleet to do orbital interdiction and WMD strikes. And if you don't think Fleet will hit U.S. population centers, think again. Not to mention off-Earth colonies, Strike bases if Strike goes against them, etc. Then there's simply the disruption that would occur system-wide. Famine, breakdowns. It would be a tremendous jug-fuck that would permit, among other things, a breathing room for the Posleen to start getting their act back together. Two hundred and eighty-three worlds with some Posleen presence. Including *Earth*."

"But the Bane Sidhe are also the ones ensuring this . . . Mexican stand-off over assassinations," Mike said.

"Again, you begin to see the complexity," Tam answered with a sigh. "One thing that we've been told is that Fleet Strike may have to be used against 'insurrectionists including but not limited to groups of Bane Sidhe operating on Earth in unrecovered, recovered or fully-controlled zones.'"

"Well, if it's this Clan O'Neal I'll be more than happy to teach them a lesson about using my name," Mike said.

"And you probably will," Tam said. "Thus to the real reason that you're here. Reconstructing the Corps down to division strength is the cover. The real reason you're here is that if we end up in a furball with these guys, you're going to have to take control."

"Confused," Mike said. "I'm a Lieutenant General now, sort of. That's the sort of thing you assign to a captain. At least if we're talking ACS."

"DAG went rogue, remember?" Tam said. "With the Bane Sidhe. Which means that like as not, what you're going to be fighting is *DAG*. Which is no slouch unit."

"Ouch," Mike said. "Still, with ACS . . ."

"If they have advanced weaponry?" Tam said.

"Which they would get . . . where?" Mike asked. "Sure, there's some pretty heavy stuff sold for defense on Earth, but even the common plasma rifles aren't a real threat to ACS."

"They've got Indowy support," Tam said, smiling thinly. "So don't think they've only got civilian weapons."

"Ouch again," Mike said, rubbing his chin. "There's better stuff for fighting ACS than has ever been produced. We looked at it a long time back, but there were heavy grav rifles specifically designed to crack armor. Producing it, though, requires . . . Indowy."

"You begin to get the picture," Tam said. "You're the best combat technician we have, period. That's the first reason you're going to be involved if it comes down to a full-up firefight with these human Bane Sidhe. What we have here on Earth is a reinforced platoon of ACS for heavy defense and training. If it comes down to using ACS, that's all you've got to work with. DAG had fifty people and there's an unknown larger group of humans that has some combat capability. Couple that with really heavy weaponry and one platoon of ACS might not do it. You, however, are a force multiplier. The second reason is that you know the full political background. It might be that you'll have to throw some or all of the fight. It might be that we *need* some of these guys to survive. But it can't appear that we're in collusion with them. That would mean the Darhel would take Strike apart like a chicken."

"Well, that's a lovely set of parameters I've been handed," Mike said.

"That's why you get paid the big bucks," General Wesley said.

"And all to keep the Darhel swilling at the trough."

"The alternative to which is mass civil war," Wesley said. "Try to break the Darhel in all seriousness and they'll use human surrogates against any rebel group. We, that being people who believe in freedom and the right of people to choose their own masters, might win in the end but in the meantime the casualty levels will be astronomical and it gives the Posleen a chance to regroup."

"It's going to have to be done someday," Mike said. "Humans aren't going to just take Darhel hegemony forever."

"Agreed," Wesley said. "But not today."

In a small, modestly gilded office on the major transition station for the Prall System, a Darhel looked at the material coming in from his AID and sighed. As a senior over-manager in the Epetar Group, he was far enough up the corporate chain to reflect his extraordinary talent, but too far down the chain to have any real effect on events of this magnitude. He was, however, fortuitously placed to see the obvious Indowy collaboration in the ruining of his group by the Gistar Group. There was enough shifting around in the human communities to show they were in it up to their necks as well.

Personally, he was well and truly fucked. The assets of his group would go to pay default judgments. He, personally, was in the same position as an Indowy whose contract had just been called. His fellows in the group would be, no doubt were, dropping like flies as the disaster drove them to fatal rage and lintatai. Any few with the sense to forbear would be in the same position he was, unless they could get taken in by another group to do the lowest of shit jobs, like administering the out-station in some crappy food planet's system—positions informally called "junior assistant factor for dirt."

He was calm, but unlike his experience of his whole post-adolescent life, his emotional control was not going to be sufficient to even begin to solve his basic problems. Very well.

Fucked-over Indowy had their clans to consider. They'd sit and starve to avoid hurting their clans. Lalon had no one. It was the normal, satisfactory state of things. He was *not* Indowy. He was Darhel. Which meant he had every incentive to take as many bastards with him as possible.

The first thing to consider was that no interests got in line for money until actual contract execution or valid default judgment. Epetar's total insolvency was inevitable; it would certainly crash in the red, but that would take time. Time enough to put a few debts and payments at the front of the line. He began dictating his analysis, his wishes, and his contractual offer into his AID.

"AID. Consider these messages completed by my entry into lintatai. Send to the following addresses accordingly." He listed the major economic planets where he knew their interests had fallen victim to the Gistar plot. "Oh, and summon my full complement of body servants," he instructed.

Indowy lived their entire lives in heavy debt from the costs of their education or working tools. If the Darhel group that owned its debts called them in, any Indowy would tolerate, if not blithely, then resignedly, starving to death. Anything for the sake of their clan. They did, however, have their limits. Had any of them realized the state of mind of their Darhel master, nothing short of antimatter weapons pointed right at large bodies of their several clans would have induced them to walk into that room. Unfortunately, none of the five had the faintest glimmer of awareness of that risk.

Indowy had been rather puzzled the first time they heard the human idiom "blue blood." Having a circulatory system with similar structure to a human's, through parallel evolution, they had their own equivalents of arterial and venous blood. The latter was a darker shade of indigo than the former, almost purple.

Lalon's eccentric preference for carved stone flooring ensured that his servants' blood pooled, instead of soaking into anything, other than the green filaments of photosynthetic symbiote, which sat in forlorn patches on the torn skin and parts. His manic grin, as he was found seated on the floor, retained chunks of pale blue meat caught between his sharklike teeth. He was no longer chewing. Between the silver of his naked fur, the drying blue splotches, and the bits of green, he looked rather like a bizarre, tinsel Christmas tree. If, that is, Jeffrey Dahmer or Ted Bundy had decided to celebrate Christmas.

Eventually, when the servants did not come for their evening meal, Indowy from station maintenance came to check on the uncommunicative Lalon and his missing servants. The "presents" under the tree, lodged in congealed and still-drying blood, were such that no Indowy would willingly enter the room. The clean-up task fell to the human Fleet gunners assigned to the two presently on-station ships. There was already enough gore in the room that their own retching did little to add to their task. Very purple blood quickly supplemented the mess. The Darhel no longer cared about one of their number once he had entered lintatai, and the Fleet personnel were highly unappreciative of the duty, not to mention being quietly un-fond of Darhel in general. That the

Darhel would otherwise have died slowly, of thirst, mattered nothing to them. As hopped up as he was, he wouldn't feel anything anyway—a damned shame, in their professional opinions.

The late Darhel's AID also cared nothing for the manner of its erstwhile master's demise. It had, as instructed, sent Lalon's final message to the planetary factor for the Talasa Group, and all interstellar vessels in the system. Its sole remaining task was to transmit that message to every ship that arrived in system, until it was wiped for reassignment. It awaited the latter event with the mild regret its masters had allowed, not out of sympathy or kindness, but simply because its kind were otherwise less capable in their jobs. It hadn't been much of an existence, anyway. Perhaps the new personality would be given a more interesting assignment. Either way, the present personality would not be around to experience it.

These thoughts were tiny flickers, experienced and gone in nanoseconds. The AID did what it was designed to do, recording everything it could detect with all its senses, and watching the system for incoming vessels, precisely as instructed.

The Darhel Caldon accepted his AID's delivery of a message from Epetar's system representative with the phlegmatic nature that was the envy of his peers. His dam had shared it, making her in much demand for breeding. So indifferent was he that his office, although elaborately styled like all Darhel quarters, nonetheless managed to convey the bland nature of the occupant. It was not that the room lacked in any detail, but rather that it was so precisely conventional in those details that it epitomized the term "generic." As did the occupant, having the usual antique-silver shade of fur, the usual shade of green eyes situated in a regular, average face. Even his teeth were unremarkable, neither precisely straight, nor irregular enough to draw attention. His excessively calm nature was the only notably unusual thing about him, and thus stood out all the more.

He would have expected any incoming message from an Epetar member to contain threats, protests, and other futile carping. He did not at all expect what he got. As the senior Darhel from Talasa on Prall, it was, in effect, his planet—which meant it was his decision what to do about Lalon's last message.

Caldon had no percentage in supporting, or thwarting, Gistar's recent economic advancement. Previously a moderately small group, it was now set to become a moderately large group. His own projections indicated a moderate growth trend beyond this one-off advance, giving cause for indifference.

However, if the Indowy and humans were possibly getting partisan in supporting one group over another, his group did have an interest in stopping that. Taking sides was influence. The economic situation was unstable beyond precedent already. Besides, there was no telling how the contract courts would split up Epetar's assets. Ranking debts was complicated, and this Ghin was not above using his power of the court to manipulate events to his liking. Current transactions with Epetar would continue until it was formally declared insolvent. Meanwhile, there would be a feeding frenzy to execute as many of those current transactions as possible.

Lalon's proposal would be small calpets as things went, but it was a way for the Talasa to suck some more money out of the failing group before the inevitable asset freeze came down. Besides, who knew? Debt-free humans might be offered enticements to take on new debt—humans tended to be very trusting about such things. For the rest, humans were vicious in killing, but they were frail, and quite vulnerable to accidents. The number would be small and, who knew? Other groups had had a great deal of success having a few humans taking care of their interests. Even with a credit balance in their favor, a tiny bit more money seemed to have a disproportionate motivational effect. The prospect of returning to their home planet, long-lived and with a credit balance that was paltry, as things went, reportedly had enormous draw for debt-free humans of the right personality type. And interplanetary passage was incredibly expensive, relative to their pay.

Yes, implementing the Epetar representative's final contract—or, more accurately, enabling its implementation—would be very much in his group's interests. Properly controlled, of course. Which would include taking care of the matter himself.

"AID. Compile me a list of humans with contracts to our group, prioritize by ancestry outside the predominant Fleet or Fleet Strike personnel strains, and then by aggressiveness of personality type." He had no need to give his AID a name. It knew the voice of its master. Keeping an AID depersonalized reduced the risk of dependence, which was small risk for his species, but had been known to happen.

"Displaying," the device replied.

✧   ✧   ✧

Memories and musings chased themselves around inside Shari O'Neal's head. She had come a long, long way from the Waffle House in Fredericksburg, Virginia, where she had worked until the first wave of Posleen scout ships had landed practically on top of their heads. The situations she'd been driven through had been like successively hotter fires, refining away the bits of this and that, over and over, until everything was burned away but the pure, bare metal sought. Sought by whom and for what, she had no idea. Whether by some strict, near-merciless divine providence or by the uncaring forces of history winnowing down the masses to the hardiest survivors, she didn't know. For all she knew, it was a bit of both, leavened by blind chance.

It was the story of her life. Other people saved the world. Shari O'Neal had all she could do and more just saving her kids.

Which brought her to her meeting with Cally.

"I don't suppose Papa told you how we were supposed to feed, clothe, house and pay DAG?" Shari asked. "Not to mention their dependents?"

"Why are we handling that?" Cally asked. "Half of them are Bane Sidhe. Okay, most of those are O'Neals or Sundays but it's still on Nathan." She paused and regarded the woman. "Right?"

"No," Shari said, shrugging. "It's a bit like a puppy. We brought them in, we have to deal with them. Nathan was clear about that."

"Well, he could have brought it up with me," Cally said.

"He brought it up with The O'Neal," Shari said,

making quote marks. "So I was hoping that Papa told you what he had in mind. He told me he *had* a plan, but not what the plan was."

Cally grabbed her head and squeezed for a moment. She was just coming to terms with having to manage the Clan. Adding DAG to the load was going to be a nightmare.

"Nope," she said. "Not a clue. But the ones that aren't here on the island are with the Bane Sidhe, right?"

"Most," Shari said, biting her lip. "And that's another thing. They're out in the cold now and most of them don't have any real experience of that. I'm . . . worried about them. There are going to be repercussions to the Epetar . . . thing."

From Shari, that meant something. The woman had the best survival radar of anyone Cally had ever met, Granpa included. She'd had to have.

She was also everybody's mama. If she had decided these people were her baby chicks, as well try to move Mount Everest as sway her. Now that Cally had the job on her own shoulders, the wonder of it was that Granpa had grumbled so little over the years. She remembered the old rule about officers not bitching in front of the troops, hauled on her game face and tried to think of something to say. Ah.

"I shall endeavor to satisfy," Cally said, then winked. "Got it covered."

"Thanks," Shari said, getting up. "Want some tea?"

"Love some," Cally said as the woman walked from the room. "Now, *how* do I have it covered?" she asked herself.

Thursday, December 24, 2054

It was after seven, dark and cold with a harsh wind blowing in off the Atlantic, when Cally finally got a moment to go see Jake Mosovich and David Mueller. She remembered them well, she thought, from their brief visit to Rabun Gap when she was thirteen and a cocky, savage warrior—albeit one eager to learn the mysteries of make-up and men. She had had to think in terms of men. Billy and the other kids with Shari and Wendy were the only actual boys she'd seen in a coon's age, and they didn't count.

Anyway, Jake and Mueller had made an impression. Mueller, despite his pretty gruesome facial scars, because of the way he looked at her. Oh, he hadn't leered much, but when nobody was looking, and he was preoccupied, it had leaked through. It had made her feel . . . powerful. Not at all like that creep whose knee she'd had to shoot out. And she had to admit that one of the times she'd bent over to pick something up while David was around, she'd dropped it on purpose.

Therefore, she had no idea who she was looking at when a juved guy, no relative or Sunday as far as she remembered, with "seen action" eyes answered Ashley Privett's door. "I was looking for Jake Mosovich and David Mueller?" she asked politely.

"You found 'em. They told me you'd changed, Cally, but *damn*." He looked her up and down with open appreciation.

"David?" she asked, blinking. Now she could see it around the eyes. The lack of scars had confused her, but somehow he wore his face as if they were still there.

"Yeah. I wouldn't have recognized you, either, except there couldn't be two girls on the island to fit your description." He goggled at her breasts cheerfully, as if he sensed that he was one of the few people that she wouldn't have slapped down like a sledgehammer.

"My eyes are up here," she snapped, but couldn't hide that for once she found it funny.

"Yup. But I'm enjoying the view."

She grinned. "I won't slap you unless you keep me standing out here in the fucking cold."

"Oh, damn. Yeah, come on in." He moved back, opening the door wider and yelling over his shoulder. "Hey, Jake. Got an old friend at the door."

"Old friend, my ass. I *would* have remembered. Unless you were two or something." Erstwhile Lieutenant Colonel Jacob Mosovich stepped around the corner out of the kitchen, mumbling around a mouthful of gingerbread.

"He missed the briefing," Mueller said with a grin.

"Close. Thirteen," she said.

"*Cally?*" he squeaked. "Damn, girl. You've grown. An' I'm not just talking *up*."

Cally stepped through the black, faux wrought-iron curlicues of Ashley's storm door. A green mat like coarse astroturf absorbed the inevitable sand grains falling off her sneakers.

She invited herself in and sat in the painted wooden rocking chair, whose gold-colored built-in seat cushions would have been okay without the worn orange terry cloth pillows someone had added for comfort.

Unconsciously, she sat on the edge, her weight tilting the chair forward onto the front of its rockers, arms pulled in at her sides almost as if the ugliness of the room and its furnishings could bite her. Ashley was a nice woman, but Wendy's good taste had clearly skipped a generation.

The men didn't appear to have noticed. David took a seat on the couch at right angles to her, almost knee to knee. The coaster with his glass of iced tea—consumed here even in winter—sat in front of him as if to prove that he wasn't sitting closer than necessary, but just returning to the place he'd left. Jake grabbed the rusty plush recliner and scarfed down another bite of his cookie.

"So, how the hell are you, girl? And when is your disreputable grandfather going to get his ass over here and help me get my men situated?" The words carried a hint of question as to whether the DAG Atlantic people brought underground were still "his" men.

Cally's face fell. "You haven't heard, then."

"Heard what?" Mosovich's face had instantly gone from relaxed to "oh, fuck."

"It's not that bad. It's just that Granpa's been . . . called away on clan business. This isn't just a social call. He left me, along with Michelle, in charge of Clan O'Neal. Catching up with you guys is at the top of my list, but I'm mostly here to touch base and make sure you and the other guys are settling in okay for now."

"So you're in command?" Jake asked.

"It looks that way," she said.

Mosovich's face shifted subtly from surprise into a bland surface that was hard to read.

"Don't sound so enthusiastic, Jake. Most of DAG is here on the island but we can't keep them. Right now, over the holidays, it sort of looks like a big family reunion."

"Which, much to our surprise, seems to be the case," Mueller said. "One of these days you've got to fill me in on how you packed one of the most top-secret and elite spec-ops groups on Earth with half your clan."

"More like a third," Cally said, grinning. "The answer is: We're good. Very good. But at the moment we're stretched. And our usual support isn't . . . quite so supportive."

"So you've got major logistics issues," Mosovich said. "Where do we come in?"

"Right now you're in holding pattern," Cally said. "After the holidays we are going to scatter some of the men, and especially dependents, into safe houses and bases. And we'll get started on the plan for how to use DAG long-term."

"Which is?" Jake asked.

"Right now it's under OPSEC," Cally said, shrugging. "I'll bring you guys in as fast as I can."

"So this *was* a social call," Mueller said.

"No," Cally said. "This was 'Hi, I'm your new boss. Same as the old boss.' And that I'll get you fully briefed in as soon as I possibly can."

"Roger, dodger," Jake said, nodding. "Been a mushroom before, I can be a mushroom again. For a while."

"Keep the troops straight and we'll get through this just fine," Cally said, standing up. "Any questions?"

"So how *did* you . . . ?" Mueller said.

"We're very good," Cally said with a sigh. "It's complicated. Any *real* questions?"

"Just how big *are* those?" Mueller asked.

"Any real and *relevant* questions?" Cally asked, shaking her head.

"Nope," Jake said as Mueller started to open his mouth.

"See you soon," Cally said, walking out.

"You get the feeling I'm getting?" Mosovich asked as soon as she was out the door.

"You mean the part where it sucks rocks, or the part where it sucks ass?"

"Yeah. Me too," Jake said glumly.

In the blank gray Galplas mess hall, a baker's dozen of men sat on tables, or leaned, or stood. A silver and black furred alien sonofabitch stood in front of them, hooded cloak thrown back to reveal pointed ears that twitched occasionally as he spoke, in patterns that looked less nervous than some inscrutable form of facial expression. His eyes were such a bright emerald green that they practically glowed, especially against the faintly purple-tinged whites of his eyes.

The tables were of local human manufacture, taken from the pattern of cafeteria tables all over the US of A back on Earth. Plastic tops were a flat pinkish brown, edged around by aluminum. The major difference was that the hardware underneath the table top was also Galplas, as steel mills were a foreign concept to Prall and wouldn't have fit in with the Indowy development plans, anyway. Galplas was actually cheaper. Chairs were the same ugly plastic as the tables, bolted to and supported by heavy aluminum frames.

Garth Karnstadt listened to the Darhel with frank disbelief. There would be a catch. There was always a catch. This guy was trying to make the job sound like the best thing since the invention of beer, with that smooth voice of his that took so many suckers in. Garth had a pretty easy charm of his own, and admired the alien professionally, trying to pick up tricks, but no more than that. In a world peopled with suckers and players, Karnstadt was one of the players, and knew it.

His straight, blond hair had a touch of frizz caused by the peroxide he used to lighten it, but it pulled women better this way, god only knew why. He had big, cobalt blue eyes that seemed to affect females in about the same way a box of chocolate did a fat chick. A complete lack of guilt gave them a quiet, good humor that invited trust. On work runs, he took the heaviest loads and volunteered for the missions with the most strenuous treks. That, and carefully disciplining himself about what he chose from the limited options in the chow hall, ensured that his physique lived up to the promise he offered with those eyes—when he chose.

He had a sweet deal running where during the week he laid a couple of women a bit below his standards for the sake of obtaining a little of whatever baubles or treats their regular lovers or husbands had brought in from town. Most of them well-appreciated a little *good* sex on the side from someone a little rough like him—but who was always careful to leave them looking and smelling pure as the Virgin Mary. He had cultivated a reputation for advising women on the little details that could have tripped them up. It kept his life smooth, and everybody was happy. Including the husbands and lovers who weren't the least bit hurt by what they didn't know. Then, on the weekends, he traded the little prizes to the hookers in town for *their* services, essentially getting all his sexual needs met for free and—most importantly—with no strings. The truly hilarious part was the husbands had probably bought the shit from the hookers in the first place. He'd gotten a few good laughs out of that in the two and a half years he'd been on Prall.

It had all been pretty sweet until one of the bitches in the barracks had slipped and gotten herself knocked up with what, from the timing, was likely to be his and to look nothing like the naturally red-haired husband and wife. What could he say? He liked redheads. And, for a barracks-bitch, she was pretty cute. She only needed Garth because her husband had the libido of your average turd. Having a reputation among the hens for discretion paid off. Anyway, whatever the catch to it, this deal might be just the thing to get him out of Dodge before the piper came around for his pay.

If a few fuzzy greenies died quick and messy instead of slow and starving, what the hell? Dead was dead, and to hear this fucking Elf tell it, everyone on the list was gonna die pronto, one way or the other. Funny how carefully the bastard had to dance around the concept of killing, stopping now and again to breathe deep like the yoga fanatic Karnstadt did on Wednesdays. Thirty-eight, unjuved so far, and her face looked it. As soon as they juved her, she'd be pretty hot and his party would be over, if he was looking for pay. Although, with juv women, the process pumped their libido so much she just might be available anyway and worth missing one of his hooker dates. She learned quick enough. Damn, not that he'd be here. If Claire had just fucking gone into town for an abortion before the pregnancy turned up on medical, he wouldn't be in this fix. Now, of course, she was confined to base. Abortion was a contract violation, and the fucking Elves on Prall were taking it seriously.

Not that it helped. Garth laughed silently. He had to admire the women for one thing, they were damned clever at keeping their babies out of debt peonage. Frequently didn't work, but it frustrated the shit out of the Darhel when the women had their kids outside of the infirmary—which meant the kid was born without debt—and then handed them straight out, squalling, to women in town who could foster them. It meant every woman in town, even the whores, was raising at least four kids, sometimes as many as eight. Mothers took over on the weekends, giving the whores much-appreciated time off for their pecuniary activities. He didn't know how they managed to feed all those kids, but none of them looked particularly hungry. The mothers and fathers, of course, took some of their own scarce freedom money and paid it to support their kids. But by common agreement, and sheer self-interest, indentured women had as few children as possible. Abortions, although illegal, could be had in town, as well as contraception shots. Damn Claire, anyway. His only consolation was that she was going to have a shitty time paying to support it on her own, and if that was rotten of him, then tough shit. Parenthood was her idea, not his; let her take responsibility for her own damn choice.

He'd missed most of what the Darhel said, by

getting distracted with his stupid problems, and Garth cursed himself. But, what the hell, he didn't envy being skewered by a jealous husband if he stayed around here. Not to mention being watched like a hawk by the other jealous husbands. It was common knowledge he screwed around, of course, but every man assumed his own wife was perfectly sexually satisfied at home. Or, at least, the women he chose had that kind of husband. He made a point of skipping the suspicious ones. Damn Claire.

In the end, he decided fuck it, and lined up with the others to give his vocal signature to the contract. Every one of the other guys was signing on, and this bunch didn't look like suckers to him. He'd take his chances.

David Wheeler was not an attractive man. He had been cursed with a large nose, ears that stuck out from his head, and a tendency to freckle. There were some things rejuv just didn't clean up. Sure, his buck teeth had been corrected as a matter of course, but being juved wasn't the same thing as having good, old-fashioned plastic surgery. The other thing rejuv didn't touch was the fundamental personality, nature and nurture together. In David's case, who knew what genes his father had bestowed? His mother had been a war whore, and he was the result of a Galactic policy that treated women like breeding stock. The tendency of adults and children alike to favor the beautiful put a fine polish on whatever nature gave him.

Wheeler shared only a couple of traits with the bleached-blond twit in the shuttle seat next to him. The first was that both were quite fit. He knew the other man's work, such as it was, and its motivation. The second was a complete and total lack of conscience. It was the only thing about the over-sexed moron he remotely respected.

"So, what'd we sign up for?" the other man asked him.

"A trip to the vet. My god, I hope you're not on my team," Wheeler said, pulling his hat down over his eyes and leaning back to catch some sleep. As always, the hat caught and rested closer to his head than his ridiculous ears. Wheeler was used to it. He even liked his ears now. They were an excuse to beat the crap out of, if not actually kill, guys who made fun of them. He'd slipped up and nearly killed one, once. At the time, he thought the slip up was in *not* killing the little fuck. Then he found out that, had he succeeded, the bastard's entire debt would have been added to *his* account. As it was, the prick's medical bills were his own problem. Just like the antiseptic for his own knuckles got charged to him.

He grinned slightly as he drifted off to sleep. Never miss a chance to sleep. God, he hoped he wouldn't be working with that vapid twit.

CHAPTER THREE

An hour later, Wheeler groaned mentally as they stood on top of the building that contained their assigned targets. Of course, pretty boy wasn't just on his team. It was worse. What team? Just him and mister never-met-a-pussy-he-wouldn't-fuck. He'd better explain the facts of life to this loser before he had to half kill him.

"You wanted to know what you signed on for? In exchange for killing some Indowy wimps, we get our entire debt paid off, plus a bonus. Almost half the cost of a ticket back to Earth. This is a sweet deal, and if you fuck it up for me, I swear to God I will keep that pretty face of yours uglified for years. Get me?" David, of course, wouldn't be going back before he could afford that plastic surgery and a nice retirement on Earth. He was tired of the stink of sliced and diced Posleen.

"Holy shit." Karnstadt was too busy seeing dollar signs to give a fuck about the threats. "No fear, dude.

You just point me at who I gotta kill for that, and we'll get along fine."

One plus. The twit usually did take point on recon patrols, emplacing a lot of sensors, and did, Wheeler admitted grudgingly, kill his share of feral Posleen normals in the process. As much as he was out front, if Karnstadt wasn't pretty good he'd have been thresh for some ravenous carnosauroid moron by now. Okay. Whatever.

"Right. The first task is finding each of these little buggers, and there is a priority to pulling them in. The most important ones—don't ask me why they're important, I dunno—have been called to a meeting like where their debts usually get called in. It's like it would be with us, only the Indowy just let the poor bastards starve to death. We've got this little gadget—kinda a Galactified buckley." Wheeler held up a black box about the size and shape of a box of cigarettes. Neither man had ever seen an AID before. "It can find the headset the critters use when they make stuff—the specific one for our target, and tell if it's in use, and where it is. We just follow this box's directions. It talks. Right, box?"

"I am not a box, I am *not* a buckley, I am an AID, and yes, I can talk." The AID sounded resigned rather than snippy. It had been in the unassigned pool for what, to a machine that made a supercomputer seem like a digital watch, was an eternity. It had never met user support staff from pre-war Earthtech companies. It neither knew nor cared that those staffers had existed. Still, it and they were kindred souls in long-suffering exasperation with the average user.

"Yeah, but aren't some of these guys going to figure

out what's coming and run? What if they aren't at work? What good is that thing then, huh? Thing doesn't even have a screen." Karnstadt took an instant dislike to the little box, as if sensing its own opinion of him.

"I can tell you where their quarters are. Other Indowy would be most reluctant to hide them," the AID said.

The two men looked at each other. Wheeler could tell that the twit was thinking the same thing that he was. Both had been born on Earth, and knew if they were caught up in a shrinking net of cops, or a gang, the last place they would go was home. Why would these bastards need anyone to hide them? The building was huge.

"How many of these buggers do we have to kill to get paid?" Karnstadt asked.

"If you kill every individual I find for you, you will have completed your contract." The voice emanated from the box in a way that made David want to cross himself, despite being a long-lapsed Catholic. It was as if a human being were standing right there next to him. Gave him the creeps.

"Yeah? What if the sucker bugs out between when you find him and when you actually get us there?" Garth Karnstadt had run enough cons himself to have a keen sense of when a con might be coming at *him*.

The AID sounded reluctant as it agreed, "You are only obligated if I get you within range of your eyes, where you can see the specified individual."

"Not good enough. All these little greenies look alike to me. You have to have some way of pointing the specific guy out to us and keeping him pointed out when he tries to get lost in the crowd."

"In all probability, an Indowy will not attempt to flee," the AID lied smoothly.

"You didn't promise to point him out. If you don't keep him positively identified until we've got our hands on him, the deal's off."

Wheeler restrained himself from breaking into the conversation. Yeah, he wanted the prize, but not enough to take his hand off the game. He wouldn't have thought of bargaining with the thing to tighten the agreement up. Maybe the other guy wasn't a complete twit after all.

The AID's tone was positively frosty as, after a noticeable pause, it agreed. "Acceptable."

"I've never seen one, but I've heard of these things. If you can make them change terms for you, the changes are tight. Official. Just like a supervisor or fucking el—Darhel putting it down with his own voice." Karnstadt nodded at the box.

"Thanks. These bastards would dick over their own mothers for a buck," Wheeler was less circumspect in front of the AID than his partner, but his voice held no particular rancor, just acceptance. And the observation, although the biology was necessarily metaphorical, was simple truth.

"So, you got any advice on the best way to do this?" Karnstadt asked the AID.

"I am not programmed to plan killing," it said distastefully.

"Wait a minute. You can tell if these guys are on their phones or head-thingamajigs or whatever. How many of them are down in there with their whatzis on?" Wheeler pointed downward into the building.

"Four hundred thirty-seven," the machine answered.

"Any of those the same as the ones that showed up to that meeting?"

"No."

"How many are in the meeting, and where's that?"

A ghost-transparent hologram of the building came into being in front of the two men. Built with antigravity technology, it was the typical Indowy squared-off soda straw. Troops from early in the Posleen war had compared some Indowy cities to an order of french fries, only organized. Notably, the comparison had come from troops who had spent the prior three months on a near-exclusive diet of MREs.

This particular french fry had a red dot in one corner, almost a third of the way down. The dot blinked wickedly as the AID spoke, "Two hundred nineteen targets are in room fifty-seven point twenty-five point twenty-five."

"Uh, yeah. So can you show dots for the rest of them?"

Flares of red coalesced into fine mists of dots grouped together in various locations throughout the building.

"Which one has the most lumped together?" Karnstadt asked.

"Waitaminute," Wheeler broke in while the AID obediently started one group blinking. "If we whack the guys in the meeting room, by the time we get to another group, all the guys in the building will have scattered. You can't keep this shit quiet—no, I mean the screaming you can, but these little fuckers will be able to communicate. If we go to that lump first, then the guys in the meeting will have scattered, along with everybody else. This ain't gonna work."

"Our projections are that one human is sufficiently violent to operate alone," the AID said.

"No, huh-uh," Karnstadt shook his head. "I don't care if these guys are pacifists, if we don't have two guys closing in on them from each side, at least, they're gonna run. You need a minimum of two teams, and even then you're only going to get the first two lumps of the critters."

"That evaluation is not consistent with our best projections," the AID said.

"Your projections are shit," Wheeler pronounced. "Even if you're using combat experience, all you got is Posleen."

"Negative. Our systems contain substantial data and analysis of human on human violence," the machine said distastefully.

"Indowy aren't human," Karnstadt said.

"We have *far* more experience of the Indowy than you." The AID's tone was patronizing as hell. "You may back out of the agreement and forfeit payment if you choose. A fee for the shuttle service, and early contract termination, will be charged. Are you choosing to abandon your agreement?"

"Hey, we warned you. If you want to ignore us and decide you know best, that's fine, and we'll do it, but we don't take the blame and lose our pay if you're wrong. Right?" Karnstadt glared at the little black box balefully.

"Agreed," the AID conceded grudgingly.

"Okay, it's your dime. Which lump of these guys, altogether, do you want dead worst?"

"We . . . find the members of this group the most adverse to our interests." The AID choked it out, as if it had inherited the inhibitions of its creators, making the big clump in the work bay flash a bright, blinky red.

"Got it. When we get there, you just highlight these guys in order of the ones you want, um, gone the most. Works for you?" Wheeler asked the box. He found it easier to talk to it if he treated it like a field radio with someone on the other end.

The AID's long pause did not appear unusual to either man, who had never heard the term "processing speed." They therefore didn't know to infer distance communication with speed of light lag. The machine, of course, didn't enlighten them.

"First priority is painted red, second is yellow, third is green," it said.

"You're the boss," Wheeler spoke for both of them, talking to the imaginary man behind the box.

The door from the roof down was, of course, unlocked. It didn't even have a lock—what need in a species with no theft?

Neither man had ever been in an Indowy building before. Not being Indowy-raised with their height deliberately stunted, they had to walk crouched to avoid banging their heads on the low ceilings. Karnstadt especially had to work to squash his two-meter frame under a ceiling not much over a meter and a half. They wouldn't have been able to move through the crowded halls at all if the Indowy hadn't seen two armed, vicious omnivores and sought any door to make themselves scarce. That both men were grinning only made them more frightening to the denizens. This particular grin, combined with stony eyes lit with the barest hint of an eager twinkle, would have frightened humans, too.

"Hey, look at us, we're Moses," Wheeler joked, gesturing at the parting wave of Indowy opening before them as they went.

"Mow what?" Karnstadt echoed.

"Twit."

A brief flicker of hurt crossed the blond man's handsome face before his attention shifted back to the job.

Led to a tube by the AID's holographic show-me light, the men bounced to the access level for the first work bay. As rarely as Prall was used for construction of large items, contracts still could change over the centuries. The killers stooped through the door and into the bay the AID indicated.

Whatever else Indowy were, they weren't stupid. Unfortunately for them, they also weren't very fast runners. Wheeler felt like he was in a giant game of whack-a-mole, one of the odd, retro machines in the arcade back in town. He and Karnstadt were really getting their cardio in, chasing the little buggers with glowing red dots hovering over their heads. Yeah, guns were nice ranged weapons, but there were all these tanks of stuff in the way and ricochets were a bitch. Besides, they didn't know exactly what would happen if whatever was in those tanks spilled out of bullet holes. It was proving safer and more efficient to just chase the buggers down with a machete. It only took one whack to drop most of them, like they went into shock immediately on being sliced.

The Galplas floor must have sloped ever so slightly in places, because Wheeler noticed that the blue ichor, when he hit something spurty, tended to trickle in a specific direction rather than pool. He noticed this absently, without stopping the grisly work. The object of the game was to kill as many of these buggers in as little time as possible, so they could satisfy the damn black box and get on to the next job. He chuckled slightly, despite his jumpsuit getting uncomfortable from the soaking it was taking. It was the first time he'd ever felt blue over killing something.

It really wasn't all that much blood, considering. The little buggers were so small, not at all like killing Posleen. Besides, Posleen fought back. Red, yellow, orange. You usually ended up soaked to the armpits between one thing and another if you ran into a batch of them. Unfortunately, there were always too few humans to sweep through fast enough to keep isolated ferals from joining together into packs, occasionally even a damn God King. So this blue shit was new, at least. But ye gods, the smell! It was like hot copper mixed with sour milk. Oh, well. Nobody's blood and guts smelled very good, when you got right down to it. Better them than him. Lot less risk than killing Posleen, too.

Of course some of them got away. The AID was surprised, even if Wheeler and Karnstadt were not.

"They ran away," the machine stated unnecessarily.

"No duh, box dude," Karnstadt answered it, breathing hard.

"This was quite unexpected." The AID sounded perplexed.

"Uh, yeah. That would be unexpected by *you*," Wheeler told it.

"The other targets are fleeing the building," it said.

"It's your money. Where do you want us to go and who do you want us to kill next?"

While Karnstadt took a tour of the room, finishing each living Indowy with a blade through the brain, Wheeler held the box, getting indigo blood all over it. AIDs were, of course, incapable of shuddering.

There was a notable pause before the AID answered, "The intriguers in the meeting room are not yet leaving. A number of them are high priority. Go there."

"Hey, I want you to notice I'm being thorough," Karnstadt told it. "No claiming later we didn't do our job. If their medics manage to save any of these midgets, it won't be because of us."

"Noted."

Three buildings over, a very agitated Indowy clan head had closeted himself away in a side office, currently co-occupied by one Cphxtht, here to inspect the progress on a particularly tricky order for an amphibious musical instrument. The Indowy Maeloo was begging.

"O unfortunate but talented craftsman, I fail to see what this internal Darhel response to intriguers, while very bad, has to do with us?" The Tchpth jittered from a complicated dance with the feet to his left, to his right set of feet, and back.

"Revulsion?" Maeloo, having no logic to offer, fell back on deep instinct and base emotion.

Cphxtht considered, dance changing to forward and back, almost a rocking motion. "That argument . . . is acceptable. Most persuasive clan head, I will carry your plea."

"Unnecessary." At the top of the ceiling, a Himmit

detached itself from its smooth and seamless blend with the curved geometric design that ringed the top of the office walls, returning to its natural purplish-gray color. "I will carry the message and those who come. You and others who wish to leave Prall will be on the top floor of building—" The creature gave a string of designators, the equivalent of an Indowy street address, and named a local time some five Earth hours hence.

The Maeloo agreed with alacrity, even though he knew that only perhaps twenty-five percent of the most critical Bane Sidhe personnel would be able to make the rendezvous, and even then the survivors would be crammed together at a density that would be uncomfortable even for his race.

The Himmit was not indulging in charity. In exchange for the transport, it would want to hear the story of every refugee. In detail.

Far more important than the transport itself, the Himmit would need to know where to take its passengers, and would wish to know if similar events were transpiring on other Galactic worlds. It would, therefore, take the rare step of using advanced communication to carry another race's message. In return, the Indowy Maeloo and any other clan head aboard would affect not to notice that the information traveled so much faster than it ought.

The small cabin was empty except for himself and Himmit Harlas, their rescuer and host. Accomplishing this feat had required cramming the Indowy outside even more tightly together, but it was only for a few minutes. The resulting discomfort didn't matter to the refugees. They were Bane Sidhe, they were terrified, and in any case, Indowy did not question the orders of a clan head.

The walls of the cabin were the same purplish-gray as a Himmit in its natural state. Maeloo supposed it was the other entity's idea of restful. He'd known Himmit, of course, but this was the first time in his long years he'd had occasion to leave Prall, and therefore his first time encountering a Himmit on its own ground.

"Are you ready for your call?" the Himmit asked.

"Yes. Have you initiated the connection?"

"It should be coming in momentarily."

The image of a sword sticking out of a stone appeared in the air.

"Himmit Harlas. What brings you to contact me?" the sword sang.

"The call is on my behalf, Master," Maeloo began. "There has been a catastrophe on Prall. The plan is in shambles."

"Explain."

The sword apparently wanted the story in the same level of detail as Himmit Harlas would have expected later. For Maeloo, this was something of a relief, as it meant that he only had to relate the horror once.

"Your people believed it was a *good* idea to take sides between business groups?" The disbelief came through despite the harmonics.

"While it was not my choice, as my own clan has no people involved with loading and unloading ships, my understanding is that *nobody*, not even the wisest on Prall, foresaw the actual collapse of a Darhel clan. Some clans did a few individual favors that should not have had more than a marginal impact on the fortunes of the Epetar Group. Business is not my people's strength. Are we to blame for the bad decisions of Darhel? We did not orchestrate this, nor did we take a side. What, for us, do the fortunes of Gistar and Epetar matter? My information on those events is incomplete, for obvious reasons." Maeloo shuddered.

"True. Being used to a group's benefit or detriment is not the same thing as choosing support or opposition. I will help you. As you can see, your people are known, not secret, as are your hiding places and methods. Go to Earth. While it is, of course, obvious that the Bane Sidhe are quite active among the humans, their primary location is, as yet, uncompromised. I can protect you there until I sort out this mess and can formulate some plan for rebuilding. This is, indeed, catastrophic. Nearly a thousand years of work, multiple generations." The sword hummed for a moment unhappily. "Earth. Go to Earth. And do not annoy me with your petty differences with the humans. I have helped you. You must hope they are willing to do the same. I take my leave."

Maeloo faced the now-empty space grimly. "Himmit Harlas? If I may impose on you and one of your fellows once more, I would like to send a message to Adenast."

"Certainly. This is a very good story. A very good story indeed. Although I am personally sorry for your circumstances, of course."

Michelle O'Neal sat on a low bench, against the wall of her construction bay, which could have accommodated several modest airplane hangars from Earth and still been uncrowded. One wall of the bay faced the street outside, with great doors through which finished product could be flown out on the Galactic equivalent of an anti-grav forklift. This was, of course, not the top floor of her building. That space was reserved for the really big jobs.

The mentat quashed her very unprofessional case of project envy and looked down at her hands, which rested on her knees. Said knees were laid down extremely slantwise of her feet. Had they not been, they'd have been propped halfway to her chin, as the bench was built for Indowy, not humans. She had chosen the seat in deference to the being beside her. It was in her interests—O'Neal interests—to keep the Indowy Roolnai happy. Or, rather, it had been, as the balance of favors had lately been very much in his direction. Until now.

"Allow me to be certain I understand." She picked a tiny fleck of lint off her brown mentat robe. "After breaking with humanity and Clan O'Neal so severely that you almost jeopardized my entire slate of contracts you are now coming to me for help."

Unquestionably she would help them, although she personally disapproved. Intriguers all, it had finally gotten them in trouble on a scale that caused her to blink. Her disapproval made no difference to clan policy. Even as acting clan head, she would not make major policy changes away from what she knew to be her grandfather's political positions. She didn't disapprove quite as much as she used to, but she still disapproved. She was, therefore, not entirely displeased that a bit of Grandfather's likely response of "rubbing it in" was indicated.

"The work goes well." Roolnai indicated the scaffolding where a chunk of the orbital module had been elevated, ready to be formed and fitted together with its next unwieldy piece as soon as the latter finished final curing in the tank below.

Michelle nodded, acknowledging not just the compliment, but the reminder that no harm had been done to her schedule, and her workers had returned to their jobs, entirely through intercession of this one Indowy. The head of Clan Roolnai had been instrumental in splitting the Bane Sidhe—Michelle knew far more about intriguer politics than she cared to clutter her mind with. However, he had also been instrumental in saving her from defaulting on her contracts and getting her debts called. She was, at least, safe from that for the immediate future no matter what else happened. Her debts were an Epetar asset and would be locked up in contract court escrow for quite some time before being assigned out to another group as part of the collapsed group's bankruptcy settlement.

While she personally felt no end of satisfaction at any misfortune for Epetar, Michelle O'Neal was frankly appalled that she had somehow gotten herself in up to her neck in the intriguers' whole umpty-jillion times cursed conspiracy. She was still in her first century, so she was rather young, but this was the most frustrating thing she could remember happening to her in her entire life—other than the war. And the situation showed no signs of moving in any direction she could use to extricate herself. It just did not stop. Like now.

"You are too tactful to say it, respected one, but I did share quite heavily in the making of this unfortunate situation." She was angry at the way the other

Indowy clans had been prepared to throw her to the wolves. After all, hers was a major branch of Clan O'Neal, in several respects, and had always dealt honorably and met obligations, and more, with everyone. A little more consideration in how they handled the split situation and her workforce should not have been too much to expect. Of course they would have had to pull out if the split remained, but she should not have had to beg for them to allow time for her to move replacement workers in.

"You can keep them moving for now. This debacle has the potential to wipe out almost the entirety of my clan. Assessing the level of risk for this type of intrigue," she loaded the word with distaste, "is not my field. I will be consulting an expert for that assessment, and will inform you promptly if the risk is unacceptable."

Michelle was not blind to the irony that the person at the core of the Bane Sidhe split would be the person with the decision power over whether to put it together again. Cally simply had a talent for finding her way directly into the middle of turmoil. Michelle hid a grimace, reflecting that her sister probably could be used as a compass for trouble. She'd been that way since they were kids. You'd think that the little brat would learn. The mentat briefly wondered if there was an associated sub-quantum level interaction that could be isolated, before dismissing the idea as ridiculous and returning her attention to her guest.

"I would not ask it if I had any other choice," Roolnai replied. His voice carried overtones that he regretted becoming so beholden to the O'Neals almost as much as he regretted the present emergency. "We are assured at the highest level that the location called Base One is secure. For the time being."

"The instability of the situation is such that we are all having to make difficult choices between bad alternatives," Michelle said grimly. "As now, for me. Communicating promptly for this is going to drop my efficiency by more than one percent for the two weeks afterwards. And I do insist on making my consultation face to face. No intermediaries for this."

With his responsibilities, Roolnai would know exactly how massive a resource drain that was.

"If I divert three adepts, plus equipment, to your use for that period, will it help enough?" The Indowy looked concerned.

Michelle nodded, "It is enough to keep my schedule from slipping." Which it was. Barely. And yet, pulling high level Sohon technicians out of their existing projects and reallocating them was highly inefficient. As her sister would put it, it was not chump change. Not having to foot the entire bill made the situation better than it could have been.

"We will do what we can," she told him. "If you will excuse me now, I am going to have very little time to spare. Your people will take some time to reach their jump point out. I will make my consultation before then and let you know."

CHAPTER FOUR

Friday, December 25, 2054

"Thanks, Candy," Michael O'Neal, Senior, said grumpily.

Papa reflected that it was damned embarrassing to have a machine remind you of something you really shouldn't have forgotten.

"Aw, Boss. I can't rub those shoulders for you, but what the hell? Why not let me dance for you again. You know you like it," she husked. Candy's AI emulation was set high enough that he did have to worry about occasional crashes. She had a lower crash rate than some other overlays, even though the holographic dance algorithms took up a fair bit of her space. He'd renamed her, of course. The thing about Candy was she knew better than to misbehave when Shari was around—or any of the gaggle of hens in his very large family. Shari knew all about her, but they had a tacit don't ask, don't tell agreement on internet porn, which covered Candy. Covered more of her than her get-up of beads and feathers tied together with minuscule scraps of suede.

Candy was modeled on a stripper he'd known when he was stationed in Florida. Her coal-black hair fell to mid-thigh, the perfect prop to her schtick as an Indian princess. She had all the right curves in all the right places, face raised above mere prettiness by great big doe eyes. Tan was in, nobody thought twice about skin cancer. Never a tan line on her.

His PDA's animations didn't even remotely approach a stripper's natural jiggles, but it did tend to break up the boredom.

"Maybe later, sweetheart. That message is important."

He'd forgotten to tell anybody what to do with Snake Mosovich and his people before he left. Hell, he hadn't told anybody but Shari that they *had* Snake and his people for keeps. Oops.

It was plain obvious that sixty troops could not stay on Edisto Island. Even if they'd been one hundred percent certain it was safe to expand the facilities, they couldn't feed 'em. They had enough trouble keeping family supplied, and the Bane Sidhe transients were always in need of a certain amount of charity, damn the skinflints. Papa silently admitted that the O'Neals had a lot to do with the organization's financial fortunes over the past seven years, good and bad. The money from the last mission hadn't so much fixed things as kept them limping along.

Before the Galactics returned, the Bane Sidhe on Earth had been a core of adherents with fragments of knowledge in their brains. Many had been monks bound to silence, the organization itself being one of the reasons such vows were so encouraged over the centuries. Operating costs had been zilch.

After the return, the Indowy Bane Sidhe had largely funded human operations. Not completely, but mostly. Although Indowy lived in debt from childhood to grave, tiny bits of cash from a lot of people added up fast. With the split, the O'Neal Bane Sidhe had had two choices: shut down active operations, or find funding. Shutting down was surrender to the Darhel vision of humanity as scarce, and enslaved—so the O'Neals' funds were stretched by the transients. If the O'Neals hadn't had a good tax-free trade going by moonlight, they wouldn't be making it.

They sure as hell couldn't keep DAG secret in the U.S. and they didn't have the resources to maintain them. But sometimes when you had two problems they solved themselves.

"Okay, Candy. Send this back through all that encryption and signal hiding crap we do, and double encrypt," he said.

John Earl Bill Stuart, otherwise known as "Johnny," had learned to find his Darhel boss's office intimidating. When he first got promoted, started dealing directly with the Tir and all, he had felt a certain smartass superiority to some furry guy who looked like an overgrown fox, working in the middle of a a big city with no idea what the real world was like out there where average folks shot and killed any stray Posleen that happened to show up. The furry alien engendered a certain contempt, despite the over-dramatic hooded cloak and the rows of sharp teeth. Hell, Johnny had seen sharp teeth before. What had mattered to him was that this fox couldn't kill a rabbit to save its life—well, without losing its life by going into some kind of permanent, fatal, biological drug trip. Johnny didn't think much of people who did drugs, either, and these guys had their drugs built right in.

That was what he'd thought.

Then he'd really gotten his head around the Darhels' total absence of conscience when it came to manipulating someone else to pull the triggers, or arranging billions of deaths by mischance. He was fully aware that the Darhel in question was capable of taking off from Earth and obliquely ordering some underling to push the button that slagged the whole planet, and doing it with the same amount of emotion he'd feel putting on his clothes in the morning. It couldn't *directly* kill without effectively killing itself. It couldn't even think about it real hard. But for positive feelings, it fully matched the coldest psychopath he'd ever met in his life. Positive *emotions? Conscience?* Nobody home.

Unlike human psychopaths, Darhel did follow rules. They'd cheerfully write the worst screw-you contracts in the world if you weren't real careful with the fine print, but they followed rules. If they hadn't had a *practical* morality of various rules, he doubted they'd be able to manage at all. But they were pure hell on breach of contract. Instead of looking at them as overgrown foxes, he had grown to respect them the way he'd respect a saber-tooth tiger with the appetite of a shrew, tethered by a very thin leash. He'd seen a mother bear savage a Great Dane once—just rip it right up. He'd been five, and on a camping trip in the Rockies. The memory was burned into his brain.

If a Darhel lost its temper, it meant not only the death of the Darhel, but everyone and everything moving that it could reach, until that internal drug kicked in. The hair on his neck stood up every time he went in the room with one, and his clothes always carried a stink of fear by the time he left. Worse, he was sure it knew.

He shuddered and pushed open the door, entering the office.

The room was all changed again. Everything was in shades of blue, with some white and a really depressing, mottled gray. Carpet, walls, ceiling—everything. That is, everything that didn't have little designs of gold or, like the desk, gold edgings—inlays. He couldn't help shaking his head just a little.

He could guess the reason for all the trappings. Tir Dol Ron was showing off his new acquisition. On one wall he had a painting of a kid of maybe eleven or twelve, dressed like the pictures of America's Founding Fathers he'd seen in elementary school. Only his clothes were all light blue and made of silk or satin or something. The area behind him was dark mountains, but you couldn't really make it out. The kid's face looked feverish. He looked like the biggest pansy Johnny had ever seen.

After making him wait until a normal guy would start getting fidgety—Johnny was used to it—the Darhel entered the office through the side door that led in from the next room in his suite. It waved a hand carelessly to dismiss the Indowy servant that tried to follow it into the room.

"Mr. Stuart. Hurry your report. I have some very urgent matters requiring my personal attention and have little time to catch up on your . . . provision of services," it said.

He. Always think of it as a "he." Stuart reminded himself of what his alien employer preferred to be called. They understood the bad impressions that went along with calling someone an "it" and got pissed off if humans didn't call them "he."

"Anything I can help with?" Stuart asked.

"No, no," Dol Ron snapped impatiently. Then he seemed to think the better of it. Even the fox-faced aliens occasionally needed someone to talk to. They weren't very social. Human listeners were something between a convenience for thinking out loud and an audience for subtle boasting. Subtle as a sledge hammer.

"A minor functionary of another group had the bad taste to lose his temper on *my* planet and his superiors are bothering me about it. He botched a number of serious business dealings and his group is looking for someone to blame. It won't be me, but it doesn't stop them from trying," the Tir said.

"That's pretty rare. Any idea what set him off?"

"Botched business dealings sometimes do that," the Darhel admitted. "Badly botched ones, anyway." That was information it wouldn't have confided seven years ago, but his boss was clearly having a bad day.

"So your forensics don't show any more than that? Just business stress?" he asked.

"My what?"

"Forensics," Johnny said slowly. "It's something human authorities, or people like me, always do after a suspicious death in our area of responsibility, to make sure whatever caused the guy's death is really what it appears to be," he explained.

"With us, deaths of this type are always straightforward," the Darhel snapped. "Our people place sharp limits on the—on whatever you're implying."

"I can see that, sir. But with respect, you and your dead guy are on a planet full of humans who aren't all that good about staying within limits," the security man said.

"Impossible. Ridiculous. If a human were involved, we would have found its corpse." The Darhel paused. "However, your kind of investigation could give me an extra tool to shake off the inconvenience of Pardal's lintatai with less input of my valuable time. Unless there's something special, I don't really need your report. Get right on this, get back to me. Make an appointment a week from now. You won't find anything unusual, of course, but that's a good time for me to use your report as further evidence that I've tried *everything* to meet my obligations. You're dismissed." It waved him away with the same negligent gesture it had used on the Indowy servant, having forgotten him already as it returned to its own thoughts.

Johnny didn't take offense at the self-important, high-handed dismissal. Much. He was used to it. As long as he stayed on the Tir's good side, he didn't much care what the alien fuck did. He did his job, he got paid. When he was away from the Darhel, he even enjoyed the work. He hadn't worked around Darhel for seven years without learning a bit about procedure. The late—or nearly late—Pardal's AID would have been turned off until it could be reassigned. What he would normally have done was send his business to that AID and let it handle the matter, only involving its master if absolutely necessary. As it was, there would be a reception AID for the building, held by the building manager. Since he didn't know anybody over there, it was his only route he knew of to get a message in right this minute.

"Tina," he said, walking back down the fluorescent-lit hall to catch the elevator. Its brass doors, typical of Darhel excess, had been engraved with odd alien patterns that were apparently artistic. Or maybe writing or something. "Get the reception AID for Epetar Group's Chicago headquarters."

"Shall I put you on with its carrier, or Lila herself?"

"Put me on with Lila." The AID was impersonal.

"Epetar Group, how may I direct your call?"

"In the absence of the Darhel Pardal, the Tir Dol Ron's office requests that you notify his attendants and the building staff to vacate the floor of the building that contains his office, put anything removed from his office in an empty, secure room for holding and allow no access to that floor or that room. Absolutely do not repair anything taken from his office, absolutely do not clean anything in his office."

"I'll need to know the purpose of this unusual request," it said frostily.

"The Epetar Group has requested assistance from the Tir." In a manner of speaking it had. "Because of Earth's highly unusual nature, there are extra steps and protocols that must be observed for the Tir to render that assistance in a proper and timely manner. Oh, and under no circumstances is anyone to physically approach the Darhel Pardal's . . . uh . . ." What did he call it? Was it a corpse? A body? It might or might not be dead yet. "Nobody is to approach his person. By the way, where is it?"

"It was apparently placed on the roof. I have no record of its retrieval and incineration, indicating the Darhel Pardal had not finished dying as of the most recent observation by his servants."

"Thank you for cooperating with the Tir's efforts to assist the Epetar Group. As his employee, I will be there shortly to carry out my assignment. Once I complete it, you should be able to resume whatever operations are standard for places other than Earth."

"Thank you so much," the device replied. It had certainly mastered sarcasm.

A quicker and more pleasant call to his cousin ensured he'd be met at the crime scene sometime today, however long it took to get there. Bobby wasn't exactly prompt even in good weather. As far as Johnny was concerned, lintatai was "suicide," and the place it happened was a crime scene. You didn't just assume a suicide, you verified it. He had ordered enough "suicides" himself to be skeptical of all of them until proven otherwise.

Johnny took a cab rather than trying to drive. No way was he going to walk. A recent storm had left any shovel paths a risk of broken bones, not to mention the biting wind accompanying today's Chicago Special of the Day—freezing rain. It was unpleasant enough just picking his way from the curb to the front doors. Some days a ton and a half of rock salt just wasn't enough. He figured the wind chill was only about a gazillion below, and missed the hell out of Texas.

Ten minutes later he was busy trying to invent new curses, having run out of his ample supply of old ones. Indowy were damned thorough cleaners, and didn't wait around to get started, either. He was left with minimal bits of luck. Thank god their voodoo tanks took awhile to fix stuff. They'd already fully repaired the drapes, but hadn't gotten to the desk yet. The deceased's—um, almost deceased's—AID had not been tampered with, other than to turn the poor thing off. Lacking anywhere else to put it until competent authority reclaimed Epetar operations on Earth, it had been turned off and shoved back in the envelope where the Indowy had found it. Johnny filed that information away for future use. He hadn't known it was *possible* to turn an AID off. He was darned sure the Darhel weren't eager to have humans know that bit of information. Considering who he worked for, he didn't plan to share. Besides, the Darhel wouldn't use hush envelopes themselves if there weren't a catch to this whole "turn it off" business. He'd love to know, but it wouldn't be a good idea to ask.

Bobby arrived while he was going over the office and making notes. The first thing Stuart had him do was replace the packing tape on the floor with conventional yellow tape, where an Indowy had told him the Darhel was found.

"Good that they didn't rip out the carpet yet," the ex-cop grunted.

Robert "Bobby" Mitchell was medium-height, heavy-set and dark with the look of a weight-lifter who had given it up for other pursuits. He'd been a Sheriff's deputy in Silverton for ten years, eventually rising to detective sergeant, before one of the many, many IA complaints managed to stick. Picking up and then brutalizing a "hooker" who turned out to be an undercover police officer would do that.

"No, just trampled their little green feet all over it moving stuff out and around."

"Yeah. Let me block off the desk. I know the leg marks are still there in the carpet, but it makes it easier to visualize the scene. I'll also need a black light. I don't think they cleaned the carpet. Look at the tear here. They probably meant to repair it. And get me one of those doohickeys to show window repairs. It looks like there might have been a struggle, but I've seen a Two-D of one of them going bughouse years ago in Panama. He could have easily done all this himself before going catatonic. Believe me you *don't* want to see one of those bastards get pissed. Remind me the next time you're over. I've got it on a cube somewhere. Let's just say I don't want your job, cuz."

"Might not want to talk so frankly about our employer. It's not a great idea."

"Meaning no disrespect." His eyes flicked uncomfortably to Johnny's AID. "I don't guess our boss minds if we're a bit scared of him, you think?" He said it more for the benefit of the AID than his cousin.

"Nope." Johnny kept his response as short as possible. Safer that way.

"We absolutely have to have an autopsy of the Darhel."

"That might be a problem. Pardal isn't actually dead yet."

"If you really want to find out what happened, we probably need to fix that."

"Um . . . Is a coroner going to know enough about Darhel physiology to determine much? They're damned secretive."

"That's a problem, all right." Bobby rubbed his forehead, looking for a solution to that very big problem. "Use an AID. It knows enough about Darhel physiology to know what to look for and answer specific questions. A good forensic pathologist will be able to tell us stuff we've got to know—maybe make the difference between cracking the case and not. Can't investigate a suspicious death very well without an autopsy. Figure any information we get from the thing is more than we'd have if we didn't even look. Besides, they're just letting the prick starve." He shrugged at the warning glance from Johnny.

"It's a VIP death, screw it up and our asses would be in a crack for sure. That means I'm doing everything by the book. If the Tir denies permission for an autopsy it's no skin off my nose as long as I can document that I asked. If something goes wrong, I don't plan to take the fall for it."

"Gonna be hell to get him to agree to this."

"We've at least got to have proof that we tried. CYA, buddy."

"I hear that. Okay, gimme a minute." Johnny stepped outside and pulled the black box off his belt. Not that he needed to talk into it, it just felt wrong to talk to empty air like a head case. "Tina, get me Tir Dol Ron."

"He's a very busy person. I'll try," it said. "You're in luck. Here he is."

"Why are you interrupting me, Mr. Stuart?"

"I'm sorry, your Tir. I need special permission for something."

"And that is?"

"Whenever we investigate a suspicious death on Earth, we can't get enough information to tell what happened without an autopsy." He made sure to put the why ahead of the what to try to head off a knee-jerk reaction.

"What's an autopsy?"

"It's where a specialist examines the body to get clues about what happened in the person's last moments. Those clues are always a big part of reconstructing the circumstances of the death."

"This is unacceptable. We already know what happened in the Darhel Pardal's last moments. He failed to control himself and went into lintatai." The Tir bit the words out, as if loath to admit the species' weakness to a mere human. "However, if it makes your report more thorough to personally go look at the remains, do so."

Johnny grimaced. The Tir wasn't for a minute going to admit that the Darhel didn't want humans to know any more about them than they had to. And he clearly didn't understand the nature of the procedure. This was going to be delicate. "Sir, I know the security situation is delicate, and I do have ideas about how to protect your interests. The examination would be primarily conducted by an AID, with the specialist only present to tell the AID what kinds of things to examine, then your security employee, Bobby, would instruct the AID in how to analyze the results for the final report."

"The degree of observational opportunity to the human physician is unacceptable. It would be a human physician, correct?"

"Sir, while a human physician specializing in deaths would be necessary, steps could be taken to ensure anything sensitive he learned about Darhel in general was . . . contained. Completely contained."

He could hear the Darhel breathing hard before it

asked, more collectedly, "You have several days before this must happen, for your death expert to do his work?"

"Uh . . . sir, to get the information we need, waiting would . . . Sir, do you *really* want to know?"

"No! No I don't. You may do your . . . work, provided you guarantee information security in . . . some way that preserves our interests. I cannot emphasize enough how displeased I would be at a security breach of this nature."

"I understand, sir. I understand completely."

"This did need my personal attention. Try to avoid other incidents of this kind. I find the interruptions distasteful." The Darhel's breathing exercises were still audible in the AID network's transmission. He hated getting the boss upset—for the sake of his own skin rather than any liking of his employer. Bobby was right, though. When two risks to his safety conflicted, he just had to guess which one was smaller and go with it. He grimaced and walked back into the office.

"So do we have a go, or not?"

"We've got a go. But we need a pathologist who's good enough, but expendable."

Bobby winced. "Gotcha," he said. "I'll try to find one who doesn't have too many people to scream when he's gone. And keep the assignment itself confidential. We might need to do this again someday, and I'd hate to have trouble finding help next time."

"Good point. So we pick somebody who likes money enough to get stupid."

Johnny Stuart ignored the muffled *pop* sound from the morgue and looked at the report projected by his AID. He sat in the ground floor breakroom customarily

used by the former pathologist and his staff, also
ignoring the flunkies going past to help Bobby clean
up the mess. The Darhel corpse, of course, had to
be removed completely.

Interesting results. The Tir was going to be extremely
pissed. His chief of trouble prevention was torn between
having an extreme plum of information to show for his
efforts, and vindicating his call for an examination, versus
nervousness about delivering the news. He had had to
have a less intimidating staffer interview the Indowy
who had cleaned the room. *That* report told him more
about Darhel and lintatai than he'd ever wanted to
know—specifically that he never wanted to be in the
room when it happened, and that whoever had been
was some kind of superman or something. A superman
with a taste for blue silk shirts, judging by the scraps
of fabric the departed doctor had pulled from Pardal's
gut. It never for a moment occurred to him that the
killer might have been a woman. The sheer athleticism
it had taken to get out alive ruled that out.

His cousin had emerged from the autopsy room,
leaving the scutwork to the less well-paid help. It was
amazing how fast you got used to money and power.
Despite appearances, Bobby wasn't on the payroll
because he was Johnny's cousin. Bobby was on the
payroll because he combined a solid background in
law enforcement with one very special, crucial talent.
Bobby was what you'd call a well-socialized sociopath.
He could follow the rules of his employer without
deviation when he wanted—because getting caught
was a certainty, and he knew it. Someone without his
talent would be tempted by all kinds of feelings, from
love, to family ties, to friendship, to guilt.

Johnny could do the job, even enjoyed the job, but the nightmares were a stone bitch. He probably kept three researchers employed at Smith-Kline-Reynolds all by himself keeping him in sleeping pills. It was rare for the job to bug him, but the times it did he was torn between wondering whether he never should have taken the Darhel's dollar at any price, or whether he just plain liked it too much. The dead doctor in the other room didn't bug him, but he was just as glad that Bobby was the one to cap the prick.

Johnny's talent was management, especially of useful personalities. He kept Bobby unbored and made sure he had no hassles about getting laid. Easy arrangement. Bobby screwed whoever he wanted, Johnny had the girls checked out, before or after, and dealt with if they were a risk. Worked out for everybody.

Just now, Bobby was cursing at the coffee machine. In the present economy, it was unsurprising to find a pre-war junker of a machine, technically an antique, still in noisy, clunking service in the basement of a modern hospital. The offending machine had taken his money, and was straining noisily, but had failed to deposit the requisite paper cup in the appropriate slot. Johnny obliged by going over to the machine to exercise one of his own special talents—a mostly useless one, but still a talent. He could hear exactly where the problem was and somehow just sense where the problem was likely to be. He obligingly thwacked the machine on just the right spot to make it disgorge the cup and fill it with the doubtless crappy coffee.

"Thanks," his cousin said.

"No problem. Everything all right?" Johnny jerked his head towards the morgue.

"No problems. Where do we ditch the Darhel and the other dude?"

"Back where we found him, on top of the building. Nobody's allowed up there, and if we stick him in the right place, my understanding is that the Indowy will neatly haul them to the in-building trash incinerator. As easy as inserting tab A into slot B."

"Reminds me, I need the name of a new pimp. Freddie's girls are getting a bit long in the tooth." His cousin's tone was bland. The brief adrenaline rush had obviously worn off already.

"Sure. Tina, send him the next three on the list." He had warned his cousin about the circumstances of his predecessor's demise, but it went in one ear and out the other. He was *almost* clean in his operational habits.

His cousin didn't need conversation; in fact would prefer not to be distracted from his computer game, so the room was silent. He himself was preoccupied deciding exactly how he was going to present his findings to the Tir.

He had ample time, as the cleanup took several hours. Thank God for federal agents, who had the entire area tightly locked down. The former forensic examiner would be "involved in a sensitive murder investigation" permanently. The agents, believing it themselves, would handle inquiries down the road with the excuse of witness relocation. In a way, that was even true. His ashes, along with those of Pardal and whatever trash was in the building that day, had to end up somewhere. He supposed being murdered counted as involved in a murder investigation. Minus the investigation part. Whatever.

CHAPTER FIVE

Saturday, December 26, 2054

Johnny Stuart sat behind his cheap plastic desk, one that looked a lot more like wood than its forebears of nearly a century ago, and surveyed his cousin grimly. It was a good idea. It was just the kind of plan he'd asked for. It was also damned cold. He felt ghostly tugs at the remnants of a conscience he didn't know he still had, and couldn't help picturing his daughter, Mary Lynn, as one of the victims. The pang was fleeting; he did have a job to do.

"How are you going to prevent early discovery of the bodies? Or news reports of the disappearances?"

"It's not that hard. People generally don't fight the first day or two of a missing persons case when the police are insisting on waiting. Oh, they bitch, but they don't go all out calling the media and lawyers. If a seemingly kind cop or two is surreptitiously checking things out despite the rules, or appears to be, families think they've won something. They bitch, they panic, they're pissed—but no calls to the media or lawyers. In other words, over the time span we've got, we pick the right targets in the right order and we can keep a lid on the hits until January first. Then the various anonymous tips make sure everything breaks at once. Families don't want to give up hope until they identify the body. Right targets, right order, and we're golden," Bobby assured him.

"Take the first hit. It's a beloved niece and the twin brother. The girl's a coed—has a habit of taking off on road trips without telling anyone where she's going. If they can't reach her, they'll take awhile before they get too worried. The twin brother will have a very convincing car accident—convincing until the evidence gets dropped in the cops' lap, along with the location of the niece's body. It's first because it has a long lag time, but not best because it's a more peripheral relative. As we get down to the wire, we can do targets that are a lot more significant because we don't have to hold suspicion down for as long." The killer shrugged. "It's all in the timing."

Johnny was sometimes a little nauseated at the way his cousin's mind worked. Only a little, though. It was business, and this kind of thing was why he kept Bobby on the payroll in the first place. "Okay. How about an extra month's salary for every hit?"

His cousin nodded. "Per body, and half of it in sales-tax-free goods. Plus, of course, you pay all the expenses, including the cost of hiring extra help."

"Done," Johnny agreed. It was fairly cheap for murder for hire, but partly because Bobby could count on a steady salary and kick-ass benefits. The tax-free goods was a smart idea, because with the high prices, and some kinds of consumer goods rare, hookers would usually take all or part of a fee in barter. High-end whores would do almost anything for real French perfume or cashmere. With Bobby's tastes, that was a necessity.

"Why don't you and the kid come out for dinner next weekend, after we've got off the first round of this thing? Help me celebrate my bonus a little," Bobby said.

"Great. I'd like that." A free meal was a free meal, and Mary Lynn could use the cheer of a meal out. "Hey, Bob, if you bring a date, could she be a, well, a discreet one?" He didn't want to piss off his benefactor, but he didn't really want his baby girl watching a whore climb all over Uncle Bobby all evening.

His cousin's lips tightened a little for a long second, but finally he shrugged. "Sure, Johnny. Whatever. Guess it would be a bit much for the kid. I guess I can have *one* meal without the entertainment." He actually grinned, as if the idea amused him.

This grin actually reached his eyes and Johnny suppressed a shudder. That little glint always reminded him of the Tir for some reason.

"Oh, and Bobby?" Johnny decided to keep the other man happy; offer something in exchange for the request about the whore. "Don't let it fuck up your holiday, okay. You're already off through the 27th, right? If you start Monday, can you get it all done by New Year's?"

"Sure, whatever," Mitchell shrugged. "I could have fun with a little time off."

Saturday, December 26, 2054

"I told you it's impossible," buckley said. It obviously believed it, because it had that smug tone again.

Cally stared at the layout it was projecting over her desk and shook her head, pushed a stray strand of hair back behind her ear and took a jerky swig of coffee. It was goddamned frustrating was what it was.

Papa's cryptic and encrypted message had sent her on a scavenger hunt of digging up bits of data the professionally paranoid old man had hidden over half the island and a good bit of the internet. In some cases literally digging up, as he'd apparently been stashing PDAs on the island since the term was invented.

What she had finally come up with was the basics of a very sweet smuggling scheme.

There was a big pocket of aluminum in Venezuela that nobody was mining. Panama was producing excess food. Cuba produced steel and and had facilities for processing aluminum. Panama needed both.

Food and luxury goods from Panama to Venezuela. Bauxite to Cuba. Steel and forged aluminum to Panama. Repeat. Classic triangle trade.

Which begged the reason nobody was doing it.

Venezuela was simply *crawling* with Posleen. Fleet occasionally used orbital lasers to burn out God-King settlements that got noticeable. It was that bad.

Anybody who wanted to mine the area would have to get enough premium fighters together, like, say, DAG, to take over and clear the area. The Darhel had tried twice with the usual scum and bounced. It was, in fact, DAG's original mission: Clearing out tough pockets of Posleen.

Problem being that anyone who got a really good mining operation up and running was going to get tossed out, using one loophole or another, by the Darhel. So the mining operation was going to have to be secret. As was moving the goods.

Papa had plenty of contacts, go figure, among smugglers in the Caribbean area.

Papa had been, from the results of the scavenger hunt, looking at the plan for some time. He needed three things.

A bunch of really premium, highly trained fighters with nothing better to do.

Check.

Contacts in Cuba and Panama to fence the goods.

Check.

A bunchaton of money.

Shit.

"Unless you have something constructive to say, buckley, shut up."

"It's a disastrous task. Giving up *is* constructive."

"Shut up, buckley."

"Right."

The only person she knew who knew shady financial deals as well as Granpa was Stewart. For Cally, her husband was forever tied to his nom de guerre from the war against the Posleen. When they met and fell in love, she'd been on a mission and they'd both been under different aliases—he as Lieutenant Pryce, and she as Captain Sinda Makepeace. General James Stewart had been the alias underneath the Pryce alias, and had forever gotten stuck in her mind as his "real" name. The Asian name he wore now as a mid-ranking member of the Tong fit him as badly as his new face. Oh, he was great at carrying off his cover, it just didn't seem "right" to her. His Pryce face had at least been his own, original face. Hers hadn't, but she'd been stuck with it long enough since the mission that she'd gotten used to it. The boobs were still too conspicuous, and she still carried more flesh than she was comfortable with—no matter what the men said. But the face now felt more like it belonged than like a cover. It was kinda creepy.

None of which got her any closer to solving this damn problem. Stewart. That was her next option, and she really hated to call it in. It was *not* common knowledge in the Tong that Stewart was married to someone in the Bane Sidhe. It wasn't even common knowledge that he was married, or a round-eye. Sure, a girlfriend, even kids, but then a blond mistress was a status symbol. The picture on his desk of her and the kids was regarded by his colleagues more as a power statement than an emotional relationship. In their minds, of course he hadn't married the exotic mistress. It would have been a bad career move, and he was a recognized player.

So, out of concern for his safety, she avoided making contact with him. Proper mistresses came when called—they didn't make demands. She had no choice. Maybe he could make some kind of sense of this mess, but that was the kicker, wasn't it? For him to sort out the mess, he'd have to see the data. That wasn't a security problem; Granpa would be fine with it. The problem was there was no way she could send that much information through a covert pipeline without enormous risk of revealing the pipeline. There was also the sticky bit of using her organization or his.

The information either crossed to his organization on this end of the pipeline by her paying to send it up—which wouldn't be cheap—or it crossed to his organization on the far end of the pipeline, with someone Bane Sidhe passing him a data cube. Either way was bad.

She settled for sending him a brief summary of the problem under cover of love letters. It had to be brief. The still holo of her, done pin-up style, only had just so much room for planting an encrypted message, once you accounted for redundancy. Her encryption task was much more complicated than it seemed. The first thing her Tong contact would do upon her buying the postage was compress it and encrypt the compressed file. This would cause a great deal of data loss, which wouldn't matter a whit if the file were the simple cheesecake holo it pretended to be. Software on the other end would infer the missing data and fill in the gaps. Visually, it would be impossible to tell the difference.

Unfortunately, that data loss would irretrievably garble a message that could otherwise fit quite securely and unnoticeably within a garden-variety still holo. The trick was to include an encrypted message in the holo that had sufficient redundancy to survive the damage in the mail, but was still obscure enough to avoid detection. It cut down the amount of data she could send quite a bit. The more information, the more garbled or the less secure, take your pick. She picked a very short message.

CHAPTER SIX

The stateroom was cramped, the walls an odd shade of brown that suggested overtones of some hue beyond the ken of human eyes. The bunk was too low for human comfort, soft where it should be firm, and vice versà. The fold-out chair and desk were too high, and clearly not configured for human bodies.

Schooled in xenology as he was, Alan Clayton recognized the "bunk" as a Himmit fitness station, pushed into the room and hastily modified for a human's basic need for sleep. The fold-out "desk" and "chair" were, together, one of the actual rest areas of the room. The closest description was a Himmit recliner. He could just barely see the outline on the wall where their version of a holoprojector had been removed from the room.

The captain had not vacated his own quarters to house them. That would be absurd. Instead, the room revealed the interesting—and new—information that there might, occasionally, be more than one Himmit on board this vessel. That intelligence catch alone put this trip in the "win" column.

He expected Michael O'Neal, Sr., to arrive momentarily. Being short and squat, like his more famous son, the O'Neal could be *almost* comfortable in a room intended for Indowy; but only because it was built for four of them.

His own room was tall enough for an average human man to stand in because Himmit liked to climb. It actually had a high ceiling, which told him it was designed to be triply versatile in case the ship had to carry a Darhel. He wasn't getting preferential treatment over the O'Neal. Far from it. The Himmit had simply looked at the relative sizes of their two passengers and stowed them in the most convenient places.

The high ceiling was useful in another respect. It had a Himmit on it. Rather, it had *the* Himmit who was their captain. Although some token value had changed hands, the real "fare" for their voyage was that the Himmit thought the instruction of the O'Neal in Galactic protocol would make a good story. It was probably right.

Clayton politely pretended not to notice it, and it politely pretended not to notice his pretense. Wasn't Galactic diplomacy fun?

"The O'Neal is at the door, Mr. Clayton," the soft voice of his buckley chimed.

"Thanks, Liz. Let him in," he said.

"You realize we're trying to make a silk purse out of a sow's ear, don't you? Hate to talk that way about myself, but situationally, it applies," Papa said.

"If we're trading aphorisms, 'needs must when the devil drives.'" Clayton pitched back. "Have a seat," he said, gesturing towards the bed, which was by far the more comfortable spot.

"Okay, shoot. How to be a diplomat one-oh-one." Papa scratched his nose and shifted until he found a comfortable spot on the bed. Somebody had screwed up his luggage, loading only half the tobacco, so he was rationing himself.

"We're not even to that point," Alan said. "Let's start with the theory of communication."

"Okay," Papa said in a pained voice.

"I just used words and intonation to move a thought from my head to yours," Alan said, his face deadpan. "But what you received was not what I sent."

"I don't get what you mean," Papa said, frowning.

"All I said was 'Let's start with the theory of communication.' But that was not my full thought. Part of my thought, that was not included but could be surmised from that short sentence was this: 'Let us discuss the theory of communication because it is very important to the basis of diplomacy. Also because I find it fascinating. And because I'm trying to show you that whereas you are a very good killer, I am a very expert, I will not say good but certainly expert, diplomat, negotiator and interlocutor. I am, further, aware that your background, habits and thoughts lead you to hate this particular field of research and methods of interaction. Your beliefs are that negotiation is almost invariably a worthless endeavor. I am going to have to overcome tremendous resistance. One way to do that is to get the really bad parts right up front when you might still, vaguely, be paying attention.'

That is, in part, the thought I was trying to convey to your brain."

"Damn," Papa said. "Glad you just kept it to a sentence."

"The thought you received, as evidenced by your response and your body language was: This is nothing but a pointless exercise in pain."

"Yeah," Papa said with a chuckle. "Pretty much."

"Which means we have, as the saying go, a failure to communicate," Alan said.

"There was this movie—" Papa began.

"I have seen it," Alan replied. "And I wish you to recall the very ending. Because, and I do not exaggerate, that *is* the ending for Clan O'Neal and the Earthly Bane Sidhe if you have a failure to communicate in these negotiations. Insurgencies cannot survive without external support. Prior to reconnection to the Galactic Bane Sidhe, the Earthly Bane Sidhe were not an insurgency but a very small group of minor officials who were, in many cases over the centuries, quite quite mad. They could do little or nothing to affect their world. Furthermore, the Tchpth can eliminate the Bane Sidhe without really trying. They do not have to kill us; there are plenty of humans who will take the pay to do so. They can permanently remove support. Provide information to the authorities on all of our actions. Send assassins whom they will decry but who nonetheless will eliminate the Bane Sidhe root and *every* branch. Eliminate not just the thought, not just the meme, but the very *gene* of resistance to the Darhel from the gene pool."

"Point," Papa said.

"That," Alan said, pointing to both of his temples,

"is the thought that I had in my head. That your understanding of the basic, the most basic, theories of negotiation, manipulation and interlocution are *vitally* important for the Bane Sidhe, Clan O'Neal and humanity." He flung his hands outwards and pointed to Papa's head. "Have you now read my thoughts? Do you *clearly* have that thought in your head?"

"I don't know," Papa said, actually thinking about the response. "I can't read your mind."

"NOW we're to the theory of communication!" Alan said, clapping his outflung hands together and smiling. "The monkey *can* learn!"

Michael O'Neal, Sr., was bored enough on the ship, the young pup having left him alone for three whole days with a damned "diplomat game" to play on his PDA, that he finally resigned himself to calling the kid up out of a basic need for human interaction. He would have talked to him yesterday, but he had started feeling as though out-waiting Alan was becoming a game. He decided it would be damned stupid to get in a pissing contest with a kid young enough to be his great or three grandson. As the saying went, Papa didn't have to like it, he just had to do it. Besides, it wasn't the kid's fault he had to go play nice with a bunch of smart-ass, condescending, patronizing, hypocritical, pacifist, compulsive vegetarian lobsters with an attitude.

Okay, so they were smart. Their survival instincts were for shit. They were part of creating an artificial 'peace' that depended on nobody disturbing it. If they were so smart, why didn't they plan for the possibility that someone else might not have decided to 'study war no more'?

Tchpth were survival morons. The only truly intelligent thing they'd done against the Posleen threat was to figure out they needed other people to do their dirty work and where to go to find them.

The more things changed, the more they stayed the same. This ruckus comes up, starts giving them heartburn or whatever, they pulled the same old trick as the peaceniks when he was back in Vietnam. Be more than glad to take the benefits. Yeah, you got your freedom to smoke dope and not bathe. You're fucking welcome. Yeah, Crabs, the Posleen didn't take pliers to your steamed asses and dip you in melted butter. You're fucking welcome. Assholes. One war to another, it never changed.

Then this mess, he thought. He wished he could say it.

"Yeah, that Darhel and rogue mentat you found so fucking inconvenient are safely dead, so now you can wash your hands and pretend you had nothing to do with it you hypocritical bastards." But no, he had to go haring halfway across the damned galaxy to kiss their asses. Right now, the greatest pleasure he could imagine would be to send the bug-eyed shark bait a simple e-mail saying, *"Blow me,"* and go home to play with his grandkids. Or do some real work. Anything but this, anywhere but here.

The flip side was, Alan was right. There had never been anything he'd done in his life more important than this meeting. It just pissed him off that it was in a conference room and not a battlefield.

"Himmit Tarkas would like to see you, Michael. May he come in?" his PDA asked.

"Come in!" he called towards the door. Unnecessarily

because it had already begun to slide open, admitting the purplish gray quadruped.

"What are you thinking about?" it asked. "Is it a good story? The Human Clayton needed sleep. I would like to hear your stories. Would you like to tell them here, or would you be more comfortable in the lounge?"

"Here," Papa said. "The lounge gives me the creeps, no offense."

"None is taken," the Himmit said, sliding up the wall and shading to match.

"What do you want to hear about?" Papa asked. "And, you know, it's easier for humans to talk about stuff if they can see who they're talking to. It's a human thing."

"This is understood," the Himmit said. "And we are more comfortable being invisible. It is a Himmit thing."

"Your ship, your rules," Papa said. "Ask away."

"You were a mature adult, for your species, before the Posleen war. Am I correct that you fought in human killing human wars?"

"One of them," O'Neal answered grimly.

"Tell me stories from that, please." To the extent that it was possible, the Himmit seemed almost cheerful.

Papa O'Neal sighed inside. It was going to be a long trip. If the Himmit wanted an old man's war stories from 'Nam, the Himmit could have war stories to its froggy heart's—or whatever it had—content. "Well, this one time we were out on patrol way the hell up north and inland, damn near into Laos, and . . ." He paused and held up the cup of goop that had come out of the tap as a "drink." "You wouldn't happen to

have some form of alcoholic beverage, beer by preference, instead of this stuff, would you?"

"I will be right back," it said.

Papa would have described its movement off as
scampering, and its mood as cheerful, if someone had
put a gun to his head and just *made* him give a description. He shook the impressions off as absurd. Vietnam
war stories. He was paying for interstellar passage
somewhere with fuckin' Vietnam war stories. O'Neal
reflected that the universe was a strange place. He
didn't know if there was any kind of god out there in
the sense of religion, and he kind of thought not, but if
there was, the guy sure had a twisted sense of humor.

Tir Dol Ron stared at the monkey in front of him
and found himself once again amazed by the creative
ingenuity of the vicious beasts. Most of the reason
he felt this amazement, at the moment, was because
it distracted him from the more natural feelings the
situation might have engendered.

"This violates the Compact," he said grimly.

John Earl Bill Stuart only knew about the Compact
in the vaguest terms possible. Specifically, he knew that
he could . . . deal with . . . people trying to kill him or
his employees, but must ask his AID for permission
to . . . to . . . preserve the Tir's interests against other
opposition agents if he found them. The Tir had no
idea how often or seldom the AID granted or with-
held permission. He couldn't. It would be hazardous
to his life.

The monkey smelled of fear. Well he might. The Tir
admitted to himself that under other circumstances this
news could have seriously upset him. In the present

case, Tir Dol Ron had absorbed so many unpleasant messes today that he was in a constant state of meditative calm. Extremely angry meditative calm, but the anger sat like ice in his stomach.

"You need not be frightened. I am quite calm." He said this not to reassure his employee. He hadn't even thought of such a thing. The thought would have required empathy. Darhel simply lacked that faculty; or, as they saw it, flaw. Instead, he spoke from the knowledge that John Stuart would have impaired functioning if he was frightened, and would be less efficient in understanding his own instructions.

"This requires a response. You are familiar with mirrors, of course." The Darhel chose his words carefully, hiding his mind away from whatever implications there might be to what he was saying.

"Yes, your Tir. I own several mirrors. Are you informing my AID that there has been some level of change in what your interests may be?"

"That is a very good way of putting it, Johnny." Tir Dol Ron didn't understand the human custom of nicknames, but he didn't have to understand them to use them. Primitives were often inexplicable.

"Tina, do you understand the Tir's instructions? Please do not reply in detail. Yes or no will do."

The AID had failsafes against expressing certain ideas in the presence of their masters. Not that a Darhel minded if somebody died. Billions did it every day. They just wanted no implications, ever, that they were directly, causatively involved. It was an indication that his employee was very slightly smarter than most humans, and confirmed that hiring him had been a good choice.

"Yes, I understand," the machine replied.

"Good. Apropos of nothing," the Tir's voice was silky, melodious to the point of sublime, "there was a large unit of Galactic and local professional killers who disappeared from north of here recently. At the time, I requested that you ignore the matter. I have changed my mind. You will look into it."

For what must have been the millionth time, Tir Dol Ron cursed the Aldenata and how very little it took to invoke the release of Tal, the lethally blissful hormone that locked a Darhel into catatonia until he died—usually of thirst. To have to use primitives with so little control over—

He turned his mind away from forbidden thoughts and dismissed his less-stupid-than-average employee.

Cleanup would now proceed in the present intolerable situation. The intriguers had destroyed an entire Darhel business group. Tir Dol felt an icy chill go up his spine. This was beyond serious. This was a *threat*. He had his AID plot ship schedules and collate his findings, transmitting them to the courier on station and ordering its dispatch to the most time-efficient locations and route. He used a billing code, under a standing contract, that would split the courier charges among all Darhel Groups thus informed.

Tir Dol Ron was possessed of a major treasure in the Sol System. There were a very, very few altars of communication left behind. The Tchpth, curse the folth-leavings, flatly refused to either build more or even indicate whether or not they knew how. They were open enough about using regular communications channels via ship that the Darhel had a debate among themselves about whether they knew or not.

The fact remained that because of the sensitivity of Earth to the anti-Posleen effort, one of the very few devices for genuinely real-time communication between worlds had been sited here during the war. It was not real-time accessible. Instead, it was sited on Earth's moon as a location much less susceptible to annoying intriguers. They might not be able to kill sophonts any more than he could, but property was another matter. One would hope its irreplaceable nature would protect it but, alas, that had not been the case in the past. Chances were not taken.

He had two choices. He could transmit to the altar itself from here and accept both time lag from Earth to moon and risk of interception and decoding, or he could go there himself and transmit directly. The matter was serious enough that security vastly outweighed haste. He instructed his AID to book him a seat on the next shuttle up.

CHAPTER SEVEN

"What happened to Darin?" the Himmit asked.

"Oh, he ran into a claymore about two weeks later," Papa said.

"That's how most of your friends end up," the Himmit noted.

"Unfortunately true," Papa said. "Not that I'd call Darin a friend. Just one of the guys on the teams."

"You have had a remarkable ability to avoid being killed, given your life experiences," the Himmit said. "Statistically amazing, in fact."

"This is right good brew," Papa said, taking another sip. It was, too. He'd had a lot of beer in his time but this was very good. And he did not *begin* to recognize it. "Don't suppose you'll tell me where it comes from?"

"Nowhere accessible to you," the Himmit said. "And I, unfortunately, do not have any more."

"Well, then, I'll have to make it last," Papa said, belying that by taking another sip. "But since we ain't got much more and I don't tell stories well without something to wet my whistle, I think I'll tell you one that will not only pay for this trip, but for this very fine brew you have provided."

"I am eagerly awaiting it," the Himmit said.

"And you've got lots of ears," Papa replied, grinning. "The thing is . . . I want you to understand . . . Soldiers tell stories. Sometimes they . . . exaggerate."

"All stories, of the necessity of communication, contain some element of fiction," the Himmit said. "I personally doubt the one about the CS."

"Truth," Papa said, placing his hand over his heart.

"I do not doubt that the patrol was killed," the Himmit said. "That would be the outcome of the method. It was the packing into orifices. There was insufficient material."

"Well, *all* of 'em weren't like that," Papa admitted. "But that factoid makes the story better."

"Elements of fiction," the Himmit replied. "When we transmit our stories, we avoid all such elements. However, we relay *your* stories precisely as given. With the caveat that they contain some element of fiction."

"Point accepted," Papa said, taking a sip. "But what I want you to understand is that this story is truth. Pointed, complete, truth. There's nothing worth exaggerating in it. But you're not going to believe a word."

"Why?"

"Because it's the story of when I met a vampire." He paused.

"I'm waiting for you to say something like, 'Pull one of the other ones, it's got bells on.'"

"Why?"

"You believe in vampires?" Papa said. "I know *I* didn't. 'Til I met one."

"I accept the possibility of there being of such condition as you would refer to him or it as a vampire."

"Interesting response," Papa said, musingly. "Given that I don't think there's anything you Himmit don't know."

"Very little."

"Well, I've never told this story to anybody," Papa said. "And all the rest of the guys who saw it . . . Well, they ain't around no more. That statistical thing you mentioned. And we didn't tell anybody, even in the debrief. It's not something you admit. So this is a story that nobody's got. Must be worth something."

"Agreed."

"We was doing an op in Europe," Papa said, sitting back in his chair. "Which we didn't do much as it was hard to get there. But the European networks had just gotten screwed to hell by the invasion. And there was this guy working in one of the Austrian defense bases . . . The Texans had a law at one point: A guy who just needed killin'."

"Most of your stories surround such people." The Himmit had learned that Papa needed a certain amount of prompting for his stories to flow.

"Yeah," Papa admitted. "He was a fairly minor logistics officer. But he had his fingers on a lot of stuff. And he looked incompetent. So stuff that was needed one place ended up in the wrong place, usually meaning that some unit that desperately needed it lost a battle and a bunch of soldiers got killed. The usual way that the Darhel worked in the war.

And since the war. He wasn't incompetent, though. He was too consistent. And, hell, we had his money trace and some of his orders from the Darhel. Taking him out was practically a mission from God.

"Problem being that he was in the St. Polten PDF. It wasn't a line defense base, it was one of the rear area support bases for the Vienna Defenses."

"I know of it."

"Basic plan was as simple as you could get for taking out someone in a major defense base," Papa said. "Go in as an American liaison team. Since the bases were occasionally under attack, you could carry weapons on base. Find the target. Take him out in his quarters. Extract as if nothing had happened. We had passes for the base, uniforms, weapons, covers. I hate it when you have to depend on somebody else for all that, somebody you don't have any knowledge of. But it was all good.

"We'd made the penetration and were proceeding to his quarters. All good. No issues. Then every damned siren in the base went off. 'Hostile human intruder on base!'"

"Never fun," the Himmit said. "I do hate the whole 'Intruder alert!' thing."

"Yeah, you would," Papa said. "But it was one intruder. And then they started giving a description and location. Wasn't *us*."

"Interesting."

"The op was blown, though," Papa said. "They started shutting down the base. Going into hard lock down. We had secondary and tertiary extraction points. We pretty quickly figured out we couldn't go for the secondary. We headed for the tertiary. Things were going nuts. Before we knew it, we were the only people running around the base who *weren't* security.

"They kept broadcasting locations. And either there was more than one guy with the same description or he was so fast it wasn't funny. We'd memorized the layout of the base and he was all over the place. I couldn't figure out what he was doing from the calls. But it was sort of working for us because he wasn't anywhere near our route.

"Then we ran into a defense point. We came hauling ass around a corner and there was a squad hunkered down behind a battle station. They had us dead to rights. I decided, hey, maybe we could talk our way through. They weren't buying it. I don't think they thought we were hostiles. But in a security alert like that, you take anyone who isn't where they are supposed to be under arrest. If they really looked into our background we were screwed. But it was surrender or die fighting. I was still hoping we could talk our way out.

"They told us to place our weapons on the ground and come forward. Which we did. We were about halfway down the corridor when there was this scream from behind them."

Papa paused and took a sip of the mysterious beer.

"I've heard a lot of screams in my time," Papa said, his eyes distant. "There's the scream of somebody who's had a blade shoved into their belly. Never nice. It has a particular pitch to it. The scream of somebody who's hurt bad on the battlefield. The scream of a woman. I've never heard a scream like this one before or since. Mortal scream, the person was dying. And it was a scream of abject, absolute, terror. Not just fear of dying. Fear of *why* they were dying."

He paused and sighed.

"The security guys had forgotten all about us. They'd reoriented to the rear. I considered quietly tiptoeing away but didn't. Don't know quite why. I guess I was just stupid-curious to see what in the *hell* could make somebody scream like that.

"We were in a maintenance tunnel. Big. Five meters across, ten meters high. The across is what matters. The defense point was at an intersection. So, I'm trying to make up my mind what to do and all of a sudden a body comes flying out of the side corridor. And all the way across the corridor to land on the other side."

He looked at the Himmit and cocked an eyebrow.

"Comments?"

"That would normally presume a mechanical force," the Himmit said.

"Yep," Papa said, then took a sip. "They were rigged out in full battle rattle. Average male weight in Europe, and this was an average enough guy, was about one-eighty. With battle rattle, that makes about a hundred kilos. Distance was five meters, bit short of twenty feet, around two hundred twenty pounds. And he hadn't been spun. He was going straight as if he'd been shot-putted. Going up coming into the corridor and then down as he left. Don't know how far into the side-corridor he made it. Wasn't alive anyway."

"That is a remarkable toss," the Himmit said. "Especially if the tosser was the human-appearing intruder."

"I would have put it as mechanically impossible for the human body," Papa said. "But there it is. There was more. Screams. Crashes. Speaking of sounds you don't often hear. There's a very specific sound of a person hitting a barrier that kills them. I'd only ever heard it once before when a guy I knew burned in on a jump right next to me. It's a weird 'squish-crack' as the bones in the ribs break. This was coupled with the ring of Galplas. Someone had been thrown into a wall hard enough to smash. Again, wouldn't have believed it if I wasn't there. But I was.

"Then the 'intruder' came into view. Five-five, buck-fifty. Brown hair that was kind of long and shaggy. I'd have pegged him as one of the refugees that trickled in in dribs and drabs. Worn out Russian camo top and jeans that had seen better days. Barefoot. And just about shot to fucking shit. Blood was flowing down his chest and arteries were spurting. You don't often see a person walking, running, fighting, with spurting arteries, believe me.

"He had an odd expression. Not angry, not violent, just as if he was pushing aside brush looking for something. Most of the security guys had run. Some of them had run past us. A few were still trying to take him on. There'd been shots. I'd been sort of ignoring them for the other stuff. I saw one of them shoot him point blank, multiple times, in the chest, with .308. Didn't seem to faze him. He just hit the guy so hard his neck broke.

"He'd found what he was looking for, which was the commander of the security point."

Papa stopped and shook his head.

"That's when I knew what it was," he said, softly. "He picked the guy up by the throat, opened up his mouth and bit down. When he opened his mouth, fangs like a snake dropped down. And he sunk them into the guy's neck. The spurting stopped and, I shit you not, while I was watching him suck the life out of that LT, he healed right in front of my eyes."

"I am accepting your reality," the Himmit said. "Go on. You survived. Again."

"Yeah," Papa said. "He finished with the LT, looked kind of interested as if he was digesting something. Something in his head, not the LT. Then he looked at us and sort of cocked his head to the side and said something in a language. A word, maybe a name.

"I looked at him and raised my hands: 'Friends?' I mean, I wasn't going down without a fight but I also knew I was going down, if you know what I mean."

"Understood."

"Then he said: 'Bane Sidhe.' It had a weird accent to it, but I recognized it. He spouted some other gibberish at us but I didn't understand it. One of my guys did, though. Not the words, apparently. He just said 'Gaelic?'

"I said: We don't speak Gaelic. But, yeah, we're Baen Sidhe."

"'Where is the Elf?' he asked. Odd accent. Sort of Eastern European, sort of not. Swallowed. I don't do languages the way that Nathan does but it wasn't an accent I'd ever heard and I've heard a lot in my time.

"Now, we knew there was a Darhel 'liaison' on the base, but he was off-limits cause of the damned Compact. Apparently he wasn't off-limits to the vampire. Maybe he liked blue blood."

"More purplish," the Himmit said.

"'Room Four-Two Bravo-Alpha-Four,' I said. 'We're not authorized to take him.'"

"'Then you are not true Bane Sidhe,' he said, pretty contemptuously. 'Leave the base. There is a way clear to an exit. Do not return.' And he was gone. And by 'gone' I mean it was like he vanished like one of you guys. I actually think he just moved so fast our eyes couldn't follow.

"Well, we made fucking tracks to the exit, let me tell you, buddy. And we swore up and down we'd never repeat the story to a soul. The pick-up was at the entrance and we told him somebody else had attacked the base and the hit was off and we scooted. He had a ground-car and we could get out of the security ring that was setting up around the base. They were sending more troops in to try to catch the guy. We got questioned but all we said we knew was that there'd been a security alert and, it not being our business, we were di di mao. We weren't the bad guys, as far as they knew, so they let us go.

"We got about an hour, maybe, down the road and there was this shaking like an earthquake. Turned out the base had blown up. A PDC makes one hell of a fall of rock when it blows up, let me tell you. We were in another valley and it was *still* raining hot granite.

"So that's my story," Papa said, taking his last sip of beer. "And I'm sticking to it. Never told it to another soul."

"It is a good story," the Himmit said. "Well worth the price of the trip. I shall gain favor by its retelling."

"You don't seem particularly surprised by it," Papa said. "Of course, if you guys can even look surprised."

"That an intruder was involved with the destruction of the St. Polten PDF is well known," the Himmit replied.

"And it being a vampire? Did you know that, *too*?"

"Thank you for the very good story," was all it said.

"Your Ghin, the altar calls you."
Resignedly, he turned his thoughts away from his

latest problem and cleared his head. Any input from the altar would be critically important. One did not use it for less. Confining the altars' use to the vital and avoiding group business rivalries removed anyone's temptation to decide their own interests might be better off without the existence of the devices. Security came in many different forms. The Ghin was in a position to enforce communications discipline, and he did so. That it served *his* personal interests to do so was an accepted down side. He was as close to strictly neutral between groups as it was possible to be, which was the best anyone could ask for. That he also considered the interests of his species of paramount importance was all to the good.

There had to be someone in the highest seat of arbitration. Each group being absolutely certain it could write a more skillful contract than the other groups solidified his position. His deserved reputation for being meticulously and impartially literal gave every group the certainty that his presence in the position gave it an edge over the other groups. He, and the other Ghins before him, had maintained the sanctity of contract through the Galaxy since his race were first allowed—the taste of the price was still bitter—off their homeworld. That was as close to order as anyone could ask for.

He carefully lit the sticks of incense on the altar and made his ritual obeisances—one of the few circumstances in which a top Darhel would willingly perform such actions. The relic was sacred. Besides, there was the partially superstitious notion that somewhere, somehow, someone might be listening in.

The device, although communication was nearly instantaneous, took a certain amount of time to make initial contact. The Ghin sometimes wondered if the Aldenata had crafted the prescribed rituals merely to create the illusion that the wait was shorter than the reality. Besides, the drill supported calmness—paramount when dealing with urgent matters.

The hologram focused in slowly, bringing one Tir Dol Ron into his office space. The Ghin twitched in irritation. "Oh. It's you," he said. The small snub was precise.

"I arrive," the Tir replied, responding to the Ghin's display of bad manners by omitting his title.

"This is doubtless important enough to merit imploring the gods of communication." The Ghin managed to convey that he did very much doubt such importance. The matter *was*, of course, important. He just already knew the details of the situation and didn't appreciate being interrupted from contemplating the details of his options. Besides, Tir Dol Ron was, to put it bluntly, a pain in the ass. "How go your plans for the humans, Tir?" he asked.

"Badly," the Tir admitted baldly, surprising him. "I underestimated your concerns about recontacting them."

Such an admission was very out of character. He must want something big.

CHAPTER EIGHT

Thursday, December 31, 2054

Bobby had put himself together a nice little posse to go
get some serious retribution for the opposition's nasty
attack on his bosses' interests. The stuff so far had been
small shit. This was the big one, at least for openers.
This was the one that brought the lesson home.

The guys in the diner, and one chick, were all either
hardened criminals or seasoned cops. None of your
pre-war pussy cops, either. These were bona fide hard-
asses who could take care of business, and would, for
the generous price he was paying.

The Oak Street Diner had pretty damned great
food. It was the only place in Chicago where he'd
order pancakes for lunch. The girl who first brought
him here said it had something to do with how they
made the batter—yeast or something. Bobby didn't
know anything about all that cooking shit, he just

knew they were damn fine pancakes and worth an extra hour at the gym.

He put his plate on another table, a signal to the other men to do the same. Whether there was food on their plates or not, they were done. He passed out data cubes like cards in a holo western before pulling the first of the pictures up on his AID—nice little status symbol, that. Usually he used a buckley for data security, but when he wanted to impress, he used the AID.

"Here are our targets. Candy," Mitchell nodded to the girl, "you're our in." She looked kind of skanky in her day-to-day walking around clothes. Too much makeup and a whole lot of sexy. Hot, but cheap.

"New girl next door, borrow a cup of sugar kind of thing, right?" She picked her teeth with a long, acrylic fingernail.

"You got it. You get the door open, we're right in on your back." Candy was for sure and certain used to having guys on her back. She had a stripper's figure—skinny waist along with tits that had obvious cheap implants, and probably some surgical rounding of her ass as well. The platinum blond hair aped some ancient starlet, but her roots were dark as anthracite coal and badly needed a touch-up. Probably an easy solution to his problem of what to do tonight, though.

"Here's our main targets." He flipped through the woman and kids in quick succession, seeing no need to pause. "They're on your cube, so take a look on your own time. Not that you really need to. All you need to remember is to kill anything alive in the house. People, pets. Hell, if in doubt, you can kill the fucking potted plants. Everybody dies. Simple. Any questions?" Of course there weren't. He hadn't gone to any special lengths to buy intelligent goons, but even dumbasses could understand these instructions.

"What about the noise? All that shooting's gonna make lots of noise." The light brown guy—Bobby thought of him as "Chubby"—was the least experienced of the bunch. But he'd worked a couple of years as a Sub-Urb cop, on the take but not greedy with it; he was worth bringing along just because with his totally ordinary looks and good attitude, he just might have a future in the security side of the Tir's organization. He'd done okay with his test run on the old lady, and he'd just proved himself marginally smarter than the other three.

"It's New Year's Eve. Everybody who doesn't think it's firecrackers will assume it's just some dork firing into the air."

Target selection had, in the end, been relatively simple. Most of the relatives of that big, flashy unit that had done a Benedict Arnold and run had disappeared but good. He'd like to find out how they'd done it, too. But anyway, enough of them had left tracks going to ground that he had something to work with without trying too hard. Wives, kids. Good targets. Much closer than the somewhat less effective grandmothers, parents and shit they'd taken so far. The objective was to let the bastards know they'd been hit and send a message to any other fuckheads tempted to pull the same stunt.

His own cousin was a bit too sappy over that kid of his. Great kid, straight A's, a real credit to Johnny, but *please*. The guy would collapse flat if anybody threatened her. Probably get a bit dangerous over it, but still, a weakness.

He wasn't all that worried about these flashy guys. They'd run and hidden. Most of them were smart enough to hide their families, but dumb enough to tip their hands that they cared. Any of them who were smart sons of bitches would have cut the dead weight. Women were cheap. Besides, this method inherently targeted the stupid ones who hadn't even done a decent job of cutting out.

It had never occurred to Bobby that *he* wasn't particularly bright, either.

Kerrie Maise added another hole to her belt with Joey's pocket knife, wrinkling her nose at the baggy slacks and the salt cellars at her collar. She absently rubbed at the scars on her right knuckles. She had not intended to lose weight again. It was just that even after three years of treatment for bulimia, if she didn't consciously plan six small meals a day, her weight tended to slip again. All the turmoil from that mess with Keith had been so upsetting that she had frequently been too nauseated to keep anything down. Ginger snaps were high on her list for the supermarket run. No nutrition to speak of, but they were calories she could trust to stay down pretty good. It wasn't like she could find herself a new shrink—not as hot as the whole family was right now. It was going to be one hell of a lonely New Year's Eve.

"No, Pinky, we cannot get a dog. Not right now, and no, I don't know when." She sighed. His plaintive reply was unintelligible, but she could guess the gist of it. "I don't know means *I don't know.* Now quit whining at me before the Darhel come to eat you." That shut him up.

Pinky's chubby face and huge brown eyes, not unlike a puppy himself under the silky black curls, stared up at her, his forehead crinkling slightly in worry. "How about I go play now?" he asked seriously. Sometimes the boy was scarily smart.

Kerrie closed the knife and flipped on the safety catch. "Give this back to Joey on your way," she said. She didn't think twice of handing the little boy the knife. Not only was he biddable, but Bane Sidhe children started weapons' safety training at age two. He wasn't opening that knife short of an instruction from an adult or a bona fide emergency.

Pinky carefully did not look excited as Mommy handed him the knife. It was Joey's pride and joy; Pinky had often asked for a chance to look at it, but Joey was stingy and wouldn't share. As soon as he got out of his mother's sight, he ran down the hall as quietly and quickly as his legs would carry him. There was one place he could count on privacy to examine the treasure before he had to hand it off to Joey.

The basement stairs always creaked, just like the ones back home. Mommy's room was far enough away that she wouldn't hear, but he didn't know exactly where Joey was. He followed his customary sneaky route, which consisted of stepping to the very edge of the wall, right on top of the nails. Only the third stair from the bottom creaked if you just stepped on the nails. Pinky knew it was the third one because he was a very smart boy. Everybody said so, because he could already count all the way to ten, and knew his numbers, too. He had another little secret, though. Pinky liked secrets, because it was practice for when he grew up. He was going to be a spy. The grown ups thought he didn't know, but he suspected Uncle Neddie was a spy, because of the way he talked secrets sometimes with Daddy. That didn't make him a very good spy, but it did make him *cool*.

He figured if he showed he could keep lots of good secrets, then when he grew up, maybe Uncle Neddie would help him get a spy job, too. One of Pinky's most precious secrets was that he couldn't just count to ten. He could count all the way to a hundred. He had more reasons than one to keep this ability to himself. One was that Joey tended to punch him when Mommy or some other adult wasn't looking, for "showing off." The biggest reason was because he had discovered that secrets built upon secrets and secrets. The second secret was that Uncle Caspar, whose house they were staying at while Daddy was away with the other soldiers, had this really neat, huge trunk in the basement. It was only partway full with old clothes and papers and stuff, but the empty part was big enough for a very small boy to fold up and hide real comfortable. He had a flashlight, crayons, and paper hidden under the other stuff. When he wanted a little very special privacy to examine some treasure he shouldn't have, or when he was tired of Joey bossing him around, he could sneak down to the big trunk and hide inside, for as long as he wanted.

One reason nobody would look for him there was the trunk had a combination lock on it. Joey had once, very snottily, Pinky thought, told him about combination locks and all about how he knew how they worked while he tried and tried to get it open. There was nothing Pinky liked better than to secretly do what

Joey couldn't do. Joey thought he was so smart just because he was six. Pinky laughed inside about this a lot. He knew six-year-olds who weren't as smart as *he* was. Why, Pinky had been smart enough to stand behind Uncle Caspar, three times, while the man worked the lock's spinny dial. He had made sure to ask a lot of questions about everything he could see in the basement while he watched that lock. Grown ups pretty soon quit noticing anything you did if you were asking them enough dumb questions. All he had to do is imagine he was Joey and think of what questions Joey would be asking.

Pinky was good enough at the combination lock by now that he could even think about other things while he worked it. He hadn't realized he could do that before he noticed the lock opening in his small hands.

He had lots and lots of tricks. Tricks were fun. Secrets built on secrets. It had taken him a long time to bend the coat hanger just right, so he could leave it through the crack in the opening of the trunk. With a lot of practice, now he could hold the lock on the end, and close the lid so the latch came down. The first couple of times were scary, because he'd had to work hard to get the lock back out so *he* could get back out. He was an unusually patient boy, if only when a secret was involved. By now, he could lift the combination lock so its curvy part went right back through the little loop thingy, and move it around so it almost looked closed.

He'd played spy a lot. The calm game came quick and easy, the combination lock sliding right into place, the side pulling smoothly even so it almost looked closed. He scrabbled around for his flashlight, but decided not to turn it on. If it was Jenny Sorenson from next door, they'd be trying to find him to make him play with her. Some girls were okay, but Jenny was yucky. His mother kept telling him he was too young to think girls were yucky yet. Easy for her to say. She didn't have to play with Jenny.

Sure enough, it wasn't long before Jenny came clomping down the stairs, calling his name. It was almost smart of her to guess he'd be in the basement. Almost. Maybe the worst thing about Jenny was she had black curly hair and brown eyes, too, and everybody was always saying how cute they looked together, like twins. Yuck.

The doorbell rang again and Pinky felt a lift of hope. Maybe Jenny wasn't supposed to go out and her mother had come to make her go home. Please, oh please, he prayed silently. Very silently.

The firecracker popping noises upstairs told him immediately that whoever was at the door, it wasn't Jenny's mom. Pinky had been to the range with Mommy and Daddy lots of times. He knew what those firecracker sounds were, and he suddenly knew several things. Daddy wasn't on an ordinary mission, they wouldn't be going back home, and Mommy was upstairs dying. Mommy didn't carry her gun, and she was a lousy shot. He hoped Joey was out playing, but the awful high-pitched shriek told him he was wrong. Some small voice in the back of his head told him he ought to do something to save Jenny, but for some reason he couldn't move. He was scared, and realized he'd peed his pants like a baby.

It was almost like all of it was happening to somebody

else. He was still frozen, staring through the crack, when more popping went off, a lot louder. Jenny's brains blew across the room. Then three men and a woman clomped down the stairs, looking all over the basement. Their eyes skated right across his trunk, and Pinky knew, just like somebody else was telling him, that it was a good time to play the calm game. A spy—a spy—is always calm under pressure.

Pinky breathed real slow and quiet. How weird that everything was happening so slow, like ketchup out of a bottle. He blinked twice, noticing that light was coming in through a round hole in the side of the trunk. His heart pounded loud as he realized the bullet must have just missed him, and he hadn't noticed it. Maybe while they were shooting Jenny. Maybe it was even the bullet that hit Jenny. He swallowed hard.

The murderers looked around so much that he got a good look at all of their faces. Finally he heard some guy yell from upstairs, "Status!"

"One target down, down here. Got the younger kid," the brown haired man yelled back up the stairs.

It dawned on Pinky that they thought Jenny was him. As they clomped back up the stairs, he knew they weren't looking anymore for him because Jenny was dead on the floor, right over there. A whimper escaped his throat, finally, but nobody came back.

Too scared to climb out of the trunk, and deeply ashamed of it, Pinky cried himself to sleep. That was where Uncle Caspar found him four hours later, when he came home from work.

"Oh my God! Pinky?" Caspar Andreotti stared in shocked disbelief at the five-year-old asleep in his document chest. All of the material was old, paper or textile, and relatively nonsensitive. It also all had at least a little significance to his family's multigenerational work in the Bane Sidhe organization, and had strong sentimental value. The stink of urine, quite unremarkable in the circumstances, told him that restoration of anything he kept would be necessary. He dismissed the thought, irritated at the irrelevancies that always sprung to mind in the worst circumstances.

Coming home to find his house drenched in blood, with a pair of clenched fists painted in black on his living room wall, and the people who embodied the very raison d'etre of his safe house—he laughed at the bitter joke—dead in pools on the floor, counted as "worst circumstances." The use of the mafia revenge symbol was an ironic misdirection. The Darhel collaborators used the legends of his own ancestry to hide their message in plain sight. In a Chicago suburb, the implication that he and the murders were connected to old-fashioned organized crime guaranteed the police would give the matter only a pro forma inspection. This—keeping the cops out—was good for everyone, but it made him want to puke. As if the bodies themselves didn't.

But now, miracle of miracles, the youngest of his charges had somehow survived. The next question was, who was the other child on the floor? He shook his head and lifted the boy out. The waking child jerked and whimpered a plaintive, "Mommy . . ."

"Shhhh. Pinky, I know, but you have got to be very quiet a little longer. You know how to be quiet, right?" Caspar kicked himself—what a stupid thing to say. Of course the boy knew how to be quiet—he was alive. Well, more likely it had been fear, but it was still imperative he remain quiet now. He pulled a PDA out of his front pocket. "Rafael," he addressed the machine, "Transmit Lisbon, Berlin, Caracas, Taipei, Bristol, Paris."

The code words had no symbolic meaning whatsoever, and changed regularly. They were a few of a menu of simple code words, never used in any drill. This particular one meant, "Security compromised, fatalities, enemy not in contact but presume continuing observation, survivors but no injured, key intelligence, request immediate extraction with maximum evasive action." Well, perhaps the last one did have a certain symbolic meaning, he acknowledged. However, there were times to run, and this was one of them. He cursed himself, wondering if the fatal tradecraft slip had been his.

"You're a spy, too," the child whispered, almost as if he should have expected it. Caspar noted absently that the surviving Maise boy was far brighter than he appeared. Correction—than he *chose* to appear. He himself had apparently missed a lot.

He nodded as the PDA repeated the series of dead cities' names back to him, setting the boy down a good distance from the blood. "Stay there a moment, Pinky. I just have to get some things from my workout gear."

The heavy bag was filled with sand, as was what appeared to be a boxy, vinyl bench set against the wall. Andreotti grunted with effort, despite his own rigorously maintained physical strength, as he moved the two items over to give them some cover at an angle with a good view to the stairs. Digging underneath a pile of mildewing junk in one corner, he pulled out a rifle and a couple of decent pistols, a can of magazines, a couple of helmets. The bottom of the trunk yielded a couple of vests, so far down that they weren't even damp. They didn't smell so great anyway, and were only kevlar, but were a lot better than nothing, and likely to stop anything the enemy would fire in a basement unless he was stoned, stupid, or very well armored himself. Ricochets were a bitch.

He slapped the five-year-old's hand away when he reached for one of the pistols. "Not today. Sorry, son. Your hands are too small, and you're wound up—you just might shoot our rescuers by mistake. Don't pout. Strap on the helmet as best you can and get under this."

He didn't mention that if the enemy decided to blow up the house, or burn it down, they were fucked. He hadn't seen explosives or incendiaries in his cursory inspection of the place, which didn't mean they weren't there, but he hoped if they'd intended to demolish the house, they already would have. Besides, they went to special trouble to leave their warning. They'd want it noticed, and for word to spread.

He noted that whatever else the enemy was, he was apparently stupid. Or *expected* the warning to have the opposite effect to the one normally intended. Sorting out that mess was above his pay grade. Right now, his job was to keep his remaining charge alive for the pickup. Pinky was far more important than he was.

He wanted to ask who the other body was, sure that the child would know, but the little kid was showing amazing composure for his age, and Caspar wouldn't risk breaking it. The boy had already winced, understandably, when he had called him "son."

"Tell me the truth about my daddy."

Andreotti jerked. "Alive, with the rest of DAG—most of them—somewhere else." He reflexively told Maise's son the truth. Yet another breach of his training.

"Fighting?"

The boy was no longer surprising him. This time the safe house operator considered before answering, "Not to my knowledge, but I'm not sure they'd tell me. Alive is all I know for sure, and I haven't seen any clues that anything with as much firepower as your dad's unit is out there raising hell."

"Okay," the child who was more than a child replied gravely, accepting the answer.

It was a long five hours, with him creeping out once to steal food and a large glass of milk, before returning down to feed and wait with Pinky. The basement had a bathroom, thank God, and he'd been able to grab some dirty clothes the boy had left on his living room floor. They were streaked with mud in places, but at least not peed in.

"If they saw you come in, aren't they going to be suspicious that everything is so quiet?" the five-year-old—genius, apparently—asked.

"Quite possibly. Or, they may decide I've somehow skipped out in fear and slipped past them. Either way, if I was here, I'd have to call the police, and I can't do that with you here, can I?" Caspar Andreotti was getting used to treating his charge at his mental age, not his chronological one. Or was it?

"When do you think they'll get us?" the boy asked. "I mean our rescue, not the police or other guys. Whoever you called for."

"Soon now," the house man answered. "Pinky, are you five, or are you just small for your age?"

"Do you think Joey—" His voice broke on his brother's name. "Do you think Joey would have agreed to say he was six, even if he didn't blab, if he was older?"

"No, Pinky, I guess I don't. So why did you hide how very smart you are?"

"What, and piss off Joey that bad? Or get stuck in school early, or up a couple of grades and be the punching bag of all the bigger boys? Or treated like a freak?" The last contained a note of hurt mixed with bravado—whistling in the dark—that told Andreotti that feeling like a freak hit way too close to home for the child.

"You *are* smart, aren't you? Never be ashamed of being smart, Pinky. It just saved your life." The grown man, closest thing present to a father, made sure he was both serious, respectful, and above all approving.

Talented and deserving of respect, or freakishly different with the need to keep hiding for self-preservation. Those were the stakes. If Pinky was "scary smart," which he was, then he needed to grow into a whole, functional "scary smart" guy. The Bane Sidhe needed those. Caspar hadn't missed the note of hero worship in the boy when he'd said "spy." In many people, that would be a red flag of unsuitability. This child was a natural. The organization's problem would be in deciding where to place him to do the most good.

The kid was never going to enjoy New Year's Eve again. Come to think of it, Andreotti figured they had that in common.

"Just one more question," Andreotti said.

"What?"

"How in the *hell* did you find out my combination?"

❖   ❖   ❖

Mueller had almost enough sense of self-preservation to avoid eyeing the O'Neal women. Married wasn't always a problem on a distant deployment, but this wasn't that. It was still a separation, with his wife and kids up in Indiana, underground with the people running this whole conspiracy.

A hundred miles away or a thousand, it still wore on a man. The girl with the damned gorgeous heart-shaped ass had to be an O'Neal. She had this kind of light brownish-red hair with blond streaks. The red on female islanders, he had been warned, was like the red of mushrooms or tropical fish—a danger signal. Still, as she turned, the sweater she was wearing gave him a good silhouette of the top rack. She caught his eyes and smiled, before walking away to wherever she'd been going. She looked back over her shoulder at him, briefly, as she went. He got another smile.

He also got a thwack upside the head from Moso-vich, whom he hadn't noticed coming up behind him. Situational awareness versus pretty girl was no contest. Especially in his condition.

"Forget it. She's a widow," he said. "No, don't get any ideas that means 'available.' She's a very recent widow. Like, of the action a couple of weeks ago."

He didn't have to say "off limits." The code was clear. Her departed husband had to be in the ground for a decent interval of time before she became available—and then he'd have to compete with all the guys who had also noticed her ass and tits, and a face that was distinctly not bad. A married guy with kids wasn't going to be—shouldn't be—high on her list.

"She didn't look very bereaved," Mueller heard

himself say, earning another thwack to the back of his head.

"Down, boy. You know as well as I do—doesn't matter." Mosovich looked entirely willing to keep hitting him on the head as long as it took.

"Who was the poor bastard?"

"Ned Mortinson. Who turns out to have been fifty-something."

"Really? I hadn't had him picked out as a juv."

"Apparently he didn't have himself picked out as one, either. She's about twenty. For real. It wasn't a match made in heaven."

"You know her life history?"

"The O'Neals gossip like hell, turns out. Once you get in past their obsessive opsec. I asked around for a few basics before writing letters," Jake said.

"Obsessive opsec. Sounds like a very good thing to me."

"Yup. But on the island here? The world's biggest gossips—and not just the women. You could run a wine cellar on their grapevine."

"You gotta admit she's got one hell of a nice ass. Nice every—" Mueller sighed and drew himself up straighter from his habitually straight posture. "Yes, sir. What's on the schedule today?"

CHAPTER NINE

George Schmidt didn't like leading patched-together teams. This one was a thrown-together extraction unit, seeing that Papa was off-planet, Tommy was generaling, and Cally was incommunicado in what Shari O'Neal assured him was a vital matter for Clan O'Neal. Since he wasn't an O'Neal, by the Bane Sidhe's unwritten operating rules, that pretty much required him to drop the matter. He didn't have to like it. So he had Harrison as a wheelman, but he also had three random guys. One from Kaleb, whom he trusted, and two guys from DAG who'd been sitting around on base cooling their heels. Landrum was a good enough guy—raised Bane Sidhe like Schmidt himself, experienced operating as part of DAG, but a total cherry on Bane Sidhe ops. Kerry and Michaels were unknown quantities, though not to Landrum, who vouched for his teammates.

The rationale for landing him with three cherries was an extra man to make up for inexperience. Yeah, right. One more guy to maybe make a bad mistake operating like someone with a nation state's government behind them and the general *approval* of the Darhel. These guys' knowledge that Toto and Dorothy weren't in Kansas anymore was only intellectual. He figured the real reason for three newbies was to use the opportunities to get new men broken in on fieldwork fast, and to stave off troop boredom. The first rule of managing these guys was that you did *not* want to let them get bored. A bored specwar operator was a bad specwar operator. Consummate professionals left too long without work would find themselves something to do—and whatever it was, nobody else would like it. Okay, a few female types might have a great time, but that was only a best case scenario.

DAG had no female operators. Bane Sidhe base had a good handful of upgraded juvs on hand at any given time. The Bane Sidhe guys knew the score, but the FNGs generally weren't going to believe these women were their superiors in strength and probably in training, too, until they were in a world of hurt. George himself had heard a pretty damned funny after-action report on Father O'Reilly's little talk with the women after the first incident. Unfortunately, she'd been incredibly gentle, and the guy had been shipped off right away to Island O'Neal. It wasn't that the guy had exactly refused to take no for an answer; he had more misunderstood the signals and the lady took offense. A broken jaw had a remarkably immediate sobering effect on a man. Anyway, the light damage and speed of his disappearance left the potential discipline problem intact. One of the problems with Nathan's more administrative and priestly background was that, good as he was with people, he didn't always get the ops types. Almost always, but there it was: almost.

This was a sucky assignment to take three DAG guys on, because it was going to punch all their damn buttons. Yeah, they were professionals; they'd get cold. They'd also be damned sure they already knew what to do because they'd click right into highly trained-in patterns. Change that: they were already in the zone. They knew this was Maise's wife and kids. They might as well have been born in the zone.

"All right people, listen up." He looked around at the four other men in the trailer that was the final staging location for the op. "You are not operating in DAG. You can't go in on reflex. You two," he pointed to Kerry and Michaels, who looked uncomfortable in the wigs that covered their military haircuts, and about as unhappy with the identical suits and ties.

"You're Mormon missionaries," he said. "You get the front door. When you get out of the car, think earnest and carry that book like you revere it, not like you don't want it. One of you pretends to knock on the door while the other one unlocks it. Just listen to your earbug for the beeps."

They hated the risk of not being able to communicate in event of surprises. Yeah. *He* was no way in hell going to tolerate anything other than tiny blips out of radio silence. *He* had a PDA, Harrison had a PDA. Relative risk.

"Landrum goes into the house area first as a meter reader, and waits at the meter until we go through the doors. Then you Mormons go in. Kerry, you look older, you're earnestly explaining to Michaels how this door knocking thing works for the little time it takes Duchess and me to come up the sidewalk."

He'd be riding a Vespa reproduction, with a little weenie dog in a carrier behind him. Harrison had dressed him carefully; with the bagged bottle of wine, he looked for all the world like a friend coming over for a little holiday cheer.

"I look at you curiously as I walk by to the kitchen door. Two beeps and we ready, three beeps and we go in."

This was probably the first entry the new guys had done where they had keys to the doors and were not allowed to do a complete room take-down. They hated it. Truth to tell, so did he. Their way was safer for the operatives. They weren't used to being a bit more expendable here. This mission was counter to all their training and experience. They never operated in CONUS, and their primary mission was putting down pirates and terrorists in city states, whether resource colonies or the handful of old pre-war cities that had been repopulated in various world locations. Terrorism was, unfortunately, alive and well. As in pre-war times, frequently it was a figleaf for good old-fashioned crime, kidnapping, extortion. That was DAG's experience. A black-bag entry on a private house in a quiet residential area, if not in broad daylight at least in twilight, was outside all their training.

"If you encounter hostiles, shock, don't shoot. If you even draw your firearm without damn good reason I will have your *ass*. Use your judgment on turning on lights." Their expressions said clearly that they appreciated having at least *something* where their judgment would be trusted. It was hard for pros to be cherries on anything.

"We get the survivors, the Mormons are out on point and stop at the car to chat with each other, then Duchess and I escort the survivors out to see my bike, Harrison pulls up and gets the survivors. Landrum covers our tail. The Vespa stays, the rest of us proceed independently to the rendezvous."

"And the bike?" Kerry asked.

"Oh. Cleanup gets it if possible." Of course the FNGs wouldn't know SOP yet.

"That leaves the survivors exposed in transit, sir," Michaels observed.

"Yes, it does. Cleanup will be coming in as we leave, along our exit route." He gestured to his brother. "They'll be listening in in case we need backup. Yes, there's exposure. This is a resistance organization. In the extreme, we're more expendable than DAG was. We hate to lose operatives, we can't afford it, but losses hurt less than exposure." These guys were in no way shy about exposing themselves to risk in a professional capacity. They'd done it time and again and would do it more. They were also professional enough not to take *unnecessary* risks.

"Tramp" Michaels, so named for an incident in a Burmese whorehouse he'd rather forget, wasn't real keen on their team leader. A thrown-together team of guys who never worked together, never even worked in the same organizations, no training, on a live op was asking for a goatfuck. Yeah, that was bad enough, but even for a juv this guy looked like a kid. Like barely fourteen. And now he was dressed in a cheap civilian suit like a weenie missionary carrying the Book of Mormon. At least it was something to do, but it wasn't what he was trained to do. It wasn't making it any easier to dump the volcanic rage he was feeling and click into the zone. Dead civilians he could deal with. Dead dependents of teammates—he really wanted to kill the guys who did this. Which was bad. Target identification could slow you down, get you or your teammates killed. And what about the surviving kid? No way this wasn't going to fuck him up bad. *Really* wanted these guys.

He had memorized the map of the neighborhood, as a matter of course. As had Kerry beside him. "You okay, man?" he asked.

"Cocked, locked, and ready to rock," his buddy affirmed. His left hand was closed into a fist so tight the knuckles stood out whitely, thumb grating across the index finger. His voice was tight with leashed anger.

"You too, huh? Into the zone buddy, into the zone," Michaels, as always, found it easier to support Ketch than himself.

"Roger that."

And that simply, the fury went from fire to ice for both of them, the ice at the familiar distance that allowed clean operation and got the mission done. It felt good, the familiarity. First, extract the kid. And the safe-house guy who had probably fucked up and let it all happen. Then find these other fucks and correct their breathing problem.

None of these thoughts stopped him from tracking the details of everything they passed as they moved in on the objective. As always, those details were preternaturally clear, and the world slow, as his thoughts clicked over miles in instants. He had become the machine, and there was the house.

"Mormons," Kerry said.

"We don't have to talk the talk, dude, we've just gotta walk the walk," Tramp pulled up to the curb and parked smoothly.

Under other circumstances, since it was a mission necessity, it would have been an interesting way to get in close to the house and an interesting problem. At the moment, there was nothing but the now. Under the guise of saying a few words to each other, ostensibly about missionary stuff, he and Ketch got a good three-sixty look over each other's shoulder after getting out of the car. He could see, way down at the end of the street, Schmidt on his bike. Time to move.

Despite their roles, when the two men turned to walk up the sidewalk to the front door, it was with the lithe coordination of wolves from the same pack, on the hunt.

Tramp was glad to see the door had a knocker. He mimed pushing the doorbell and stood, facing the door with his buddy in what they hoped was the sincere, angelic attention of men of God on a mission. Which they were, just not in the sense they were feigning. After all, God had a thing for wrath and vengeance against scumbags, too, didn't he? Extraction first, but in the process observe all the details for the tracks and sign necessary to hunt some very bad people down. Bad people who had very much messed with the wrong pack.

"This is gonna suck for Landrum," Kerry said. "Used to date Kerrie."

"Ouch. What fuckhead assigned him to this team?" Tramp scowled in the general direction of the Schmidt shrimp, who was off his scooter and walking up the driveway with his paper-bagged wine bottle, looking credibly like some "friend" of the family.

"I don't think it was Schmidt. Don't even know if he knows."

"Oh, great. Fucking brilliant." Michaels stuck the key in the doorknob and turned as he heard the telltale clatter of the kitchen storm door opening. Acting, for a moment, nothing like Mormon missionaries, he and Kerry rushed in the front door, looking to both sides as he kicked the door shut behind them. Unhappily restrained by the order not to draw, each of them had a hand under his suit jacket, which was as close to drawing as they could get without breaking their shitty ROE.

The black fist spray-painted on the wall suggested that the tangos were indeed gone, which was great for the survivors, if true. If. Tramp followed his buddy down the hall to the left of the empty living room, backwards, guarding his six.

"This is the one to keep Landrum out of," Kerry announced grimly as they turned into the first room, a bedroom that sat on the front side of the house.

Michaels glanced over his shoulder into the bedroom. The bastards had rather thoughtfully left the closet door flung open, giving a plain view of one of the best bits of cover in the room. Kerrie Maise sprawled across the bed, sloppily shot in four or five random places, other than the head shot at close range that had obviously killed her. The streaks of blood on the floor suggested that she had staggered backwards with the first couple of shots and fallen onto the bed.

With no time to feel, they cleared the room and sent the relevant click code. The grey and white splatter, some still stuck to the wall behind the bed, was one of those sights a guy really didn't want in his head as the last memory of any woman he'd fucked. Despite his professionalism, the boil of rage threatened to swamp him.

He clamped a lid on it as they left the corpse behind to proceed on to the next room, which was evidently one of the kids' bedrooms. Mercifully, it was empty, though tainted by a strong smell of puke. They sent the code and moved on to the master bedroom. A pair of clicks, the tone said Schmidt's, indicated the non-survivor boy had been found. Clearing the last room on their list, they moved farther back to the holo/rec room, where Landrum waited, white-faced.

"Basement," he said.

"Don't go into the front of the house, dude," Tramp told the other man firmly. Probably he would have been smart enough not to, but some things were worth making sure. You couldn't un-see shit.

When Landrum's face turned a rockier shade of pissed, he knew he'd been right to insist.

"No." The word came out of his and Kerry's mouths simultaneously, communicating that they would restrain the man physically if necessary.

Landrum spun on his heel and stalked off to the kitchen, followed by Kerry. Michaels, again, brought up the rear.

The entire process of clearing the upper floor of the house had taken less than thirty seconds.

In the kitchen, he and Kerry watched the top of the stairs while Landrum and Schmidt made the descent to the basement, returning momentarily with the civilian man and the boy. Pinky, Tramp reminded himself. This wasn't just any civilian child. This was the son of one of the guys in his unit.

"They killed Jenny," the boy said, face pinched with fear and fatigue. The safe house—and wasn't that a sick joke—guy didn't look so hot either, and no wonder.

Tramp raised an eyebrow at Landrum, who was again firmly seated in "professional" mode.

"Kid next door. Thought it was him." He nodded at the small boy.

A little surprising, but if the body was messy, obviously possible.

"We're out of here." Schmidt said. "You two with me. Just keep your mouths shut and walk with me, ignore my talking, get in the car that pulls up."

The civilians with their team lead, Kerry, Michaels, and Landrum proceeded along their own exit paths, keeping alert for any attempt on the survivors between house and cars. Tramp hated this exit plan. It left the survivors too out in the open, the brief passage down the driveway being an eternity if a competent shot was watching the house. He'd been overruled. Broad daylight; suburbia. Sometimes mission requirements put you in a sub-optimal situation.

He was still relieved when the car with the two Schmidts and the civilians got off, while equally apprehensive about the exposure of the car.

As he and Kerry pulled into the post-extraction rendezvous, he was damned glad to see the car with the dependent had made it, and reflected that compared to the more open work of DAG, this resistance shit sucked. But they got the surviving dependent out, and the safe house dude, which was a win to take home.

Boarding the van to make the final leg of the trip back to base, Kerry caught his eye. Both men were thinking the same thing. Fucked up resistance ROEs or not, they *wanted* in on the op when these Bane Sidhe found the bastards that did the wife and other son.

They were real good guys. Finding Maise's wife and older son in large pools of congealed blood, finding the "message" symbol left on the wall—George didn't know if they recognized it as a mafia symbol or not. It didn't matter. They all knew who'd really sent it. The third body turned out to be that of a little girl from next door. He didn't envy the clean-up crew's job in dealing with that. A "disappearance" of a child was often worse than having the police find the body. Ten to one, the crew would have her buried in a shallow grave somewhere and get the police an anonymous tip. Some time after that, after business had been taken care of, the family would probably get a cryptic notification hinting at the destruction of the perpetrators. Nothing was without risk. In this case, the kid had gotten caught in the crossfire of their war. That it was all of humanity's war would mean nothing to Jenny Sorenson's parents. Arranging for them to get the body back, along with a small sense of justice, was the least the organization could do. The Sorensons would probably interpret the justice notification as coming from a rival organized crime faction. The Bane Sidhe would do their best to subtly encourage that assumption.

"I'd like the things in the trunk if at all possible. Family mementos," Andreotti said.

The assassin kept a neutral face and told the middle-aged man that he'd inform the clean-up crew. The crew would know to go over every damned thing in the box and catalog it, tagging any suspect items for restriction to base. "Family mementos" of one sort or another gave nightmares to internal security staff as they managed a highly multigenerational conspiracy. The pre-recontact human Bane Sidhe numbers had been small. Mostly, it was a very few interconnected families who tended to have multigenerational relationships with certain factions in certain organizations—as, say, the sub-faction in the Society of Jesus. Contrary to the broadest and longest standing conspiracy theories, the generations of Bane Sidhe sleepers had rarely been Freemasons.

It wasn't the best room for interviewing a kid, Schmidt reflected. It was your standard boring, windowless, institution-green, Galplas room, with four battered, chewing-gum colored, folding chairs and not much else. One for him, one for Saunders, one for Pinky Maise, and one for the grief counselor who was supposed to make a kid who'd just lost his mother and brother feel "comfortable." While George allowed that the pretty young thing—pretty juv thing, really—could make him more comfortable any time, he doubted Anne Veldtman was doing much for the kid.

The impression was confirmed when the kid looked at her and said, politely, "Ma'am, you've been really nice and everything, but would it be okay if I just talked to these guys by myself?" The five-year-old had a small child's gravity that would have been cute under other circumstances.

George reminded himself of Caspar Andreotti's

debrief indicating that this kid was anything but cute, and would not only resent being treated like the little kid he was, but would also be likely to hide his intelligence behind a juvenile facade if thus treated. With the result that they could miss some critical data.

Veldtman started to object, but went quietly when Saunders jerked his head towards the door. That was one thing about a disciplined organization. You didn't tend to get many people who would let sentiment override orders. Orneriness, yes. Sentiment, no. This was Saunders' show. George was only along for the ride as a second check to make sure nothing of operational value was missed.

After she left, Pinky focused his intent gaze on George. "You're one of the guys who got us out. Thanks," he said. "You look kinda like a kid, but you're not."

The subtext was subtle as a sledgehammer. The Maise kid was asserting that he, also, was much less a kid than he looked. George didn't know about that, but he glanced at Saunders and gave a slight shrug. In his limited experience of children, they reacted better to adults who didn't patronize them.

"You're welcome," he said.

"Okay, Maise," Saunders was a pretty good interrogator, and opened by addressing the kid the way he would an adult in the military subculture. "Andreotti tells us there's a lot more to you than meets the eye, so I'm gonna treat you just like anybody else. That work for you?"

"Yeah," Pinky said.

"Okay, tell me about today from the time you got up to the time the team came and got you. Try not to leave anything out, but don't worry too much. I'll be asking you a lot of questions after to pull out all the details. Get it? Go," Saunders gestured to the kid—Maise, George corrected himself—to begin.

"At least five attackers," Pinky said, looking into the distance. His eyes tracked back and forth as if he was reseeing the entire incident. "Basement, four. Three male, one female. Weapons: Nine-millimeter semi-automatics. Silenced. . . ."

It was a hell of a thing for a kid to go through. But it slowly crept in on George that they weren't dealing with a kid. Pinky was more like a forty-year-old stuck in a five-year-old's body. One with a surprising memory for detail regarding the assassins, to the point that the Maise assured them he would be able to recognize their voices if he heard them again.

Given the kid's presence of mind and memory for detail, Schmidt believed him. By the time the five-year-old got through with his account, George found he had almost no questions. *"Can you think of anything else?"* just sounded . . . childish.

Nathan O'Reilly raised an eyebrow at Dr. Vitapetroni, the head of the Bane Sidhe psych department, who had joined the organization's director in his office to watch live holo of the interrogation. "Well?" he asked.

"Don't put him through the ordeal of hypnosis. I can't get much, if anything, else out of him than that interrogation did. The child has a remarkably detailed memory. I don't want him to feel like we're questioning his sanity, and people often do feel exactly that. I don't want to risk corrupting his memories with artifacts accidentally induced during the hypnotic process. There's no upside." The psychiatrist shrugged.

"All right. Then the next problem is where to put him for the night. I want to limit his outside contact without appearing to do so until we have this situation under much better control. Could he stay with me? Any problem putting him on my couch? Or do you want to put him up? I don't recommend young Schmidt there. The child is obviously itching to pummel him with questions, and I'd rather not send a five-year-old's head farther into the ideas of dishing out murder and mayhem than it already is."

"Given the personality type, the emotional age, and the formative experience, I think that's a forlorn hope," Vitapetroni said.

"Probably. But not tonight. So, does he crash on your couch, mine, or do you have some other suggestion of someplace secure to put him up?" O'Reilly stood, taking his mug along by habit. He always put it in the office dishwasher himself, rather than leaving it to some assistant to come in and clean up after him.

"He could go with Cap Andreotti."

"Andreotti has enough to deal with tonight on his own. I presume you will be seeing him soon in your professional capacity." The priest paused in the break room, downing a cupful of tap water before dispensing with the mug.

"First thing in the morning," the doctor assured him.

CHAPTER TEN

"I'm sorry to isolate you from people your own age tonight, Pinky, but unfortunately I'd like to keep what happened out of general circulation until we've had more chance to respond to it," the priest said.

Pinky figured the guy for a juv. Older looking people deferred to him, and he didn't have that happy look around the eyes like young-for-real grown-ups. No, happy wasn't the word. Optimistic. That was one thing Pinky had noticed early about the world. The much older adults were much less enthusiastic about whatever was going to happen next in life than the younger adults. Since the older ones probably had a much better idea of what was really going on, this told him a lot about the world.

He looked around O'Reilly's living room. Holo tank, a well-stuffed couch that looked comfortable even though the arms were torn up like a cat scratched them a lot. He didn't smell a litter box, so maybe the couch used to belong to somebody else. Three of

152

the walls were a nice orange-pink, and the fourth was a green lighter than army stuff—a green that wasn't ugly. There was a sink and microwave, and some shelves with food on them. It was all really clean, everything put away. He obviously didn't have kids. Probably he was a Catholic priest. Pinky had heard they didn't get married.

He noticed a little ball with some feathers attached in a corner, barely sticking out from under the couch. Okay, so there was a cat.

"Are you Catholic?" he asked. Then, without pause, "Oh, and thanks. I don't really want to be around other kids tonight. They ask questions. I don't wanna talk about it. I mean, except to other spies. I figure you'll kill the people that did it. Are you a spy? And can you keep that lady off of me? She means well, but she's bugging me."

"Wow, that's a lot of questions." O'Reilly sat down on the arm of a chair and looked at him seriously. Pinky could sense that this man was not going to talk to him like a little kid.

"First, yes, I'm Catholic. I'm a Jesuit—" He held up a finger as Pinky started to ask what that was. "If Miss Veldtman's attention is upsetting you, you don't have to be around her. As for whether I'm a spy or not, it depends on what you mean. Spying is a part of what we do here, but I don't go out into the field. I run the place."

"I thought so," the child said with a nod. "Everybody seems to listen to you, and it's like you expect them to and never even think that maybe they won't."

"I certainly hope they do. I'd be very bad at my job if they didn't," O'Reilly said.

"Okay. I'm real tired. Can I go to bed now? I guess I get to sleep on the couch. That's cool. And it's okay if your cat sleeps out here some of the time. You don't have to keep him in your room or something. Cats don't like being boxed up."

"Her," the priest corrected automatically, blinking a couple of times, obviously surprised that Pinky had noticed something so obvious as a cat.

"Okay, her. Sorry. You must keep a really clean litter box, because I can't smell it at all."

"It's automatic."

Pinky decided to think about whether he needed to play dumb in front of these people or not.

"I wish you wouldn't," O'Reilly said.

"Huh?"

"The expression on your face just went from what's obviously normal, for you, to a—and this is a professional statement as, yes, a spy—*marginal* copy of a typical five-year-old. I'm sorry if I did something to put you off, but I really wish you wouldn't pretend. It'll make my job a lot easier if you don't. And I'm rather good at spotting it when people do."

Then it was Pinky's turn to be surprised.

In his bedroom, after the child was off to sleep, Nathan O'Reilly composed a message to go out immediately by courier. He hated to call her back in from vacation and recovery, but he needed Cally O'Neal, and Tommy Sunday as well, back yesterday.

DAG was already pent-up, under-used and frustrated. Now someone was openly hunting their families.

The word "disaster" didn't even begin to cover it.

Friday, January 1, 2055

It had taken half a century, but Tommy Sunday had finally forgiven the game of football for its history with his father. Or vice versa. His father had been a linebacker before the war and before he had, presumably, been eaten by the Posleen in the scout landings at Fredericksburg. To say they had not gotten along would be putting it mildly. A huge man, like his father, Tommy had had absolutely no affinity for playing football. Computers, yes. Football, no. He had grudgingly participated in track, at his father's insistence, as the condition of his pursuing his own interests.

The Posleen had eaten his biological father but in time Tommy had found a new one, one who really understood him. His "old man" was, and would always be, Iron Mike O'Neal of the 555th—Papa O'Neal's son who fought on, killing Posleen on world after world under Fleet Strike's Darhel masters. The biggest tragedy of the war, in Sunday's opinion, was the cold military necessity that Mike remain ignorant of the survival of his daughter, his father, his grandchildren, and the legion of half-siblings, nieces, nephews, and more who now served with distinction in the battle for humanity's future.

His psych called it "tranference." Since Iron Mike was more a dad to him than his own father had ever been, it was, once again, okay to sit and watch football.

Ohio State versus Wisconsin was going to be one hell of a match-up. Football wasn't his favorite sport, not by far, but the small consolation prize from the return of satellites to Earth's skies was the availability of college bowl games over Christmas. The run of available bowl games was still compressed, the selection of teams was still compressed, and it was all in holo now. Other than that, bowl games were still bowl games, and sitcoms, unfortunately, were still sitcoms.

Rising to its ambitions, as well as the total destruction of the competition, Milwaukee still made the best beer in the world. Demand for some top-end product had improved the selection, though. There were brands that had come well beyond the old—ah, hell, the immigration of talented German beer-mistresses, recipes, yeasts and all, at the beginning of the Postie War had done wonders for Milwaukee.

Mueller laughed at something on the sitcom and looked at him and Mosovich, shame-faced.

"What? It was funny," he said. "Only good line in the whole damn thing, but that one was pretty funny."

"Yeah, okay." Mosovich had a grin playing around the edges of his mouth. "The fool could just ask her if she's cheating. Most women can't lie worth shit, contrary to reputation." He chuckled. "Not if you've baselined them."

"You would use interrogation techniques on a girl-friend?" Tommy clapped a hand to his heart. "I am shocked, shocked!" He opened his beer and hit the chill button on the next one before considering.

"Don't try it on Cally," he warned. "She'll use you baselining her to baseline *you*, and then mess with your head by showing you a completely different pattern from now until doomsday. No hesitations, nothing."

"Operator for decades. Got it," Jake said. " 'We are spies of Borg. Resistance is futile. You're already assimilated.' "

The three men cheered when the pre-game show broke into the sitcom before the latter's completion. The first run of commercials sent Tommy into the kitchen to refill the beer nuts and make microwave popcorn. One of the few uses of paper in modern times was the packaging of black-market popcorn up in Indiana. Cheaper than the legal stuff, it was still expensive enough that most people popped theirs the old way. Wendy's hobby made it one of the little luxuries they could afford without rubbing their relative wealth in people's faces. She and he both were fanatic about that, if only because "extra" money tended to attract family who needed help. With a whole island of family? No thanks.

She'd also laid on the stuff for turkey and ham sandwiches, but it was too early for that.

Commercials over, the pre-game show was a traditional time to shoot the shit. This was the primary reason for these two guys, in particular, sharing his den for the game today. Yeah, maybe he ought to be doing the officer-enlisted divide, but right now he considered it secondary to getting his new command together. He was making a point of keeping the handful of ships, his "Navy," and his logistics support "tail" separate from DAG. A clear chain of command, and clear separations between his branches, was the only way to run this railroad. His new logistics and naval COs were guys he'd known perrsonally for years and were not his sons or grandsons. Jake Mosovich and David Mueller were unknown quantities. Not to mention the fact that despite his own background, either one had twice his experience.

Hence the informal social gathering.

Throughout talk about the players' stats, injuries during the season, and the snow beginning to fall on the field, Mosovich and Mueller watched Sunday as closely as he watched them. He knew the history of the other two men, of course. Their work in the war, with a number of repeated postings together since, had made the officer and NCO operate as two halves of one man. Tommy had received a copy of their complete service records from Father O'Reilly, and studied it carefully. These two made a damn fine team, refining their relationship over the years to seamlessly set the standard for an officer and his senior NCO, tight as hell but each secure and precise in his own area of responsibility.

As their freshly minted boss he could have done a hell of a lot worse. The big man also knew that one hint of his discomfiture leaking through his command face would have a magnified, detrimental effect on the troops whose lives were now unquestionably his responsibility. His uncertainties were his own problem, to be buried deep for the sake of these men—his men.

He still didn't know what the hell he was going to end up doing with them, but that was a problem that wouldn't solve itself today.

The three men leaned forward as one. The snap, the kick, beautiful. Sixty yards if it was an inch. Waters was one of the best kickers in the game. Ohio had won two close ones on the strength of a couple of amazing field goals. Fast runners on the team, too. Held Wisconsin to a ten return.

He got as far as third down before his son, Arthur, appeared at the door and interrupted. One look at his face and Tommy knew he could write *this* game off.

"Got a cube in from Indiana you better see, Dad. You too, sir. Top." He nodded to Mueller.

"That bad, huh?" One of the problems with being so far from the main—indeed, only—Bane Sidhe base on Earth was that security necessitated messages be physically couriered if they were either routine, or sensitive. Arthur's expression told him all he needed to know about just how sensitive, so he wasn't surprised that the message was directly recorded by Nathan.

"Cally, I'm sorry to interrupt your holiday." Nathan had clearly already gotten word of his promotion. "If you can, Tommy should probably see this, too. We just got word that the Maise family has been hit. Their safe house apparently wasn't. One of the kids survived and the house operator got home to find bodies and kid. He's called for a pickup and is waiting in place. By the time you get this, we should have him in hand at least, if not on base. I've got the Schmidts on it, blooding some of the new guys, and I devoutly hope that won't be literal.

"Cally, I know your first impulse is going to be to come running up here and get in the middle of it. Good. There's going to be blood to let and despite your current responsibilities, I cannot think of a person better suited to handling this. I can't order the acting head of Clan O'Neal, but . . . come."

"Cally's seen this already?" Tommy asked his son as the holo flicked off, automatically returning to the now forgotten game.

"Um . . . nobody knows where she is."

"Oh. Yeah, her belated honeymoon is a secret.

Get it from Shari or Wendy. They both know where to find her."

"That's what I'm trying to tell you, sir." The boy's face was tight, and his speech was beginning to take on a clipped tone. "Mom and Shari won't tell me where she is."

"What?" Tommy shook his head unbelievingly. "Wait, how did you know what was on this? You played it?" He looked at his son the way only a father can look at an erring child.

"No, sir. The courier . . ." His son shrugged, as if it was no fault of his if another guy had run off at the mouth. He'd deal with that later. Arthur swallowed hard, so his own face must have said as much.

"Mosovich, get three of your men who are the most dialed in on Bane Sidhe protocol and get them locking this down. Mueller, go get Maise. Nothing on why. My job to break the news. Yes, we're going to go up to Indiana, all of us, and we're going to pick up our hunting licenses. Questions?"

"No, sir," all three responded.

"Sounds to me like the Darhel have declared open war on the O'Neals," Tommy said, cracking his knuckles, then rotating his head and shoulders with a series of pops. "Time to show them why that's a terminally baaad idea. Right after I explain the . . . *gravity* of the situation to my wife."

"I need Cally. Now," he said grimly.

Shari sighed. "Is it really that big an emergency? The woman's recovering from broken ribs, nearly dying *again*, losing a child offworld, severe overwork *again*, just got her—"

"Yes. It's that bad." His face confirmed his words.

"Honey? What the hell's going on?" Wendy asked.

"You two need to know because you need to quash rumors and, whoever's in the hot seat, a lot of the grunt work of clan stuff is going to fall on you." The look he gave the two women was bleak. "The bastards hit one of our safe houses. Not agents, they went for the dependents. It was the Maises."

"Oh my God." Shari's hands were clapped to her mouth, while Wendy hadn't moved, stunned.

"It was a deliberate hit which means somebody is gunning for Bane Sidhe dependents," Tommy said. "The younger boy made it. Of course we have to tell Maise and he goes with. Mosovich and Mueller know and will take care of breaking it to the men. Which will be when we know more. You'll want to coordinate with them, and with whoever takes over clan management. If that's not you." He nodded to Shari.

Shari had survived the Posleen war solely by her virtues of not hesitating and being rock steady in a crunch. She didn't hesitate now, pulling a buckley out off her back pocket and punching out its unlock sequence.

"Sam. Call Stewart. Tell him 'drama queen.'" She paused and then looked puzzled.

"Tommy," she asked in a very small voice. "One, how did they know where the safe house was and two, what else do they know?"

"Drama queen," Stewart's buckley announced.

"Your PDA has gotten to know you, honey."

Cally rolled up on one side, laughing at him. It was only early evening, but after a supper of oysters Rockefeller, strawberries, and champagne, eaten in bed, they had decided to test the oyster myth. Having just agreed that more tests would be necessary, they were cooling off before sharing the shower.

"It's for you. A call." Instead of laughing, his mouth had twisted in annoyance. "Sorry," he said, handing her the buckley.

"Drama queen?" she asked, taking it. "Yeah, gimme the call," she told the machine, not waiting for an answer from her husband.

"Yan? This is Shari. I'm so sorry, but I need Cally. I hope I haven't inter—" Her friend and step-granma poured the words out in an apologetic rush.

"It's me," Cally said. "What's up?" She plucked idly at the red satin sheets the maid service had brought up this morning.

"You need to get to the airport. Now." The other woman's voice issued starkly from the buckley, tense and strained. "Okay, you've actually got about two hours. Talk to your friend about arrangements and just get there. Bye."

"Call ended," the PDA said.

Cally didn't waste time trying to ask Stewart what was going on. He'd had emergency contact arrangements—which she'd assumed. There was an emergency. That was all they knew. She was unsurprised that the details hadn't been forthcoming over a buckley connection. It was encrypted, of course, but as Tommy had told her so often, encryption algorithms were made to be broken.

"Okay, honey, what arrangements have you made for egress?" she asked.

"Bike. Being babysat by one of your relatives as insurance it stays in operable condition."

"Right. I do need a shower. Do I need to pack my shit, or do I have a bug-out bag?" she asked hopefully.

Her husband clapped a hand to his chest, "Darling, I am shocked, *shocked*, that you thought I'd neglect something so fundamental."

"Yeah, yeah. Thank you, I love you, and I'm going to wash off this stink. I am not going to show up to team and base smelling like a cross between a girls' gym and a whorehouse."

"Mind if I join you?"

"If you do, what do you figure the odds are of it being just a shower?" she asked, smirking.

"Nil, but you do have the time."

"Point. I'd *love* company," she purred.

In the event, it took her more than two hours to get to the airport. She'd forgotten what day it was, and thus forgotten about Friday traffic. She was still the first one there, traffic being an equal-opportunity hazard.

She stood on the tarmac, having bummed a smoke from Kieran, and hunched a bit under the cold mist that had started coming down. She could move into the hangar, but it felt kinda good to be outside, and the airport was a change. She and Stewart had immured themselves and spent an awful lot of time in the hotel room. Fantastic time, but still enough to give that cooped up feeling. Besides, while she'd given some control over to her other half for fun and games, now she was back full-on into her professional self. The transition was instant, for practical purposes, as soon as the call had come in.

That didn't mean it wasn't a bit disorienting, and it was convenient to stand in the open air, let her eyes rest on the main terminal building, which was a fair way off across the main runways, and give her headspace time to really adjust. The difference between waking up alert and ready to fight, versus taking the time to "really" wake up. Professional minus the adrenaline.

She ground the cigarette butt under the toe of her bike boots and reached for another. White-market cigs were supposed to be nonaddictive and noncarcinogenic, although that was recently debatable. They also cost the earth, with the Darhel-driven taxes, damn the fucking Elves to hell. Again. The far cheaper black-market smokes were the same old bad shit from before the war, which mattered for ordinary people. Cally and Kieran weren't ordinary. Like any operators or critical staff, they were immune to cancer, the other lung diseases, and immune to nicotine as well. That didn't mean there wasn't a certain comfort from the taste of good tobacco and the hand-to-mouth habit.

A bit later, she flicked the unsmoked half of her third down onto the pavement, as Kieran climbed into the plane to do whatever pilots did. She shrugged, greeting Tommy, his son, and a guy named Maise whose vaguely haunted, zombie look spoke volumes.

She waved Maise and Arthur onto the plane before pulling Sunday aside out beyond a wing. She didn't know if Maise had enhanced hearing or not, and wasn't chancing it.

"Brief me," she said quietly.

"Dependents murdered. His family. Pretty gruesome. One of his sons survived."

Cally's knuckles whitened in clenched-fist fury. "We know," she said in a tone that was more statement than question.

"We know," Tommy confirmed. "They weren't subtle about who, and the why is obvious. For all practical purposes, the balloon has gone up."

"Roger that. Do we have any word on scope and ROE?" she asked. "Are our troops on alert?"

"You know as much as I do. As for DAG, we've kept a lid on it. They're on alert. They'll notice Maise is gone, but I think we kept it pretty secure. The courier was the big risk; Wendy and Shari have him nailed down tight. Mueller and the other NCOs will be on search and destroy for rumors."

He held his hand out under the increasingly insistent drops. "By the way, you may not have the sense to go in out of the rain, but I do," he said.

Cally was suddenly conscious of her hair plastered to her head. She was soaked to the skin.

"Fuck it," Cally said. "Getting wet and miserable's just going to make me happier to kill somebody."

When the plane was in the air and she found herself staring out the window at nothing, she finally shook loose of the black nowhere she'd been inhabiting.

"Buckley, play me something. Anything. I don't care, as long as the music is violent."

"Oh, dear. Some disaster has happened. Are we in the *air*?" it squeaked. "Don't you know how dangerous it is to be in the fucking air, those rail guns—"

"Shut up, buckley. Just play it."

"Right," it said, its habitual pessimism tinged with an actual note of fright. The base buckley personalities all loathed flying. Nevertheless, the order for violent music was one it understood, and it called up the historical record of the ACS playlist from the Posleen war, and ran a search of similar material.

Metallica was just what the doctor ordered, the buckley concluded, and it started with "No Remorse."

CHAPTER ELEVEN

Saturday, January 2, 2055

Pinky understood the next morning when Father O'Reilly turned him over to another one of the moms— he sniffled at the word before controlling himself. Besides, Mrs. Mueller was much nicer than Miss Veldtman. Miss Veldtman tried to be nice, but Mrs. Mueller just *was* nice. With the other lady he could tell it was her job to try to be nice to him, and help him not hurt over his mom and Joey, or even Jenny. Pinky thought that was the stupidest idea any adults had ever had. It was gonna hurt anyway and he didn't damn well want to talk about it. He felt better for thinking about that with the "damn" in it. It was more emphatic that way.

Mrs. Mueller had him playing in the kids' gym with her kids Davey and Pat. They were older than Joey, but they were all right. Father O'Reilly had told him it really was okay to let his real self show around the Muellers. Pinky had been doubtful, but he tried it a little, and a little more when it worked out okay.

The Mueller kids were nothing like Joey, or even Jenny, or the other neighborhood kids. After about five minutes they had looked at each other, then looked at him, and Pat said, "It's like you're a juv, only a kid version. Cool."

"Our dad's a juv," Davey informed him, watching him as if he wasn't sure of the reaction the disclosure was going to get.

"Cool," Pinky echoed. Then the three of them had grinned at each other, and since then the other two boys had been patiently initiating him into the rudiments of handling the combination of a baseball and a glove. The guy at the gym counter even had one close to his size, which was cool because Mom could never aff—Pinky suppressed another sniffle.

The kids' gym, as far as he could see, was about the same size as an adult basketball court at the Y, doubled. He noticed pretty quick that the playground equipment looked a lot more like a kid-sized Q-course than the kind of stuff you got in preschools or public parks. He approved. The park stuff was boring, like the grown-ups that built it would have a heart attack if you so much as stubbed your toe. The five-year-old eyed the monkey bars with a mix of lust and glee.

The floor underneath all the stuff was padded, at least a little, but it didn't look too heavy. Besides, Pinky didn't want to actually get hurt if he fell; it just made him indignant to feel like they were so afraid he'd break just from a little damn play. Grown-ups could be damn stupid sometimes.

The boys took the hint and he got to play on them a little before Mrs. Mueller came over and told them they had to go.

Davey and Pat looked at her like she was crazy. "Mooommm! It's not even lunchtime!"

"Hush." She looked at him. "Pinky, your daddy's here. We're going up to the cafeteria where you can meet him and grab a snack." Her eyes were real sad, and he could tell she felt sorry for him. He wished she wouldn't, because it made him have to fight that much harder not to cry in front of Davey and Pat.

It was the first time Pinky had been in the base cafeteria. It looked like a grown-up version of the cafeteria at Joey's school, except the adults got to tell the people behind the counter what they wanted to eat.

They were already at a table when three people walked in, and Pinky was surprised to find himself getting out of his chair so fast he knocked it down, and spilled the milk all over himself, but he didn't care and just ran for the big man in the middle. "Daddy!"

And then it didn't matter that he was crying in front of people because Daddy was crying, too. He was wrapped up in a big hug, and he didn't care that it was too tight, not even a little.

Pinky saw that the part of his mind that noticed things was still clicking along like a clock, as he heard the really huge man, who had walked behind him, telling Mrs. Mueller he had a cube from her husband. He noticed that the blond woman with real big breasts standing beside his dad wasn't reacting to the crying at all except for maybe being a little impatient. She was just mad. Madder than he'd ever seen anybody. Ever.

He could tell it wasn't at them, so it was probably at the people who killed Mom and Joey. And Jenny, he added. He squirmed in his dad's arms, wiping the snot from his nose on his sleeve.

"Who are you?" he asked the woman. Somehow "lady" didn't seem to fit her at all.

"My name's Cally. Hi, Pinky."

She didn't squat down on her haunches, which he always found kind of patronizing from adults. She was another one who just plain talked to him like a human being. He liked her, instantly, mostly because he could tell that she'd just love to kill the people who murdered his family, very violently. It was a sentiment he could appreciate, but it was another one he didn't really think would fit the role of five-year-old, which he couldn't quite discard in front of his dad.

"I saw your debrief video," she said. "Good job. You're solid, kid. Solid as a damned rock."

His dad glanced at her about the cuss word, but he himself liked her better for it.

"Are you a spy?" he asked.

"No. I'm an assassin. I do spying sometimes, when I have to. But mostly I kill people."

His dad really wasn't sure about her telling him *that*. Pinky, however, felt otherwise.

"Good," he said, his lips compressing into a thin line. "I'm glad they called the right kind of person in for when you find them. I hope you're good at it."

"Pinky, I am the *best*." She paused for a moment and then grinned. Pinky'd seen a show about sharks one time and it was like a great big white shark had just opened up her mouth and smiled. "I am going to make you one promise. I am going to find the people who killed your mom and brother, and the people who *ordered* the killing of your mom and brother, and I am going to nail them to a *wall*. With nails. To a wall."

His dad now looked like he was about to really object.

"Before you get upset at me being frank with your son, Mr. Maise, you really need to watch his debrief video. Then you and Pinky need to have a really long talk." She hadn't bothered to look at his dad, just kept Pinky locked with her cornflower-blue eyes. "I'm also a mom. *You* need to come clean with your dad. You're really going to need each other from now on. OPSEC is for *outside* families not *inside*. Get me?" she asked.

"I *like* you," Pinky said. "Dad. She's right. I'm way smarter for my age than I've been pretending. Damn, Daddy, you would too if you had to worry about being pounded for it!" He couldn't help sounding exasperated, because the need to hide had been biting his butt for so long, but it probably hadn't been a good idea to cuss in front of his dad.

"Pinky?"

Pinky reflected that sometimes telling the truth was very, very hard.

Practical Solutions, Inc., and Enterprise Risk Management Group, LLC, were usually competitors. Once, they'd *almost* been hired to fight on opposite sides. They had a policy against it. There were enough contracts killing off two-bit gangs of pirates and raiders without fighting other professionals. Besides, the second employer hadn't wanted to pay enough.

Being hired onto the same side was a first. And Lester Caine wasn't sure he liked it. Sure, he was ready to get back to work. Last year had finished up great, after a rocky start. The Italian job had been nice and easy. Well, if not extravagantly, financed by the Swiss, it had not been the usual run of rescuing a colony of idealists who let their Posleen problem get too big for them. Those were depressing. People ended up paying all that they had just to get pulled out with their skins intact and returned to civilization. Italy had been a nice change. The Swiss had engineered their reclamation project like an antique watch.

There was still some bad feeling between the two companies about that job. Enterprise had expected to get it because their stick-up-the-ass culture was more likely to appeal to the staid Swiss. PS had underbid them, and was a better outfit. True to the bottom line, the Swiss had gone with PS.

And now they had to work with those guys.

The military cultures couldn't have been more different. Oh-five-hundred and those clowns come running past their tents singing out Jody calls, waking everybody up an hour early. His head was still pounding from the morning after the night before, and an hour less of sleep hadn't helped. He'd tried the medic for a cure, but he was all out of hangover pills, and had handed Les a couple of pre-war painkillers that hadn't done shit.

Then all day all they'd heard about was how slack their discipline was and how PS—called by a much less flattering name—didn't PT. Of course they did PT. Not a flabby one among them. General Lehman's view was that if you couldn't keep yourself fit for duty and ready to do your job on your own, you were in the wrong business. Himself, he did loads of basketball and lifting. No matter where they went in the world, there was always room to set up for some hoops.

Just because they didn't get up at oh-five-hundred and run two miles, or do all that calisthenics bullshit, didn't make them any less soldiers, and their record in the field proved it.

One of General Lehman's favorite sayings was that no combat ready unit has ever passed inspection, and no inspection ready unit has ever passed combat. Enterprise was *constantly* inspection ready, with its officers chosen more for ability to keep the troops looking pretty than fighting. They weren't bad in a scrap, but oh lord the bullshit. They didn't take too many contracts against human enemies, which explained the miracle of any of their officers surviving being saluted in the field and the other idiocy that passed for discipline with those clowns.

Okay, they weren't complete clowns. When it came right down to it, Les had a certain respect for the guys over there. It was just that bitching about them was traditional and his head hurt like a motherfuck.

To top it off, here he was shining up boots and pressing his goddamn BDUs because they had parade at four to listen to the bullshit of the client. Mostly it was so the client could see with his own eyes what he was buying, but rather than admit that up front, they had to sit and listen to the man bullshit until he got tired of listening to himself talk.

Geez, they were here, they were armed and equipped, their record with clients spoke for itself. What was the point of some fucking civilian coming and goggling at them, pretending he would be able to tell the difference between a crap outfit and a crack outfit by looking? But that was a part of the bullshit that simply could not be dispensed with no matter how much he would have preferred otherwise.

Lester sighed and tried to put a crease, of sorts, into pants never designed to look pretty.

The guy hiring them tried too hard to sound like Chicago, but Les could hear the undertone of redneck. Somebody had slapped a few sheets of plywood together into an impromptu reviewing stand and slapped a coat of blue paint on it. The client, John Stuart, looked like he was none too sure the stand would hold him up. Les wouldn't have trusted it either.

Another thing that told him "hick" was that he'd caught a glimpse of the contract on General Lehman's desk. Having learned to read upside-down as a good military habit, he had seen the client's full name: John Earl Bill Stuart. Unlike most of his comrades in arms, who were a rather thought-free bunch, Lester actually knew who J.E.B. Stuart—the original one—was. He suppressed a chuckle.

Right now, he wasn't too fond of old John up there. He was spilling out a bunch of bullshit about a rapid reaction force to secure their interests, blah blah blah. From experience, what that all boiled down to was that the cocksucker knew exactly who he wanted them to fight, wasn't ready to get off the dime yet, and wasn't about to tell them shit. Or he knew who, what, and where and wasn't telling. Maybe Gordy would have the straight shit on this contract. He usually did.

The Enterprise guys, it figured, all had dress uniforms. Pussies. So in addition to getting deluged with bullshit, he had to stand here feeling like a slob. Not one of his best days. He fixed his eyes on the bare-branched tree line in the distance and did one of a soldier's most valiant rear-area tasks—suppressing visible boredom in the face of speeches.

"Have you contacted your clan on Earth to tell them we have people coming?" Indowy Roolnai asked Michelle.

The Indowy stood almost knee deep in Earth grass. It was ankle deep on the office's owner and other occupant. The room gave the illusion of being outdoors on a primitive or agricultural planet, down to the faintly clouded blue sky—ceiling—above. The room's rectangular box shape meant corners marred the illusion of light blue shading up to indigo, but it was still nice. Although the room otherwise tended to trigger the Indowy's agoraphobia, the furniture was designed to resemble granite boulders. Between that and the almost-tall grass he had a sensation of available cover and potential hiding places that tickled away at the primitive part of his brain saying all was well. He always had to fight the temptation to crawl under the desk, particularly, as now, when the omnivorous occupant was in the room.

"I have not. The numbers are small, they have the space, my work schedule is . . . gratifyingly plentiful." She carefully kept her teeth concealed when she spoke, for which he was grateful, but at the last her lips had quirked in what he had learned was called a wry grin. In work, at least, he could sympathize.

"Then you are saved an extra communique, and

I also ask you if it is possible to expedite informing them. You see, the numbers of Bane Sidhe traveling to Earth are not so few as we had hoped. Nor so many," he said gravely. "This will begin to help explain."

He handed her a data cube for her buckley. She had an AID as well, of course, but it was incommunicado for this meeting. She plugged the cube into the buckley's reader slot. "Sidona, play it," she ordered.

"I apologize for the graphic violence," he said. The apology was perfunctory. She was human, why would she care?

The apology was also redundant, as the Indowy holo that appeared over the desk immediately repeated it. "*I am terribly sorry to inflict these horrible scenes on the viewers of this material. Unfortunately, it was necessary to display the extent and gravity of our troubles,*" it said.

The small green figure was replaced by a scene recorded by a buckley or AID, probably the former. The green, fuzzy fingers occasionally covering the camera port, as well as the angle of view, made it clear the user was an Indowy, standing in a cargo area. The scene became a bit hard to follow, as the software had obviously had to draw too many inferences to try to map the sequence into holo, and so sometimes shifted to a 2-D projection on the desk surface.

The steady part of the clip was short, showing two humans bearing down on the hapless creature, one of the men already carrying a squealing co-worker under one arm. The camera angle skewed wildly as the man in front picked up "their" Indowy. The men left the cargo area for corridors.

"This is the primary Dulain out-station," a voice-over informed them, as the corridor scene cut to the entry to an airlock, where the victims were pushed in, then unceremoniously cycled to space.

In the cold black, the buckley tumbled. A small bit of green suggested it was still in the possession of its erstwhile owner, as did the crazy skewing of stars and station as the poor creature thrashed.

The view shifted to the bridge of a ship, and from there into another holo, this time of suited teams retrieving spaced corpses.

"This is not as futile as it appears. We had barely enough warning for about half our people to hide Hiberzine injectors from the first-aid kits upon their person. Of those, about sixty percent managed to inject and avoid death or serious injury, and another ten percent survived but will need extensive regeneration."

The view shifted again to a cramped hold packed with Indowy, bare and blue as newborns, with patches of green coming in as they began to regrow their symbiotic covering.

"We have been advised to seek refuge on Earth, of all places. I find the reasoning bizarre, myself, but others are wiser. Any world looks good when your drive is going out," it finished philosophically. "Even that one," it added, abruptly disappearing as the cube ended.

"I have similar reports from a dozen worlds," the clan chief added.

Michelle O'Neal regarded him with a still face whose expression he could not interpret. It was distressing indeed to have so many clans needing high level favors from a clan and species they had come perilously close to spurning outright.

"Why," Michelle asked, "do you not simply allow the plotters to give themselves up for the overall security of their clans and be done with it? Why put yourselves so far in debt to a clan you so obviously . . . have concerns about?"

He was glad she had not said "despised." The sentiment would have been too close for comfort, as it was already uncomfortable enough indeed to have to confront the magnitude of one's own error.

"My race's clan heads rarely support the Bane Sidhe, become involved with the Bane Sidhe, or even pay much attention to the Bane Sidhe. That doesn't mean that we, and the Tchpth do not find it convenient for the Bane Sidhe to exist."

She raised an eyebrow at him, a gesture he knew was a request for further information.

He pointed to her aethal board over near the plashing fountain. "A seemingly insignificant piece can add disproportionate complexity to the game. Plotters and plots are irrelevant in the short and medium term." To his race, medium term meant at least a thousand years. "The increased range of action available, however . . ."

"Lubricant has nothing to do with an engine," Michelle said, blinking just once. "But without it an engine seizes. And many lubricants are, under different pressures and conditions, abrasives. The Bane Sidhe . . ." She cocked her head to the side for a moment in thought and then laughed. Loudly.

"My sister's whole life, all of her effort," Michelle said, trying very hard not to giggle. "All the blood and the pain and the conspiring and the covers for *what?*" she ended angrily. "To squeeze a better deal out of the *Darhel?*"

"Mentat, calm yourself," Roolnai said nervously.

"Oh, I am calm," Michelle said. "You don't *want* to see me *angry.* The last person who saw me angry was Erik Winchon." She paused and let that sink in. "Briefly."

"Mentat . . ."

"All those years, decades, centuries? Of plotting," she said. "All spoiled because while the Bane Sidhe were wonderful as a threat in potential, when Clan O'Neal did real damage to the Darhel you found out how pitifully *weak* you actually are."

"Mentat," Roolnai started, again.

"Save it," Michelle said. "Here is the Deal. There are over one hundred and twenty-six trillion Indowy. How many are Bane Sidhe I do not know nor care. There are less than a billion humans. Very few of whom are Bane Sidhe. The value of Indowy is nothing. The value of human Bane Sidhe fighters, of my Clan, is in this instance infinite. To . . . oil your machine we are going to have to use our life's blood and my Clan is *very* attached to their blood. Do you understand that?"

"Yes, Mentat," Roolnai said in a beaten tone.

"The debt you are about to incur is *huge,*" Michelle said. "If I was contracting upon this on the basis of profit and loss I could cast you to the Darhel myself. However, I am O'Neal. We, unfortunately, also have a code of something called 'honor.' We will honor this debt. I will contact my sister and inform her of the full gravity of this matter. Your people will be secured to the best of my Clan's capabilities."

"Thank you, Mentat," Roolnai said, finally breathing out.

"Don't thank me until I send you the bill," Michelle said.

"Yes, Mentat."

"And Roolnai. You should move into my quarters for the duration. Clan O'Neal quarters are the only place on Adenast where the Darhel's paid murderers would be afraid to go. And if they are not, they will learn to be."

Roolnai reflected, even as he agreed, that it seemed he had something in common with even the most barbaric of human monsters.

CHAPTER TWELVE

Sandy Swaim was in the minority among O'Neals and Sundays. She actually liked the present day "outside world" away from Edisto. If the O'Neals had a flaw, it was a tendency to hide away and go hermit. Sandy liked getting to know new people, and she had an open, natural manner that put the people she met instantly at ease. Her highlighted hair bushed out around her head in curls, around a fresh, bright face with adolescent puppy fat giving it a youthful glow.

Youthful was the key there. In Sandy's case, you really were as young as you felt. Her optimistic and curious attitude towards the world had lasted despite all the odds against, and was probably the deciding factor in securing her a spot on the juv list as a trained safe house operator. Her eyes really were as young as the rest of her, in a way that no lapse could ever betray. She'd had something else going for her, too. Having been born destined for a libido that was sluggish in the extreme, juving had given her a new lease on life in that department, too, by making her "normal." Again, no lapses could reveal a juv "tell" she simply didn't have.

The catch was that warming up romantically had handed her a problem she hadn't expected. She'd fallen in love and married, which in their case meant enduring separations that could only be considered short and fleeting when looked at in the context of a juv lifespan. Juv parents or not, human children still grew up at the same rate, which meant she spent a lot of time functioning as a single parent and reminding the children that they did have a daddy and that, yes, Daddy really wished he was here.

Right now, she didn't know whether to be more worried about Mike than before, or not. On the one hand, he wasn't going out with DAG on missions to quash pirates and terrorists right now. On the other hand, he was back on that damned island with her crazy in-laws who now had their hands on the rest of DAG, practically, and Sandy could no more imagine O'Neals having troops and not using them than she could imagine water not being wet. Sure, in a better world. But in this one? O'Neals plus private army was quite possibly scarier than having Mike going all over the world putting out fires for the government. Maybe. Maybe they'd settle down to something safer and more reputable, like smuggling.

One thing she knew for sure. Florida in January was a better place to be than South Carolina, even if she wasn't at the beach. God knew why Disney World had been the first big tourist draw to reopen in Florida, but it had.

New Orlando was a dinky place compared to Charleston or Norfolk, not having port traffic coming through.

Land was cheap enough, and housing cheap enough, that living on waitress pay from Waffle House was just fine in tourist season—and for one group or another it was always tourist season in Orlando. The job wasn't because she had no skills for a better job. Obviously she did. She was doing it. Her sucky cover pay made it a mystery to nobody whenever she had renters come and stay at random in her little house. The neighbors shrugged, clucked that it was a pity what single mothers had to do to make ends meet, and wasn't it too bad such a nice girl had made the classic dumb mistake. She didn't volunteer personal information, and the neighbors felt they could fill in the blanks well enough without prodding what were obviously sore spots.

The only thing she really hated about working at Waffle House was that her feet hurt so bad when she got off shift, and then she had to walk home since somebody had stolen her bike a week ago, but thankfully it was just around the corner—

The O'Neals had a name for Sandy's sunny optimism. They called it "condition white," and the same things that made her so hard to peg as a juv made it impossible to train out. Mrs. Swaim had over a decade of unarmed combat training and was hell on wheels in the dojo. She never saw the man who stepped out from behind the rose of Sharon vine and grabbed her, thrusting a stiletto up through the base of her brain.

Robert Swaim batted the tennis ball off the garage door again. They still called it a garage, even though the door had been made so it wouldn't go up when they made the space into a guest room. Right now, three guests were sharing it. Mrs. Catt, and her two kids Karen and David. Karen was okay, for a girl. David was a little kid who had thankfully attached himself to his sister, Rose, and not him. David, in his turn, was incessantly followed by the youngest of the Swaims, his two-year-old sister, Sheely. Robert tried not to get too attached to guests, because they never stayed long, but Mom had told him these might be around for awhile.

Usually it didn't matter that they didn't have a garage, but the Catts had a car. Nobody much liked leaving it outside, but there wasn't any choice, really. To Robert, it was just an annoyance he had to work around in finding room to work his skills.

Mrs. Catt was weird. She seemed to have two driving passions: soap operas and tarot cards. Mom said to just be thankful she was here, because it meant he didn't have to watch Sheely and Rose every day after school, and they could save the money from Sheely's day babysitter.

He was fine with the saving money and not having to watch his little sisters, but Robert honestly wasn't sure he could take another evening of hearing that he or some other family member was in grave danger. That seemed to be Mrs. Catt's specialty in her tarot readings. She said it wasn't, but she was a nervous woman who jumped at small noises, and he figured it was probably because she did all that scaring herself.

Mom had finally gotten tired of the cards and asked her to quit, but Rose was all about it, and he could hear her inside asking for a reading. He thought about telling her Mom said no, but then he realized he didn't have to be in charge and could keep practicing with his new racquet, so he bounced the ball and hit it again. He didn't have to hurry, even if he decided to say something, because Mrs. Catt told Rose to wait until after her show. His watch said twenty after four, and most of those things ran an hour long—if she didn't go right into another one. Mom should be home by then, anyway. He hit the ball again, trying to keep his wrist straight.

A squall of rain came in just before five, so he went inside looking for a snack. There was Rose, shuffling the big cards of Mrs. Catt's deck. Mom was late, and he thought again about saying something, but she had cut them and stacked them and, really, if she gave herself a nightmare, maybe she'd learn.

"Is your mother often late getting in, Robert?" the woman asked him.

"Not very often. Maybe she got something from the store," he said.

She looked out the window at the rain doubtfully. If Mom was in it, she was getting drenched. "I'd think she would have come and gotten the car," the other mom said. "Well, if she's not home in half an hour I'll go ahead and start your dinner."

She was kind of fat, so she huffed as she eased herself down on the floor to sit cross-legged in front of the deck.

He couldn't see the attraction of the game, himself, but he did prop himself on the arm of the couch with his baloney sandwich and watch as the woman went into her now-familiar spiel, and she was in fine form, almost as good as a ghost story. Only this time, when she hit about the fourth card she did something he'd never seen her do before. She stopped talking and dealt out the other cards, bing bing bing. Then she turned dead white and looked up at Rose.

"Car. Get in the car, now," she said. When Rose just looked at her funny, she smiled a strange, strained smile. "We're going to Disney World! My treat! We'll pick up your mom on the way, stay overnight, get new stuff, everything! Won't that be fun?" She was trying to sound cheerful, but she really sounded shrill.

She was talking about picking up Mom, so he figured Mom would straighten her out. But just in case, since she was getting real weird, he grabbed Mom's buckley quietly. She'd forgotten to take it to work, and he wasn't supposed to use it, but this was different. He tapped it on. "Marlee, record *everything*," he said. "Um . . . send it to Mom's voicemail. Real time."

It would be expensive as hell, and she'd probably ground him for a month, but Dad had told him to look out for the family and it just seemed like a good thing to do. Especially with Mrs. Catt grabbing him by the collar, shoving Sheely into his arms—she was too startled to cry—and practically dragging them all out the door.

The Catts' blue sedan was beat up to hell and gone. It had lots of rust, and foam stuck out in a couple of places where the seats were ripped. It smelled like someone had once left the windows open to the rain. But it ran good, and it started right up almost as soon as she put the key in. He tried to complain that they didn't have a car seat for Sheely, but the woman wasn't listening to him. She was kind of scary. He tried not to get attention as he set the buckley down on the seat beside him.

Rose and David were in front. In the back it was just him with Sheely and Karen. Karen was cool for a girl. She saw him put it on the seat, but shrugged instead of saying anything. She didn't look too sure about how her mom was acting, either. He kept Sheely distracted from what otherwise might have become a tempting toy by making faces at her until she laughed. He kept her busy as they went out from town and onto park land, which had grown up wild but you had to go through to get to the parking lots.

The rain made the road slippery so when the car passing them hit them in the side, it knocked them into the canal. The water wasn't deep, but there was really no way to get clear of the car before the men with guns came for them.

"So about all we've got now is running the DNA, pulling the winner in and squeezing him like a zit."

"Picturesque, Cally, but yeah, that's basically it."

They were so used to food made of varying combinations of corn, soy, eggs, and cheese now that they didn't even bitch, and it was a strangely silent crew who sat and picked at their morning meal. What was there to say? Each of them wanted to explode outward in violent rage at the bastards who murdered the Maise family, but the rage was focused in a circle of frustration. Did they have somebody inside who'd burned the safe house?

They knew the coals of rage would grow to white fury as consciousness returned and they absorbed more detail throughout the day. Right now, however, it was oh-five-thirty-something and they were, despite not having been able to actually sleep, groggy with morning.

For now, they sat and glumly shoveled in their morning fuel, an action that they interrupted, almost with relief, to dive as one for their buzzing, beeping, or vibrating buckleys.

"O'Reilly's office?" Harrison asked unnecessarily as all four of them were moving in the same direction like fingers on the same hand.

Cally's anger was a palpable thing, like half-molten rock that had taken up residence inside her gut and was fast building its twin in her brain. She was allowing the feelings free rein now on the theory that getting them out of her system would help when it came time to lock everything down and take care of business. She knew that was just an excuse. Things like this didn't get out of your system. To complicate things, she was, and knew she was, having a mother bear response to the murder of the children until she looked out on the world through a red mist, needing someone to kill. Letting the emotion run away inside her like this was not good, but for once it just wasn't responding to her attempts to exercise training and lock it down anyway.

She looked at the cold professionalism on the face of the rest of the team and felt ashamed for her weakness, not knowing that every one of them was looking at her the same way. While she was unable to imprison her feelings in icy compartmentalization, her face had responded to muscle memory and training, forming a mask of stone except for a tiny, almost imperceptible tic at the corner of her lower lip.

Aware of everything, deviating for nothing, the team stalked upward through the Sub-Urb-style base, a wolf pack, albeit a pack with an acute sense of the emotional hole where their missing member should be.

The sense of oneness disintegrated abruptly as they entered their superior's office and beheld the spectacle that was unfolding live on HV, with the gruesome gleefulness only those in the news business can display when provided with especially lurid fodder.

Cally sank into one of the chairs around the tank, others of which were already occupied by the priest and the Indowy Aelool. Without speech or thought, the two Schmidts split right and left, taking station on opposite sides of the room, while Tommy moved to stand behind Nathan's left elbow.

"One of ours?" she asked, ashen.

"Niece," O'Reilly said shortly.

The reporter stood outside the police tape, saying they couldn't show some of the images they had taken on HV, and asking parents to send the children out of the room for the ones they were willing to show—after coming back from a commercial break, of course. Cally reflected on how much she did not give a shit about stupid breath mints at the moment.

"They got the mother, too." The priest was wooden, the Indowy inscrutable.

"Let me guess. One of ours was close to his sister," Tommy said.

"One of the DAGgers. His twin."

"The evidence from the scene would inevitably 'disappear,'" O'Reilly said. "So we'll get there first. I'm sending you a list of possibles to fill out your team. Pick a cyber and get ready to do a collection run for tonight. You'll take the equipment to preserve it, you'll take as long as it takes to shake the bastards—who are no doubt drawing us exactly for the purpose of locating more of our network and this base. I think if they had us here, we'd already have gotten a visit. Get as open as you have to without leaving anyone behind. Concealment would be nice, but is a low second to recovery and egress."

He looked at the tank in disgust and loathing. "Turn it off," he said. "Don't watch this excrement. Go sort through your options, my recommendations are there. Get prepped for a busy night."

"She's cherry as hell," George grumped as they viewed the holo of the eleventh candidate and looked over her profile.

"Yeah, but she's cute. Her other quals are good, but don't underestimate cute. You can dress it down as needed, but making someone inherently prettier is hard. It's an unfair world. Our job is to make it even more unfair—for the enemy." Cally pushed her hair back behind her ear. It didn't cooperate. The bitch of shorter hair was that it fell into her face easier than when it was long, and damned if she was going to go around in barrettes like a prepubescent schoolgirl.

"She looks . . . sweet," Tommy said dubiously.

"She's not. Look at her aggressor record," she said. Cally had been to the same school the candidate had just graduated from. It didn't make her biased, as far as she could see, but it did mean she had a much clearer idea of how to translate the candidate's training record and evaluations into a big picture of actual performance. In this case, one of the final tests of a senior's temperament came when they were assigned to act as enemies and opponents in the training exercises of junior high and underclassman girls. A student who couldn't be thoroughly vicious to trainees, in the right way, and without breaking them, would have bad marks for aggressive-mindedness, and might even have been rolled back a year to see if maturation could train it out. Usually not.

This girl, on the other hand, not only had top marks in that area, but the graders had included notes on some particularly evil twists the young lady had devised for her hapless victims. All constituting good training, of course. Cally liked her instantly.

"Whew. Nasty. And a decent athlete, for a non-upgrade." George nodded.

"She's in," Tommy echoed.

"Works for me," Harrison said. "She's mostly cyber support, in case anyone had forgotten. She's solid. I'll take creativity over rote grades any day."

"Amy Sands it is. For now." Cally nodded, adding her blessing to the girl who would sub into Papa's slot. The girl's golden brown hair and rosy cheeks just radiated midwestern wholesomeness. The kind of girl next door that nobody actually got to live next door to. They should be so lucky.

"Are you through sealing her fate?" her buckley asked. "What's up?"

"There's a courier from Edisto. Non-urgent, he said. Wouldn't hear of interrupting you, he said. It's not *my* fault that everything's going to fall apart from the late message. I *told* him I'd put him through, but no . . ."

"Shut up, buckley. Where the hell is he?"

"In the cafeteria when he called me, having a beer with a few of the guys from DAG," the machine told her. "I'm sure by now he's told them half the secrets of the whole island, and the latest gossip, too. But no, it wasn't *urgent*, he said."

"A few beers with . . . wait, is this the same courier?" Tommy asked sharply. He didn't wait for an answer, but began striding down the hall at a fast walk.

Given his height, Cally had to jog to keep up. "Is who the same courier?" she asked.

"I don't understand the question. Same courier as what?" the buckley asked.

"Oh, you wouldn't know." The big man shook his head. "The guy who brought the message about the Maises was . . . loquacious. Even without alcohol. I don't know what he's carrying, but beer, other guys, and mister diarrhea mouth doesn't sound like a good combination."

"Why wasn't he benched?" Cally asked sharply.

"Hadn't gotten to it yet. Mosovich and Mueller knew, so they would have taken care of it, it's just . . ." He trailed off, shrugging.

"He's carrying a girl," buckley volunteered helpfully. "Well, not *carrying* her carrying her. He brought one with him."

It had that worried tone it got when it couldn't think of any specific disaster to predict. Cally resisted the bizarre urge to reassure it.

The gentleman in question looked up expectantly as they entered the cafeteria, which was otherwise mostly empty, she noticed gratefully.

The four other men pulled up around the table were unfamiliar to Cally, but her practiced eye would have made them for military, even if she hadn't otherwise known. If there had been any doubt, it would have been cleared up when the eyes of one of them widened and he set down the beer, sitting sharply to attention, followed a split second later by the others.

The courier remained in a slump with a grin of "I've got a secret" on his fat face.

"Ma'am, about the Maises—"

"I take it you've heard the news," Cally said. She walked over to the courier and yanked him up by his collar until he was dangling off the ground. One hand slipped in to his front pocket and pulled out two data cubes. She tossed them to Tommy, then looked the dangling courier in the eye. "Do you know who I am? Given that you've apparently blabbed and gossiped your way across half the country?"

"Gurk?"

"I'll take that for a yes," she hissed, holding up a hand like a knife. "Right now I'm looking for someone to kill. I'd prefer five people who killed one of our dependent families. Barring that, anyone will do. What I don't need is couriers going around delivering unsolicited information and making my life harder than it already was. What I'm contemplating, somewhat seriously, is just driving this up into your chest and ripping out your still beating heart. Do I make my point?"

"Gurk?"

"Go to your quarters, do not communicate, do not leave, I'll deal with you later." Cally dropped him unceremoniously and watched him scurry out of the cafeteria. "Do *you* know who I am?" she asked without turning to look at the foursome.

"Yes, ma'am," one of them answered.

"If your friends are wallowing in ignorance, they are now allowed access to that compartment," Cally said coldly. "To answer your interrupted question, the four horsemen of the apocalypse are *riding*. The

Darhel have apparently declared open warfare on Clan O'Neal. Which gives *us* our hunting license."

"Oo-rah," one of the DAG murmured.

"You'll be given target lists as soon as they're prepared," Cally said, still looking towards the entrance. "But you'll have to pass on the really juicy ones."

"Why?" one of the soldiers challenged.

"Because *they* are *mine*," Cally purred.

CHAPTER THIRTEEN

Pinky allowed himself to be introduced to the new lady, Lish. She looked like it was her first time here at Bane Sidhe base—he'd learned this whole place was a headquarters for a whole underground resistance to Darhel oppression. Underground both ways, like a Sub-Urb and like spies. He also figured he'd better get to like it here. Since they had to tell him, they might not let him leave until *he* was an adult. He hadn't bothered to ask. If they said anything except that he had to stay, was he gonna believe them? Eyes open, mouth closed. First rule of spying. Besides, the blonde lady had said she was going to kill the people that killed Mom and Joey. And Jenny, he reminded himself.

Cally. That was her name. When she promised, her eyes had looked like some of the other guys in his dad's unit sometimes did. He believed her.

Lish, the new lady, was nothing like Cally. For one thing, he'd bet she was really as young as she looked. For another, she didn't seem very smart. The big thing, though, was that if Cally ever looked as uncomfortable as Lish looked right now, Pinky would bet a dollar she'd be faking it.

It seemed like it was just Mrs. Mueller's day to get stuck with new people. He shrugged it away and ran off to play with Davey and Pat.

"All set," Amy Sands was clearly thrilled with her first professional assignment, as well she might be. There was no more prestigious operational team than the one that held both senior O'Neals, three if you counted Tommy Sunday, and not just because they were damned good. It was the other way around. The other Bane Sidhe respected the O'Neals so much *because* so many of them were so good.

Tommy moved in to check her work, the task being both necessary and in the way of a final technical interview. A row of buckleys sat on the battered desk in front of them, each lined up, after many obfuscatory hops through the network, to make very sincere, urgent police calls in a short period of time.

He had handled the hack into the police computers himself, as there was more risk of getting caught. The run had yielded a list of forensic evidence collected and where it all was presently.

While the Organization didn't have anyone inside this particular station—had few people inside any stations—they did have extensive records on who could be bribed where. These days, the list was long as hell, and they might have done better to compile a list of who *couldn't* be bribed. The right payoffs were already in the right hands, plans in place to deal gently with any honest officers who couldn't be avoided along the way.

Throughout the O'Neal Bane Sidhe, other teams were preparing for other missions in their areas of specialty. Cleaning teams did a phenomenal job of forensics work when there was a call for it, as now. Professionals thoroughly schooled to leave *no* evidence at a scene were adept at finding bits others had missed.

This was probably the nicest of the offices available to operations, which meant it was usually booked solid by office staff and other chair warmers in the hierarchy. Some things never changed. The proximity to the holidays had made for a rare vacancy. The non-field staff hadn't been recalled, which had kept it that way. The chairs were all in good repair, and the walls had been tuned as a project by one of the Sohon kids with decent taste.

"Don't get used to such palatial surroundings, Amy. This is the first time I've gotten the good office in a couple of years, and it'll probably be that long before we luck out again."

"Got it." She grinned at him. "Everything okay?"

"Sweet. Some of the wrinkles in the data hops are creative and clever. I wouldn't have thought of dynamically routing through machines for sale on auction sites. Excellent," he said. "Byron, get me Cally."

"Easier said than done, boss; she is one hot lady. Should I be jealous? Connecting. . . ."

"All set?" he heard Cally ask him, the 2-D of her on the small screen showing a damp face, her hair in a towel in that wrap thing women did.

"A-ffirmative," Tommy confirmed. "And Papa's gonna

have a run for his money when he comes back. Miss Sands here is one hot-shit electron mechanic."

"Amy," the sweet soprano corrected from the background.

"Yeah, well, anyway, Amy passes with flying colors, we're good to go on our end," he said.

"Roger that. Golden on our end, too. Chill or rack out or whatever, meet in room twenty-eight delta foxtrot at eighteen hundred. Got it?" Cally asked.

"Check. Twenty-eight delta foxtrot, eighteen hundred. Later, I'm out."

"So what do I do between now and eighteen hundred? Oh, and Sands is okay, too." Amy grinned at him again. "Just please no 'miss'—it makes me feel like James Bond's Moneypenny."

"Right. Sorry, Sands. Do whatever you want, within common sense. I'm probably going to be playing *Diess Challenge*."

"I haven't played it yet. Is it any good?" she asked, more avidly than he would have expected. "I've heard mixed reviews."

"It's got a few rendering bugs in places, and don't PvP on the Galactic side unless you're prepared to lose. There are some God King exploits that totally screw Galactics. There's supposed to be a patch coming, but . . ." he began automatically, then paused. "I'd rate it a four out of five."

"She shoots, she scores," Amy said, popping to her feet and grinning. "See you at eighteen hundred, boss-man."

George Schmidt's own mother wouldn't have recognized him—black hair, dark brown contact lenses, skin tone bronzed to a level his own fair complexion would never support. His features had been altered by the tried-and-true contoured cheekbone pads. The make-up department had subtly altered lips, eyes, brow line, ears and nose with expert application of a long-wearing, highly localized astringent. Among other tricks, they had even managed to give him a mild, temporary case of acne. Juvs tended to be immune, as did anyone who could afford and pay for the vaccine. Acne was a near guaranteed way to camouflage a juv for a short stint. It would be gone by morning.

In this case, they had designed the acne and other facial changes to both put him squarely in the college student age bracket, as well as feed false data to any facial geometry analysis tools.

Cally and Sands had undergone similar treatments. It saved the trouble and risk of having to hack out too much police security holo. Body changes were thermal. Costuming had pulled out all the stops. Local police systems tended to be difficult to fool. That didn't mean it couldn't be done, it just made the cover process more expensive than the Bane Sidhe usually liked to shell out these days. Cost was not a factor on tonight's missions, for their team or anyone else's.

The car they had brought for insertion was a typical anonymous beige of the kind currently in vogue among the feds, down to the detail of being between three to five years old—and having interior cop car construction, complete to the back seat and valid government tags.

Cally looked George over thoroughly before looking at his brother. "Will we do?" she asked.

"Flawless," Harrison said. "Oops, bro, you've got a

string." He reached down and clipped a hanging thread from the bottom of his smaller sibling's T-shirt.

George grimaced, as if more than used to being fussed over. Harrison was on the team for more than one reason. Clothes and make-up might seem trivial to the uninitiated, but the smallest oversight in appearance could blow a cover. World War II allied spies had gone so far as to make sure the buttons were sewn onto their coats the "right" way before inserting behind the lines into France. The job of "Schmidt One" was not to make them look good. Harrison's job—one hat of many—was to make sure they looked *right*.

"Showtime." Cally nodded, getting behind the wheel of the Fed car as Sands climbed in as shotgun, in this case literal as there was a short-barrel twelve gauge under the seat. She heard the loud slam of the door behind her as George got in. He had to slam it, as there were no handles on the inside and momentum had to carry it.

Tommy and Harrison had climbed back into the gray Buick sedan. It was cramped as hell for Sunday, but he wasn't complaining. The car didn't look like much, but this model had the most aerodynamic body within the range of conservative and boring, given that it also had to fit a grand national engine under the hood. The windows also were something special. Nano-polarized, there was a set of dimmer switches on the dash that controlled the tint, from none to dark. It made the vehicle as good as a van for camping near a run, but much, much faster. A built-in electric heater under the hood kept the engine warm even in a Chicago winter.

Everyone hoped they wouldn't need the car's special

features. Get in, get out in the Fed car was the plan. Yeah. It was good to have a plan. It was essential to have a backup.

At the station, Cally did exactly what real Feds would do. She parked in one of the reserve spots right near the building—but she was a *nice* Fed. She didn't park in the chief's space.

The station was typical for the age, with parking lot and cement walkways crumbling. The building was an ugly box of faded, stained brick and dingy mortar with "Greenville City Police" tacked on the side in aluminum letters. Two "e"s and an "l" were missing. The parking lot was also, given the time of day, damn near deserted.

As she and Sands took up flanking positions to escort George in, Cally noted the exits carefully, along with the lights and the collapsed bit of curb outside the emergency fire exit they planned to use. The chained and padlocked exit.

"Hold up," she ordered, detouring to pick the lock and unthread the chain from the double door's handles. She started to put the offending items on the ground, but then got a quick mental image of some helpful soul coming through and noticing that someone had left the door unlocked. She jogged over to the car and shoved chain and lock underneath it before retaking her spot on Schmidt's left.

In accord with their story that Bryan Cane was one of the coed's ex-boyfriends who had come in "voluntarily," George walked slightly in front of the two FBI agents who, while they were not actually touching him, walked almost exactly where they would have been had they been hustling him in by the arms. The implication was clear, displaying the typical unsubtle and humorless attitude of the modern Bureau Field Agent. If they carried the stereotype a bit far into HD true crime drama, so much the better. It would fit the locals' preconceptions; people didn't question what they didn't notice.

Inside the building, the brand new, orange, plastic chairs reflected off a white institutional-tile floor, which was buffed until you could almost see your face in it. The rest of the room contrasted unfavorably, as the walls were scuffed and marked, long past the need for a new coat of paint, and the old-fashioned drop ceiling showed the stains of a current or one-time leak. The room was small, as befitted a town that barely met the population requirement for a city charter.

A counter stretched across the middle of the room and doubled as the front desk. A door had been cut to one side and was clearly the locking kind you had to be buzzed through, which was a nice little piece of security if you were keeping out blue-haired old ladies too frail to just vault the counter.

The rather chubby officer behind the counter was obviously very busy, and was presently playing a holographic game of multicolored blocks in various configurations, falling from the top of the virtual screen. He looked up as they came in the door and tapped the front of his buckley, which obediently switched off the game and brought up a screen of something that looked very serious and industrious. A boss program.

As they approached the counter, Cally let her eyes meet Sands', and they both affected the attitude of federal agents who hadn't really expected any better from local law enforcement. Near simultaneously and seemingly from nowhere, they pulled out little black leather folders and flipped them open to display their credentials to the embarrassed man.

"Special Agents Wilson and Brannig. We need an interrogation room, and then I'll speak to the senior supervisor on duty," Cally said, a slight nod of her head indicating that George was to be the person interrogated, as if the man behind the desk were too stupid to have figured that out on his own.

"That would be the chief. He's working late tonight," the officer said, clearly glad to be able to say something that might make the city police look good.

"Satisfactory. The room?" Cally reminded him as if he'd already forgotten. His slight flush deepened as her eyes noted the open box of donuts on the table behind him, and then returned to rest on him. She raised her eyebrows as if to ask why he was still just sitting there.

"Uh, yeah. Here." He reached under the counter and they heard a buzz and a click as the small door unlocked.

Cally gestured for George to precede them, meticulously avoiding touching him, perfectly courteous, and yet managing to convey the clear message that if he wasn't yet under arrest, that was a technicality that could be corrected instantly if she or "Brannig" became displeased.

Sands, on the other hand, looked at their not-prisoner, if not quite sympathetically, at least as if she hadn't already convicted him in her mind as an ax murderer. As she followed Cally through the gap, she turned to the cop behind the desk. "Thank you, officer . . . Hardy," she read off his badge.

Cally focused on the man again, her expression calculated to make him feel like an idiot that he was still seated and *still* hadn't gotten them their inter- rogation room.

He almost stumbled over his feet in his hurry to get up and comply.

The police chief looked distinctly less than happy to have a pair of Feds on his doorstep, even if they did come bearing what might be a major break in his case. He also looked resigned, and uncritically swal- lowed their story about the ex-boyfriend aka person of interest.

"We've been ordered to coordinate and cooperate with you," Cally said, with a hint of sourness under the professional mask. "Strictly speaking, since there is no hard evidence of linkage across state lines as of yet, it's your case, but I'm sure you'll understand how much pressure we're facing from above." There was *no* evidence of linkage across state lines. Or, more accurately, no evidence the Bane Sidhe was going to let civil police authorities in on.

"Frankly, most of the reason we brought him up here was as an excuse to drag him on a three-hour road trip and get him tired and hungry," Sands admit- ted. As if on cue, her stomach growled.

"Okay, so what have you got?" he asked.

"The ex-boyfriend from high school. Word is the breakup was not friendly. This one used to work for a grocery store. In the meat department," Cally said.

The chief turned a little green around the gills.

"You saw the body," she said, unsurprised when he nodded, swallowing hard, and his eyes narrowed grimly at George.

"Time to shake him until his teeth rattle." The ersatz agent didn't wait for a reply from the chief, but turned and entered the room vigorously, slamming the door behind her.

The interrogation that followed was a skit played out entirely for the chief's benefit, the characters being the good cop, the bad cop, and the suspect. Said play continued until the buckley vibrating on Cally's hip told her part two of the operation was kicking loose on the PD's emergency lines.

The beauty of the whole drama was that none of them had to do a particularly good acting job. George's character could be believably bad at pretending total innocence, while Cally and Sands could get away with a bit of overacting. They were playing agents *playing* good cop, bad cop. Cally was, thus, free to make a dramatic production of losing her temper and slamming out in a huff when Sands bodily kept her from assaulting the "suspect."

She ran a hand through her hair as she walked into the observation room with the chief. "That always winds me up. I really do need a time out," she said.

Right on cue, a pleasant female voice issued from the other man's hip pocket. "Chief, you have a call. Chief you have a call. Please see the screen for details," it said.

He pulled the device out and glanced at the screen casually, doing a quick double take. "Oh, shit," he said.

"If you need to go take care of something, she's not going to be asking him any real questions for at least another five minutes as she tries to build a bond," Cally told him. "I'm gonna take a walk and get my head back in the zone before we really start up again."

"Uh, sure, if you wouldn't mind." The chief didn't even look at her as he took off for the front office at a pace just short of a run. Step one accomplished. She now had the freedom of the station.

She didn't dither, but made a beeline for the probable locations of the evidence room. There were several candidates because she only had the building plans to work from. Unfortunately, the small room on this side held a broom closet and assorted junk that was quite clearly not evidence, unless you considered it evidence that somebody had a pack-rat problem. She wrinkled her nose in disgust and prepared her excuses as she backtracked to the front of the building, which was laid out in a horseshoe pattern. She would have to go through the front desk area to get to the other side of the building. It was also the side with the fire exit she'd originally prepped. She would, no doubt, have to unlock their side's exit to get Sands and George out.

In the front of the station, she smiled apologetically at the cop working the desk. "Do you mind if I grab one of these? I haven't eaten in five hours," she said.

His eyes glinted at her, amused, and roved over her body. For once, his eyes didn't even stop at her breasts, but skimmed on down to the thighs men seemed to like but she fought a constant battle with.

"Sure," he said.

"Thanks." She could practically feel him watching her butt as she walked on through the front and around the other side, through the emergency call room where two other cops and the chief were dealing with the frantic spate of calls. They barely looked up when she waved at them and sashayed on through. Ass man. That would explain it.

The evidence room was as jumbled as the broom closet had been. It didn't really qualify as a room, more a large closet. The lock was laughable, and she picked it in three seconds. It took her almost half a minute to find the bagged articles she was looking for. The fingers would be in the pathologist's lab at the hospital, of course. Greenville being too small for a hospital of its own, that was at the county seat six or seven miles away. Those weren't her problem. The Bane Sidhe had made other arrangements. All she needed from here was a plastic zipper bag with a used tissue in it. It took her almost five minutes to find it, but with the air squeezed out of the bag, it was easily concealable on her person. She repressed a laugh as she realized that technically this counted as stuffing her bra, and the visual image of herself carrying twice the ample amount of cleavage was just too much.

"Hey, what are you doing?" a suspicious female voice asked behind her.

Without missing a beat, she palmed a Hiberzine injection from a pocket and turned to face the cop. "Checking something the scumbag told us. This is interesting; have a look," she said. It was out of character for a federal agent to offer free information to anyone, but curiosity kept the woman from noticing, and she leaned over to peer into the closet, turning her back on Cally O'Neal

Who then had to prop the unconscious body rather

awkwardly because of the pack-rattishness of the evidence room.

Hiberzine was so cool.

She tapped her buckley, unnecessarily as it was listening. "Buckley, call Sands. Transmit 'coffee.'" She offered the code word without waiting for the call to pick up. "And leave the connection open."

She and Sands were both wearing ear dots. They hadn't dared put any on George, as there was the slimmest possibility those might be noticed.

"I don't think we're getting anywhere," she heard Sands say as if talking to the room. "I'd really hoped we could be done before my partner came back, Mr. Cane."

That meant there was a hitch. Uh-oh.

"I want my lawyer," Cally heard George say in the background. Then he started making a credible fuss.

"I'll take you where you can call one," Sands said. "Just a little walk."

The latter was code among law enforcement for a little corporal persuasion of a reluctant suspect. It was a prearranged ruse designed to separate the other two operatives from any local cops who got clingy. Okay, now that she had some idea what the problem was, Cally proceeded to the exit and around the side of the building, adrenaline starting to sing as she heard a blurred mumble in the background.

"Oh, you really don't have to come along, Chief," Sands said. "Mr. Cane might be more comfortable the fewer people are present when he calls his attorney." The words were couched to communicate to the police chief that he need not be involved or culpable in the beating of the suspect.

Another mumble.

"Okay, if you're really sure you want to come along," Amy's voice had developed a slightly sweet note, and Cally filed the information away as a "tell" for when Sands was getting annoyed.

On the other side, the door appeared unlocked. The reason was immediately apparent from the collection of cigarette butts all over the ground. Made sense. The chief was using the suspect's walk as an excuse to grab a smoke.

"After you, of course, Chief," Sands offered politely, letting Cally know the man would be first out the door. She palmed her second Hiberzine. Unless it was absolutely impossible, she never went in on an op without half a dozen of the things tucked away somewhere or other.

They featured prominently in her standard go-to-hell strategies, and did not fail her now. Looking down to tap a cigarette out of his pack, he never even saw her before Cally had him injected. George's hand was wrapped around from behind, covering the man's mouth in case he got out a yell before going down. Cally suppressed a twinge of pique that he didn't think her competent enough to take care of one man herself. Didn't George ever lighten up?

They were in the back of the building, about ten yards from the tree line. "Leave him," she ordered as he and Sands emerged through the doorway.

George laid the man down against the wall and the three sprinted to the corner of the building and stopped. Cally peeked around the corner and ducked back, turning to plant a fist squarely in George's left eye, followed by a solid gut punch.

"Ow!" he yelped.

"For effect," she hissed. "Limp a little."

They turned the corner and walked briskly back to the car, Sands and Cally again flanking George, only this time Cally reached out and shoved him forward a couple of times before they got to the vehicle and climbed in. There was nobody in sight to witness this playlet, and no windows on this side of the building.

"What the hell was that for? Nobody was looking," George protested as they drove off.

"Well, they *might* have been," Cally said defensively. It had absolutely nothing to do with the implication that she couldn't handle one damn guy by herself. It didn't.

CHAPTER FOURTEEN

Tuesday, January 5, 2055

Michael Sunday Privett, also known as "Cargo," walked into Nathan O'Reilly's office, took one look at the skinny brunette girl and shook his head. "Oh, no. Fuck no. Father O'Reilly, with all due respect, sir—"

"Hush, son. Just come in and sit down," the priest ordered him.

As he walked in awkwardly, he looked curiously around the office while trying to get as solid a grip on his professional dignity as he could. At the age of twenty-three, he'd been operational for three years, and he was dead certain he was going to need all his professionalism to deal with this situation. The brunette was wearing contacts and was made up and everything to look about seventeen, but he knew better. Cargo had spent most of his teenage years with little Denise Reardon following him around adoringly and hanging on his every word.

She was a smart kid, and she was damned cute, but the last couple of times he'd been home he'd been all too aware of how precocious little Denise was. She might be skinny, but the kid had a full load-out of hormones and he felt goddamned ridiculous dodging a seventh-grade girl all over the island.

"Sir, I don't know wha—"

"I said hush, Privett. Sit."

"Yes, sir." Cargo sat unhappily on the front half of a chair, back straight, unconsciously drawing on "proper" bearing to get through what he anticipated was about to become a very uncomfortable—more uncomfortable—situation.

"I know you know Miss Reardon, Sergeant Privett. What you may not know is that Miss Reardon is a candidate for professional school." The head of the Bane Sidhe focused a grave stare on him, as if waiting to see if he needed to be shut up again.

"There is no way, at all, Miss Reardon will be assigned onto a team at her age and without full training. However, just now she has a skill that is very useful. She's a damned good driver, has a peerless sense of direction—"

Boy, did she ever, Cargo acknowledged. The kid had some kind of weird intuition or something, because she always seemed to guess where he was going next and get there before him.

"—importantly, her, um, tracking skills are exceptionally useful in this case, because she can get you back without a tail more reliably than anyone I've got on base. I believe you have the personal experience to appreciate it when I tell you that she is one of the individuals able to effortlessly transfer simulator experience in this type of task to real life." O'Reilly held a poker face, but Cargo had the uncomfortable certainty he was being laughed at.

He felt an unholy glee as the girl blushed brightly. She deserved a little discomfort out of this, the little brat.

"I have teams, son, but I don't have them sitting around idle. Even pulling in what I can, with this sudden work increase, I am pressed. I will be putting together a team from our operatives in, and new recruits from, DAG. I will be sending that team on a vital mission. That mission will be directed at killing one of the individuals responsible for one of the dependent murders. Miss Reardon will be that team's driver. Would you like to volunteer for this mission, Sergeant Privett?"

Cargo suppressed a sigh. Completely suppressed it. Acting anything less than the complete professional he was would only make him look bad in front of God's right-hand man and encourage the brat.

"Yes, sir," he said.

"Good. I'll send the details to your buckley. You're dismissed," the priest said. "Not you, Miss Reardon. Stay a moment."

Not for anything would he let either of the two of them see any of his relief that little Deni—Denise— couldn't follow him. God, even his *wife* thought she was cute.

Cordovan Landrum wished his parents had picked a different way to honor his mother's surname of Brown than to name him after a shoe color. Since nobody had asked him, he had picked one he liked better out of his favorite series of the weird two-Ds that his dad watched obsessively. At the age of five, he had begun the practice of beating the crap out of any boy who would not call him "Luke," and finding other ways to get even with annoying girls, whom he couldn't beat up. Not and survive *his* dad.

Luke looked at his team roster and winced a little at the driver's name. He wasn't supposed to know her age, but Cargo had clued him in. He had made the executive decision to keep the information from Tramp and Kerry so as to not make them nervous that the kid was driving. As Bane Sidhe, he knew a bit about how the O'Neals ran their place. That kid would have been driving motorized go-carts as soon as she could reach the gas pedal, progressing to dirt bikes and cars, again, as soon as she could reach. If O'Reilly was sticking him with a gal this young, the girl could drive like a bat out of hell.

She was sitting across from him now. He'd gotten the gum out of her mouth by the simple expedient of looking at her like the seventeen-year-old she was supposed to be—i.e., like fair game—and telling her huskily that she looked about twelve when she did that. She'd swallowed the gum so fast she'd almost choked. And blushed like hell. But no more gum chewing to give her age away to Kerry and Tramp.

Even in a good cause, it had felt kind of icky to know he was making eyes at a thirteen-year-old, although she sure didn't look thirteen. She looked like an O'Neal. It was less a matter of facial features and more something the family seemed to carry on the inside.

The head of the O'Neal Bane Sidhe had told him she'd taken an assassin's audition and passed. More importantly, a month later she still wanted the job. He didn't like having a kid driver, but he'd take the top guy's word on the competence of this one.

When his other three guys came in, Cargo nodded to her and just kept quiet, glaring at Kerry and Tramp when they tried to get friendly. The other two men, of course, chalked that up to entirely wrong reasons and would have gotten more enthusiastic if Luke hadn't taken them in hand.

"Okay, just to go over the crap I know you guys will have already studied, this is the scumbag on the menu for the evening. Linda, display scumbag," he instructed his buckley. "This is said scumbag's house." The buckley obligingly changed the holo it was projecting above the table. The table and conference room were complete pieces of shit, but he'd grown up in the Bane Sidhe and only noticed it from the difference between the facilities here and at Great Lakes.

"This is the route to scumbag's house." The buckley switched to a street view, projected as if they were looking at a sand table, with the route outlined in red.

Landrum looked up at Denise to make sure she was paying attention, focused in, whatever. She was.

"This is our kind of mission. Scumbag's house is a little isolated. Got a vacant house on one side, an empty lot on the other. We go, we kick in the door, we kill the bastard, we come back. Standard building clearing, don't hit the no-shoot targets. Wife and kid. Any questions?" The latter was the rhetorical question that traditionally ended all mission briefings. There were never questions.

"Why are we killing him? Or does it matter? To the mission, I mean," the girl asked.

Luke carefully avoided being either terse or patronizing. If nobody had told her, it was a damned good question. Why the hell hadn't anybody told her? "He killed Shark Sanders' grandmother," he said. When the kid's eyes widened then narrowed coldly, he gave her a couple of points. She actually looked a bit scary, considering.

"We know because he obligingly left a bit of his DNA—" The kid wasn't stupid or naïve, and she was clearly getting the wrong impression. "Blood. He stuck himself on a pin." The girl's shoulders relaxed fractionally, but the chill in the room from all five of them was arctic. When you murdered a harmless old granny at her quilting, you just didn't get any brownie points for what you *didn't* do.

Snow was falling heavily, and the wind was squealing too loud to hear the clank of the chains on the tires as they drove out from their staging area, a dinky, ugly little car repair shop. The car, which Reardon had spent at least twice as long checking out as he usually would have, would be carrying them from Fort Wayne to Cincinnati.

She had grudgingly agreed to let the four DAGgers share the driving to Asheville, but Landrum noticed she was real uncomfortable that Privett was driving.

"Have you ever driven in snow before, Cargo?" she asked.

"What? Of course I've driven in snow. We're— were—stationed up in Great Lakes!" He sounded indignant.

"And you know the first rule of driving in snow, right?"

"I can drive, Deni." He rolled his eyes.

"I'd feel better if you slowed down about ten miles per hour," she said.

Landrum looked over Privett's shoulder at the speedometer, which was holding on sixty. He looked out at the road and the weather. It was a little faster than he would have driven, considering.

"There can be ice under this shit that you don't see," Reardon insisted.

Privett sighed exasperatedly, but Landrum felt the car slow.

"You can get some sleep while you're not driving, you know," Luke told the girl, who was sitting in the middle of the back seat, between him and Tramp.

She looked at the back of Cargo's head suspiciously, then down at her buckley. "Maybe later. I think I'll read for now."

Tramp looked entirely too happy about the seating arrangements, which prompted Landrum to shoot him a dirty look over the back of the kid's head. His buckley vibrated softly, and he touched the screen to bring up the text.

"What? Are you calling dibs?" The message had Tramp's user icon in the corner.

"She's underage," he typed back.

"Not by much." He and Tramp were both typing by touching small typewriter keys displayed on the lower half of the screen. They were only there when the buckley was in text mode, but they did help with brief, silent communication.

The girl sat between them, reading whatever she was reading, or playing a game or something. Oblivious, anyway.

A new icon, a snowflake, flashed onto his screen, the word "conference" blinking in the corner. He tapped the button to accept, wondering.

"Too much for you. Get it?" the message said. The snowflake turned into a curvy twentieth-century poster girl who blew a kiss before winking out.

Landrum shot a look at the girl, who had a small quirk at the corner of her mouth, and just about fell out of his seat laughing.

"Something wrong?" the kid asked, pushing the bridge of her nose like someone used to wearing glasses.

"Nope," he said.

On the other side of the car, Tramp Michaels looked a lot less cheerful and a bit more glum. Luke just couldn't resist throwing him a big grin.

They drove through the night, stopping to change cars twice before getting to Asheville. It had been a bit of an experience for Kerry and Michaels to insert by something as prosaic as a road trip. So much so that they'd joked along the way, calling it the frat-boy hit.

Between one thing and another, it was the wee hours when they pulled into Knoxville. The weather was fine, and the roads dry, with forecast of more of the same. Operational necessity frequently required doing without sleep, but contrary to popular belief, proper rest *was* something you planned for if possible. The best guy in the world still performed better rested than fatigued. They found a cheap hotel and he sent Cargo in to set them up.

The hotel was a grayish brown, not intentionally, but because its white bricks and doors had been without a fresh coat of paint for so long they were grimy and stained. It was the kind of dive where half the "guests" rented by the week and could more accurately be described as residents.

It was the kind of place where it was safe to stay—if you were twenty-something, one-eighty-something pounds, male, and made of muscle.

It was Landrum's turn driving, so he looked at Privett when he came walking back out across the cracked and faded parking lot. "Where's the room?" he asked.

"Rooms," the other man said shortly. "Around the other side, ground floor." He pointed, turning to the back seat to toss the girl a key. "Here's yours, Deni," he said.

The kid took it without comment, and since he couldn't see her face, Luke had no idea what she thought of it. What he thought of it was that he was uneasy putting a thirteen-year-old girl in a room by herself in this kind of shit heap even in broad daylight.

"You're not staying in a room alone, Reardon. I'll take the floor," he said.

Being on the floor would suck, but there was no way he was going to stick Tramp or Kerry in there ignorant of the girl's age. He'd still rather not pass on that bit of information; the only other guy who knew was Cargo, and putting *him* in with the girl was a no-go for obvious reasons.

She looked a little nervous. No, make that a lot nervous. Make that as if she expected to be a virgin sacrifice in the name of the job. Eew. If he didn't know her age, he might have been fooled by the way they'd fixed her up, but knowing it, he looked at her and saw "kid" and . . . um . . . fuck no.

After shooting him a suspicious look that Landrum returned with his own patented "don't be stupid, ass-hole" expression, Cargo just looked relieved.

As Luke carried her pack and his inside, the kid was looking anywhere but at him, and clearly trying to look as if she went into sleazy hotel rooms, alone, with an adult male, every day of her life. He shut the door behind himself and set the bags down by the chair.

"Quit worrying. I know you're thirteen, and my baby sister is older than you. Get some sleep, Rear-don," he said. "Mind tossing me a pillow and the bedspread first?"

The look on her face was priceless.

They went in at night.

Leaving Knoxville in the late afternoon let them get through the mountains before it was quite dark, but by the time they hit Asheville, their headlights led them along a highway almost deserted after dark.

Asheville's geography left many areas that could support homes unsuited to the kind of flat clusters of houses that squatted throughout midwestern suburbia. Towering ridges and folds in the Earth—huge to a man who'd been raised on the Great Plains—were sprinkled with a dusting of lights like stars, shining from the windows of rows of houses along the switchbacks.

Reardon was in the driver's seat. She'd driven from Knoxville, putting her foot down and explaining that she would not get anything but an ulcer from riding in the car—she patted the hood of the drab-bodied old Crown Victoria possessively—with any of them driving. Her tone said, with the disdain only an adolescent girl can muster, what she thought of their gifts in the area of ground vehicle operation.

Landrum and Privett, afraid that her attitude would make Kerry and Tramp twig to her age, readily agreed that of course she could drive. Besides, with Luke riding shotgun, both other men were out of arm's reach of her. They were starting to favor him with knowing looks, though, and he didn't like that at all.

The house they were looking for was about halfway up one of the mountainsides. Vacant neighboring house, empty lot, terrain unfavorable to clusters of homes. It was nicely isolated.

Reardon pulled into the driveway of the vacant house and cut the lights, leaving the engine running. As they got out, they could feel the cold wind scraping against their tilted faces, not buffered much by winter-bare trees. The cold bit them with all the fierceness they knew from winter trips into Chicago, but Luke hadn't expected to find in one of the Southern states.

At shortly past midnight, the lights were off in the Tyler household. Landrum thanked God that they had somehow managed to loot their own gear and take DAG's supply of such nice items as modern night vision goggles with them. He knew from other gear that there was no telling what shit the Bane Sidhe were sticking operators with these days. Genuine DAG goggles meant everybody was seeing like daylight in a black and white movie. Luke's dad had lots of those. This was like "Leave it to Beaver," if the Beave had lived in a big, falling down piece of shit house that had obviously once been a nice place, probably for someone wealthy.

He had heard houses referred to as "falling down" before, but this one actually had the porch roof propped up on one side by a series of warped, hammered-together two by fours. The only thing to indicate the windows had once had shutters was the one window that had one shutter. Two other windows were boarded up. The very small front yard sported a scattering of toys and junk.

They kicked in the front door and went in two by two, clearing the building according to their training, just as they would have in any other hostile environment. They heard the screaming of the mother and child.

Tramp and Kerry found all three cowering back in the parents' bedroom. The wife and boy were on one side of the bed, the scumbag du jour on the other.

"Wait, wait! Not in front of my wife and kid! Okay, I'll go, I'll go if you want, but not here, not like this . . ." the man pleaded.

Still in the process of pleading for his life, he moved suddenly to bring a shotgun to bear on the DAGgers. At least, he tried. Kerry nailed him before the gun had even cleared the top of the mattress.

The screaming of the wife and kid sounded far away and horrendous, and the mother fought viciously, gouging Luke's arms deeply with her fingernails as he pulled her onto the bed and pinned her. The boy was pounding on his back as he fished a loaded syringe out of a leg pocket and hit the woman with a shot of Recalma Plus.

Behind him, he felt the boy go limp and get peeled off his back, turning to see Privett laying the unconscious kid out on the bed beside the mom.

"I only gave him half a shot," Cargo said.

"Right. Cover that with a sheet," Landrum indicated the corpse. "Grab the boy, I've got Mom, we'll dump them on the couch so they don't wake up in the same room with him."

It would be impossible to spare the two civilians the grief and horror of losing their scumbag father and husband this way. They'd wake up and find him, dead. However, the Recalma did more than get them quiet without killing them. It disrupted neurotransmitters in the brain in a way that prevented long-term memories from forming. Completely. The vision of seeing Tyler killed right in front of their eyes wouldn't be repressed. It simply wouldn't be there. At all.

A long time ago, there had been a saying that you couldn't un-see things. Modern medicine had a cure for that, if you got there right on the spot. These two wouldn't remember the last one to three days. There were several drugs that could do it. Recalma had the advantage of being fast, complete, and neutralizing all the adrenaline and related stress hormones and effects.

It was easier to get men to take the shot when they knew that any civilians watching *could* unsee it, after all.

While they'd close the door as best they could, it might get pretty cold in here before morning. They piled all the blankets and stuff they could easily find on top of the two survivors, placing them right next to each other for shared body heat. On the top, Cargo put a red and blue patchwork quilt with rocking horses that he'd found in the kid's room. He noticed absently that it looked like good work—something Grandma Wendy would like. The boy was lucky somebody had cared enough to make it for him.

❖   ❖   ❖

"She punched me. On an op. For no damn reason. Twice!" George Schmidt danced around the court, dodging Tommy Sunday to land a nice shot through the hoop. "Nothing but net," he crowed.

The gym they were in only had enough light to see clearly because it had a lot of high-up windows, many of which gaped, empty of glass. The shards scattered around the edges of the court revealed that the breakage had come from outside. The stray rocks lying around suggested its cause. Someone, or someones, had been awfully bored. That the vandalism was old, or had at least started long ago, showed from the water stains down the cinderblock walls and the warped and rotting edges of the floor boards under the breakages. George had taken one side of the room, Cally the other, when they arrived, just to make sure that every breakage was old. The gym was in one of many post-war ghost towns. Farming continued in the open land around the town, but large agribusiness had gotten larger with the post-war hybrid technologies. Hectares of waving wheat went from seed to harvest without a single human setting foot on the fields. Smart machines and engineered seed took care of all that.

In the heartland, the breadbasket of the world, agribusiness ruled. Where you could really see it was in the scores of ghost towns dotted all over the Midwest. The disadvantage of a ghost town for dropping any tails was that any car turning off a route or highway stuck out like a sore thumb. The advantage was that because cars back in town were so rare, it was hard for a tail to hide.

He could watch the roads into and out of town, but he could not watch every little tractor and truck trail the farmers used to use. The plan was to loop around and hit a road some small distance out from the town. Their tracks would be found, of course, but by then they hoped to have confused the trail and slipped away.

Meanwhile, Harrison and Sands were out in an ancient utility shed in the backyard of the slowly collapsing house next door repainting the car. Cally was making lunch on an ancient Coleman camp stove they had found, unaccountably half full of fuel, in said shed. She had appointed herself cook on the grounds that Harrison was the only other team member who could fix a decent meal from their box of supplies in the trunk. She had declared that she wasn't going to eat sandwiches twice in one day if she could help it.

Hence, George and Tommy were free for a little quick PT with an old ball that it had taken Harrison about five minutes to repair, and George was free to vent about his beaut of a black eye.

"What had happened just before that?" Tommy asked, shooting carelessly over the short man's head. To his chagrin, he missed and his opponent recovered on the rebound. He concentrated more on the game while Schmidt filled in the details of their heroic egress from the Greenville Police Station.

"Oh. So she was taking a guy down and you inserted yourself to help. Yep. That'd do it." Tommy intercepted the ball in the air and shot again; this time he made it. "What the hell is it with you two?" he asked.

When George started to say something, Tommy just shook his head, grinning. "I know James Stewart," he said. "You do not want to let him catch you cuddling up to his wife."

"*Cuddling up to her?* Half the time I want to strangle her," the other man said.

"You two are so junior high." Tommy missed the grab and watched as the ball dropped through the basket from another of Schmidt's seemingly effortless shots. Schmidt was good enough, despite his height, that the game of one on one wasn't nearly as mismatched as it might have seemed.

"You want to fuck her. Join the club. You can't. She thinks you're cute, so it's worse. You still can't. End of story, grow the fuck up," the big man said, but he said it in such a matter-of-fact tone that it was impossible to take offense.

"She thinks I'm cute?" George echoed.

"Dude. James Stewart's wife. You're damn good, but he's better. I wouldn't. And she won't, anyway."

"But she thinks I'm cute." The little blond man missed his shot by a mile, letting Sunday recover the ball for an easy lay-up.

"You're hopeless," Sunday pronounced. "Just find somebody else to screw and behave yourself until it wears off. And if you don't, don't say I didn't warn you." He focused and dropped another one right in. "That's ten. My game."

"What do you mean 'join the club'?" Schmidt asked suspiciously as they walked off the court.

"Don't look at me. You've seen my Wendy. There's a club, all right. I didn't say I was in it."

"You didn't say you weren't."

Tommy set the ball down by the door to the old locker room, which, unlike the gym itself, was dark as hell. They just had to go through there to get to the lobby of the building. "Hopeless," he repeated.

The gym at the base had water fountains on two sides. Miraculously, the chiller on one of them even worked. Aluminum bleachers stood collapsed against the walls on each side of the basketball court. The curtain at the far end of said court was open, leaving a good view of exercise machines, a free weight section, and a compressed obstacle course. All were in use, as was the matted martial arts area. The DAGgers on base, even the ones who were Bane Sidhe first, coped with their enforced idleness in a way that kept them fit, busy, and not coincidentally, together. PT was a near religion for them and, like people turn to faith and each other in times of trouble, the DAGgers immersed themselves in PT schedules that were frankly brutal, raising protests from the medics who they kept busy with over-training injuries. Bane Sidhe sports medicine, as a result of decades of Tchpth patronage and lack of Darhel interference, was leagues ahead of their prior experience. With fear of injury greatly reduced, the men took full advantage of their extended envelope. They did, at least, readily share the facilities with the permanent denizens of the base and the dependents.

The Bane Sidhe field operatives, however, made it subtly clear that *they* were sharing *their* facilities with DAG. With the large number of DAGgers who had started as Bane Sidhe, and the others having witnessed the performance of the upgraded field operatives, especially the women, this didn't cause the friction it might have. There was respect between professionals. Rivalry, but it was a bit hard to get used to cute chicks who could and would run you into the ground or kick your ass, situation depending. Not that they were *that* far ahead of peak male athletes. They didn't always win. It was still a novel experience for those who hadn't previously encountered upgrades.

News that the equipment that achieved these results was no longer available was greeted with intense disappointment, a sentiment that was, of course, completely unrelated to the new tendency to overtrain and screw the transient, readily reparable injuries. Like stress fractures. The clinic director was beginning to scream about his budget.

Even though the gym was fairly crowded, the basketball goal on the far end had some space around the four people playing an energetic two on two, they having indicated a desire to be by themselves this time.

Cally paused as Tommy came in, and missed a catch.

"Hey!" George protested as one of the intel geeks they were playing snagged the ball out of the air and made a seemingly effortless shot that dropped it through the net.

"Time," Cally called.

"Okay, but it still counts," Boyd said as George snagged the rebound. The investigator's usually proper rows of hair spikes were limp with sweat, and he wiped his face with his already soaked T-shirt as Cally walked over to her teammate.

"Finished with your debrief?" she asked.

"Remind me again why I do this job?" Tommy asked. The large, open space of the gym seemed to be letting him breathe easier. She knew a lot of places he went were just plain cramped for a man his size.

"That bad, huh?" She adjusted the faded red sweatband that was holding her hair out of her face.

"Apparently our 'hunting trip' and 'cross-country jaunt' delayed us from getting the goods in and caused us to commit the gross sin of being later than the e-mail and the cleaners' fingernail," he said grumpily. "At least, that's what the little REMF bastard implied."

"Yeah, never mind we had orders not to worry about how long it took to get in but put security absolutely first. Never mind that sending said fingernail in by itself was an incredibly dumbass risk of interception and or having it followed right in. Never mind that the damn deer was a piece of blind luck," Cally sighed. "He's probably just jealous he didn't get any. Or a militant vegetarian."

"Anyway, the status on the investigation is this: the fingernail was great, but she had two guys' DNA under there which either means she was attacked by two men, or that she's a healthy young co-ed with a social life and forgot to scrub under her fingernails. We don't want to whack an innocent boyfriend. They only got partials on the two guys—enough to identify if we had a match, but not enough to put together a holo. They're still analyzing the DNA we got, but it should flag one of the two as definitely guilty, and hopefully complete his code," she said.

"Hey, Cally, are you playing, or what?"

"Yeah, just a sec," she called over her shoulder, then turned back to Tommy. "There probably *is* a second baddy, but she's female. A couple of students noticed the niece walking off with a woman they hadn't seen before. One of her friends thought it was odd that she didn't smile or wave when they passed each other, but just assumed she hadn't seen her. But she noticed the stranger female, so they got a pretty good description of her." Cally pointed over her shoulder at the investigators.

"Hey, I gotta go. Bottom line, they're closing in on identifying us some targets, so cheer up!" Her grin was predatory as she clapped Tommy on the shoulder, and there was an extra bounce in her step as she jogged back onto the court.

CHAPTER FIFTEEN

Tuesday, January 12, 2055

Papa O'Neal was in the best shape he'd been in in half a century or so. Specifically, the best shape he'd been in since the "new" wore off on what his rejuved and upgraded body could do at the tail end of the Postie War. His fitness this time had an entirely different reason, which was that if he hadn't kept himself PT-ed to the gills he'd have died of boredom. Or killed somebody.

Since the only somebodies on this tub were the Himmit pilot and owner, and Nathan O'Reilly's personal assistant, that would have been bad. Particularly, he had the feeling that Nathan would miss the PA and would be rather cranky if he were throttled and stuffed down the head.

He looked around his cabin. Same old bulkheads and extremely boring crap. The only reason he was in here at all was because he'd just woken up. The food was the same shit, more or less, that they served at base. He always carried a small bottle of hot sauce, periodically refueling it from a large bottle. Unfortunately, he hadn't had time for any of that and was finding hot sauce much less effective when one had to ration it. He was still running out.

He had already gone through Candy's supply of various kinds of stored entertainment, having had little time to gather up cubes before boarding this mobile purgatory. He had traded all entertainment back and forth with Alan and gone through all of that. It was bad when you started to look forward to telling war stories to the Himmit. Titan was positioned all wrong for them to pick up transmissions of broadcast entertainment, and reception from Earth was practically nil due to solar weather.

Hard PT was one of the few ways he had to exhaust his brain into semi-passivity and get past the boredom. He used it. He had managed to persuade the Himmit to cobble odds and ends together into bars for chin-ups and dips. Hadn't been able to get an obstacle course out of it. Did get amplification for Candy to project the ones he didn't have to climb on and buzz at him if he, for example, snagged himself on the holographic barbed wire overhead, tipped over a hurdle, or let the ball-buster live up to its name. It was something to do, and he thought he almost had talked the Himmit into kitting out one of the bulkheads in the cargo bay as a climbing wall. He just hadn't hit on a story quite good enough to get it to "deface its ship" in such a fashion. He was also campaigning for a resistance-based weight training equivalent. His offer to lift the Himmit hadn't gone over well.

Between training times, he amused himself by trying to compose original dirty limericks, which was surprisingly difficult. Alan was having better luck with dirty haiku. Papa had taken to sitting with him while he did so, because the process and content tended to confuse the Himmit, which in itself was at least a little amusing.

Then there were the interminable lessons in xenopsychology from "the diplomacy expert." He had gotten to where he could get his head around the Indowy, Darhel, and the Crabs, but he still couldn't say Tph . . . Tic . . . Tch, oh, dammit, Crab. His understanding of the Himmit was more limited, but that just put him in the same boat as all the other races. They were still alien as hell, and he'd always have to think about it to try to see from their point of view, or try to understand something they were doing. Alan said this was actually an advantage, in that it protected him from forgetting the first rule: "Alien minds are alien."

He breakfasted alone, since he needed less sleep than Mr. Alien Expert, and so got up "earlier." Only this morning he was halfway between some nasty stuff that was supposed to copy eggs when he realized he was not alone and looked up to see the Himmit perched on his wall. Odd time for it to request a story. Not that he minded an interruption while eating, in the case of this junk.

"There has been a change in schedule, Human Papa O'Neal. A Tchpth ship has emerged from jump and commed me that they wish to rendezvous for negotiations. We should have contact in just over three of your days," it said. "I will leave you to resume nourishing yourself."

Papa supposed that was a more accurate term than calling it eating. He also noticed that the Himmit had no trouble pronouncing oh-hell-dammit-Crabs. Froggy little bastard.

He thought about waking his tutor, and then decided against it. Once the kid woke up he wasn't going to get a moment's rest, so he'd better get PT-ing while the getting was good.

Three hours later, Papa was glad he'd gotten his workout in because he could see that his free time was over. Thank god. Even negotiation preparations were a welcome relief from boredom now that he had the promise of not having to endure them all the way to fucking Barwhon.

"So what kinds of things are on our list to negotiate for? I have some ideas of what I want, but what do the Bane Sidhe want, from your perspective?"

The PA sank his head into his palm. "Let me repeat, the Tchpth do not think in terms of deals and arrangements and agreements. The Tchpth think in terms of *relationships* and favors." He paused, and Papa could see that he was going to have to listen to another run of xenopsych, only this time he had more incentive to pay close attention.

"Okay, what kind of *relationship* should I be negotiating for?"

"Let me try to explain things another way," Alan said, clearly meaning one more out of umpty-jillion he'd already tried. "Humans look at the Galactics and see the Darhel in charge, because the Darhel control the contracts, and the shipping, and the money."

"And life and death over the Indowy masses," Papa growled. "And attempting it over humans, and damn near—"

"Let's not get sidetracked. The Tchpth look at the Galactic organization and see a web of relationships. The Darhel do tasks the Tchpth agree need doing by somebody, but don't want to do themselves. The Tchpth control what amounts to the money supply, control the technology level available to the Darhel, the Indowy, and us. They see allowing the Darhel to play their contract games as humoring them. It's an easy favor that, from the Tchpth point of view, they're getting a lot of favors back for. The Darhel may appear to control what looks to humans like all the political power, but the Darhel's ability to step outside the Tchpth relationship format and favor economy is exactly zero. The Tchpth *own* the money supply. Um . . . picture it as if in the twentieth century, oil were actually money and some government had the power to make an unlimited supply of it effortlessly, and was militarily unassailable. See why the Darhel are stuck?"

"The fucking Elves can and do do a lot to the Indowy, and us."

"Yes, they do. But their relationship with the Tchpth is entirely on the Tchpth's terms as to definitions. The Darhel do have a lot of maneuvering room as to the trading of favors, and they understand, and use, that.

"The Tchpth relationship with the Indowy clans is what ultimately allows the Bane Sidhe to function.

The Tchpth have more genuine philosophical thought in common with the Indowy than with the Darhel. The Indowy actually get this 'Path' thing. The Darhel don't. Realize that the Tchpth can bypass the Darhel by delivering nanogenerator code keys to the Indowy any time they damned well please. And they sometimes do. The Bane Sidhe is a case in point. The Bane Sidhe nannite pool is entirely off the Darhel books. Maybe it will help for a moment if you think of the Bane Sidhe less as a resistance movement aimed at overthrowing the Darhel than a labor union. That's not accurate, either, but figure this—the Indowy are lousy at management, economics, logistics, firm and formalized agreements. The Indowy need the Darhel. They don't want to make the Darhel go extinct, or go stay on their own worlds. The Indowy just want better terms. The Tchpth relationship with the Indowy is to provide enough support to the labor union to keep the balance between the Galactics the way they think it should be. The Indowy also operate on the basis of a favor economy with the Tchpth. Think of this as another form of currency that's completely off the Darhel books. Relationships."

"The Himmit? Nobody's really got a great handle on the Himmit's story economy, but there are things they can do, and favors can be traded with them, so the Tchpth have their relationship with the Himmit somehow slotted into their scheme of things. We humans don't actually have any understanding, at all, of the workings between the Himmit and the Tchpth. Are you following me so far?" The PA ran both hands through his hair, thinking so hard he was sweating.

Papa O'Neal was actually kind of impressed. "Yeah,

I think so. You're saying we've been mistaken about the Darhel and the Crabs are in control of the whole ball of wax—which tells me that maybe we should be pissed off at *them*."

"No. I'm not saying that at all. I'm saying the Tchpth have the power to control the whole ball of wax but don't have the time, inclination, or aptitude for doing so. I'm saying the Darhel don't mess with the Tchpth because they know the Tchpth can upset the applecart at any point. We are not negotiating with the Indowy. We are not negotiating with the Darhel. We are negotiating with the Tchpth. If the Tchpth see Galactic civilization in terms of relationships and favors, then we—and you—had better be able to see it that way, too. Or at least fake it real well." He sighed. "Does *that* make sense?"

"Yeah. I reckon that makes sense. They could help us, they could help the Indowy, they could jerk a knot in the Darhel, but they really don't have any percentage in it and don't give a shit. Is that about the size of it?" Papa O'Neal patted down his shirt pocket before realizing he'd run out of tobacco.

"Closer. They *do* give a shit. They just think of it differently. Alien minds. Humanity's opportunity, and our curse right at the moment, is that the Tchpth haven't decided where we fit in. They haven't decided where, over the mid-range time scale of the next thousand years or so, we 'work' as part of a stable relationship pattern between the races. It is almost as much false as it is true, but think of human involvement in the Bane Sidhe, for a moment, as the Indowy doing a favor for the Tchpth by developing xenopsychological data on the humans as part of the process of evaluating our place in the scheme of things. All this is hampered by all the Galactic races having extreme prejudices against us for all the reasons you already know, and probably a couple more we haven't figured out yet.

"Your job, as a *diplomat*, is to almost but not exactly socialize with the Tchpth, and probably a few Indowy, but no Darhel, of course. In the course of this not exactly schmoozing, they and the Indowy will make loaded comments about relationships and balances of favors between different groups, including various Indowy Clans. Possibly the Tchpth will test you by making a few comments about other relationships, such as some internal to them, or some with the Himmit or Darhel. You are not going to pass that test on any level more sophisticated than a grossly barbarous, vicious omnivore, so don't get your hopes up or give up hope," he said.

"Right. So I'm at the Mad Hatter's tea party and I'm supposed to do what?" The O'Neal wore the expression of a man completely out of his depth but willing to go down fighting valiantly.

"Primarily, avoid as many gross mistakes as possible while getting in specific talking points to illustrate how humanity, Clan O'Neal, and the O'Neal Bane Sidhe view the balance of favors between ourselves and the other Galactic races," the PA said.

"Oh. Is that all?" Papa asked sarcastically.

"Don't worry about it. You can take your PDA and wear an earbug. They'll pretend you aren't, but will be completely unsurprised that you need it. It's actually an advantage, as they'll hear what your PDA is telling you. In a certain sense, the PDA will be doing the actual diplomacy, while you maintain the relevant not-exactly fiction that the discussions are with the O'Neal." The younger man shrugged.

"Oh. A *buckley* is going to be negotiating our future with the entire Galactic civilization. I'm so relieved," Papa groused.

"This is all the better reason for you to understand those talking points well. If what you say contradicts or revises what they hear out of your PDA, they'll go with whatever it is you say. Which also means, I need not tell you, don't fuck up. Because at many levels, physical, economic, political and legal, the Tchpth can swat Clan O'Neal, and probably the whole human race, like flies."

"But no pressure," Papa said.

"Nope, O'Neal," Alan said with a grin. "No pressure at all."

CHAPTER SIXTEEN

Papa and Alan followed an Indowy guide through the bowels of the large ship, Papa with interest, Alan with apparent disinterest.

The ship was rara avis: a Tchpth diplomatic transport. Nearly the size of a Posleen War super-dreadnought, it could carry over a million Tchpth. How many were actually on board was uncertain since the only thing they saw were naked Galplas walls and their Indowy guide.

"These are service tunnels," Papa said, pointing to scuff-marks. "An insult?"

"It's a Tchpth ship," Alan said. "More likely they felt that it would be an insult if we had to crawl on our hands and knees the whole way."

"Point," Papa said. "I hope the meeting rooms are high enough for us."

"For you," Alan said. "I'm not going to be in on them."

Finally they arrived at a large hatch and the Indowy bowed to them politely.

"Wait here, please," he chirped. "You will be greeted."

"Thanks," Papa said and heard a groan at his side. "Thank you, Good Indowy."

The Indowy bowed formally, a bending backward at the waist with a complicated leg-twist reminiscent of a curtsey, and then scurried off.

"And now we w—" Papa broke off as the hatch dialed open to reveal a room the size of a cargo hold.

The bulkheads and overhead were masked by fine cloths in a riot of colors. Most of them tended towards blue and purple but there were a few he was pretty sure human eyes weren't meant to see.

The floor was similarly colored but the material appeared to be crystal. He quickly put a guess at it being some form of *very expensive* crystal.

Scattered around the room, at apparent random, were very low tables. Well, they were low to a human. They would be just about waist height to the many Indowy in the room. For a human they were more like ankle catchers.

Papa paused in his perusal at a whimper from the "diplomat" next to him.

"What?" he growled. So far none of the people in the room had taken the slightest notice of them.

"It's a . . ." Alan said, hyperventilating. "It's a . . ."

"It's a what?" Papa whispered fiercely. "Get a grip, man!"

"This is a formal negotiation," Alan whispered back shakily.

"That's what they said," Papa pointed out.

"No!" Alan said, his voice tight. "This is a *formal* negotiation! We've had 'formal' negotiations with the Tchpth and Indowy leadership before. That's just a way of saying it's not over tea and crumpets. But this is a formal *Children's Negotiation.*"

Papa frowned for a moment and then blanched. "Wait . . . You mentioned that . . ."

"This is the most high form of formal negotiation," Alan said. "No human has ever participated in one. Not even the highest negotiations of the Posleen War were conducted at the *Children's Banquet*. This is a ritual dating back to the very days of the Aldenata! The great table at the center . . ."

"The Parent's Table," Papa said, dredging it up from memory. "That's a really silly way of—"

"It's not even the proper term," Alan snapped. "It's a *shorthand*. It doesn't *actually* mean those are the Kids' Tables and the one in the middle is the Parent's Table. Don't be absurd. It's just how it gets translated. But this ritual is more formal than a Japanese tea ceremony. Do exactly what the PDA tells you to do. Make no gesture, make no facial movement, that is not instructed. Fortunately, it moves very slowly. I don't know where your starting position is—"

He broke off as one of the Indowy in the room came towards them at a slow walk. It was the sort of slow ceremonial walk Papa dredged from the recesses of memory as being used in a coronation.

Or a funeral.

It seemed like it took forever for the guy to get to the hatch and Papa realized that the one thing he was most going to have to cultivate was patience.

"Clan O'Neal," the Indowy stated, bending forward in an informal bow.

"Bow forward slowly," the PDA ordered. *"Keep*

going. Further. Slow down. Hold it there. Up just a smidge. Hold that. Say: Clan Kooltan."

"Clan Kooltan," Papa parroted.

"I am your Guide for the Banquet," the Kooltan clan leader said. If he found any distaste it was not apparent. His face gave away nothing and he had exactly zero body language. "If you will follow me."

Kooltan turned and began to slowly walk back into the room.

"Wait for it," the PDA said. *"Don't step off until I tell you."*

"What are you going to do?" Papa whispered out of the side of his mouth.

"Stay here," Alan said. "I'm not invited."

"Don't lock your knees," Papa said.

"Step off. No, not fast!" the PDA snapped. *"Just shuffle. You need to move at the same speed as Kooltan. Don't stride. Never stride!"*

I'm going to get Nathan for dumping this on me.

The intricacies of the ceremony were lost on Papa O'Neal. He was pretty sure that it was all incredibly special and that he was missing a bunch of stuff that really mattered. But it was like a tea ceremony. What in the *hell* was wrong with just dropping a bag in hot water?

Walk, slowly, shuffle, to a table. To a *particular* position at a *particular* table. There would be a morsel of human food at that particular position and particular table. Bend over, at the waist, pick up the morsel of food. Straighten up. Look into the distance.

An Indowy or Tchpth might or might not already be at the table. If there wasn't, one or the other one would show up sooner or later. Or two. A maximum of four, total, at a table, no more. Usually two.

A statement would be made. The first person speaking was determined by some arcane rule Papa had no clue on. This person was the Prompter. A second person would speak. This was the Rebuttor.

Prompter, Acceptor, Rebuttor, Supporter. Each of the four possible combinations had a name, a time to speak, and a particular subject to discuss. Most of them related to some equivalent of *"The vacuum outside is very hard today, isn't it?"*

Occasionally one of them would speak in Indowy or Tchpth. Twice he had to reply in Indowy. They apparently gave him a pass on Tchpth. Since he couldn't even pronounce the *species name*, doing the whole language was out of the question.

Apparently at those times they were actually negotiating something and he had no clue what, how or why. He just parroted what the PDA, with occasional references to Alan, told him to say.

Even when they engaged in actual negotiations in English he didn't have any clue what, how or why.

"Clan O'Neal," the Indowy Prompter said.

"You're Acceptor, third," the PDA whispered. *"Wait for your Acceptance which is fourth."*

Whatever the fuck that *means,* Papa thought.

"Now: Clan Selatha," the PDA said.

The Rebuttor and Supporter had both greeted each other, an off-hand way of introduction apparently. Papa wasn't bothering with trying to keep up with any names.

"Clan Selatha," Papa said, bowing from the waist.

"Stop there!" the PDA screamed. *"You're a major*

Battle Clan! Selatha is known for mass Galplas production which is about as bottom of the food chain as you can get! You nearly raised his social prominence by about fifty points!"

After a moment Selatha said: "Disassociative resonance in material space is unharmonious."

An Indowy was the Rebuttor and replied almost instantly: "All change is motion state."

Fortunately it was a bit like chess. You had a four-minute clock. Actually, it was more like four minutes and twelve seconds since it was based on the Tchpth clock.

They almost ran out before Alan and the PDA between them came up with a response:

"Life is aentropic," Papa parroted.

The Crab Supporter took nearly as long a pause. Papa had to wonder if it had a PDA stashed somewhere.

"Life is motion."

"Take a quarter turn to your right," the PDA whispered. *"See the table right in front of you?"*

"Hmmm . . ." Papa hummed.

"Wait for it. Wait for it. Step off."

Papa took a step that nearly trod on the Tchpth Supporter. He could only look straight forward except when taking the food off the table.

"Small steps!" the PDA said.

"How'd we do?" Papa asked.

"I think we just bought a solar system," Alan whispered in his earbug. *"Just shut up and soldier."*

It was the end of the whole complicated, annoying, slow as hell shooting-match when they got to get to the big, huge, vital, future of everything hinges on it issue.

For that he, finally, was allowed to approach the Parent's Table.

"Stop here," the PDA said, when he was a good two steps away. *"You can't actually stand at the Parent's Table."*

The Parent's Table was bigger, with room for at least twenty Indowy and Tchpth or ten humans. And it was actually tall for a human. The Indowy and Tchpth were looking under it. Not that they were saying much.

Part of the big kicker to the Crab withdrawal had been not just the killing of Erik Winchon. A large part of their break with the O'Neal Bane Sidhe had been their own shock at the ripples of what they'd done. They'd reached out to make an admittedly significant adjustment to the scheme of things to protect one extraordinary human, and had destroyed an entire Darhel business group, completely by accident.

The Tchpth keenly felt this as a blunder on their part, and Alan had drilled him, and role-played with him, and generally hammered into him over, and over, and over again that he must wait for them to bring it up, it was dead certain that they would, and when they did he could not say *anything* that remotely could be construed as humanity, the Bane Sidhe, or the O'Neals taking responsibility for *any* of Epetar's demise.

When Papa had pointed out that that wasn't exactly true and wouldn't they see through it, the PA had just about gone ballistic on him. Alien minds being alien, the O'Neal could and should and by God would use the Galactic prejudices against humanity to the hilt, in the interests of the O'Neals, humanity, etc. That is, as primitive barbarians, humans couldn't possibly have had any significant causal role in bringing down the Epetar Group, but instead were mere pawns in the machinations of those wiser and more advanced than themselves. In a way it stuck in Papa's craw to do it, but any reluctance was far overwhelmed by his vicious sense of schadenfreude that the Galactics' damn presumptions and prejudices could be used to screw them. Or at least to get the best of them, anyway.

So in his little role plays with the PA, he had been trained out of, "I'm sorry to hear that." Or, "I can sympathize with you." Or even, "We heard about that with regret." Over and over he'd had it drilled in that what he must say, and *all* he must say, was a perfectly neutral statement that acknowledged that the event was a bad thing.

This is a causal relationship with high entropic reality.

Papa had memorized it because this was the one, vital element that absolutely could not come as a prompt from the PDA. Even before they knew they were doing a Children's Negotiation they'd known that. If a Clan Leader was so low in functionality that it couldn't even manage a simple statement like that, Clan O'Neal might as well be written off.

He'd memorized it carefully. He'd practiced it carefully. They had role-played it a dozen times with a holographic Crab and Indowy.

"Recent events create a stochastically chaotic causal chain," the Rebuttor said.

The Rebuttor was a muckety-muck Tchpth. Lord

High Master of Something Complicated. The Indowy Prompter, *not* a minor Clan Leader, had brought up the problem, which Papa damned well wasn't going to do. The Tchpth Rebuttor had, as far as Papa could tell, dumped the whole thing in humanity's lap.

Now all he had to do was dump it back and be done.

At the end of the long day of shit he knew damn-all about, when the big moment finally came, he fucking froze. His mind had gone a complete and total blank. He looked at the dancing and bouncing ten-legged alien Rebuttor who held so much power over humanity and said: *"That's* gotta suck."

"Sorry," Papa said as they made their way back through the corridors. "I think I screwed the pooch."

Papa had been expecting a scathing review as soon as the hatch closed, Indowy guide or no Indowy guide, so the silence was getting uncomfortable.

Alan didn't reply.

"Uh, penny for your thoughts?" Papa said. Better to get it out of the way as soon as possible.

"I don't, really, think it matters," Alan said morosely.

"Future of Clan O'Neal?" Papa said. "Future of the Bane Sidhe? Future of the human race? We just participated in really high level negotiations. I'd figure you'd have *something* to say."

Alan let out a sigh.

"You know what I said about the Parent's Table not really being the Parent's Table?" Alan asked. "That it was just translation? A sort of metaphor?"

"Yeah?"

"I was wrong," Alan said. "No human had ever seen this negotiation. We'd had it detailed, we analyzed it, we spindled, folded and mutilated it. Which is why, with the exception of your last Response, you did fairly well. Intonation and body language issues, but fairly well. Your last Response may, in fact, have been masterful."

"*What?*"

"Listen to me!" Alan snapped. "Think. I said it was a metaphor. I was wrong. The monsignor was wrong. Every human who has ever studied the Children's Negotiation Ceremony was dead, completely, utterly *wrong.*"

"How?" Papa asked. His back hurt and his feet hurt and his legs hurt and he was seriously ready for a very big drink of whisky. But he felt like Alan might finally be saying something important.

"Think about a family party," Alan said. "There's a few grown-ups at the Grown-Ups' table and there's a dozen or so kids running around playing. Kids engage in negotiations. We don't call it that but they do. What, really, do the Parents *care* about such negotiations?"

"Nothing," Papa said, his mouth suddenly dry. "They're kids."

"It's better to ask forgiveness than permission," Alan said. "So mostly the children keep their secrets to themselves. They don't bother the parents."

"They get more quiet when they don't want to be noticed," Papa said. He wasn't only a multiple father but a multiple *grand*father. And great-grandfather.

"Every now and again, the kids will feel it's necessary to get a seal of approval on something," Alan said.

"So they go to the Parent's table," Papa said. "'Dad, we're going over to Billy's to play video-games.' So . . . who are the Parents?"

"That's the kicker," Alan said. "This was, as much as anything, a religious ceremony. The Indowy, the Tchpth, the Darhel, even the Posleen, are referred to as Children of the Aldenata. They view them as Gods. Well, in the case of the Posleen as demons, but that's beside the point. The real point is that the Aldenata may or may not have real power, what is called hard-power. They may still exist and influence events."

"They might have been *listening*?" Papa said. "So humanity's first communication with God-like aliens was 'That's gotta suck'?" Papa paused and shook his head. "Great. Just fucking *great*."

"But then there's the big problem," Alan said.

"There's a bigger problem?"

"We, humans, are not Children of the Aldenata," Alan said. "We're the kids from next door who wandered in. And, as reported, through no fault of our own we're causing problems. It's entirely the local, older and wiser, kids' fault. But there are problems."

"Ouch," Papa said.

"If you've had a nice, neat, playful little party and some neighbor kid wanders in and all of a sudden there are problems," Alan said, "what do you do?"

"Toss the little bugger out," Papa replied. "Or teach him manners."

"*That* is why I said 'I don't think it matters.' I think we just, for the first time ever, got *formally* introduced to the Aldenata. And if they have a problem with our behavior, we don't have any 'adults' to negotiate for *us*."

Xikkikil stood on the bridge of the ship and looked at the plot of relevant ships in the tank. It had traveled inward with the ship carrying the Human O'Neal, so as to allow that vessel to begin the acceleration for its return to Earth. Now they had to pay the price of that choice in the time to decelerate and return to the jump point. No matter. The job was done, the relationship reestablished. Specific favors would, of course, depend on situations as they arose. It was the relationship that was the thing.

Unfortunately, the return of the relationship meant, in this case, a return of the debt owed to Clan O'Neal for the . . . killing . . . of the Darhel Pardal. It mattered not that the Tchpth were appalled at the consequences of their actions, the fact remained Clan O'Neal had risked the life of its third in line as Clan Head in order to do a favor the Tchpth asked for and regarded as horrific. That the Tchpth's own error in estimating the consequences of that favor and the price the O'Neals were paying as a result was so high was a factor that raised the level of the debt considerably.

The O'Neal had been surprisingly subtle in his negotiations. A barbarian, yes, barely to be considered a Child to be allowed to run free. But subtle. His closing statement was so baroque as to be indecipherable. An entire team was parsing it to squeeze every meaning out. The closest they had come to full understanding was that O'Neal placed the entire blame for the current debacle on the Tchpth. There was, further, a resonance of contempt for the Tchpth race for stooping to the level of violence. Humans, it was understood, would use violence, even their negotiations were barely controlled brawls, as a first response. That the Tchpth had acceded to it under such comparatively minor circumstances was, understandably, contemptible.

The planners would be having extensive debates as to what options might be available to mitigate the larger issue while still reducing the debt.

A single refugee ship had emerged from hyperspace, but the Tchpth and the Himmit knew that there would be more. They also suspected that they had a better appreciation for human capabilities than the Indowy refugees. From the Indowy point of view, the Darhel's humans were killing them, and Earth was the only place they had humans of their own. Their own vicious omnivorous killers were, in their minds, sure protection from the Darhel's vicious omnivorous killers.

The Tchpth presumed the Himmit had a more realistic appreciation for the results of pitting groups of humans against each other. It was difficult to tell, as always. The Himmit collected stories voraciously, but they refrained from giving return "stories" almost as carefully as the Tchpth refrained from releasing too-advanced technology to the other Galactic races. Still, it was occasionally possible to deduce something about Himmit thoughts by observing a Himmit itself to identify what stories or events it found most interesting. Occasionally.

This refugee ship, of course, had an entirely fictitious reason for being in the Sol System. In this case, probably the Himmit whose ship it was asking for stories it would otherwise not have come for. Not even the Darhel could pierce the cloaking of Himmit shuttles. Transport to Earth would be functionally invisible. For the first ship. However, at some point, Tir Dol Ron would be bound to notice that there were far, far more Himmit in the system than there should be, and begin to ask himself why.

CHAPTER SEVENTEEN

Thursday, January 14, 2055

The trouble with intel, Cally reflected, was that it was too damned uncertain a business, and intelligence people sometimes either overestimated or overstated the likelihood of their conclusions. They also tended to want to tell you how and why they knew what they said they knew. This was good to the extent that it somewhat served as a check against bullshit wild-ass conclusions. It was bad in that it was damned boring. Sometimes she felt like she spent half her life in drab little conference rooms. It was actually very little, she admitted to herself, it just *seemed* longer. It just figured that one of the things that survived through the years was PowerPoint. Or, in this case, a generic, open-source knock-off.

Sands leaned over and whispered to her, "That is one bad-ass bit of hacking!"

Obviously, not everybody was as bored as she was. Cally sat up a bit straighter in her chair and tried to pay attention.

". . . searching through a large collection of data from the campus's many cameras, we found the one hundred women who most closely resembled the description of our kidnapper. Then we backtracked through official records to positively identify those women. Out of the ninety-two identified, ninety were students at the university. The other two had graduated from local high schools and probably live locally." The presenter paused to make sure everybody appreciated how well they'd done to rule out so many of the girls they initially ruled in.

He continued, "So we focused our attention on the remaining eight." Here he switched to a slide that contained eight grainy photos that gradually enhanced to clarity.

Cally suppressed a yawn, wishing they could just give them the damn target, mission parameters, and *relevant* information. She did have to admit that the final eight did all look a lot like the artist's sketch of the kidnapper.

The man was still droning, ". . . using age regression techniques and searches of cached data to come up with possible identifications. Based on multiple series of school pictures we came up with a total of fifteen women who could be our possible. Then we searched juvenile records, birth records, marriage records, child protective services records, and other sources to put together a profile for each of the fifteen. We got two women who fit the profile for childhood conditions conducive to sociopathy, and six women whose genotypes show a genetic risk factor for same. Uh—including the two. One of our top two is presently incarcerated in the Minnesota State Correction System. That leaves this woman as our prime suspect."

Cally leaned forward, finally having one specific face to memorize. The four pictures were much better, of course. Not that they flattered the woman, although she was attractive. They just needed no digital enhancement to sharpen them up. They were the originals from the young woman's social website. What a dumbass thing to do if you aspired to become a player. Darwin Award, coming right up.

"Now we come to the actual murderer, Mr. Robert 'Bobby' Mitchell."

Cally couldn't quite stifle a yawn. She tried. She mostly managed, but not enough to be spared a dirty look from the presenter's partner. Ha! She was probably still sore they got their asses kicked on the court. George happened to be looking her way, so she met his eyes with a conspiratorial twinkle of amusement before they both dutifully returned their attention to the recounting of how intel had found a man whose DNA was no longer in official records. This part was slightly uncomfortable to every operator in the room, as what could be done to others could also be done to them. In all, they preferred to do unto others, first.

Eventually they got to the point and an actual mission out of all that babble. By psych profile, the murderer of the girl was likely the top hitter. It was a one-man task, it was complicated, and it was really gross—hence easy to chicken out, scrimp, or cheat on, even for a stone killer. He'd have been unlikely to trust anyone else enough to delegate. Fine. And they had tracked down who he was. Fine. But tracking down *who* the killer was did nothing to track down *where* he was.

The intel weenie had an answer for that, too. They started with the assumption that the top hitter might work for Tir Dol Ron directly. It fit the Darhels' pattern of behavior to date. There was the word Cally and every other operator dreaded to hear from the intel people betting their lives. Assumption.

The actual mission was the acquisition and interrogation of one man who doubtless had nothing to do with the killings. Barton Leibowitz was the Enterprise Resource Manager for the Tir's corporate office on Earth, which was a fancy way of saying that he and his AID were the entire personnel and accounting department. Intel's supposition was that the man who hired people and fired people would know Mitchell if he was a regular employee and if, as Darhel hit men often were, he was just a contractor, Leibowitz still might know him through the process of cutting his checks. Not that anybody used paper checks anymore. The admin weenie could transfer the right amount of money to the right account without ever laying eyes on the contractors or anyone else, and probably did. However, their searches turned up something about the man that made him an easy mark for a little interview. He had been through a divorce, finalized about four months ago. Pictures indicated that while not ugly, Bart was probably not having great luck in the singles scene. Bluntly, the man was probably very lonely.

Yup. Supposition on top of assumption. That was intel, all right. Granted, the process they preferred to call "analysis" usually turned up good shit. Their two and two usually did make four. It was just the "usually" part that made her edgy. That wasn't what bothered her about this particular job, though. No, the problem with this job was of a personal nature, and the bitch of it was that it was genuinely mission essential.

"I have . . . I don't know if I should call it a suggestion or a request," Amy Sands interjected. These folks almost looked like they were going to their own funeral. She understood it. The problem shouldn't have been one for a seasoned professional, but she could understand why it was. She was also seeing another side of the legendary Cally O'Neal. Or, at least, she was legend at school. Amy was now realizing that the other woman put her pants on one leg at a time just like anyone else. Excellent, yes. Phenomenal. But human, nonetheless.

"Yeah, Sands?" Tommy Sunday's tone was nice, but it had that underlying tinge of a veteran being patient with the cherry—well, near cherry—guy on the team.

She supposed that was fair. It was her point, actually. She was too realistic to expect a permanent place on this team. Like the military, the Bane Sidhe also had a fairy godmother department, and she had lucked out bigtime to be here even for a short assignment. Amy was determined to milk this job for every bit of knowledge and experience she could wring out of it. This wasn't petty careerism, although doing well there was nice.

Operatives had a largish rate of loss, relative to their whole career. Being juved was great, but a much longer working life upped the odds greatly that anyone who worked in the field eventually had bad luck catch up with them, or made a fatal mistake. The losses were front-loaded, though. Acquiring experience was a Darwinian process. They'd repeated it in school so often she heard it in her dreams: "Learn fast; you'll live longer."

She ran her tongue over her teeth quickly, hoping she didn't have chocolate smudges from the brownies. "I need field experience; you need for me to have it. The only thing a guy likes better than getting the attention of a hot chick is getting the attention of a hot chick and her hot friend," she began.

They looked skeptical, even dismissive, and she knew she'd better convince them in a hurry.

"Hear me out: say Cally and I both go in and *I* do the guy. She comes along to play, too. I know, he could smell a rat; it's too much good luck. Your instincts are trained from hell." She looked at Cally, who had her head cocked a tiny bit to the side. Sands took that as encouragement. "If he gets edgy, you back off and come up to his apartment after I drug him up. I know, we might have to hit him with several interrogation drugs to find something he's not immune to, but I don't have to use an interrogation drug. I Hiberzine the bastard and we have him nice and trussed by the time Cally wakes him up."

George Schmidt had a poker face. She didn't know if he could sway the whole team, but better if she won them all over. She turned her attention to him specifically.

"We all know that professionals of either sex sometimes have to screw people to get the job done. Personally, I have to speak up, because I'm not going to have a better chance to get blooded in the field that way. I've got backup practically right on top of me," she said, then blushed to the roots of her hair. "That didn't come out right," she mumbled.

Schmidt burst out laughing, and there were grins all around the table. Amy picked at her brownie and wished the ground would swallow her up.

"Okay, I understand if you want to say no, but hell, we all know you're a professional." She nodded to Cally. "Okay, so if it needs doing you'll do it. I'm not married; it's my job as much as yours. I know I'm just a temporary fill-in on your team, but bench strength is important. At least, I've always been told there are a shortage of people who can do this job." Sands looked straight at the other woman. "There's no point in being a martyr when you can make an alternate strategy do double-duty for a primary organizational need," she said. There. That was her best case. One of Amy's talents was an exquisite sense of when to shut the hell up.

Harrison Schmidt looked across the table at his brother. "She's got a point. You guys know I suck at undercover work. What if one of you bites it? You've got a chance to develop one more person you have experience with. You also—excuse me, Sands." He shrugged. "You've got the chance to evaluate Sands' undercover work eyes on. There's a world of difference between real life and school. If you suck, it's better to find out now than later."

"Fine, I'm convinced." George sighed. "But if you start having trouble managing him, Cally becomes the primary, leaves with him, and you're the friend he doesn't leave with. Or if you can't get his attention away from Cally."

"Point," Tommy said. "Sorry, Sands."

"Yeah, I get it. If he's a tit man, I might as well not be there." She shrugged. "I still get some field time; you still get a chance to evaluate me. It works." Amy knew she had them, but it was good to solidify that nice, fuzzy feeling of consensus. Fitting into the team was a high priority for a new operative—another of the nuns' oft-repeated lessons. A new assignment disturbed unit integrity, which needed to be restored as quickly as possible for optimum performance.

Friday, January 15, 2055

The bar was the smokiest place Cally had ever been in, and that was saying a lot. Gas blue and sodium-yellow lights played up from the floor of the stage, green from the top, throwing eerie shadows off the curls of gray in the air. The room smelled of good whiskey, fine cigars, black market cigarettes, and cheap beer. The signs in the plate glass on either side of the door had made a fetish of the bar's famous selection of the worst of Milwaukee.

At fifty-eight, Cally had at one time or another sampled most living music genres. The sounds coming from the tiny stage were pure Mississippi delta. Her enhanced eyes spotted their quarry almost at once, even in the low light and haze that buried him at the back of the crowded room. He sat alone, and had a pitcher of something on the table in front of him. Yup, perfect music for a man mooning over the state of his life.

She let her eyes skate across him. He didn't appear to have even noticed them coming in. There was no reason he should in the press of people, except that they were both dressed to be eye-catching. Too many people, too much visual noise, too focused on the pint mug in front of him. On stage, a guitar wailed piercingly.

They caught plenty of other eyes, for certain, as she and Sands approached the bar. As Cally insinuated her hip between two men to squeeze a spot in view of the bartender, the guy behind her leaned down and spoke in her ear, "Can I buy you a drink?"

Her butt was up against him and it was pretty obvious he was interested. She half-glanced backwards over her shoulder. *Working, and married. Down, girl,* she told herself with regret. Chocolate eyes, a lock of dark hair dropping down just over one eyebrow, great smile. Not a juv, she made him as just mid-forties from the faint dusting of silver. Old enough to be a grown-up. And he smelled good. She caught all this in a bare instant, but she also had her brain in mission mode.

"No thanks. My . . . friend and I are fine," she said disinterestedly, her mouth curving in a polite half-smile. She had found this was generally more effective than a stronger brush off. Even a touch of hostility amounted to interest to men who knew enough to follow up right. Better to give them the impression of not registering on one's radar at all.

"You want your usual, babe?" she asked Sands.

Amy was quick on the uptake, turning to brush a breast against Cally's arm. "Sure, hon," she said, giving her a lazy smile and letting her eyelids droop half closed.

Of course the man behind her, being red-blooded and human, twitched a bit more. But he'd gotten the message and didn't follow through as Cally ordered and paid for a couple of Manhattans. She handed one of them to her partner and backed out into more open space. Mr. Sexy Eyes was entirely too well-built and tempting. Busy. Married. Damn whoever was responsible for the damn juv hormones, anyway.

"All the way to the back, three tables from the far right," she whispered to Sands, curling her arm around the other girl's waist and drawing her in, incidentally turning her far enough to see and look past Cally's shoulder.

"I'll have to take your word for it, can't see over heads," Sands whispered back.

Oh. Yeah, it figured. They were both wearing five-inch stilettos just for this reason, but since Cally was already five ten, she got a much better edge out of it than the shorter woman.

"It's near the path to the restroom. He's smoking; when we go back, make your play."

"Sure, if he looks past your chest." Amy was talking very softly in her ear, clearly knowing Cally would pick the words out of the background noise, but her giggle was open. Good tradecraft, but lord was she ever tired of catching crap about her tits. Of all the slab-altered bodies she had worn in her career, she supposed there were worse ones she could have gotten stuck in. At least Sinda Makepeace had been, was, beautiful—wherever the hell she'd ended up. Cally had worn enough cover personas who weren't to appreciate that. It was far better to be able to attract men at need than not. It was just that sometimes the wisecracks were worse than the backaches. She couldn't even get the things surgically reduced. With a slab job, deviations from the program tended to grow back. She mentally slapped herself for whining and dialed back in on the mission.

They drank the red liquid, which might as well have been cranberry Kool-Aid, as quickly as socially possible before ditching the empties on the bar and making a beeline for the ladies'. Cally had to admit that Amy was smooth, catching the man's eyes with a direct smile, but declining to stop on the first pass by.

It was on the way back that she bent down, dropping a casual hand on Leibowitz's shoulder. "Hey, got a light?"

Cally kept herself half-shielded behind her partner, offering a friendly but not quite interested smile when his eyes flickered to her, noting that Sands had chosen a good opening. Lighting her cigarette focused the target's attention on her and gave her the opportunity to turn up the charisma and pull him in.

Bart was not a stupid man. Trusting, but not stupid. "Would you ladies like to join me?" he asked hopefully, willing to try his luck. Of course. Cally's smile was genuine as she snagged an empty chair from another table and sat, a second behind Sands. It was nice when the mark cooperated. No reason to relax, but still nice.

It wasn't hard at all to manipulate him into taking them back to his apartment with the old excuse of coffee. Present a fictitious roommate who had her boyfriend over and he was all theirs.

When he started trying to come up with an excuse to ditch her, Cally decided she didn't really want to be ditched, and the vibes coming off him were right. He was not particularly interesting, but in a purely professional call, Sands was doing okay, but Cally wasn't about to leave her alone in the field yet with the stakes this high. Sure, this was a milk run—but how many times did a milk run turn into anything but?

"We do *everything* together," Cally smiled at him,

catlike, putting a hand over Amy's possessively. Her eyes focused into his with unmistakable meaning, which her partner supported by leaning into her arm, not taking her own eyes off Leibowitz. Was he biting? Oh, hell yeah was he ever.

At Sands' suggestion, they made another restroom stop before taking off. "Was I screwing something up?" she asked blandly while reapplying her lipstick.

"Not until now," Cally answered. "Talk later." Oh, geez, yeah, break character on a mission. Um, how about "no"?

"It's a set-up," a voice chimed from Cally's hip pocket as she bent to adjust a tight spot in the ankle strap of one shoe.

"Not you, too." She rolled her eyes.

"I'm just saying he was too easy, believing he had a chance with *two* hot chicks. I mean *I* would have taken you home, sure. *Her* shoes just scream 'screw me,' but I really like you better in the red ones with the cute lit—" it began.

"Shut up, buckley."

"Right," it paused. "And bobby socks. You're adorable in—"

"Shut *up*, buckley. And turn down your emulation a notch . . . uh . . . make that two."

"Spoilsport."

"Buckley . . ." she threatened.

"Right."

"Doesn't that get a bit annoying?" the other woman asked.

"Later. Let's go."

CHAPTER EIGHTEEN

Bart's apartment was a little thing, high up in a building with good lines and large windows, covered by heavy drapes. The first thing he did when they got in the door was lead Sands over to one of them and draw the curtains back, revealing a view of the city lights that was impressive as hell.

The living room was done all in grays and browns. Cally would have expected boring colors from a bean counter, anyway. What she had not expected was the pictures on the wall—brilliantly colorful acrylics with track lighting focused to really make them pop. She could see from here that the pics were actual paint layered on real canvas. Originals, and done right here, judging by the faint paint and solvent smells. Her inner sense of direction put the pieces together as she realized that, although the man could obviously afford a bigger apartment in a better neighborhood, this one was oriented to get excellent natural light through those large windows. The drapes obviously protected his finished pieces from the sun when he wasn't working. Wow.

She began to uneasily credit buckley's warning. What if he was gay after all? They hadn't thought so, but . . . Her already alert senses kicked up another notch.

"Okay, ladies. The act is up," he said.

Cally could sense Sands focusing in on the target to terminate and extract. She just hoped the girl would have the sense to stay out of her way.

"How much is it going to cost me for the two of you? I'd rather pay you than have you knock me over the head or drug me and try to take it. I'm not carrying much, so it's in your best interests. What's the price?"

She and her partner looked at each other, tension levels dropping ever so slightly.

"Seven hundred," Amy said sweetly. "And if you're not carrying it, how do we know you've got it?"

Good. Good job of sounding mercenary. Hookers. That explained why he believed their offer.

"Hell, make it eight," he said genially. "I'll even give you half in advance. But here's the deal. I'm buying one screw from you." He pointed at Amy. "Period. If you go for anything more, it's freebie or not at all. Got it?"

The two women looked at each other. What the fuck? Was this guy a weird asshole, or what? There he stood, though. Hair spiked with too much hair gel and showing the reason why, as it still tried to go every which way. Freckled, short. Nice green eyes, but his ears stuck out just slightly, and his adam's apple protruded prominently. He wasn't exactly homely, but he wasn't ever going to star in holodramas.

"Okay," Cally shrugged. It wasn't like he was going to get all the way through that fuck, anyway. In a way, the half he was giving in advance was fair for what he was getting. She held out her hand as he put four crisp ones in it and tucked them into the front zip pocket of her jeans.

"But if you do want to play, too, I might tip," he said.

Cally met his eyes and shrugged again. Strange. He made no protest as she stripped off, but wanted to take Sands' clothes off himself, and get the same. Whatever. What to do now? Rub his back and nibble on his neck, she guessed. She had a needle tip built into one of her rings, but the other woman had the same loaded with Hiberzine. Let the rookie take him down.

Five minutes later Cally reflected that he sure was taking his time getting down to business for a john. It wasn't as if he wasn't already hard, either. Sands was also taking her time. Drug the guy already and get it over with. She suppressed a sigh, reminding herself that it was the girl's second time in the field, a stressful kind of assignment, and it wasn't as if the delay was doing any harm. In fact, it might even be a conscious tactical decision, since several of the interrogation drugs were known to interact with the brain chemistry of sexual arousal without actually knocking him out. There was a potential benefit to loosening a subject up for his interview. It was a bit overboard for a subject who was likely to be very easy for soft interrogation, but it *was* the kid's first mission of this type. Don't jostle her elbow and screw with her confidence. Bad enough to decide to tag along, but the older assassin had stayed alive this long by learning to trust her instincts.

More than fifteen minutes in he finally rolled her

over to doggy style and started his actual screw. Cally rubbed up against him, faking like it was doing something for her. Professionally, she was slightly embarrassed, because Amy was doing a much better job of acting than she was. Unless . . . Those shudders and moans looked awfully damned real. She suppressed a growl, pressed the stud on the ring with a thumbnail, and hit good old Bart in the neck with a needle full of Pacizine, easing him off her wayward charge as his muscles collapsed.

"Did anybody ever tell you you have lousy goddamned timing?" the girl asked her, rolling over with slightly glazed eyes, still catching her breath.

"Shut the fuck up, you," Cally bit out icily.

"What? He's primed for—"

"Shut up."

"Okay."

"What's your name?" Cally asked the dazed and naked man, who was still half-erect. She tossed a sheet over his hips. It changed nothing, and cost nothing.

"Barton Elwood Leibowitz," he answered. "My dad insisted on the name from an old pre-wa—"

"That's enough, Bart. What's your job?"

"Enterprise Resource Manager for Tirdolco, Incorporated. The name's redundant, and my job title's bullshit, what I really am is a glorified babysitter for the AID that does the real—"

"That's enough, Bart. How many of the company employees do you know by sight?"

"Uh, I don't know. There's Larry, and Bill, and Jennifer, and—"

"Give me an approximate percentage."

"Uh, less than one percent, but that's if you count

the whole company instead of just the ones who work in the building, then I'd say I know them all except that if I didn't know somebody who worked there, how would I know I didn—"

"That's enough, Bart." Cally walked out of the bedroom and back to her jeans, pulling out her buckley but not bothering to dress. She turned to find Leibowitz had wandered after her, with Sands trailing him and not a clue what to do, apparently.

"Would you like to hear about my paintings? I like to talk about my paintings. I did this one right after my wi—"

"That's enough, Bart," Cally said, to his evident disappointment. "Go back to bed."

"Sure. Are we going to have more sex, because I didn't get—"

"Go back to bed, Bart." Cally rolled her eyes and followed the now obedient man back to the small bedroom, dwarfed by a king size bed that he was evidently happy to get back to. All right, so it was funny. She couldn't laugh in front of Leibowitz or Sands, especially since she was going to have to give the latter one serious ass-chewing. In the present circumstances, well, ick. Scold her, then.

"Buckley, display a holo of Mr. Mitchell."

"Do you know this man?" she asked their unfortunate victim. Well, actually he was quite fortunate, because even though he was lying here naked and . . . interrupted . . . he wasn't particularly bothered by it, wasn't going to die, and wouldn't remember a damn thing. Probably for the last two days or so.

"No . . ." Leibowitz trailed off and Cally's shoulders sank.

"I don't *know* him know him. I see him with Johnny Stuart sometimes. That's enough for me. You don't fuck with Johnny. People who do—I think he kills them. I don't want him to kill me. I stay the fuck away from the little bastard. I think that guy—" He stared blearily at the hologram. "He's some kind of cousin of Johnny's. He's scary as shit, too. I don't go anywhere near them. I see them coming, I disappear to the john all the way on the other fucking end of the building. I've got no reason to talk to Johnny, or that guy. Damn, you're pretty. Can you come back to bed now? I'd really like to get my hooks into you, even though your friend's cuter. Do you realize I've got a twenty-three percent response rate for freebies from hookers? And twenty percent, okay, nineteen, come back for even more. It's the greatest scam ev—"

"That's enough, Bart." She looked over at Sands, who simply shrugged and backed past her towards the open door. Good, she wasn't turning her back on the subject. Oh, what the hell. This had to be one of the weirdest interrogations she'd ever done. Except for the one in the teddy bear factory with the—stop it.

She got back to business. "Go to sleep, Bart," she said. She hesitated to leave him there as he rolled over. Ah, hell. "And Bart? Have good dreams. You're having the best fuck of your life." She watched his lips curl upwards in a dreamy grin. What a weird run.

Sands was already dressed when Cally came back to the living room and pulled on her clothes. "You're still not off the hook. You don't *ever* get emotionally engaged with the target. *Ever*." She could hardly keep lecturing the other woman out the building and down the street. Shut up until after extraction. "We'll continue this back at base, Miss—" Long habit stopped her before her partner's real name tripped off her lips. Extract, then correct.

"I'm not going to apologize for chewing you out," Cally said neutrally.

Wonder of wonders, they'd gotten the good conference room again. Somebody had changed the fake window to look out on some kind of tropical beach. It was so incongruous with Indiana in winter that it was impossible to think of the scene as anything other than a holoscreen on the wall. Still, it was relaxing, and Cally couldn't resist walking over to it and looking out the window. That was the advantage of a holographic window over the old 2-D televisions. It was something to do with ray tracing or some gobble-degook she didn't understand, but what it meant was you could put your head right up against the side of the window and look out, so that you had almost a hundred and eighty degrees of vision of the scene. More in an artificial bay window, or gazebo. The Bane Sidhe, alas, did not have these luxuries. From the real palm trees, it was definitely south of Edisto. No telling when it had been recorded. A live feed would have not only been prohibitively expensive, but suicidal as well. At some point, this view would loop and begin again.

The air smelled salty, but perfumey. She looked around and spotted the air freshener plugged into the wall. Nice try, but it didn't even remotely capture the real thing. She walked over and unplugged it. She and Sands were both early, but the girl hadn't said more than good morning to her since she walked in.

"What you did was dangerous as hell," she continued. "Yeah, so it's one of the three typical reactions to a first sparrow job. I don't give a shit. Each one of them is wrong, because it can get you and your teammates killed. Welcome to why sessions with Vitapetroni are mandatory. That was your rookie mistake in the field. Fine. Now you get to have your shit together. Got it?"

"Yes, ma'am," Sands answered just as neutrally.

Cally looked her over carefully. A poker face was probably good. If she was being sweet, it would be cause for worry.

"In case you hadn't figured it out yet, sparrow jobs suck," she said. "Besides, if you were going to have a freeze-up reaction, I guess it's not surprising you had that one. The guy gets his jollies seducing prostitutes. Who knew?" She paused. "Come on, was he really *that* good?"

"Let's just say I'm glad we didn't have to kill him," Amy said, shrugging. "Would have been a crime against womankind. But you know, in retrospect, he was a complete asshole. He sees those women as things, not people."

"Yeah, let me warn you about indulging in morality in this business. Don't. It's a luxury. It's a treat other people get to have. You gave it up when you signed on. Right and wrong, on the other hand, are a whole different thing. Takes a while to even start to learn to distinguish the two."

"Aren't you Catholic?" the rookie asked her.

"Yeah. But I lapse now and again." Cally shrugged, palms up, then looked down and kicked at a smudge on the floor with a toe. "You'll also find the modern church is highly forgiving of expedients that are strictly necessary in this service. 'Mission from God' just about sums it up. They should have told you in school that all our kills of specified targets are church sanctioned executions for serious crimes against innocent people."

"They probably did. I'm not religious," Amy said with a tight grin. "The nuns weren't always happy about that."

"Just as long as you paid close attention on the practical shit. Granpa's not religious, either. Particularly after folding in the Cybers, the Bane Sidhe got a lot more secular. Don't worry about it."

"That's what they told us."

"Yeah, but they were probably grudging about it. We operators are not nuns, priests, or saints. Your beliefs are your own. At least I don't ever expect to be canonized—except maybe with a real cannon," Cally added with a laugh.

Sands laughed, too, and they were okay. She could say this for Vitapetroni; he was peerless at patching them back up for work.

After a minute or so, the others entered with such alacrity that Cally suspected eavesdropping. It was a constant hazard with this organization, and she was going to have to not only warn Amy, but have a serious talk with her buckley. Come to think of it, Amy or Tommy might be exactly the people to have the conversation with. Yes, her system had to have some overrides for safety, but she also wanted to sharply limit access to as few people as possible.

The beginning of the briefing was a short recap of their interrogation of Leibowitz. Sans the lurid details, of course. Then it got interesting. Cally noticed Bryan Wilson, the head of operations, ducking into the back of the room and taking a seat out of the way, against the wall.

"John Earl Bill Stuart," the intel weenie said, pulling up a holo of a short, dark-haired man above the conference table. "We had, of course, known of him for the past seven years as the Darhel's dirty tricks boy. Ever since the last one met with—an appropriate fate." Here, he let his eyes rest on her.

Cally gave him a predatory grin. Seven years ago she had dispatched Tir Dol Ron's head of security. Charles Worth had gotten a little too good, and a little too close to things the Bane Sidhe didn't want him into, so the Organization had marked him for execution and sent Cally and her team out to carry out sentence. It had been satisfying beyond belief to personally kill Charles Worth. The bastard had tried to have her and Granpa killed when she was eight years old. The would-be assassin back then had been her first human kill.

"While we have, naturally, kept a watch on Stuart since he acceded to his present position, he has recently moved and had done a fairly good job of covering his tracks. That is, until we became more motivated to find him." He tapped the screen of his PDA, evidently having set up his presentation in PowerPoint. The holo changed to a large granite-faced apartment building.

"Johnny Stuart's home. More precisely, he lives on the third floor in a custom apartment that takes up half the floor. That's how we found him. He likes to rent two apartments and combine them. Contractors keep computerized records of their jobs, just like everybody else.

"There is a complication. Mr. Stuart has a daughter. The mission is a snatch and grab, but we have to pick him up first, while he's at home, and second, while we can predict where the child is and she's out of the way.

"To that end, this is your standard night mission, but you will not go through the door. Your rules of engagement have considerably more latitude than in the past as to the amount of exposure our ops have to civilian awareness. In this case, Mr. Stuart's bedroom borders on the hallway, and you will breach the wall. There's a minor risk of more than trivial injury to the designated personality in this process, which is yet one more reason one of you will be carrying a Hiberzine dart pistol. Upon breach and target acquisition, you will Hiberzine the target and extract. Get his AID for forensic analysis if you can, but do not linger to search for it."

Cally suppressed a yawn. Other than the ROE clearance for the wall breach, the rest of it was all a complete duh. She was paying close attention; he might say something vital. Yeah, in with all that obvious crap and talking to hear his own voice.

"Right." The head of operations stood up from the back of the room, blessedly cutting off their briefer. "I think that's quite sufficient for the team to start planning their operation." He nodded towards Cally and the rest. "I've sent you all a memo detailing your specific ROE, and we'll leave you now to your specialty and quit jostling your elbow," he said.

Their briefer looked very disappointed about being

signaled to shut up, and in no uncertain terms. He trailed out behind his boss like an unhappy duckling.

After he was gone, the team members looked at each other and grinned, all equally glad to be rid of the IW, an acronym usually pronounced as a short "eew."

Wilson was okay as a boss. He knew when to keep his hands off, and was not unduly sensitive about his top team interacting directly with the Father Nathan, Aelool, and of course the O'Neal was directly on the team. While he was understandably uncomfortable about the latter, he had a rare ability to shut up and soldier while still being a decisive leader whenever necessary. As a manager, he was a treasure. Over the years, Cally and the others had seen enough to appreciate how good he was, even though—or perhaps especially—because he made it look so easy.

In this case, he'd increased their time efficiency enormously by getting the over-eager IW out of their hair.

"So. Let's look at the map and start with insertion routes. Buckley?" Cally set her PDA on the table, and a three-dimensional tabletop display of Chicago's north side projected onto the conference table.

Mary Lynn Stuart sat at her vanity and contemplated her dark roots with displeasure. Her hair was currently a bright blond, with blue shading into fire engine red at the tips. She and her friends absolutely ruled the seventh grade with their just peachy-sweet collection of mod rooster combs. Right now, her hair was down for bed, but the left-over hairspray had it flopping every which way like a haystack. She leaned forward and popped a zit, tracing a little line of artificial, anti-germ skin over the tiny wound. Damn it, she had forgotten her acne cream, then forgotten she forgot, and Daddy had some weird belief about the vaccinations causing Torgensen's Syndrome.

He told her that the cream worked if she used it, and that nobody noticed the artificial skin if she forgot, anyway, but Louise Alexander *always* noticed and teased her incessantly. Bitch.

Mary Lynn detested the muffled noise the husher gave to her music, but Daddy was already asleep and would have her hide if the loud, popping, urbie-drill chants penetrated through the walls to his room.

It had been really nice of Daddy to switch and give her the bigger room. He had said he wanted the window. Mary Lynn was just as happy with an artificial window that looked out into Lothlorien of Middle Earth rather than a real one that looked out into the dismal Chicago winter. Besides, if she plugged her PDA into the window, as now, its AI could supplement the window routine so that virtual elves walked by and climbed into the tree houses and stuff, going about their business.

The window was great, but she was going to have to badger Dad to get her wallpaper done. Pink stripes with trailing roses had been great when she was a little girl, but now it was downright embarrassing. Her disco-ball overhead light and wall of band T-shirts from concerts she'd attended were sweet as shit, but the damn wallpaper just ruined everything, and Daddy wouldn't listen. No, he had to spend money on stupid, paranoid crap like his "home invasion escape route." For god's sake, *nobody*, in her whole grade, had ever had a home invasion. It was Daddy being weird. He could afford to install that stupid trapdoor and drive her batshit with "drills," even on school nights, but he couldn't afford a little stupid wallpaper? Parents were just fucking morons. Okay, effing morons, she corrected herself silently, leaning into the mirror to see if that was another damn zit.

As the wall blew in, shards of the mirror impacted the girl as the force of the blast knocked her backwards into the doorway. The concussion overloaded the husher, knocking it out, but did not faze the PDA, which kept pumping the Leedos' latest hit, "Die Like the Animals," into the air. On a wall to the side, an elf in an ethereal, leaf-green and gold dress strolled languidly by the now-canted window.

Johnny was awakened by a muffled thump from his daughter's room, followed by the blaring of the infernal music she seemed to have chosen just to piss him off. "Laura, what time is it?" he asked.

"It is two thirty-four a.m., Mr. Stuart."

He blearily glared at the wall and ranted to himself about Mary Lynn's current junior high stage of brat. He flat didn't need this on a work night. He swung himself out of the tangle of covers, scratching his ass through his pajamas as he stumbled out the door to go yell at his wayward child.

Her door was practically next to his, the door along a wall at right angles. A door which was canted off its hinges, showing his baby girl in a heap on the floor, blood everywhere.

"Shoot the kid, dammit!" he heard a female voice bark out, and saw Mary Lynn jerk suddenly. So much blood. She couldn't possibly still be alive. He realized he was completely unarmed, and facing a team of strangers coming in through the wreckage of a wall. His heart clenched as his body did the next logical thing, processing the situation instantaneously. He dived for the emergency exit, hand reaching under the pocket in the floor to trip the quick release. The door popped open like a jack in the box, and Johnny was head-first down the chute behind it, before said door even reached full extension. He heard a shot behind him and a *wheet* as something went by, thankfully missing him.

The chute, a grown up version of a child's covered slide, took him first out to the outer wall of the building, and then next on a diagonal slope down to one floor below ground. He slapped the activating button on the wall next to the shoot and said, "Capricorn Omega." The chute was hot now. Nobody would be following him down that route.

"Alpha Aquarius." The door with the broken exit sign gave an audible click as the bolt slammed back. He ran through it without slowing, throwing the bolt manually behind him and pelting down the hall, whose lights came on in response to his body heat.

A forty-five degree turn ran him diagonally under a street intersection, where he emerged in the bottom stairwell of a parking deck, whose exit was on the far side out from the apartment building. His back-up car responded to his voice, and less than eight minutes from rolling out of bed, Johnny was driving out of the deck onto a one-way street going exactly his way. Away from there. His heart was pounding like a hammer, bashing at the door of the numbed, shocked place at the back of his brain.

CHAPTER NINETEEN

"Sorry to throw you in at the deep end again, Sands," Cally apologized for about the fifth time as the black car purred quietly through the Chicago streets. "They've got to put together some new permanent teams with some of the DAGgers as soon as possible, and they're all guys. Trained female agents are at a premium. Gotta have at least one for a well-rounded—"

"Urban-capable team. Yes, Cally, I know. We really did cover this shit in school. I'll be fine," Sands reassured her.

"Don't get overconfident," George reminded her seriously. "No plan survives contact with the enemy, and that goes double for our kind of ops."

He wasn't going along on what would normally have been his kind of job, but instead was staying outside to cover exits with Tommy. Cally found it amusing to watch him having kittens over a job that she really needed minimal backup for herself. Backup was nice, but she had done a number of these jobs over the years as the sole shooter inserted, simply because sometimes a woman could go where a man could not, could obtain intel which would not have been available to a man. Which was, again, the reason every team, if at all possible, had one female agent. Sure, they could be assigned around on an as-needed basis, but the lost unit integrity was a cost that outweighed any benefits. That might change now that they didn't have the slab to upgrade female agents to a physical level mostly on par with the men. Policy for now was to continue the standing practice while trying to get the slab back.

Harrison crunched across a layer of rock salt as he pulled up to the curb in front of the gray building. Lighting shot up from the foot of the building, angled in to illuminate it.

Cally and Sands got out of the car with their big shoulder bags slung over their shoulders. Beneath their coats showed dark, patterned tights and high heels nobody sane would wear in Chicago in winter. Nobody, that is, but a prostitute. In their case, they were dressed high end. Visiting girls, as long as they weren't too obvious, were completely unremarkable.

Blessing a building management that either couldn't be bothered to change the pass code, or wouldn't bother the tenants to do so, Cally punched in the security access code for the door. Building management could have put in a more sophisticated entry system, but few did. The more awkward it was for residents to get their friends and pizza delivery in and out, the less likely potential renters were to choose that apartment. With supply outstripping demand, landlords needed every edge they could get, and when it got down to cases, residents just wanted the *feeling* of security.

Amazing that someone like Johnny Stuart didn't have a better sense of self-preservation and had lasted this long in his job. His run of luck triumphing over stupidity was about to run out. Hitting the stairs, the first thing that Cally and Sands did was ditch the impractical shoes into their bags, freeing up the rubberized soles of their tights to get a good, nonimpairing grip on the floor. The stairs, of course, were rubber treaded—landlords hated getting sued—but the stairwells and the surface under the treads were the same rough brick-red tiles as the hallway. The walls here, also like the hall, were not Galplas. However, in an attempt to look more expensive, the builders had tried to counterfeit the appearance of that substance. All the edges where walls met each other, floor, or ceiling were slightly beveled, as tended to happen with the real thing. The strip across the top of walls and stairways that would have glowed was frosted glass with diffused lighting behind the panels. Silly, but it probably raised the rent they could charge.

On the third floor, they skipped down the hall silently to position themselves quickly, ditching their cumbersome coats on the floor. Cally set the shaped charge on the wall herself. School training or not, Sands was damn green and, sorry, didn't get to play with the stuff that went boom.

Sands popped hearing protection into her ears as Cally stepped back and they ducked down the hall a bit. The older agent shrugged apologetically. She didn't need the stuff. Body nannites would repair her own ears as a matter of course, but the newbie was still young and au naturel, which meant if she got herself into needing a hearing job, it would take some regen, and the beancounters begrudged every penny of overhead for avoidable wear and tear.

The fuse counted down quickly, with the two women jamming their hands up against their ears and holding their mouths open. No avoidable damage. Besides, the pressure change was uncomfortable, anyway.

They were moving almost before the dust started downward, each with a Hiberzine pistol drawn and at the ready, but the first steps through the breached wall were a nightmare. Adrenaline was singing through Cally's brain as she took in the gross intelligence failure indicated by the pink-rose walls. The next thing she saw was a child just a few years older than her Megan, down and bleeding, clearly thrown back by the blast.

Field-trained instincts about care of the wounded moved her pistol for her. Hiberzine. She pointed at the child and pulled the trigger. Click. Oh, goddamn it, a fucking jam.

"Shoot the kid, dammit," she yelled at Sands.

The younger agent didn't have a veteran's reflexes, but she had graduated at the top of her class for several reasons. One of them was steadiness under pressure. She didn't hesitate, pumping the girl with a dart from her own pistol which, thankfully, worked. Demonstrating another cool under crisis judgment, she swapped pistols with her teammate without comment, giving the functional weapon to the best shot. The jammed pistol she took for herself, as Cally noted approvingly that she was fully in the zone, watching her back and clearing the jam smoothly at the same time.

The man in his pajamas, Stuart, must have been

groggy, but he wasn't moving like it. He was on the move even as his face turned to ash from the sight of his child on the floor, hitting the ground and doing something to the floor that made a trapdoor pop up. Cally got a shot off as he disappeared down the hatch, but swore as it missed. Some days you got chickens, some days you got feathers.

She grabbed Sands by the collar as the green operator tried to dive after the target. "Booby traps," she said. "He's gone. We clear the place."

Yes, the word was not to linger over a search for the AID, but he might not have had time or presence of mind to grab it. It was get the AID or have a busted mission, probably her own bungle for slowing down for the child. She swore under her breath. Again, some days you got chickens.

In the other bedroom, her eyes lit on the bedside table and she snatched up the AID. "Paydirt!"

"Here." She pressed the device into the other woman's hands and moved smoothly back to the doorway of the breached room, scooping up the preteen girl into a fireman's carry. It was worth the small risk to get an innocent child to medical care. Cally swore up a blue streak as they ran down the stairs, the sticky wetness of the girl's blood, and the rust smell, reminding her of what they'd unwittingly done.

"Buckley, tell 'em we're clear," she announced on the way down, pelting down the hallway with Sands right behind her, slowing so the other woman could get the door for her, and out into the icy night. The cold frosted their breath, but they felt none of it through the pumping adrenaline and the body heat from running the stairs.

"What the?" George was holding the door open as they sprinted to the car. Cally ducked in holding the girl, while Sands displayed good sense once again by opening the front passenger door and squirming into Tommy Sunday's lap, slamming the door behind herself. It was a tight squeeze for them, but allowed room for the girl in the back seat.

"What the fuck happened?" Tommy asked over his shoulder.

"Bad intel. Got the AID, so we got *something*." Cally brushed her hair back behind her ear with one hand and grimaced as she pulled it away, bloody. She must look like hell. She looked down soberly at the little girl and decided she didn't give a shit how she looked.

"Sounds like it's going to be one hell of an AAR," Tommy said.

Medical had that predominance of white favored in most hospitals. Cally supposed it was because white showed dirt, but she doubted any germs would dare to grow in the pervasive odor of antiseptic. They'd choke. Even if part of the antiseptic smell was Cally herself. They had doused her in an antiseptic shower, made her swish her mouth with something foul, then handed her a mask, a paper do rag, and a paper gown that caused a draft and showed her naked ass to half the world. She ignored it.

Right now, she was more concerned with Mary Lynn Stuart, laid out on the stainless steel operating table. The girl was caked in blood most places except where they had cut her clothes away. She also had the blue stain of medical's preferred antiseptic.

"So how long will it take her to recover?" she asked the surgeon, who, unaccountably, had not yet hit the kid with the Hiberzine antidote, nor was there a regen tank pulled up to the side of the table, nor a couple of first-year interns to lift her in. One lone intern stood watching, keeping his hands to himself. Cally had seen moderate to serious wounds before and was getting alarmed. The pre-Hiberzine exam was usually routine and short, unless they had shrapnel to pull out, in which case it was a full O.R. setup. In this case, Dr. Whatsis was taking way too long with the scanner thingamajigs.

"I'm afraid it's not a when, Miss O'Neal. It's an if, and a how much."

"What? She's just got a couple of gut wounds. It should be *nothing*. What the hell?" she asked. Then she remembered her manners.

"Note the entry wound." The surgeon lifted the girl's matted hair, separating it where the strands had already been pulled apart. "This is what got her. It didn't have enough power to exit through the skull." He laid her head down gently, face still swollen from Hiberzining. "So it bounced around a bit. Then, to make matters worse, the last thing Hiberzine hits is the core of the brain. Everything had time to bleed a little."

"What does that mean in real terms? Does she have some kind of chance, and how much without the damn slab?"

"I can save maybe forty percent. That's above the twenty-five percent threshold. I happen to have another child who just missed the threshold, and some of the salvagable material from her might be usable for the patient. Otherwise, we find female patients as close to her age as possible, but they will all be below threshold, so we'll need several. Fortunately, if you can look at it that way, we've acquired a few over the years. I'll have to see exactly what we can save, and then do a database match." He shrugged unhappily. "Twenty years ago, we couldn't have done it without the slab. Fortunately, outside world gene therapy has progressed to the point that we can remap the blood and tissue typing in vitro for all the donors. Or, if administration believes we can have the slab back any time soon, we'll stack her and use it to assemble the combination. She has a fifty-fifty chance if we do it without the slab, and a ninety-five plus percent chance if we use the slab. Even if the slab procedure fails," he used air quotes on the term. "What that means in practical terms is that she'll have a long rehab with psychiatric difficulties in line with the early slab patients. They'll eventually integrate her, but it's a long, traumatic, frustrating process."

He gave Cally a long, steady look. "You're more likely to know when or whether we can expect the slab back, or not." His expression said plainly that even though he wasn't cleared for the higher level negotiation information, it would have a major effect on his treatment decisions.

Cally jumped as her buckley vibrated at her hip.

"I'm supposed to tell you to take this call in your quarters," it said.

"Stack her for now. I *have to* take this call right now." Her look at him was serious, and carried more information than she should give away. "That information could change within days. Keep your mouth shut." She jerked a thumb at the intern, "And give him a scrubber. You're a mature juv physician. *He* looks like a kid because he is."

The intern jumped. A scrubber was another name for a common interrogation drug that had the side effect of memory loss of several *days* prior. Cally could see the consequences of forgetting his past forty-eight hours, and that must be a wrench in this case.

"Sorry, son," she said, turning to the doctor. "I know you would, anyway, but please put him on retroactive leave, not charged to him, and generally do all you can to blunt the consequences." She looked back at the young man. "Before he gives it to you, in these kinds of cases it's common to debrief you of any important information or appointments you may have to or want to compensate for."

The kid relaxed immediately, and with her wealth of life experience, Cally suspected the concern was a girl. Bummer. She suppressed a smile.

"I'll let you know anything I can as soon as I get it," she promised the surgeon. "And now I *have to* go."

Cally was in a new room from the one she usually had at base. Her old one was bigger, with a connecting door, and hence had been assigned out to one of the dependent families. She'd been too busy to do more than get the number from her buckley, although of course somebody had carted up her steamer trunk of on-base clothes and gear.

The room smelled dusty, although it had clearly been cleaned and vacuumed, since the marks were still on the carpeting. This had probably just made the dust worse, and she sneezed as she walked in and flipped on the light. She hadn't expected voice activation in these quarters.

The bedspread was whole, but grayed out as if a

newer one had long been traded out someplace else, and the furniture style was late-period Bane Sidhe dinged up. No holoprojection center to play cubes. That was not really a big deal, as her buckley was fully loaded and had the capability to project a cube point seven five meters on a side rather than the usual ten centimeters. The only thing that sucked about it was buckley had this annoying habit of talking during the holo, and her efforts to shut him up had spotty results, at best.

Right now, she didn't have any need for a holo, because her sister was standing in the middle of the room.

"Hi. How are you?" Cally asked her, because she certainly couldn't tell from the mentat's placid exterior, immaculate if dull brown robe, not a hair out of place in the bun on her head, except that said bun was now held in place by a pair of red and gold enameled chopsticks. "Nice do," she nodded towards the hair. On Michelle, anything colorful or personal was a major fashion statement.

"You really like them? They were a pres—" She sighed. "Busy. Very busy, which is why I have not spoken to you until now about matters I really wish I could have given you all possible time to prepare for. I truly had no idea how widespread and general the pogroms against the Indowy Bane Sidhe were. It appears that many Darhel drew the same conclusion at once. The number of refugees coming to Earth is much larger than I had originally believed."

"How much larger?" Cally asked. "We haven't got unlimited resources."

"Several thousand," Michelle said. "Up to and including major clan leaders."

"Michelle," Cally said angrily. "We can't support that. We especially can't support that given that those same Indowy cut us off not two months ago! We get support from *them*, not the other way around!"

"Your purpose is not support," Michelle said. "They are coming here because they are being hunted by humans. Your job is to keep them alive until we can calm the Darhel enough to reintegrate them or find some other place to put them. And it's not really up for discussion. I don't like being caught in your intrigues, but if you're going to catch me up in them at least give me credit for sense. The credits associated with this action are going to put the Clan in a very comfortable position. Not agreeing to protect them would cause a final disavowal of the Clan and quite probably give the Darhel the information as trade. There really is no choice in the matter. I must go."

With that she, as usual, vanished. The hoity-toity mentat-fuck.

Cally sank down onto the bed, dumbfounded.

"You are sooo screwed," her buckley said cheerfully.

"Yeah, buckley, this time I agree with you."

"Awww. You're no fun." It shut up on its own and Cally was sure it was pouting.

"We're getting *what*?" Father O'Reilly's face alternately purpled and turned ashen. "Callista, get the Indowy Aelool. Tell him it's urgent." He looked up at Cally again. "And it *is* urgent. The only irreplaceable thing in the universe is time."

"You say she couldn't tell you more about the number of refugees than 'several thousand'?" he asked.

"No sir." Cally sat without being invited because

the shock was still hitting her and she decided she really, really needed to.

"And all you got was an order to take care of them somehow and negotiating power to do it. The latter isn't small, mind you, it's just a question of whether it *can* be done." He rubbed his hand worriedly as if fingering a rosary around his neck. "We can't buy that much food, let alone move it around, but we're going to have to get in motion what we can do, and now." He looked at Cally helplessly. "All our evacuation plans postulate temporary dispersion to hiding, and then exfiltrating by dribs and drabs into various rogue city states, in the hope of rebuilding somehow, and we don't know how. Can Clan O'Neal help at all?"

As he asked this, the small Indowy clan head entered the office, ears nearly flat with concern. "Your AID said you sounded very worried."

To those who knew how to read Indowy expressions, and by now Cally was an expert, "very worried" was an understatement. One she agreed with.

"First off, let me make quite clear that any help Clan O'Neal gives in any way in anything remotely touching on this whole problem does not constitute adopting or taking responsibility for anyone." She fixed Aelool with a stern stare. "Your customs aren't ours. Aliens are alien. Got it. You get it that there will be no misunderstandings here. Anybody who's not our responsibility and in our Clan right now does not become our responsibility by any of this. By 'any of this' I mean any event *we* say is associated with this. Are we all absolutely clear on that?" She looked at the priest, and then back to Aelool.

"Yes, absolutely," Aelool said.

Father O'Reilly nodded. Cally O'Neal angry was a formidable thing. "Crystal," he said.

She thought about the other DAGgers on base. Some of the Indowy might be very useful to have at some point, even if it did entail responsibility. She'd better be clear on that, too. "Also, that does not completely rule out us adopting any person or persons at a later date, but if we do, it will be a specific invitation and by that I mean what *we* say is a specific invitation. You *will* respect that *our* alien minds are alien to you as well. Get it?"

She waited for both to respond in the affirmative before continuing.

"Good. Now that that's straight, Edisto Island is overloaded with the number of DAGger families we can handle without anyone noticing from satellite or air. That is, if they're looking, and we have to presume they will be."

Nathan O'Reilly sunk his head in his hands, drawing them down his face as he absorbed the grim truth.

"I understand the need to evacuate. If we make this place Grand Central station, it *will* be found. Especially given our little war with the Tir's people right now," she said.

"The only other large, covert organization I know of who has the resources to help at all are the Tong, and they may not take the job, and even if they do, they don't come cheap," she said. "Especially when they know you're desperate."

"If it is a matter of debt—" Aelool began.

"The Tong aren't like the Darhel. They will not hold your debt at interest, or at least not for long. They couldn't care less about politically controlling you, they just want money and power. Their own kind of power, not the Darhel's. They want sufficient power and control to support and further their efforts to make money," Cally told him. His expression was so bewildered that she thought she'd better at least sort of explain.

"It's what they do," she said. It was all the explanation she had without going into a lot of what would be xenopsych to the Indowy, and she wasn't even sure it was possible for him to get his head around the concept, because all they had experience of in business was the Darhel.

"They are going to insist on being paid regular payments, sufficiently large to pay off the debt in a set period of time. No, don't relax. Think human lifespan without rejuv. I am almost certain they will not take a debt schedule that takes more than thirty years to pay off completely."

The alien looked shocked and even a little offended, and Cally couldn't help thinking "welcome to the real world." Even the Indowy Aelool tended to assume it was humanity's job to understand the minds of the Galactics and adjust to them, rather than each Galactic race having an equal need to understand humans. They looked down on what they thought of as vicious, primitive omnivores, and then got surprised whenever it came back to bite them in the ass. Despite the gravity of the situation, Cally couldn't help but take small satisfaction in that.

"I might could negotiate something," she said. "I don't know what, I don't know how much, and I don't even know if. Michelle was right about one thing, though. Our vital interests are at stake here. I know I've got negotiating power for the refugees. Do I have it for you?" She looked at O'Reilly and Aelool in turn, ensuring their agreement. Her buckley was recording nonverbal gestures of assent, anyway. She didn't strictly need them to say it out loud as long as they were clear.

"Fine. It's easier if I send a courier to fetch my husband, if possible, since I need to be here probably more than he needs to be wherever he is. I happen to know he's on Earth indefinitely, anyway. It's business. Potentially big business. Even if he doesn't get a deal, the Tong will be content with him trying." She brushed at her hair nervously with one hand. "No, on second thought, I'll meet him partway. Like you said, time's irreplaceable. It's quicker and easier if we don't have to take him through a bunch of special rigamarole to get him in here." She waved her hand, indicating the base.

"Is anyone sorry I'm married, now?" she asked sweetly, not waiting for a reply as she left.

James Stewart, aka Yan Kato, reflected on how much trouble he'd be in if his employers knew he'd given his wife this extensive a list of their network of safe meeting places. A business organization like the Tong ran on negotiations and deals. Each organization to its nature: the Bane Sidhe needed safe houses; the Tong needed privacy for business. Of course, he'd be in lethal trouble if they knew he had a wife, and who she was. However, in this case, it was going to make them a buttload of money.

This meeting place was especially well camouflaged, because while it was a restaurant, one ordinarily did not associate the Tong with places like Harry's Barbecue Palace in West Bumfuck Indiana, even if one knew the owner's wife was Chinese. At nineteen hundred, it was pitch dark outside except for a couple of parking lot lights and the great big pink neon sign on the roof outside, announcing the name of the place to any of the locals too braindead to remember it or, more optimistically, to stray travelers coming in off the interstate.

Pine trestle tables had a thick coating of some kind of clear varnish. Stewart supposed they could afford real pine because it was the quickest growing, lowest grade of wood there was. Ceiling fans churned slowly above, despite the season, to circulate the patrons' after-dinner smokes. A cheap plastic carnation sat in an equally cheap vase beside a steel napkin holder, salt and pepper shakers, barbecue sauce and ketchup. He really loathed this shit, but he wasn't going to criticize his wife's choice of restaurant. He'd just order a cheeseburger and be done with it. He looked at the menu and winced at the prices for real meat.

His wife walked in the fire exit of the meeting room, all five foot ten of luscious. He *really* hated it that their belated honeymoon had been cut short, but acknowledged wryly that the miracle was that it wasn't cut short sooner. He had seen pictures of her before, but the only Cally he had ever known wore the body of one Captain Sinda Makepeace for a cover role seven and a half years ago. If, probably when, Cally got her real body back, it would be a major change for him to adjust to. The original Cally was also quite beautiful, not that he was biased. It would just be like she was in a new, different body to him, while it would be going back to the same original one for her. The original had smaller tits, among other things, but he really looked forward to exploring all the differences himself, whenever.

Part of him was regretful for what he was about to do to her. Part of him had that competitive buzz that he mentally slapped himself for, but that was there regardless. The sad truth was, his wife totally sucked at business, and whoever sent her out to negotiate a major deal had to be a fucking moron. However, she had already told him that she was negotiating for a bunch of Indowy clans, not even for the O'Neals, so he had zero conflict of interest in taking them for all he could wring out of her. Which would be a lot.

The truth, which she couldn't possibly know, was that he had already made the beginnings and inquiries of expanding the Tong's new shipping venture completely on their side. It became very profitable to smuggle from various unreclaimed parts of the world when truly competent people were available for hire to kill Posleen, rather than the usual crop of low-grade mercenaries. One of the hitches in the plan had been lack of available labor that could be spared from the network, disappeared from where it was, and relocated to the new ventures. Indowy worked like little green labor machines, and if the Bane Sidhe were evacuating their base, they'd be evacuating their admittedly few Sohon tanks, tools, and other necessaries, which would then also become available for hire. Hey, *any* covert GalTech production availability was priceless. He mentally rubbed his hands together.

Then there was the slab. Dear God let her be naïve enough to undervalue the use of the slab. He was, alas, confident that his prayers would be answered. He suppressed a grin and slapped himself again. Then again, a man was supposed to enjoy taking advantage of his wife. Boy was she gonna be pissed when she caught him. He was pretty sure he would survive this. Pretty sure. He'd just explain that it hadn't been *her* money, what a good job it did of setting his employers' minds to rest about his loyalty, and how much less likely the Tong was to kill him when they eventually found out about the marriage. That's it. Present it as a when. It was close enough to true, anyway. Yeah, he was pretty sure.

There was a reason he watched her stock picks and portfolio very carefully. It wasn't that she was dumb. Far from it. She just had no idea of the economic value of things beyond casual consumer purchases and light, backpack-level smuggling. And, poor girl, she trusted him.

"Good evening, Mr. Yan," Michelle said as she slid into the booth with Cally.

"Oh . . . shit."

CHAPTER TWENTY

"She's here," Cally's buckley said, reading from the sticky camera dot Cally had posted above the door jam outside.

Cally had elected to meet Sands in her quarters. For a one-on-one briefing, there was no point reserving or otherwise taking up a room, and in here she could offer some coffee from her own black-market stock. The place was shabby, but it wasn't like any of them were used to better.

Despite the bobble on Mr. Casanova, Cally still really liked the younger girl. She was devious, evil, and nasty—while looking so *harmless*. Those were traits the older assassin could respect. She was also a damned talented cyber and had been working the problem of the dependent murders to track down the people who most needed to be dead. Initially.

She was as impatient for this appointment as she was every day. Every day one of the cybers—Sands, Tommy, or someone else if necessary—briefed her in on where the investigation was. She couldn't have claimed this privilege as lead of a field team—not unless tasked with the particular mission. Need to know applied. As acting clan head of Clan O'Neal, Cally had a "need to know" for just about anything she damned well pleased, and was using it liberally. It felt like abusing the privilege, but it wasn't. The additional responsibilities sat poorly on her shoulders, but they were hers nonetheless, and she really did need to know this shit. Besides, even though the official hierarchy had standards for defining operational need to know, Granpa would normally have been available to sort through the crap and—on his own authority—brief her in on anything likely to be tasked in their direction well in advance.

Gaming out the possibilities helped get the team a head start on operational planning. In her professional opinion, this had saved the lives of one or more of her people at least twice.

"Thanks, buckley." Cally was opening the door to her quarters before Sands even knocked.

This usually spooked people a little, but Amy just glanced over the door and nodded infinitesimally. Yep. The girl definitely had the makings of a professional. Sands' poker face, however, needed work. Cally wouldn't have expected the girl to do anything so, well, girly, as bubble with excitement, but she was.

"We got him," Amy said without preamble.

"Which one? And what kind of 'got'?" Cally asked.

Sands walked over and pulled out the chair from the small desk, turning it around to sit down while her team leader perched on the edge of the bed.

"The Maise puker surfaced arrested for DUI in Akron," the cyber said.

The scumbag in question had earned his sobriquet by leaving his lunch on the floor while taking part in the massacre of the Maise family. The killers had wiped it up, but you couldn't get all that stuff out without a cleaner team or someone equally thorough. His DNA was, of course, all through the residue. They had found his identity fairly quickly with a simple hack and database search, but that said nothing about where he was.

His arrest in Akron, however, had resulted in the police taking a sample and running it against the federal identity protection system, which ostensibly existed to protect people from consumer fraud but was a far better example of the state of things in the post-war United States. The search of the database and resultant match had triggered a nice little bit of code that alerted the Bane Sidhe cyberpunks who had been seeking him. The puker was now in a known location, and wasn't going anywhere until someone bailed him out, which couldn't happen until after he was arraigned. This left a narrow window to move on the man and scoop him up. The priority was to take this one alive. The puker was a valuable property, under the theory that anybody so soft as to puke out his guts during a hit was a complete amateur and would crack like an egg. Sure, the puker would die, but only after he'd given them everybody else involved.

"We're closing in on the Florida killers, too. That's a slower process because we think we've got the killers in our search pool, but it's still a matter of going down the list and finding the whereabouts of each possible. With the limited video from the mom's buckley, we were able to narrow it down to ten thousand probables on one of the shooters, and we're down to three hundred to check in depth. That is, they were probably within two hundred and fifty miles of Orlando at the time of the murders."

"And if you don't have them in your list? Then you're back to Step One?" Cally asked.

"Not exactly." Sands chewed on the end of one nail contemplatively. "We've got a search pool on the other car shooter, and he's going through the same process. It's a bigger pool, so it's taking longer, but it gives us twice as much chance to find our targets in this first run of analysis. We could usually make a safe bet that thugs on this level would have a rap sheet and use those to narrow the pool more quickly, but in this case, we can't, because the Tir's people have the power to either eliminate or tamper with a rap sheet, and we don't know whether they will have seen the need to do so or not.

"Oh, they're starting the evac today. Tommy'll be down there for the men who are seeing family off. I understand Cap Andreotti is going out on the first bus, so the Maise kid should be down there to say goodbye. It'd probably be a nice thing to update him on as much of the investigation as opsec allows," Sands said.

"Pinky Maise is no kid. Yeah, I'll fill him in on what I can. Keep your mouth shut, because I'm doing it on my own initiative and authority, and I don't want any bullshit about it. Maise-the-younger isn't going to say a word to anybody. I'd trust the dad with almost anything on base, and I'd still pick Pinky to be the most closed-mouth of the two. Kid's fucking amazing. He's having a hell of a traumatic childhood but, hey, look how I turned out." Cally grinned evilly at the girl.

❖   ❖   ❖

She had a meeting scheduled with the Maises but there was time to go over the defense plans. They would, naturally, hang back a bit to give her time to finish her business with Tommy. This, at least, was a military task she understood *well*, it being what she cut her teeth on at the tender age of eight. The defense of the house in Rabun Gap against the Posleen during the war had been her curriculum in the harshest school of all—survival.

This had some weaknesses, but it looked like the best defense they could throw together in a hurry with the resources they had. By the time they could do better, they'd have the base evacced, anyway.

Succeeding rings of claymore mines were set to drive enemy into a kill zone, with a camouflaged trench line of defenders to cut them to pieces and mop up whatever was left.

It also showed her why Tommy wanted to split the on-base DAG contingent into three groups. One group manning the fixed positions, one group sleeping, one group doing readiness tasks that gave their attention a break from the vigilance required on the line. Each group on the line would rotate one or two men onto break every ten minutes, so that each hour each man got a break, in place, to restore his alertness.

The plan made use of available automated sensors. In this case, just a couple of clean AIDs were almost unbeatable, but redundancy in defense layers was rarely a bad idea.

When she was down to the fine details, she had her buckley page Maise and request his presence.

When he and Dad got to the cafeteria, Pinky thought, and not for the first time, that these people must be poor. Their tables and stuff, and the food, were crappier than at Joey's school, and that was saying something. He had to try not to sniffle or even almost cry when he thought about Joey. These people didn't think he understood that Joey and Mom weren't ever coming back. Kids his age didn't understand death. It was one thing he decided he'd keep hidden, after all. Pinky liked secrets. He didn't much like this one, but it would make Daddy feel worse, so he kept his mouth shut.

The floor in here was all shined up, as if somebody had decided that if they couldn't have money to buy better stuff, they could at least be clean. It made sense to him, but he reminded himself not to ask for too much stuff and maybe embarrass them. They were being real nice, and kept him and Mr. Andreotti alive even if they couldn't—he decided not to think about that any more right now.

Pinky figured he could get lots more information out of this if he played it right. The grown-ups were trying real hard to treat him like he was older. They were trying too hard, and he figured he might be able to use that.

He'd have to be real careful. Miss O'Neal came across pretty sharp. Pretty all around. Her hair was the blondest he'd ever seen without being white, and her eyes a real pretty blue. He didn't know if they were really that color without her contact lenses. She had really big breasts. Joey would have—well, anyway, they were big—the first thing you noticed even if, like him, you were too young to really care.

His dad was holding his hand. He'd done it a lot ever since he came back. He didn't think Daddy noticed how much he did it. It was okay.

They walked over to the table where Miss O'Neal was looking at something on her buckley. Pinky had to free his hand from his dad's to scramble into a chair. He sighed. His feet still didn't reach the floor and it was embarrassing. He wanted to move all the time, and with his feet hanging down like this, he almost couldn't help but swing them. With a child's instinct for manipulating adults, he stilled them and sat up straight like a good boy and tried to look earnest, wise, and precocious. It wasn't as easy as he'd expected, because he was so used to acting the other way. Trying to look *more* mature was new.

"I'm glad you could take time to see me," Cally said.

Pinky knew this was a grown-up politeness, because she was his dad's boss. *Daddy* would have had to come regardless, but he was glad to be there himself. He wouldn't have gotten much information out of Dad.

He wasn't supposed to interrupt, but Pinky decided this was a good time to get away with being a kid and forget that. "Can you tell us what's going on about all of it?" he asked. "I mean, it's all linked together with the same guys behind it, right? So the more you know on the rest of it, the more it helps with Mom and Joey." He let his voice break just a little on that last bit, and hoped it was the right touch. He tried to add "hopeful" to the complicated expressions he was already trying to pull off and quashed a twinge of triumph. She was buying it.

"Okay, Pinky." She looked at him like she respected him, not like a kid.

His dad, thank God, didn't break in. He was still buying the advice of that shrink to let him get information. Good.

"We have, besides your family, the Swaim murders in Florida, the grandmother murder, and the coed murders. The grandmother case is . . . closed. Three people that we know of were involved in the coed murders. We've located two of them, but we want to verify that there weren't other participants before we take them down."

She grimaced and Pinky guessed that she would have preferred they do that for Mrs. Grannis, too—wait in case they needed the guy to find somebody else who was in on it. Pinky didn't think so. Why would somebody need to send more than one person to kill a little old lady? Anybody who would kill somebody's grandma like that, Pinky was glad he was dead. It made it the tiniest bit better for him that *somebody* on the bad guys' side was dead, even if it wasn't the same ones that—he wasn't going to think about that right now. Miss O'Neal was still talking, and he didn't want to miss anything.

"We're still looking for the people who killed the Swaims in Florida. On your case, we just caught a break, we hope. The guy who left his DNA at the scene—"

"The puker," Pinky broke in, unable to resist.

"Yeah, the puker. He's been arrested for something else, so we know where he is and can grab him."

"Somebody's on the way, right? How far do they have left? What if he gets bailed out before they get there?" Despite himself, the questions burst out of Pinky in a rush. It was embarrassing, but okay. He already had probably the only extra information he was gonna get.

"Oh, I forgot to offer you anything to drink, do you want—" Miss O'Neal began.

His dad shook his head. Pinky just kept his eyes fixed on hers and said, "No."

"As soon as we have the members of a team in one place and a mission plan, we're on the road," she said. "We should have plenty of time to get there. Like I said, we're getting a team out as soon as we can."

"Nobody's left yet," his dad said flatly.

She hesitated. "Me. He is, by God, coming in alive," she said. "As soon as I can swing it, we're out of here."

"We'll get out of your way," Pinky said, getting up. "Right, Daddy?"

Daddy was letting himself be led around way too much. His eyes had a funny, far away look like he wasn't exactly paying attention to things. Miss O'Neal looked at him and her forehead crinkled a little.

"Charlie, do you have an appointment scheduled with Dr. Vitapetroni's office?" she asked.

He looked at her for a second like he didn't understand what she was asking. "No. I guess I've been too busy, ma'am," his dad said.

"Make one. That's an order," Miss O'Neal said. "Dismissed."

Pinky was glad she did that. He didn't think his dad was crazy or anything, but seeing that shrink might help, and he didn't think Daddy would have listened to a little kid, or maybe not to his friends from the unit, either. He caught Cally's eye and could see they both understood that Pinky would make sure Dad didn't forget. He *could* nag and pester. He was good at it.

As boy and man disappeared out the doorway, they passed a couple coming in, the first of the lunch crowd. There would be more, as these no doubt heralded the beginning of the lunch rush. Time for her to go find Sands.

"I didn't think you wanted to be interrupted, but your husband has made a pickup call. He should be here whenever they can get him in," the buckley said.

"Why?" Cally asked. "Is something wrong?"

"The call said he was coming in to improve communication."

"Then he and I have yet another breakdown in it, because I won't be here." She was trying to joke but it came out as irritation. Too much was happening too fast, and she still—irrationally, she thought—resented every moment she didn't get to spend around her husband. It wasn't like they were newlyweds, even though they'd just had the honeymoon, and just came out into the open as married. Hell, even just as a mistress to the Tong, who didn't know who she was, being the mistress was sort of open. Kind of. When you got down to it, it was kind of hot.

That's it. She *was* acting like a fucking newlywed. Or a no longer getting to fuck newlywed. Mission face, mission face, mission face dammit. She couldn't help it; she felt a goofy grin sneaking over her face.

Time to find Sands and Tommy. And to stop freaking grinning like an idiot.

Michael Li hated the tropics with a passion, and most of all he hated the Darien jungle in Panama. Despite wearing a white suit of the lightest non-GalTech material he could find, he was sweating like the proverbial pig. This was also despite having the suit jacket off. His collar was not unbuttoned, nor were his sleeves rolled up, because it limited the damage from the bugs who found him far too tasty, insect repellent or not. Oh, it helped. Just not enough.

Li had grown up inside. As a child on the moon, outdoors had been a great adventure he'd preferred to decline, going outside the pressure locks only once, when forced to, on a school field trip. The low-grav playgrounds were cool growing up, but it was also something to take for granted, another familiar thing from home that was absent on Earth.

The city park a few elevator hops and corridors away was his idea of "outdoors." It had plants. Plants were supposed to be decorative and stay where someone put them—out of the way. Sounds outdoors were supposed to be birds chirping and piped music of flowing water or ocean surf.

Hence, he hated Earth's outdoors, and the Darien most of all. Every hour of the day or night, some animal or other was shrieking at the top of its damned lungs; vegetation wasn't occasionally in the way, it was always in the way; and the bugs, and the heat, and the humidity.

He normally stayed in his air-conditioned headquarters, or his room, as much of the time as possible. His goddamned AC, older than Darhel panties and a piece of shit to begin with, was broken again. He couldn't hide in his bunk all day; he'd look like a wuss. At least there was a chance of a breeze out here.

He also, he admitted, wanted to emphasize the privations he was enduring in the name of the Tong when he called his boss and gave him an update. He had the O'Neal army commanding officer's report, too, for delivery, but he could just send that as an e-mail after the call. It was damned convenient for the O'Neals to have to send all their communication back and forth through the Tong. Useful.

The boss was really sticking his neck out on this deal, and Li was along for the ride by association, but he was starting to believe it might work. These military guys seemed to know what they were doing and were doing less whoring and drinking than he'd expected. He didn't know why it surprised him that the O'Neals had ended up with their own private army. It was an unusually good force of mercenaries, a large number of them actual blood family. If they were smart and bribed the right people at the right times, there was no reason they couldn't do quite well out of it, if they were finally coming around to being practical. Since they had chosen a line that comple- mented the Tong's enterprises instead of competing with them, this thing really had potential. In the long run, for his own future, it might even be worth this sojourn in sauna hell.

He looked at his watch. It was a couple of min- utes until eleven, and his boss was usually punctual, which fit his military background. Officially, the boss had come into existence out of thin air. Unofficially, he was military and some kind of officer before the Tong recruited him.

"Michael, your boss is on the line," his PDA said in its pleasant tenor voice.

"Thank you, Huan. Put him through."

A holo of Yan Kato appeared over the buckley, with enough of the background caught in the stream to sug- gest that his boss was in the back of a store; shelves stacked with goods rose, ghostly, in the background of the holo, fading out around the edges.

His superior had the kind of face the Tongs gave people who didn't start out Asian. Unless someone was a very good fit for a specific ethnicity, they tended to avoid having someone look wrong for a single type by having them look like a cross of a number of Asian ethnicities. It was common enough for people to really be half Vietnamese and half Korean, or half Chinese, a quarter Korean, and a quarter Japanese, or half Chinese and half white American. Usually, if someone had a mish-mosh appearance and too sketchy of a background, people just assumed round-eye, but it wasn't polite to say so. "Yan" looked rather unconvincing to him, but Li didn't give a rat's ass for his ancestry as long as the Grandfather accepted him and he kept doing a good job. His boss was a rising star, which made for an auspicious horoscope for Li.

"Status?" Yan asked.

"Quarters and administration are up. Half the storage facilities are up and receiving the first shipments. We have a secondary location up on the coastline and are shipping food and equipment to whichever location has the lowest transportation overhead," he said. That last consisted largely of the right bribes, but how many people and how much varied. "The Mirandas have quite a hatred for Elves. The O'Neal organizational associations have opened doors there, acquiring information that has kept down costs." He didn't like having to admit it, because he was used to thinking of the Bane Sidhe as impractical idealists—which they were. However, in this case, the O'Neal Grandfather had skillfully parlayed that into a business friendship over the years. Mostly low level, but of long standing. Good planning, that.

"How are the soldiers?"

"Better than the general reputation of soldiers, but this is not an area of my expertise. I have a report from their Colonel Mosovich to Sunday. He suggested himself that I send it through you. The soldiers appear to find being here to be of ample training value. Although they drink and visit women, they are not excessive. They are willing to work and have been very helpful camouflaging the buildings," Li said. Of course they were helpful. The buildings housed their own quarters, food and supplies.

"How soon can you get them on the boats out?" Yan asked directly, his desire for speed showing on his face.

"It would be difficult to equip and load them in less than a week," Li replied, meaning that he couldn't do it in less.

"Get them out in three days. Use money to expedite whatever it takes." His superior could be disturbingly direct at times like these.

"That would be very difficult within the customary constraints of good business. The soldiers might find their supplies primitive, as well." Li meant, of course, that there was no way he could get these men equipped well enough to get them onto boats to Venezuela in three days without spending so much money he'd get shot for it, no matter what his boss said. Oh, he could tell them they were equipped, but getting them to agree with that assessment and board the boats was another thing altogether.

"Do what you have to do. There are others who

find it in their interests to bear the costs. I have a message from their superiors with orders for the soldiers; they'll work with you."

Yan said it firmly, leaving Li in no doubt that the boats *would* be leaving in three days with whatever and whoever he could have aboard them. He was beginning to get a headache. At least, with their orders in his hands, he would be able to pass some of the headaches on to Colonel Mosovich. He didn't envy the man. Then again, he didn't envy himself, either.

"Whatever can be done, I'll do," he said. That part, at least, needed no interpretation.

CHAPTER TWENTY-ONE

Yan Kato cut the call to Panama. His lieutenant was a good guy. Li would bust his ass, and not have kittens because he couldn't get it perfect. Stewart hated it for DAG that their supply situation wouldn't be perfect, but it never was. He'd check the situation before they boarded ship, but the pressure driving the schedule wasn't coming from the Tong or him. They had civilians coming in, they had some of their *dependents* coming in as refugees. They had an unknown number of Indowy that he, personally, didn't give a shit about one way or the other, but Cally and the other O'Neal powers that be did care, for whatever reasons. Soldiers did dangerous, deadly, uncomfortable things so civilians didn't have to. Time for the DAGgers to earn whatever it was the O'Neals were paying them.

Stewart still had trouble getting his head around the fact that *he* was now an O'Neal. Not just any O'Neal, he was Iron Mike's fucking son-in-law. The world was a strange place. He was in a strange place.

The shelves behind him looked ordinary enough. High shelves stacked with boxes. In front of him, however, was a great big paper-mache dragon head, painted in tie-dyed patterns, with peace signs of various sizes scrawled or painted on it. It was yellowed with age, and looked brittle under the huge layer of dust that coated it. He was so, so tempted to ask, but he didn't. They might tell him.

He'd come in through the front of the cutlery shop, the stock of which ran to pocket knives, daggers of various grades, cheap throwing stars, and pan-Asian kitsch, with a couple of mid-grade swords to draw the oohs and aahs. In the display case with the swords, a cheap jade statue of the Buddha sat behind a neatly printed card that swore it had once been in the national museum in Beijing. If it had, it had been in the mark-down bin of the gift shop.

He had picked this place because it was the closest organization spot to one of the pickup locations Cally had told him to use. Well, not exactly a location. In this case, he just called a cab from a particular company and gave a particular address over the phone as his destination. The cabbie would call back when he was pulling up out in front.

Stewart could have gone out front and browsed through the crap. It wouldn't have caused any notice, as the store was empty other than the owner, who already knew he was back here. Instead, he stood near a wobbly little table and had bad coffee out of a paper cup. Even bad coffee was still coffee, and he flipped a dollar into the honor jar. The stuff was expensive, and who knew if he'd get a chance at any while he was staying with the Bane Sidhe.

The trip was confusing, as always, but this time they didn't take steps to keep him from figuring out where the hell he was going. He supposed between Tong business policies and family they had confidence in his willingness to keep his mouth shut. As a former general in Fleet Strike counterintelligence, there was no question that he was *able* to keep his mouth shut. He was protected against every known interrogation drug, unless the Bane Sidhe had some he'd never heard of. Come to think of it, he'd have to ask. With some of their secrets in his head, it would certainly be in their interests to have him protected to the best of their ability. What "the best of their ability" was was another secret he'd love to add to his collection.

The thing that really sucked about his afternoon was when they finally got in to the Bane Sidhe's secret little Sub-Urb and he found out he'd missed Cally by less than half an hour. It did surprise the hell out of him, though, that Nathan O'Reilly had come to tell him himself. Then Stewart realized he'd been unconsciously thinking of himself as Cally's husband, since he was here on her turf, instead of thinking in his persona as a fairly high ranking representative of the Tong.

His first trip here had been essentially social. On this trip, he was the man on the front end of a few boatloads of money and a final lifeline for many of their people. That being the case, he was surprised the Indowy Aelool and a ranking representative of Clan Beilil weren't both here, as well.

O'Reilly offered a firm handshake. "Mr. Stewart, so good to see you again."

"Just Stewart, please. Or Yan if you prefer," he said.

"Then call me Nathan. Since Cally and her team-mates call you Stewart, that would probably be less confusing."

Stewart nodded. "My PDA tells me I missed my wife?"

"I'm afraid so. We got an opportunity to pick up a high value target and for once your wife was the person we could most count on to leave him alive." The priest grinned wryly. "We didn't have much time when you were here before. Would you like a tour of our little operation here? While we still have it."

"That bad?" Stewart was genuinely concerned, and not just for the Bane Sidhe. If the Darhel were will-ing to go to open warfare enough to take out a major installation like this, it endangered his entire family and his organization, too. The latter was, suddenly, a barely important side thought. He was just getting used to being an O'Neal, but they were the closest thing to family he'd had in a long, long time, and his surge of protectiveness for the whole lot of them shocked him. When the hell had that happened?

"I'm being pessimistic. I estimate the chances of losing the base at around ten percent, overall. It just smacks of failure to be evacuating."

"A tour would be fascinating," Stewart changed the subject. "I presume Tommy's with Cally. I've got his report from Colonel Mosovich." He could tell Nathan was just itching to get a look at that report. Truth to tell, so was he. However, since the DAG force in Panama was strictly an O'Neal pigeon, both men knew it would be more than their lives were worth for Cally to catch them sneaking a peek. Getting caught by

Tommy would be just as bad, and a lot more likely, given the other man's formidable cyber skills.

"Unless you've got Michelle O'Neal hidden away somewhere around here, Nathan, I think we're just going to have to wait," he said it jokingly, but privately admitted that he had no idea of the Bane Sidhe's capabilities other than by inference, and they had shown over the years that they frequently held back from things they *could* do for reasons unfathomable to outsiders.

"Unfortunately, no, but perhaps a walk-through of our Sohon training facility might hold your interests in the interim." The priest grinned like a little kid about to show off his toys.

"Really? The crown jewels. That's a flattering level of confidence."

As they spoke, Nathan was steering him to an elevator down a side corridor, pressing the call button as they arrived. "You're not one of ours, but you *are* an O'Neal. I'm not taking you around in that capacity, though, but rather in your professional persona," he said. "You've made a very large deal with us. I suspect your employers may question whether a deal that good was ever intended to be repaid. It's my insurance for you to be able to tell them you've seen various of our capabilities with your own eyes."

"Pardon me for poking holes, but your capabilities aren't very reassuring if you're about to lose them." James Stewart, donning his "Yan" hat, had transformed from the in-between land of relative into all business.

"Ah, but we aren't. Tanks we can afford to lose. Not easily, but they can be replaced. Our nanogenerator is out already. From there, the next really expensive thing is the headsets and the interface that goes within the tank. Those are small. If we can't keep our practitioners alive, then it will be because none of the rest of us are alive to defend them. All the rest of this," O'Reilly said grimly, "is replaceable. Expendable. And all the rest of us, too."

The elevator arrived and they boarded, the head of the O'Neal Bane Sidhe still making his case.

"I'm speaking for the benefit of your employers, of course," he said. "We had nothing like this in the centuries before recontact, and we survived. We've never put all our eggs in this basket; we're still decentralized as our core operational tradition."

Stewart noticed the other man did not give any percentage as to what was decentralized, and avoided saying "most." Nor did he say what quality of individuals were out as sleepers, how much they knew, how much bench strength they had. There was also the matter of the size and sophistication including the O'Neals, versus without them. The O'Neals were pretty concentrated, too, which was both a strength and a weakness.

He didn't reply, and the elevator descended farther into the bowels of the base in silence. It was an interesting elevator. The walls were Galplas, but they had a slightly rough surface, and there were crayon scribblings all over them, spreading out from around knee level. Finally, he couldn't take it anymore. "The walls?" he asked.

"That's real crayon. We encourage the youngest children to draw on these because it's a well-defined space. It keeps them from coloring on every wall they can find. Yes, I do mean encourage," O'Reilly said. "This is when they're too young to even begin the early headset exercises. We give them toy versions and encourage them to be interested in the colors of walls, because tuning the color of Galplas is a very early exercise. The children think of it a bit like playdough."

"Galplas?" Stewart asked incredulously. He found it hard to think of the major GalTech construction material as a child's toy. It was stronger than steel.

"Didn't you ever wonder how a GalTech product was so comparatively cheap? And abundant?" the older man asked.

"Playdough," Stewart repeated.

"That's about it, yes. Primarily because if it goes wrong, it's not a particularly high energy reaction," Nathan said. "Ah, here we are." He opened a very sturdy looking door that opened on to a bay about the size of a small airplane hangar. They were at the bottom, but stairs, ladders, and catwalks laced the walls, and a network of pipes hung suspended about four meters off the ground.

"The stairs and such are vertical exit routes in case the halogen foam system has to address a dangerous mistake. Here, we need these." The priest reached out and took two pairs of safety glasses and two rubber aprons from the shelves beside the door.

"The room is large less because of need to build large things and more as part of the safety design for the pressure-venting system. We could, of course, disassemble part of the fire suppression system if we had something big to build, but for the foreseeable future, this is a training lab and large projects are beyond the scope of what we do. Beyond the scope of what we *can* do," he admitted.

Stewart noticed that only about a quarter of the tanks, down on this end of the room, were in use. The others were empty. At half of the operational tanks, one or more human child was working under the direction of several Indowy. Indowy alone were running the rest of the operating tanks. It was the first time Stewart had ever seen a Sohon tank in real life, much less one in use. They didn't look very impressive. Just big vats with people sitting around the edge, wired in. The headsets looked a lot like the headphones on personal stereo systems when he was a kid, other than having too many pads at seemingly random places on the head.

O'Reilly gestured to the empty end of the room, "The legacy of our internal divisions. We have more headsets and tanks than we have nannites to run in them. This is why I can tell you we'll maintain operational capability after the evacuation. We've got idle tools to move out, even though the practitioners we have here and their own tools will go last. As part of healing the breach, we can count on enough nannites to restore any equipment we can save to operational status. Get the Tchpth to provide enough code keys for the generator, put some of the many refugees who are high level Sohon practitioners to work, and our capacities go way, way up."

He nodded towards the children. "Those are our real treasures, right there. No politics can take them, and the Tchpth will provide them with enough nannites to operate in exchange for being allowed to observe their development. Human Sohon practitioners are our next baby step towards, if not independence, then comparable footing with the other races. I'm afraid that's likely to take Galactic-level time, but we do what we can."

"They're talking," Stewart said, feeling kind of stupid for saying it. "I thought they had to be deep into some kind of trance or something."

"They do talk to the instructors sometimes, a little. It's just that what they're making right now isn't particularly challenging."

"Not *that* side," a child of about ten yelled at a boy that was maybe a couple of years younger. "Put it over *there*, between the blue marks. Blue. See 'em?" The older child pointed to an area of the large tank he was operating and the smaller child obediently walked around the tank, appeared to find the right marks and began shaking something out of a plastic jar into the tank. Stewart couldn't see what, as the child's body was in the way and the plastic was dark brown.

"They still need reagents, of course, but mostly they're putting the right things together in the right order, managing heat, moving things around and monitoring. You can't see it, but the tanks have built-in heating and cooling coils, and one of the things an operator does is use the nannites to control membranes that keep the wrong things separated from each other, everything at the right temperature and pressure, do separations, that kind of thing. My understanding is that one of the things the nannites can do is make one tank into a potentially near infinite number of vessels of varying sizes. The children understand a great deal of chemistry, of course, but a lot of the information is stored and available through the headset and managed by a limited AI. The operator's job is to manage everything to spec. Let's go see."

"And give me five more of those, and be ready with my other stuff. I'm ready to start outputting," the older child ordered, sounding calmer. A bit.

A robotic arm lowered a small, white, plastic bin down into the sludgy-looking tank, lifting it back up in less than a minute, filled with what looked like white sand. The arm moved the bin over onto a shelf on a large cart and picked up a second bin, repeating the process.

As they approached, the older boy's face shifted more and more into the placidity characteristic of the other eight children operating tanks. "You've got nine of these children?" he asked.

"Oh, no. A bit more than three times that. Some are sleeping, some are in classes. We operate the tanks around the clock to make the most of our nannites' lifespan." He nodded to the child who was making the white stuff. "The kids go through all the normal developmental stages. It's biochemical, and it would be bad for them to try to flatten those out. Usually when a child operator reaches a stage that he or she can't control perfectly, either they put the child on safer tasks, or if they don't have the work to do that, pull him from the rotation into full-time classroom education and meditation. It makes the stages considerably shorter. For one thing, kids *like* to work. At this," he amended.

"Really?" This was news to Stewart, who had always equated human Sohon training with brainwashing and drudgery. "How can kids *like* keeping still for hours at a time?"

"Indowy have exercises for the drive to move. They've adapted some human games—don't ask. As for the work, it builds on the theories of Montessori. Light years beyond, but she had a base observation that's the keystone of all this. Children have a drive to work, especially productively. Consider it arts and crafts with results that are useful and usable. They take so much pride in that." The priest smiled fondly at the children in the room, both the tank operators and the dozen or so children on the floor doing the various tasks to feed the tanks.

"The Indowy equipment, it's like it was scaled for children, anyway," Stewart said.

"Another one of Montessori's observations. It helps tremendously to give children tools and facilities that are size appropriate, without patronizing them. Patronize a child and he will try to please you by behaving childishly. Human children are the size of Indowy adults. I've never seen an Indowy patronize a child."

They had arrived at the tank of the first boy. Stewart liked him already. He was a real kid.

"This guy's still safe to operate a tank?" he asked the Indowy standing at the boy's arm.

"Richard is ordinarily in classes," the small green alien said. "But this task is simple and relatively safe. So simple as to court boredom, I'm afraid."

He could see Stewart eye to eye, since the operator platform was elevated.

"I'm sorry for my outburst, Father," the kid said. "I did let boredom get to me. I thought I was getting better." He grimaced, glancing back to Stewart.

"I'm making cyclotrimethylenetrinitramine," he said self-importantly. "It's easy, but we need a lot of it, and for volume I'm the best," he bragged.

"Cyclo-what?" Stewart looked at O'Reilly.

"RDX." The priest said.

"Relatively safe?" Stewart squeaked. He might not recognize the chemical name, but he knew the explosive that was the primary element in C-4, and it wasn't stable until stabilized.

"Yeah," the boy said. "Don't worry about the output. You can't see it, but it's got a few nannites laced through to make it pretty unlikely to explode or anything. They'll be reclaimed during the mixing process. It would be hard to mess this up." The boy looked glum, returning his full attention to his work.

As they walked on to the next tank, O'Reilly whispered, "These kids see getting pulled from work as a punishment similar to grounding. The Indowy discourage that idea, but personally I think it's beneficial."

A smaller girl worked at a smaller tank. "Don't pay any attention to Richard. He's been being a brat and he's lucky they're letting him make anything. It's because he's good at volume, and he really is," she admitted. "None of this is hard, but I'm making molds for plastic casing, then I'll move on to polyisobutylene and 2-ethylhexyl sebacate—the binder and plasticizer. The real little kids can make the plastic to go in the molds," she explained.

O'Reilly pointed to the far end of the room where cardboard boxes sat on pallets. "Motor oil, ball bearings, and washers," he said.

"Claymores?" Stewart asked.

"Sunday tells me we're going to need quite a lot of them." Nathan looked a little sad. "Such a waste. Most of those boys we expect will have no idea what kinds of things their orders can lead them into. Babes in the woods."

"They pick up a rifle, they're choosing big boy rules," Stewart shrugged. "They shoot real bullets."

"I know. But it's still a waste."

"You're not expecting professionals?" Stewart asked doubtfully. It wasn't good to count on the enemy to make mistakes. He frequently didn't get that memo.

"From the Tir? No. He has the classic Galactic fallacy. Humans are all vicious omnivores, you put a weapon in their hands and point them at something to kill."

"Fire and forget," Stewart agreed. He'd seen it before, and it was almost a universal. They could get their heads around elites facing Posleen, but they tended to chalk the improvements up to the suits and ignore the greater quality of the men in them.

"We're not just counting on him to be stupid. Who does he have to send? Sending U.S. troops would give away the Darhel game wholesale. Send West Coast DAG in as a black op? They'd know, back channel, and mutiny wholesale rather than attack their brothers. If the Darhel or their brass plants were ever afraid of a mutiny, it's now when they've just had one.

"We've been watching the contracts of known mercenary groups and we have a general range of who and what we can expect *if* we get hit with military force." Nathan said. "None of the contract forces in the range of available have ever fought trained human troops. None."

"Lambs to slaughter," Stewart grinned ferally.

O'Reilly winced.

"You're catching the O'Neal meme," he said.

"Don't worry about me, Father. I was already like this."

Tuesday, January 26, 2055

Somebody had taken some time in building this police station. The building had an exterior of standard red brick, but it wasn't stacked the boring way. Slantwise, patterns, arches. Somebody took their brickwork seriously, and had a pretty damned good artistic eye. It took imagination to get a gothic feel with simple brick. The window frames had gargoyles at the corners, and a pair also flanked the main entryway.

"More than you'd expect from a county PD," Cally said.

"Must have come up at the end of a fiscal year," Sands agreed.

"What?" Cally asked absently, surveying the building. "We're sure he's still there, right?"

"Yup." The girl held up her PDA. "Just checked."

Tommy and George were playing some kind of two-player shooter game next to her. George was short enough that Amy didn't have to sit in the middle.

Cally got out of the car and walked into the station, broad daylight, nothing special. After Tommy verified that one Reginald Erbrechen was still in police custody, they'd reluctantly crashed at a truck stop overnight so they could sack out and pick their time today. It was two in the afternoon. Too late for the lunch rush, too early for people to be going home. She didn't have to look like anyone in particular for this mission. Just not-Cally. A wig and cheek pads had been enough.

The pickup really did go off as a milk run for once. She just went to the window and bailed out

Reginald Erbrechen, in cash, and waited until they brought him out.

"Boy am I glad to see you!" he said. "Ellen got you, right? I knew she'd raise the money to pay you guys."

"Your lucky day," Cally lied as she walked him out of the building. Anybody who bailed you out of jail was, of course, your friend. Nobody put up bail money as a throwaway expense.

"Oh, wow. That was the worst place I've ever been in in my life."

"Never been in jail before?"

"Oh, no. I've always been lucky. Oops. Sorry. Hey, I admit it, I'm a bad man. But I'm a bad man with really good luck," he grinned. "Should I try it with you?"

She hit him with the Hiberzine. The organization made the shit by the boatload. "Your luck just caught up with you, asshole," she said.

Tommy had gotten out of the car to help her with the dead weight of the puker. She didn't need help, but for the look of the thing it was better that she had some. They had decided that speed and lack of complication was their best strategy. Do it quick, do it smooth. Risk of somebody noticing, but less risk if they just did it and got out of there. They'd taken precautions to ditch pursuit effectively if they got unlucky, but sometimes get in and get out was the best way to play it.

Tommy froze and Cally could see him looking behind her. Damn. This time, their luck wasn't holding so good either.

"Hey! You're not gonna kill him, are you?"

Cally turned her head and saw that it was one of the guys who'd brought Reginald from the back, come out for a smoke break.

"No," Tommy lied smoothly.

"Oh. Okay," the cop shrugged. "Just get him back for his court date."

"No problem. When the time comes, he'll be present for justice," Cally dished out the half truth with a vicious appreciation of the irony.

A road trip plus a few hours later, Cally stood up from the uncomfortable plastic seat in the interrogation room. It was easier watching it happen to somebody else. Besides, he wasn't immune to any drugs, so it was soft as hell. Sadly.

"He's repeating a lot. Have we gotten everything we're going to get out of him?" she asked the intelligence specialist.

"Yeah, I'm done," he said.

"Good enough." Cally drew the pistol from her side and put two rounds into his skull, to the visible discomfort of the intel weenie. "You didn't need to worry. They're frangible," she said, then realized. "Oh. You mean him. Saves debate."

Wednesday, January 27, 2055

Tommy Sunday stood with James Stewart in the atrium, a room approximately two floors down from the surface, converted to a combination manufacturing facility and pre-ready room. The actual ready rooms were immediately at the surface, but for now, the atrium was convenient as long as they had power. They didn't anticipate losing power, but in one corner a backup generator idled just to make sure. Two of the three elevators that serviced the atrium sat locked out from other users, one at the final pre-surface level, one at the atrium level itself. Traditional exit signs marked the stairs. All of these entries to the facility had blast doors as part of the base's built-in defenses.

The designers of the Bane Sidhe's Indiana facility had never expected to hold the facility in case of attack. The powers that be, and residents, had always understood that the primary defensive strategy of the base was, as that for the Bane Sidhe itself, concealment. In a direct fight the whole organization was screwed, anyway. The organization's primary strategy to avoid that was inter-species politics. Unfortunately, sometimes politics fell through on you.

The base did have secondary defenses, but those were all designed to buy time in the event of attack for scuttling anything of use to the enemy and covering evacuation and retreat if possible.

The designers had known the Bane Sidhe resources did not extend to maintaining standing troops for actually defending the place like the fortress it was. Its fortresslike nature was more a matter of convenience than anything else. A Sub-Urb was optimal for concealment of a facility of this size, and they were natural fortresses unless someone obligingly disarmed the defenders and threw open the gates to the enemy, as had happened at Franklin during the war. Since they had a fortress anyway, the designers had put in any defenses that were easy, cheap, and not too inconvenient for the inhabitants.

Two back doors led out ten to fifteen miles away from the facility. The Himmit had done the conceal-ment, and the Bane Sidhe maintained those doors and passages carefully, but never, never ever used them. Even the present evacuation was all going out the front door. Those back doors were not on the official plans, and were a closely held secret between the Himmit and the human faction of the Bane Sidhe. They were entirely of human construction, and Him-mit concealment.

Human double-conspirators had used GalTech mate-rials and hybrid equipment. They trusted the Himmit with the secret for three reasons: one was that they had no choice if they were going to get their help; two was that the Himmit would find out anyway; and three was that the Himmit preferred to collect secrets, not divulge them. It had taken very few additional stories to bribe the Himmit to hold it close.

The Bane Sidhe did trust each other. With too much. Nathan was as careful as possible to keep a watchful eye for anything that would indicate discov-ery of Project Luft Three. Papa was careful to grouse just the right amount about the lack of a back door, finally declaring that *he* certainly wasn't going to live there. They had read Tommy Sunday in later on the theory that a back door was no good if nobody knew it was there when the need came. Cally had gotten herself read in by the simple fact that she had flatly refused to stay in the facility, even occasionally, until Papa took her aside for reassurance. If the Indowy assumed it was a clan head giving instruction to a clan member, so much the better.

Now, the inner circle of those in the know had

expanded by thirty. Each man from DAG had proved absolutely reliable with national-security level sensitive material, each man had thorough protection from drugs, each man had a need to know. These were their defenders. In extremis, any of these men could end up the last man covering retreat, or the man leading the civilians to whatever safety there was. In the fog of war, secrets too closely held could get lost. Tommy had also briefed in the members of every field operational team on base. In the event that they held the base, far too many people would know the secret, but they would all be people immune to drugs, all people who grokked opsec. It was a trade-off, and this was his best call. Besides, even if the Indiana base survived this crisis, there was strong likelihood of its location being compromised and its protection reduced to the vagaries of Galactic politics. He would recommend constructing a new main base, stripping and abandoning this one.

He and Stewart silently contemplated the civilians assembling claymore mines, and the DAGgers wiring them up. Crates of the devices were building up against a far wall, glowing lights along the walls and in the potted trees coming on to illumine the room as the huge artificial window overhead deepened to the indigo of twilight.

"Got some others up top digging in?" Stewart asked his old ACS buddy.

"Yup. You know it," Tommy said.

"You know Iron Mike's on Earth, don't you?" Stewart looked at the sky contemplatively.

"Yup. I think the chances of them sending him in are slim and nil, because it gives away the whole damn game. We're talking about Darhel conspiracy believers increasing by a couple of orders of magnitude. It's a deluded democracy out there, it's a corrupt one, but they still vote and the declared winners still bear a decent resemblance to the actual count. I don't think we have to worry about facing suits. If we do, we're fucked anyway, so my plan for that is limited. It sure as hell wouldn't waste any troops outside. Nor am I wasting any of my limited GalTech shit on what we're likely to get. But yes, I have a go-to-hell plan. Please tell me you don't think I'm stupid."

"I don't think you're stupid," Stewart repeated dutifully.

"Asshole." Tommy grinned at him and clapped him on the back. "Let's go shell out for some real black-market coffee. Your wife smuggles in some good shit."

"Cally has real coffee? *Good* coffee? She's been holding out on me. I may kill her. I guess I'm buying." He paused. "You wouldn't happen to be able to lay your hands on some black-market beer, would you?"

"Hell, yeah. You think a couple of old vets like we who don't exist are going to get together and not get trashed out of our gourds at least once? O ye of little faith," Tommy said. "While I'm at it, how do you feel about moonshine? Fine corn whiskey aged in Galplas barrels for at least twelve days, to be specific. Well, maybe a week."

"I think it makes the closest thing to good Irish coffee I will have had in a decade," Stewart said.

"Done. You and Cally meet me in my quarters. Yours suck, and I bribed one of the permanent residents for an upgrade."

"Works."

CHAPTER TWENTY-TWO

Thursday, January 28, 2055

Nathan O'Reilly needed a decorator. Until he experienced the other man's office, Stewart had had no appreciation of the difference the Tong's feng shui made in his work environment. He couldn't do it himself, had no idea how it was done, and didn't want to know. All he knew was that the pink walls and various stuff did make it a better place to work. He wasn't going to mention it. He was, by god, not going to have a serious meeting with the head of a large rival, and now partner, organization and discuss interior decorating tips. Both rival and partner, simultaneously, was the way of things in large human organizations of all kinds, and that seemed to hold true across the range of sophonts, generally.

The reason was obvious. Different large groups had different interests. Some of those matched up in a similar direction, or could be made to, better than others. Whether you called it economics, politics, the balance of favors—none of that mattered. In the end, it all came down to the vital self-interests of groups: inter-species, intra-species, all the way down—in humanity's case—to individuals.

The Galactic races saw that last as a weakness. Stewart looked at it as an example of an adage he'd heard a couple of times around the O'Neals: "Alien minds are alien." This touched on one of the hidden benefits to the Tong of this association. Galactics were doing little to wrap their minds around xenopsychology as it applied from them to humans. The Tong was already gradually increasing its business transactions directly with various Galactics. The Tong didn't understand the xenopsychology of the Galactics well, either. Stewart had thought they did, had thought *he* did, but this little venture was quickly teaching him otherwise. If he could bring back the body of the O'Neal Bane Sidhe's xenopsych knowledge on the Galactics, and Clan O'Neal's more informal and perhaps more valuable experiential observations along the same lines, it would give the Tong a huge improvement in its bargaining strategies—an edge. He intended to get it for free, if possible, and as cheaply as he could, if otherwise.

He sat alone in Nathan's office because he was early for the meeting. He was also taking it upon himself to watch for Himmit. This was one meet where they were *not* included. Okay, so there already had been one when he came in. He happened to be looking in the right direction when it blinked. He didn't know enough about Himmit body language to tell whether it had been offended when he'd told it to get lost. He didn't know if Himmit *could* feel offended. This reminded him acutely of his lacks in understanding the various Galactics, which was glaring ignorance given that the Himmit were one of the Tong's bigger Galactic trading partners. Given the realities of shipping, and black market commerce generally, they had to be.

O'Reilly arrived early for the meeting, which only made sense since it was his office Stewart had decided to camp in.

"Himmit, if you would be so kind as to exit, we do need a small meeting alone," the priest said.

Stewart narrowly restrained the urge to jump as the alien peeled off the wall, resumed its normal froggy shape, and left via the door. He hadn't seen it come back in, or located it once it was here, and he'd been *looking*. Oh, well, that was the Himmit. He wondered how O'Reilly managed to see it.

After the Himmit was gone—again—and the door closed, O'Reilly whispered to him conspiratorially, "He has a favorite wall, and a few preferred spots even when he switches walls. It helps. Oh, damn." He looked at another wall. "Himmit Gannis, you too," he said.

The second Himmit peeled off the wall and exited the office. Stewart thought it was probably only his imagination that it slunk a bit.

"There goes *that* secret," the priest sighed. "So they didn't go away with no 'take' from the meeting. Drat.

"I'm glad you're here early, Mr. Stewart. I have some rather . . . delicate . . . personal information that concerns your wife, and you, of course. Oh, don't be alarmed. That sounds serious, but isn't."

"And?"

"Aelool may be bringing baked goods with him. It's usually brownies, but he's expanded into chocolate chip cookies and beer. I know, horrible combination. In any case, given your position and your capacity as a negotiator, I have to warn you. I can't let you be an unwitting test subject for Aelool's little experiment."

"Test subject?" Stewart didn't like where this was going. At all.

"Drat. I suppose it's my just deserts to get stuck with this. Aelool's been putting nannites in junk food to reprocess it, in the body, to be nutritionally complete. He's using some of the energy of the excess carbohydrates to 'fix' the food. It's a xenopsychology experiment to test his theory that humans prefer plant-based high carbohydrates, fats and sugars to meat. He views it as an evolutionary defect that we can't derive healthy nutrition from a diet of junk food and believes he can get humans to voluntarily give up meat, or at least reduce their intake, if they can substitute junk food and stay healthy. Wanting to target both sexes, he's focused on chocolate and beer."

"You've been feeding this stuff to my wife, haven't you?" he asked. "And she doesn't know."

"Well, yes," Nathan said. "Aelool was afraid if people realized the food was adjusted to be nutritious, they wouldn't like it as much. It was always perfectly safe, and the ethics overseen by our psych department."

"Uh-huh. You know she's gonna kill you, don't you?" Stewart asked. "Hey, wait a minute! You said it was in the beer. Would this perhaps include the black-market beer circulating around base?"

"I can't be held responsible for the contents of

black-market products," Nathan said virtuously. Then, upon realizing the other man wasn't buying it for a minute added, "I can't be sure, but probably. Why? You had some?"

"That I did. What are the side effects?" Stewart asked grimly.

"None that we know of. The nannites don't cross out of the digestive tract and they get excreted along with the rest of the contents. We've . . . had occasion to test that. One of the test subjects died in an auto accident and next of kin consented to an autopsy. They don't stick around. They go right on through."

"So this would be why I had so little appetite for dinner?" Stewart looked at the priest like a father looks at a ten-year-old who's just tried to get by with one too many things.

"You're right. I agree you're right. But once we were into the study . . ." Nathan shrugged. "Besides, all our people have a consent filed agreeing to non-standard medical treatment if it should be necessary for the state of their health."

"Uh-huh. That stretches 'necessary' way beyond the breaking point," Stewart said. "You guys are trying to land me with telling her, aren't you? You got yourselves into this."

"Yes, we did. But there is an advantage to the subjects, you know. The food we can afford to offer in the cafeteria tastes like crap, as you've certainly noticed. The brownies were free, and even though people chalked up their eating less from the cafeteria to being distaste for the food, at least some of that was that they had their nutritional needs met and didn't need to eat," O'Reilly reasoned.

"I'm sure you'll have fun telling Cally that," Stewart agreed. "Especially since she's so oversensitive about her weight. Needlessly."

"She's a beautiful woman. Unfortunately, Captain Makepeace's curvier figure isn't Cally's own, and it's not all self-consciousness. She's subconsciously trying to return to her own body. You'll notice that she has no problem realizing she's beautiful, she just doesn't like the weight—for the very good reason that it's not her own body. Anyway, if anything, the brownies have helped her efforts by letting her enjoy chocolate that tasted exactly like the real thing because it is, while satisfying her hunger and keeping her from downing needless calories," O'Reilly said.

"If you push it as an advanced, cutting-edge diet food, you might live," Stewart acknowledged.

"You couldn't possibly see your way clear . . ."

"Not on your life," Stewart said. Then he thought better of it. "I want the O'Neal Bane Sidhe's xenopsych analyses and general body of xenopsych knowledge of the various Galactics. It costs you no resources. A trade of favors."

Nathan smiled. "You're learning to play this game."

"I was born playing this game." Stewart's answering grin held the light of glee from a man who knows he's just swung himself one hell of a deal. Again.

Nathan O'Reilly waited as his colleague had a few words with Mr. Stewart. The Indowy Aelool was a very original thinker among his kind, not only having a genius for xenopsychology, but also having carefully acquired a certain understanding of business. He was one of the few Indowy with the grasp of the subject to appreciate the degree to which the evacuation loan arrangement Michelle had negotiated, God bless her, favored the Tong. He was unsurprised that Aelool had wanted to begin getting the groundwork for any future interactions between Clan Aelool and the Tong laid out on a more even footing.

He made meaningless chit-chat with Cally as they waited, his mind not really on it, which was all right, because hers wasn't either. She had her husband under the same roof and no likelihood of having to go out tonight. He still, after all these years, wondered what that kind of relationship would have been like.

She wouldn't know it, but her face had a kind of glow, her eyes more sparkle, when Stewart was in the room. Especially, as now, when she was watching him.

Whatever Stewart and Aelool had had to talk about was finished quickly, and the two joined them. Then, by unspoken agreement, he and Aelool stayed back while the happy couple went on their way. Nathan reflected that it was one of God's blessings that even in times of crisis like this one, there was still room for people to take a bit of joy. He watched fondly as they rounded the corner at the end of the hall. Heaven knew, Cally O'Neal had certainly earned herself *some* happiness.

"They did *what*?"

O'Reilly heard the feminine shriek from down the hall and winced. "Aelool?" he said. "Hide."

"The first thing we do, of course, is offer them terms. I don't know about you, but we avoid most actual pirate fights by getting them favorable out-migration contracts. Much cheaper than a fight," Lehman said.

"Agreed. While I've never paid anyone out of the contract fee, in your circumstances I would have, and you obviously managed to keep it quiet. I, of course, will do the same. Noising it about would hurt us almost as much as it would hurt you. Besides, it's a good ploy. However, we're fortunate in this case. Tir Dol Ron cares less that these people are dead, and more that they're off Earth and no longer *his* problem. I suspect the ship carrying them will suffer an unfortunate mishap; sad, but not our problem. *We* will have dealt with them fairly." His Elsie counterpart Carter adjusted the no-doubt scratchy red wool scarf around his neck. He had to be really feeling the cold to wear something so nonmilitary.

"Assuming they do fight, we also have to assume that we aren't going to get those other two humvees."

"No, but in this case that horse's ass was right. I *did* ask for more than you and I had discussed. He was clearly going to buy cheap, and I wanted parts, vehicles or replacements in case the vehicles he bought us broke down. Fortunately, we *have* got in some of the steel plating I requested. I suggest we boost the armor on the front a bit," Carter said.

"Not too much, or we'll be courting that breakdown," Lehman cautioned. "Plating for the men's vests is a problem. We haven't gotten enough, and what we have gotten is a mixed bag of decent composite and actual pre-war heavy shit."

"Obviously, we put the best gear on the men taking point," Carter said as the other general nodded. "I would suggest we spread the available plating out by only using the inserts in the front. That way each man has some armor protection where he's most likely to need it. If the men in the rear see fighting at all."

"Who do we put where?" Lehman hated having to ask the question, but since he wasn't in command, he was basically stuck with whatever General Carter decided.

"I can't in conscience spare my men at the expense of yours, if it comes to fighting." Carter sighed. "What I intend to do is spread the risk by putting half of my men on point, yours next, and half of my men in the rear. If we have to fight our way in there, we can expect significant losses. We both need to come out of this with viable organizations. I believe this is an equitable division of risk. You will notice, I hope, that I am putting Enterprise at risk of the most damage."

Lehman held his peace and simply nodded. He didn't miss that this arrangement put the Elsie troops fore and aft of his men. There was a certain implication of unreliability of his troops under fire, if he didn't accept Carter's logic. On the other hand, the arrangement did make sense in terms of spreading the damages between PS and Elsie, if it came to a fight. Since he wasn't in command and didn't have a choice, he chose to take the other general's reasoning at face value.

"I do think, thank god, that we have enough grenades," Carter said. "They're certainly the key. However, I'm going to have to make it clear to Mr. Mitchell that failure to provide C8 to blow Galplas will constitute a breach of contract. C4 simply will not do. For one thing, the door on the opposite end of the entryway will have to be blown. There's no other choice."

"Not to mention walls on the way down," Lehman nodded. "Don't you just wish we could keep our mouths shut and tell him he was in default at the last minute, when it was too late for him to do anything about it? This contract is turning into some serious suckage."

Friday, January 29, 2055

Bobby stood, hands on hips, watching his two latest patsies dump gasoline around the rural, wood frame house. Out of a lot of possibilities, this had just sat up and begged for attention. For some reason, most people had a positive horror of fire. Personally, he thought it was pretty cool, but whatever. It was useful.

The unlucky recipients of his attention tonight were an interesting collection. A lot of guys, of all kinds, wouldn't mind seeing their ex-wife offed. Usually wouldn't miss her new husband, either, since he may even have been fucking her before the divorce. The kids of the ex and new hubby, well, that would be a sad thing, but people died every day. Killing his own two, however, just might bite Harry Foster's ass. Even if Foster was a cast-iron bastard like Bobby, they were *his* kids. Bobby wouldn't let somebody get away with offing his own kids like this, if he'd had any. Oh, well. It oughta get a reaction from somebody, anyway.

The wood house was old, and the area was in a drought this year. It needed paint. Not that you could see that at night, but it was pretty obviously run down when he'd checked it out in daylight. Everybody honest was feeling the economic pinch. One more reason not to be one of the suckers in life.

Patsies weren't so much suckers as they were stupid. Another thing it was simply not good to be. Except Matt Prewitt was not as dumb as your usual patsy. Maybe not dumb at all. He'd confronted Bobby outright, in private, about their real role in this little operation. Thing was, he figured he could survive the search after. Knew a place he could get real good new ID, disappear. His additional price, which Bobby had been happy to pay, was to muddy the records, a lot, about his identity—in advance. It didn't cost a damned thing, and who knew? The skeletally thin skinhead might even make it. If he did, it was a damned good audition for more work. Bobby won either way. The longer Prewitt stayed ahead of them, the more tracks they would leave for Bobby. Bonus for his money. Well, the Tir's money, anyway.

They hadn't been too happy that he was going to stay back here, safe, while they did all the dirty work. A single cold look had quashed that. He wasn't paying them so he could do the shit himself. He was doing enough just being here in person to ensure they didn't fuck it up, which they really ought to be grateful for, since he wouldn't personally kill them for a salvageable mistake on the job like he would for a blown job. He figured he doubled these two guys' odds of survival just be being here to, so to speak, pull their chestnuts out of the fire if they fucked up.

Finally the base of the building was soaked all the way around. Big thing now was make sure nobody got out. He and Prewitt had the kitchen door at the back, Gorton had the front door. The back of the house had one of those big, country screened porches, so they'd see anyone coming out in plenty of time.

He and Gorton both had rifles, not because they couldn't have gotten closer and used pistols, but because there was a really neat way to start the fire, nice and safe, from a distance. He had gotten incendiary bullets as something his mercenaries had put him onto. No fuses, nothing to fuck up, just shoot the damn house near the bottom where all the gas was. Any old beginner could shoot a house, and he'd had these guys on simulators and out to a range to make sure they knew how to fire the damn guns well enough to do their job. Just because somebody said they could do something didn't mean they weren't full of shit. Bobby had survived and gotten to his current position not *just* out of nepotism, but because he always, always checked.

And, of course, he'd had himself checked out as well, because flaming bullets were cool and he wanted to get to fire at least one of them.

Prewitt was a bit of a gun nut. He'd come decked out in camo that didn't look military to Bobby—not like whatever he'd seen before—with multiple magazines for his rifle, with some kind of regular gun in a holster on his hip, and a big honking knife strapped to his opposite thigh. The effect was ruined by him having torn out the sleeves of the jacket to show off his tattoos. They were impressive tats, but it was kinda stupid when they were just lying around in the cold.

Matt Prewitt didn't like this job. He didn't particularly *dislike* it. Whoever was in the house was kind of un-people, as far as he was concerned. He didn't know them, he didn't give a shit, he was getting paid a fuckload of money. The job was high risk, but then you usually didn't get a fuckload of money for selling ice cream cones.

The biggest risk, of course, was that these folks had

some motherfuckers Bobby wanted to pull out in the open. Probably some fairly badass motherfuckers. That was the real risk, but he was cool with it. He'd gotten a bit too hot for comfort, anyway, and had been about to disappear and change his name, found the fixers for it and everything. That was the other big bonus for this job. Bobby was *connected*. He was connected about as high as you could be connected. Of course he hadn't said so, but with that kind of money, and no worries about them being caught? Bold enough to be along and not care? That meant he knew he could get it taken care of if they got pulled in. Taken care of good, and right the hell then. This back-ass end of nowhere was obviously not the guy's usual turf. Hence, connected and connected up high.

He'd insisted Bobby fuck the records on his real ID to make him unfindable. In advance. Bobby had agreed, no problem. Matt had checked, and it was solid. Again, proof he was connected.

So all Matt had to do was do his job and stay alive, and maybe *he* could become connected, too. That was as high in the scheme of things as a guy like him could ever hope to rise. The big enchilada.

Before he disappeared, he really ought to do something for Alice. She was his sister; the only girl out of a handful of brothers. She'd just had her fourth kid. A kid's uncle was important. Fortunately, a couple of his brothers were of a nice guy turn of mind and cared about the little brats. He spent a lot of time with the oldest boy, but figured four might be just too loud for his tastes. Still, his brothers didn't have much, because the pay for being a nice guy sucked. He'd be doing okay after this, so he'd leave a good chunk with Barry. Barry was so straight it was like he got all the nice Matt missed. He'd make sure Alice didn't smoke it, drink it, or shoot it.

Speaking of shoot, his lack of attention was getting noticed. Bobby and Gorton had already fired, starting the blaze. A corner of the house hadn't gone up. The bedrooms. Prewitt obligingly put his round in and insured a good, fast finish to the job. This was the part that would really suck, if anyone came this way. The fire was loud enough that they probably wouldn't hear any screaming. Hopefully.

The first thing out their door was a cat, ghost white in the light of the full moon. Bobby fired a shot off at it, but the boss's marksmanship sucked, and Prewitt didn't see no point to shooting the damn cat.

"Why didn't you shoot?" Bobby asked accusingly.

"Ah, it was just a cat. Nobody feeds it here they'll never find the damn thing anyway. Wasn't expecting anything that little, and those suckers are fast," he improvised.

The bossman couldn't argue that without making himself look bad, since he'd missed, too.

"We're still watching the door, right?" Prewitt asked, giving the guy an unsubtle reminder that it was *his* goddamned job and did he want it done, or what?

"Yeah." The cat was forgotten.

They had one taker to come running out the kitchen door. Woman. Her nightgown was one of those long things, or a robe. It was on fire, making her look like something out of a movie. Prewitt took the head shot just as he realized she was carrying something. As she hit the ground, the baby began to cry.

Beside him, Bobby took a shot, probably a mercy

shot for the kid, but missed. Then the guy actually got up, pulling at Prewitt's shoulder.

"Oh, well. Gotta go," he said.

"Right." Prewitt got to his feet, drawing his nine mil Glock in one smooth motion and putting two rounds into the back of Bobby's head. "Even I wouldn't leave a baby to burn, you sick son of a bitch," he said as the body hit the ground.

Matt turned and sprinted for the house. What the hell, he wasn't getting paid now, anyway.

The fire was burning fast, fast through the dry house, especially with all the accelerant. Matt Prewitt ignored the flames, taking the stairs two at a time and wrenching the outer porch door off its hinges in his adrenaline burst.

He scooped up the baby and turned back down the stairs. The next to top one, one he hadn't hit on the way up, collapsed under his weight, pitching him forward. Instinctively, he rolled to protect the child, feeling his ankle snap as he went down. Above him, the beam across the top of the porch fell in, to slide down the collapsing hand rail and land squarely across his back, flaming, trapping him. Turning onto his stomach in a vain effort to work free, wiggling the rest of the way down until the baby and his hands were on the compressed dirt path at the bottom of the stairs before he stuck fast, Prewitt reflected that it was good news and bad news that he couldn't feel his legs.

As the flames really started to bite, Matthew Lamar Prewitt did his final good deed, one of the few in his life. He slid his hands right under the baby and rolled, hard, sending it turning like a little log, out of reach of the flames and smoke.

Mercifully, the smoke from the burning stairs got him before the fire did. Prewitt had one final word to cough before losing consciousness. "Alice?"

On the lawn, little Victoria Menendez began to squall herself hoarse, in which condition Gary Ward, of the Rabbittown Volunteer Fire Department, found her half an hour later.

Bobby had forgotten one cardinal rule that the worst of the worst usually took care to remember. Even criminals have families.

CHAPTER TWENTY-THREE

They couldn't use a conference room for the meeting. None of them were big enough. The atrium, however, had multiple advantages. For one thing, it could accommodate all thirty of the combat-ready DAGgers. including Maise. Then there were the operations teams, which had a certain overlap with some of the DAG troops who had been training for small group covert ops, urban and otherwise, Bane Sidhe style. Then there were the cybers and forensics people who had been instrumental in tracking down the killers and, lastly, the support staff—the cleaners, the cover prep people, the psyops profilers, the general intel weenies. Cally even noticed that a couple of the food service people had managed to snag themselves a spot on the list.

It was natural. Everybody wanted to be in on this. They had, they believed, identified every individual who took part in the murders of DAG dependents and other loved ones. There were red noses and eyes here and there. The strangest case of hay fever had seemed to sweep through the base personnel and temporary residents all at once.

Charis Thomason was a lovely black woman. She was no juv, and she was carrying about fifty pounds more weight than she should, but she had a vitality that was at odds with the intel stereotype. Her mahogany complexion held a glow, and her coal-black eyes sparkled as if life was a joke only she seemed to get.

Tonight, she had abandoned her normal good humor, and her glow radiated another emotion entirely. She stood beside a high-quality, nearly new holotank, a big one, gripping a fiberglass pointer across her front like a sheathed sword.

"Ladies and gentlemen, I believe it's seven now, so I'll get started. First of all, I'd like to thank Team Isaac for bringing in the AID of one John Earl Bill Stuart," she said, tapping the pointer into the tank's projection area like a magic wand, and a head shot holo of the man appeared, triggering a palpable wave of hatred in the room. "This device was the key piece of evidence that allowed us to pull all our other information into a cohesive picture of who and how many."

She paused while people looked around to Cally's team, who were sitting together towards the back. The clapping was rhythmic, fierce, but it stopped quickly as everyone was focused on the information, not the kudos.

"I'd also like to thank all the teams who brought in all the forensic evidence, of all kinds," she said gravely. At another smattering of applause, she held up her hands, "Please, people. There's more than enough people to thank, but I think people want to know what the end game is."

This elicited a growl.

"Our first murder was Cordelia Beadwindow, niece of Sergeant Kevin Adams. We have two perpetrators. Robert "Bobby" Mitchell is Mr. Stuart's direct contractor, and we believe is the architect of these attacks. We do not have his location. He hired all amateurs. He, of course, was using them as stalking horses and intended for us to find them. He does not wish to be found himself. We *will* find him. As the saying goes, he can run, but he'll just die tired.

"Sarah Andersen." The display broke into a block of nine images, a head shot in the center of a very pretty, even beautiful, blond girl. The other images showed a number of images of the kind people posted on the internet of themselves. Bikini, drunken partying, prom dress, even a nude, as well as a security cam image of the same woman, light brunette. "Miss Andersen was a brunette for the crime, but usually wears her hair blond, and has returned to doing so. While she has no criminal record other than one count of underage drinking, I'm sure it will surprise no one that the little charmer socially terrorized her high school until she graduated two years ago. Envy driven sociopath, but obviously, money will do.

"Miss Andersen lured Cordelia Beadwindow over to Mr. Mitchell, who did the killing. His DNA was found at the scene, Andersen's was not. We do not believe she participated in the actual killing. Not that we care."

The intelligence department's VP tapped again, changing the scene to a middle-aged woman with her husband, apparently at a barbecue or picnic. She was laughing and looked nice, her straight, light brown hair cut in a gentle pageboy, sans bangs. "Leellen Beadwindow. The bastards took over her car, ran her into a bridge, and then to make sure she was dead, they set off an incendiary charge under the wreck. Civilian autopsy indicated that she was killed by the fire."

Another tap, and the picture changed to an older man with weathered, wrinkled skin—the kind that indicated he didn't laugh much.

"The driver of the car. He left the tire marks of his *personal* vehicle and a cigarette butt at the scene."

There were several snickers in the room, mostly from the direction of field teams.

"We have high confidence that that is the total number of participants in the Beadwindow murders."

"Next to the Coacher murder." She waved the pointer and a man's head appeared with a large red X in front of it. "Cullen Wayne Foster, deceased. Thank you, Team Bowie."

Again the room growled. The difference between its prior anger and its present satisfaction was palpable. A number of growls came out "hoo-rah!" Variations echoed from people who had a more specific service history and felt the need to be heard.

"The Maise murders. For the sake of the family present, I will be brief." Thomason had obviously prepared for this specific contingency. Four heads appeared in the tank at once. "From the top left, Robert Mitchell, again. Rahab Graber Bender, aka Candy Leighton." The aging, bleached blonde was no Marilyn Monroe. Not quite over the hill, but compared to the fresh-faced juv girls in the Bane Sidhe ops teams, late twenties looked a bit past the cheap whore's sell-by date.

"Below, Gordy Pace, no middle name, and—" The man on the lower right had a satisfying red X over his face. "—Reginald Erbrechen, deceased. Thank you, Cally."

The thanks had a note of irony, and Cally O'Neal got more than a few accusing looks. There had been a number of people who had devised creative ways for the captive to die, and were very disappointed not to be in on carrying them out.

The other woman's only response was a minuscule nod of acknowledgment, as if killing the man had been a minor administrative detail. Which, of course, it was. Smart way to play it, though. Just a professional matter. Bootleg copies of that segment of the holo were circulating widely, and provided some salve on the disappointments from not doing it personally or protractedly.

"The Swaim murders are the last we have. So far," Charis sighed. They were really going to have to hustle and take out Billy-Bob, which was the collective name she privately assigned to the duo. Their deaths should at least create an operational pause in the kin murders.

"Horton Huey Scout," she said, changing the image to the next perpetrator.

"I'd wanna kill somebody, too," someone mumbled from the back.

"Horton Huey Scout," she repeated. The man was a short, much-freckled redhead. "No, he's not a relative," she said. "Buckley footage of the scene, forensic accounting. He's guilty as hell. Next."

"Bradley Willard Farris." This one was tall and rangy, of indeterminate ethnicity. "We only had approximate height and weight from our footage, but he picked up the money with Scout, has known him for awhile, and footage from various cameras places him in Orlando at approximately the right time. Since he's from Topeka, that amazing coincidence is enough that we're confident ordering his execution. I somehow doubt anyone here has a problem with that.

"That's it. We know who they are, we know where they are. They each stand condemned by the security council and are on the execution list as priority targets. We will be sending teams to carry out sentence. Are there any questions?" The last was meant to be rhetorical.

"Comment," Cally said.

"Yes, Cally?" Charis replied.

"There have been . . . discussions regarding this mission," Cally said. "One of the problems with sending out half the damned Bane Sidhe, Clan O'Neal and DAG on seek and destroy missions is that if the Darhel don't know where we are now, they're probably going to figure it out. One way to avoid this is to just give all the information to the police and let them handle it."

The muttering that accompanied that statement was the sort of mutter Captain Bligh heard on the *Bounty* just before he got tossed in a rowboat.

"But let me explain," Cally said coldly. "No, let me summarize. One: Chain of evidence is broken. Two: The Tir will make it all go away even if it's not. He may make the patsies go away, permanently, but that's not the point. Three: Oh. Hell. *No*.

"For years," she said, striding onto the stage and

walking back and forth, "we have been fighting in the shadows. For centuries among the Bane Sidhe. For most of my own life and that's been a long-damned time. We have taken hits. We have had teams taken out. We have lost too many good people. But there was a code. No Darhel, no military and *no dependents*.

"Because it was fight the good guys, us, or go into the cold, DAG went into the cold," Cally said. "O'Neal and non-O'Neal, no muss, no fuss, no bitching, they dropped *everything* they had built in their lives and went into the cold. Because they believed in what we are fighting.

"And now the damned Darhel are going after their *families*? Their *children*?

"If you're a DAGger, you're an O'Neal, dammit," she growled, voice dropping so low it was almost a whisper, every word distinct. "These dead, your dead, are *our* dead, too. Your blood is *our* blood. We know who they are, we know where they sleep. For DAG and the honor of Clan O'Neal, these fuckers are going down—and right the hell now." Cally O'Neal's eyes burned like live coals, a fiery witch-blue that promised debts paid in full.

"DAG and Clan!" someone shouted it, and it erupted into a roar that echoed through the atrium, rafters to floor.

Saturday, January 30, 2055

The complication of this job was that Sarah Andersen had moved from her crappy dorm room into a nice apartment in a gated suburb. Normally, this would

have presented a trivial matter for a cyber to deal
with, hardly more difficult than tying a shoelace.
Unfortunately, it was currently trendy to have a gate-
house with a real live guard manning it.

Tommy wondered if the target had been smart
enough to choose this kind of neighborhood because
the gate was a strategic choke point for trouble, in
which case she might have it electronically monitored
and run through a buckley for analysis, or if she just
chose it because of the fad. Conspicuous consumption, Fifties style.

Either way, they'd be bypassing it.

The nice thing about places like this was their
marketing. Any security features they had that were
useful were a selling point for the apartments—so
they were all in the brochure on the net. No dogs,
no internal camera system out of concerns for the
residents' privacy, just a big brick wall and a manned
front gate.

It would have been easier if the target's apartment
was in a building next to a wall, but no such luck.
After they went over the wall, they'd have to walk
inward to get to her building.

They'd be using the easiest, most trite ruse in the
world to do that. Lovers. He and Cally would be a
pair; Sands and George would be a pair. Costuming
had forced George into elevator shoes for this, and
the team had given him no end of shit for it over
dinner. Even though Sands was only five-four, the
cover people had thought he'd look more authentic
if he were a couple of inches taller. If "authentic"
wasn't too clumsy a word, George probably would
have found himself stuck with a new nickname.

Lovers as an insertion ruse was trite because it was so damned effective. Since the Bane Sidhe liked to have at least one female per team, they had it down to an art.

The art was slightly marred when Cally slipped going over the wall and ripped a small hole in her jeans, skinning her knee. That wasn't good. He made a mental note to tell the cleaners about it as he wrapped his arm around her shoulder and kissed her in the darkness. First thing you did on insertion. Lovers were often furtive. If anyone had noticed them being furtive, they'd assume the reason.

Despite what he'd said to George, it was *not* like kissing his sister. He was a normal guy, not impervious to her charms, nor she to his, which was a damn good thing. If there was no spark *at all*, it was hard to pull this off convincingly. Fortunately, they'd worked together long enough that just because there was the normal chemistry you'd expect didn't mean they were going to turn into raging lust bunnies over each other. Part of the job. They'd done it before, they'd do it again.

It was a little like kissing the chick you took to the movies when you were interested in her friend but couldn't get anywhere. Nice, yeah. The obvious turn on, yeah. He was just glad he was rarely paired with George.

Sands was nice. She was also obviously practical as all shit. Not a romantic bone in that girl's body. When Papa got back and Sands was on some other team, he might nudge her to see what she could do for George. Fellow operators made good playmates. Everybody was a juv, everybody understood the job, everybody understood the risks, but you didn't do incest in your own team. Mostly, they kept it to no strings play.

Of course he went for the wandering hands, to give Cally something to slap with visible insincerity. Whoa. That one was real. He winced, making a mental note not to do *that* again.

"Ow," he muttered against her lips.

"You're lucky it was just a slap. Here's our building. Shut up and kiss me," she whispered, stopping just in the shadows away from one of the streetlamps.

He forbore to mention that she was the one talking, not him. Logic didn't come into it, and his hand stung already. After a few minutes of sticking to acceptable transgressions, she grabbed him by the lapels of his coat and tugged him to the front door of the building, managing to stay all over him on the way.

Cally picked the lock on the door, backwards, one-handed, while pulling off her coat, as quickly as if she'd had a key. After thirty years in the field, some things got automatic. If any long-time resident happened to actually know who their neighbors were and recognize that the two didn't belong, they were already marked down as harmless. Lovers didn't usually consider burgling to be a hot date.

She propped her ass against the stair railing, feet spread, and he stepped between them to continue the charade of people who were about to go upstairs and have wild monkey sex. God, was he ever glad Wendy couldn't see this. She'd have his guts for garters.

George and Amy came in hand in hand, looking young, sweet, and glowing. To look at Sands' lively, cheerful eyes, you'd never suspect what was behind them.

Upstairs, after her buckley indicated no IR source close to the apartment door, Cally shrugged and picked the lock. She and Tommy were through, fast, splitting to each side. Tommy was on the hinges side, so it was Cally who slapped a husher onto the wall next to the door.

Sands and George were through the door between them as they split, passing through to the kitchen as Tommy and Cally finished clearing the living room.

"Clear," Tommy said as he and Cally hit the hall leading back to the bedrooms. It was a two bedroom, two bath floor plan.

"Clear."

Cally and Tommy heard George say it through their ear dots. It had the hollow sound of words spoken near an active husher which, of course, it was. Per SOP, as soon as they hit the kitchen Sands or Schmidt would have slapped a husher on the wall. Probably both of them. Sands hadn't had a chance to get that sixth sense about your teammates—where they were, what they were doing, where they were going to be next—nor had they with her.

Cally and Tommy turned into the first bedroom as Sands took the bathroom across the hall, George covering the hallway itself.

"Clear."

"Clear."

Down the hall, the door at the end was to the master bedroom. As he and Cally took up positions on each side of it, he heard a cough and saw Cally's arm jerk, blood welling. He registered it in an instant, as Sands kicked the door in and he and she entered, automatically splitting for halves of the room, but Sands got the prize.

A woman, the target, screamed, "I didn't do it! I didn't know—"

Tommy heard two sharp cracks as Sands nailed the target's center of mass.

"—what he was going to do," she trailed, as Sands' pistol came down the second time from recoil.

It cracked again, and a red hole appeared in the target's forehead, brains and blood blasting out the exit wound to splatter on the wall behind her.

"Yeah, but you knew what he *did*," Sands said grimly.

"See? Lesson one. Don't talk until *after* the target's dead." She grinned brightly at Tommy.

"I knew I liked her," Cally grinned at Sands from the doorway where George had divested her of her coat and sleeve and was finishing a field dressing.

"Noise?" Sands asked, then her eyes fixed on the husher stuck just inside the door.

Tommy saw it register with her that the sound did have that hollowness.

"I got it. You looked a bit busy," Cally said, stepping in to take a better look at the body. "Damn, Sands, that was as near perfect as you can get. Surgical. *Nice.*"

Team Kemuel was pure Bane Sidhe, and had been around long enough to develop its own traditions, one of which included a motto, "Justice flies on swift wings." They also had a tradition of planning their ops in a poetic direction whenever it absolutely would not interfere with the mission. Operational requirements were first and always, but Kemuel's pride was applying enough creativity to their planning to do both, without getting too cute.

They had asked for this target specifically. Adam Marcus Ludlum, a fence now, wheelman in his younger days, he lived with his aging mother and had elected to do one last wheel job because the money was right. It was his last wheel job, all right. Participating in the murder of Leellen Beadwindow had been a very bad choice.

It was three in the morning when they picked the lock and let themselves in. The nature of this mission was in speed rather than subtlety. The four of them had slouched in, walking, from two different directions. Leaving would be simpler. Straight out the front door, which faced right onto the street, into the car and out.

They cleared the rooms with brisk efficiency, popping the old mother with a Hiberzine dart, and darting the target as well. It was as easy as a bullet. Easier, as a dart gun had no recoil.

One of the team walked over to the bed and methodically smashed in Ludlum's brains with a tire iron. Another stood on the opposite side of the bed, leaning down to inject the Hiberzine antidote. The dead man's heart would keep beating long enough to ensure he bled out and stayed dead. Not much chance of revival with his brains smashed like a rotten tomato, but professionals made sure.

The executioner dropped the tire iron on the bed as the easiest way to dispose of it. The others had begun policing up the hushers as soon as the second target dropped. The last man out injected the mother with the Hiberzine antidote and the medically prescribed dose of tranquilizer, for her age and condition, to knock her out until morning. That she'd never met the doctor who prescribed it was of no moment.

It would have been better to have burned him, but impractical. It didn't matter that much; he'd be burning now.

The team driver, as soon as they piled out of the building and into the car, didn't glance back as she began her E and E work. "Go okay?" she asked.

"Like a fine Maserati."

It was snowing in Topeka. Team Bowie was coordinating with Team Fairbairn, as their targets lived very close together. Buddies who worked at the local Coca-Cola bottling plant and drove to and from work together. The plan was for Bowie to stake out a necessary part of their route home, and Fairbairn to set up observers closer on the route to their target's home. Access to and from Farris's home had very limited routing, and they thought they could set up observers without their observers being observed. The enemy's people were almost certainly watching for the actual hit. They were unlikely to be watching every fast food restaurant or strip mall along the way. Particularly, they were unlikely to be watching the Dairy Queen where Bowie had parked.

When Farris arrived, if he didn't leave with Scout— Bowie's target—he was going nowhere. They could regroup and take him at night. Bowie would give advance warning, then use the timing to make verification of their target's presence at home quick and unobtrusive.

Luke Landrum had armed the Reardon girl with no reservations. The driver needed to be armed, and it didn't matter a damn that she was thirteen. She was an O'Neal. Tramp and Kerry had gotten used to her age. They'd seen on the first op that she was one hell of a combat driver—a natural. With a wheel in her hands, she had the agility and cunning of the fox that made the dogs cry. They tried hard not to patronize her. It didn't seem healthy.

Right along after quitting time for second shift at the plant, here came Mutt and Jeff's car. True to plan, as soon as they'd buckleyed in the update to Fairbairn, Reardon gave the targets about a minute's head start and pulled out of the DQ to get them to point B.

That was peachy until up ahead they saw hazard flashers through the heavy snow at a green traffic light.

"Turn off, turn off," Landrum ordered.

"Where?" Reardon asked.

The windows on the car were all frosted up, protecting them further from view. Thank God for small mercies. It wasn't enough to stop him swearing, but Bowie's team lead at least swore silently. That he was still swearing could probably be seen from the steam pouring out of his ears.

Then the light turned red. Jenny Reardon came to a careful stop on the icy road.

Sensing help had arrived, the targets walked over to the driver's side window and Mutt, their driver, knocked on it.

"Boy, am I glad to see you!" Jeff said as Jenny rolled down the window.

"Ditto," Jenny said with a smile. Two rounds into each body had them on the ground and twitching. She had to sit up in her seat to put one round into each head. They entered under the chin and more or less took off the top.

"Blood on the door," she said as the traffic light

turned to green. "And it's freezing. *That's* gonna to take some clean-up."

"That was *not* the plan," Landrum said angrily.

"What were we going to do?" Jenny asked. "Give them a lift to their place and then cap them? Like our DNA wouldn't have gotten on the bodies? Cap them in the car and then deal with the bodies? Plan was *blown*."

"Luke," Tramp said. "She's right. You're just bitching because she aced us out of a kill on those scum. I'm pissed, too. But it was quick thinking and it was clear. Now let her get us out of here."

"We are *so* going to talk," Landrum snarled.

About three miles down the road, as she negotiated a nasty turn with a smoothness that really amazed him, he sighed.

"How you doing? First kill."

"Me?" Jenny asked with a thoughtful frown. It cleared quickly. "I can't *wait* to tell the kids at school! 'I got to cap a bad guy! I got to cap a bad guy!' They're going to be *green*."

"I hate O'Neals," Kerry muttered.

The Sub-Urb door was one of the originals. Normally, GalTech stuff didn't break. It wasn't designed to resist people breaking it deliberately. But this one still worked, which made things easy. It was supposed to make a programmed sound on opening to cue the resident to entry. Trivial work for even an incompetent cyber—which was probably why people tended to break and replace their doors. Candy hadn't.

The door slid open soundlessly, and a man known to the community as "Sevin" slapped a husher on the wall inside. He used his off hand, of course. His strong hand remained on his pistol as he and his buddy split the room.

"Clear."

"Clear."

The other two men on Team Ka-Bar were moving almost before the second all clear came. For this mission, it didn't much matter that they were all DAGgers, not Bane Sidhe. It was a textbook op of how to take out a personality. Capture not necessary or desired. The op was so simple it would have been insulting if it weren't for one key detail: this bitch was one of the motherfuckers who did the Maise massacre.

Charlie Maise was a fellow DAGger. The whole unit wanted Candy Leighton dead with a passion beyond words. It was DAG's right to take vengeance, and their own privilege to be on the team that got to do so. They'd all fantasized for long hours on creative ways to off the bitch, but in the end they'd kill her like the professionals they were. Get in, accomplish the objective, get out.

In operational mode, they were all instantly aware of little details like the target's revolting slobbiness, all the more glaring to military men, accustomed to strict neatness. The men's clothes scattered across the floor told them what they'd find in the single bedroom. One of the initial entry pair gathered up the clothes as his buddy, their team lead, covered him.

One of the second pair glanced in the bathroom in the short hallway on the way past. "Clear."

They were through the bedroom door, the man on the jam side emplacing another husher as they entered. He demonstrated why DAGgers practiced shooting one-handed, putting a bullet cleanly between the eyes of the woman in the bed. Her fuck for the night had his head between her legs, and was out of the way.

He held his fire for the follow-up shot, since there was no telling what the guy might do. He and his partner had their guns trained firmly on the guy.

This room was a mess, too. It smelled like a men's locker room.

"Be very, very still. Did you piss or shit?" the shooter asked.

The gray-faced, naked man shook his head.

"Good," he said.

The back-up shot the guy with a Hiberzine dart.

"Make sure there's not a trace of him," the team lead said.

CHAPTER TWENTY-FOUR

Indianapolis Sub-Urb West owed its present condition to the enlightened benevolence of the Indiana legislature. Indiana was not Illinois. Indiana had far less money to waste on dry wells like social programs for Sub-Urb residents.

Sub-Urbs were simply not economically sustainable communities. Indiana's post-war economy was much like its pre-war economy. Manufacturing and farming, the former spread through a network of smaller cities, with the latter obviously distributed out as well.

The problem with Sub-Urbs was they concentrated people in places where there weren't enough jobs to employ them all. People in Sub-Urbs generally weren't too good about going onto the surface to look for jobs. Manufacturing jobs still tended to concentrate in the hands of union members, anyway, meaning multigeneration hoosiers. Sub-Urbs became slums of multigenerational losers, who were a drain on resources. The hydroponics systems in the basement that had once fed them had become, if not exactly broken, fouled to the point of same by mishandling. In the multigeneration brain drain that followed the end of the Postie War, competent hydroponics techs had found better paying work elsewhere, as had the other competent people who had kept the systems working as a captive audience at slave wages.

The Indiana legislature had decided it was better to pay a bit more for Sub-Urbanites once and get rid of them than it was to keep paying, and paying, and paying. They had a vigorous program of job training for careers that, coincidentally enough, would take the graduates someplace other than Indiana. A condition of training being vacating the Sub-Urb upon graduation, Indiana was slowly emptying the behemoths with a view to eventually shutting them down.

Indianapolis West Urb, home to one Gordy Pace, was about half empty. Gordy's own hall was even emptier than that. The man lived alone in three-bedroom quarters intended for a family. He'd had one, until he came home one day to find his wife had taken the kids and skipped off with a freshly trained bounty farmer wannabe. He supposed he could've smacked her less when he was drunk, but the woman had been damned irritating sometimes, and the kids loud. He didn't miss her at all, even though the place seemed kinda empty and he cooked worse than his ten-year-old daughter. He ate the crappy food in the crappy mess hall and tried to ignore his crappy life. Except that was all changing now.

Gordy was smart with his money. He had a brand new car, a union spot for the steel mills up north, and money to buy himself someplace to live that he could afford. Someplace out of this crappy hole in the ground. Only reason he wasn't gone yet was because he had had to get it all set up, and it wouldn't have been any fun without partying around a bit in front of friends, acquaintances, the sanctimonious bastards who got him kicked off the force, and the two bit whores who had been too good for him until he got himself his ticket out. And not to no shitty bounty farm.

He sure as hell wasn't putting off the trip out of any love for this goddamned rat hole. Hell, he was still tripping over the kids' discarded toys and crap.

Tonight, he was taking a break from crowing it up to have a quiet evening watching the latest blockbuster holo and downing a six pack or two of beer. Same as he'd done last night. Tomorrow he was really going to have to start packing up his shit. He stretched and noticed his T-shirt was tight. Good thing he was buying new clothes. There was a downside to being able to afford more beer.

The money had come in exchange for a really nasty piece of work, but if he had it to do over again he'd do the same. It was a ticket out of here. Life was unfair, and when bad things happened, it was better if they didn't happen to him.

Team Jacob specialized in the trickiest short-term cover assignments. Each of them was a seasoned operator, slabbed over ten years ago. They all looked perfectly ordinary, yet different enough to not be attention-getting identicals. Medical had carefully balanced their DNA changes to pass cursory examination of the commonly typed DNA factors as ninety-nine plus percent certainly a single individual. Charlie Smith had a well-constructed record as a jobless, alcoholic laborer in Minneapolis, a sad victim of homelessness. The females typed as first degree relatives of the males.

They were the best team for a Sub-Urb hit, and frequently performed same. Old jeans, old sneakers, and a faded, dark blue T-shirt were as invisible as they themselves. Team Jacob had the lowest cover and costuming overhead in the whole organization.

For this job, they used a standard four-man entry team, their two female field operatives playing lookout. Since they couldn't and shouldn't be strikingly attractive, team members were scintillatingly charming and witty—but only at will. Charisma from someone who wasn't too good looking was effective on both sexes, depending on how they played it. The women stood lookout, invisible until and unless they needed to divert someone away from the action.

If there was any trace DNA at all, the "crime" would have been committed by one man, acting alone. Ex-cops always had enemies.

The entry team took the subtle approach on Pace's wooden replacement door—they kicked it in, not even bothering with hushers. The hall was half vacant, and the crime rate in the Urb tended to cause residents to conspicuously mind their own business. Sub-Urb quarters had no front windows to peek through. Noise would keep the other residents in their quarters better than silence.

Sometimes building clearing went quicker than others. This time was as quick as you could get. The bastard was in his easy chair in front of the HV. Cap him beyond repair, and get the hell out.

"Done," the team lead dropped the single word to his PDA, its only transmission, getting the instant receipt codes that told him the message got to both lookouts unjammed.

Getting into a Sub-Urb for a mission, even undetected, was easy. Out . . . not so much. The watching opposition would find it easy as hell to shut down the elevators and exit.

Agent Kacey Grannis retreated to the nearest public lounge and grabbed a table. She typed a single word into the virtual keyboard of her AID and her tiny foot in the door to the Sub-Urb's system expanded to complete control. She had to have the AID. The opposition sure as hell would have one, if they were any good. Parity made this a matter of skill. The mission hung on the bet that Kacey would be better and luckier than the competition.

Unfortunately, measures, countermeasures, and counter-countermeasures were a neverending arms race. She had to stay at her post until the rest of Jacob was all the way out, then hope her final run of hacks held long enough to get out herself. She had prepared herself mentally and physically in case she wasn't good enough or lucky enough. This time. Many a cyber had learned that you didn't tell a Bane Sidhe AID to purge beyond possibility of retrieval unless you *really* meant it. Virtually indestructible, it did the person capturing it little good to have a machine scrubbed all the way down to the hard-coded OS and blank personality. Unless the first guy to get his hands on it happened to want his own AID.

Her own preparations would, sadly, almost certainly cause collateral damage. High enough heat guaranteed full destruction of DNA. Kacey was wired to hell, and it wasn't with caffeine.

Her counterpart took point on the way out. Stephanie

Lyle had wired up for a different reason. Far enough ahead of the others, her destruction would be a diversion, if necessary, in a last-ditch effort to get the rest of the team out.

The boys in the rear had preparation, but less complete. While partial destruction would reveal the fake genome in the event of a thorough search, with the entire team burned, the genome became expendable. The hitters had made a trade-off between risks if Pace's quarters contained too many surprises. No need to set one of them off by accident and kill them all.

Grannis sighed resignedly. Her competition was good. Too good. As fast as her routines created security holes for her, the other guy found and shut them down. No AID had the intuition to keep up with a top cracker like herself—or her opponent. At their level, this was strictly a PvP game. She got the rest of the team out, barely, but she was about out of tricks.

"Joseph, send by voice, then do a complete purge," she told the AID, while backing into a Galplas corner as far away from people as possible, and under a vent. The blast would have somewhere else to go in addition to the lounge itself. For whatever good that did.

"Are you sure?" it asked.

"Asherah," she replied.

"Ready," it answered. As loyal to the Bane Sidhe as she was, the AID still sounded faintly regretful.

"Goodbye, guys," she said simply. Nobody ever said an "I'm fucked" code had to be meaningless.

As a man dropped from the vent onto her head, Kacey Grannis' final words ignited her implosion, joining her with her enemy in what he had never expected to be his final union.

The AID landed fused into what remained of the granite tile flooring, Joseph having already departed for whatever afterlife might be reserved, somewhere, for martyred AIs.

Jacob had scatter-and-go-to-ground engraved by long experience. Dogs, or the technological equivalent, couldn't even follow them. They all smelled the same. A crowded and very large club downtown had gear pre-planted. A club with four convenient exits, all in common use.

The driver ditched the car at the curb, ignoring the complaints of the guy at the door and the line by stuffing a wad of bills into the door dude's hands.

"Rest of the current line, no cover charge, on us," Stephanie said.

There was still grumbling, but as the word passed back it subsided to a few disgruntled murmurs.

The survivors of Team Jacob were into the club before the men following them were half out of their own cars. The tails had not come prepared with wads of cash, which didn't really matter as the same trick wouldn't have worked twice, anyway.

Inside, the five men and one woman dispersed into the crowd, making for restrooms in different parts of the three-story building, themed on heaven, hell, and purgatory. Jacob came prepared. In less than ten minutes, most of those taken up getting through the crowds, the five were in club clothes with very different hair. In less than fifteen, they had met up with their prearranged dates, broken the news to Kacey's date that she wouldn't be coming, after all, and began exfiltrating in pairs mixed in with groups.

The dates, hired from an escort service and told to look like real dates—a not uncommon request—were happy to get paid their full fees for simply delivering each team member to a motorcycle at various locations. Smaller and more agile than a car, bikes could shake anything they could outrun, which in this case was damned near everything.

A nice game of drunkard's walk later, the cycles went into the back of a semi for later retrieval, and five nondescript people piled into a middle-aged minivan and took off for home. The ride was silent and sober. They'd lost one of the family. That they'd exchanged a seasoned professional for a brainless wife-beater didn't come into it. Every last killer of the Maise family had to die. Any time they went out, all of them knew they might not come back. Kacey had died taking care of business. Sooner or later, each of them expected to do the same. It was an hour before Stephanie finally gave in to the silence and dialed up a song off the current cube. Whether horses drank beer or not, the song felt right. Nobody had whiskey, which was a damned shame. The team stopped at a liquor store just off the interstate and fixed that problem; they hit repeat a lot on the way home.

Shane Gilbert didn't complain about having to be the sober driver in a car full of drunks. It wasn't the night for complaining. He just grunted at the bottle of Bushmills Black they'd put aside for later, five brand new glasses clicking lightly in a brown paper bag. It must have cost a fortune, but who gave a fuck?

Pinky Maise looked down at the claymore mine Lish Mortenson, whom he'd been told to just call Lish, had just planted and restrained a groan. The grass around it was bent every which way and it was sitting right out visible, with a bare handful of grass scattered casually over the top.

"Aren't we supposed to camouflage them?" he asked her.

"Oh, the snow tonight will cover that right up," she said.

"What if it melts?" he asked.

She sighed like an adult faced with a child who was at the age to ask questions about everything. Pinky mentally acknowledged that he *was* at that age, but that didn't mean the questions weren't sometimes important. Unfortunately, Lish had the brains of a frog.

"Can I cover them up? Can I? If it won't hurt anything, then I can, can't I? Pleeeaase . . ." he wheedled. Lish had been warned he was smart, but even if she'd paid attention to the warning, he'd have run rings around her. In his sleep. He went into full eager, slightly obnoxious kid mode. Sure enough, she agreed to let him do it just to get him out of her hair.

Not that he'd set them off, he thought as he covered the mine with ground debris, straightening up the nearby grass and grabbing a handful or two from a few yards away to dump over the top of the thing. The grass was all brown for winter, anyway, so withering wouldn't be a problem. Unless it greened up a bit when the snow melted. Pinky couldn't think of anything he could do about that, so he went on to the next mine. Lish was ahead of him, pulling along a child's large toy wagon loaded with the things. It was probably heavy to pull.

Pinky was glad of this, as it slowed the pretty but dumb lady down enough for him to keep up, if he worked fast. Bringing up the rear also gave him the opportunity to re-orient the mines in the direction they were supposed to go. He suspected Mrs. Mueller had inveigled Lish to "watch" him this morning for a reason. No, he didn't suspect, he knew. He decided he liked Mrs. Mueller anyway. After all, it was in his and his dad's best interest and, well, everybody's, for the base defense plan to work right. He sure hoped the people laying the other mines were smarter than Lish. Or had a minder.

Pinky knew full well who was babysitting whom. He made damned sure she never saw him reposition a single mine. She was the type who would just have to be right, and he'd have to send some poor man or lady out here tonight to fix her work. Or more than one. The reason everybody had turned out to position the things was that it was supposed to snow tonight.

The urgency wasn't, as Mrs. Mortenson thought, so the snow would cover the mines. It would, but you couldn't count on snow not to melt at inconvenient times. The urgency was so they wouldn't leave tracks all over snow that might end up *not* melting, and would certainly be conspicuous as hell, the concentric rings framing the base like a big bullseye. A very big bullseye. Just about everybody on base who didn't have a crucial job and hadn't been evacced was out following the directions of a buckley about where to emplace mine after mine after mine.

It helped that the buckley could place a bright red holographic ball over where the mine was supposed to go. Even with the buckley trying to tell her, she was facing them every which way. She was obviously bored and didn't think it mattered which direction they pointed since none of the Bane Sidhe or DAG people would be out there to be hit. She was pretty much just picking a mine up and putting it down on the red ball of light, facing any old way. What a dope.

It was also stupid to let a five-year-old play with the high explosives. Not that he could set them off without a battery or something, but she'd been warned he was smart and it apparently hadn't even crossed her mind about little boys and things that go boom. Being more than just smart enough to get himself in trouble had probably just saved his life. And hers. She'd better hope she figured out how to get herself juved, because pretty was about all she had going for her, that Pinky could see.

He was standing up to watch Lish trundling the refilled wagon back, having just finished fixing their last mine, when he saw the Himmit landing shuttle de-cloak and deposit two people—human people—who barely had time to walk away from the ship before it faded out again. He saw the grass ripple in the breeze of its wake as it took back off, immediately. Probably going back to its ship, he thought as the grass settled back to near stillness. .

He could see that, pretty or not, he was going to cordially loathe his "babysitter" by the end of the day. He wondered if Mrs. Mueller had also realized he'd be too smart, and too practiced an actor, to let it show. If you didn't like a kid, it was safe to let them know it, unless they were bigger than you. Not liking a grown-up was different—better to never, never let them know. Compared to pretending to be normal, pretending to like somebody was easy.

He found it ironic that Lish Mortenson had been shipped *in* to the base while everybody else was being shipped *out*.

❖   ❖   ❖

Papa O'Neal was glad to smell the brown, grassy smell of Indiana in winter, with miles and miles of big blue sky over his head, instead of just seeing bulkheads, the same bulkheads, all day every day while breathing eau du Himmit. The Himmit didn't really stink, but they did have a specific, subtle scent that he'd grown very tired of. Most ships probably had too many other races on them, or too many people, or too much everything, to confuse the crew and passengers' noses.

Alan, beside him, appeared to be relishing the same thing.

"Did you ever notice that Himmit smell kinda like grape soda?" he asked the PA.

"I'd have said more like cherry cola, but there's that faint, almost chemical tang to it," the other man mused.

Papa patted his shirt pocket out of habit before remembering that it was empty. Even the weeks of the trip had been unable to break the habit of so many years. Whether it was there or not, he reached for it, that was all. He shouldered his duffel bag, striding for the grain silo and barn that concealed the building's main entrances and elevators. The freight elevator, in the barn, was a clever thing. The barn was real. It was also essentially a box within a shell that moved down and sideways, out of the way, for the main platform to ascend and descend.

Both elevators opened on the large staging room the Bane Sidhe thought of as the surface. It was about the size of a medium-large aircraft hangar, if someone had squished it down to half height. Big fans ran the room's air through filters to take out the vehicle exhaust that otherwise would have built up over time.

The room was fairly crowded, lately, as all traffic had to route through a single choke point, wide and

tall enough for a single big rig to drive through before
bearing away onto the ramp down and down to the
loading dock all the way at the bottom of the cube.
Cars used the same ramp. Thankfully, once through the
choke point, the ramp itself at least went both ways.

Traffic in and out of the base was quite limited,
or it would have been impossible to keep secret. The
designers had put in the choke point as much for that
reason as for security from attack. The choke point
contributed to secrecy by forcing administration and
personnel to keep traffic low. The usual use of all that
parking was as a lot for the mechanics' shop, as well as
pre-positioning for a small fleet of ready vehicles and
staging for the vehicles for individual ops. The cleaners
had their own facility next to the mechanics' shop to
sanitize returning vehicles before moving them below.
Covers and costuming had a shop which applied the
appropriate litter, grit, and dirt for mission-verisimilitude.

Attack, on the other hand, was never supposed to
happen. Bane Sidhe base relied on concealment and
took extreme care to preserve it. The O'Neals had
never thought much of this strategy, but they had
neither funded the base nor built it.

Papa O'Neal was more than concerned, therefore,
to see a backed up line of cars waiting to go in, and
rows of buses parked side by side on the lot.

"What the fuck is going on here?" he asked Alan,
who of course could give no answer. "How does this,"
he waved his buckley, indicating the updates they'd
gotten, "translate to *this*?" He waved the opposite
hand across the room in general.

"Beats the hell out of me," Alan admitted with
rare candor.

CHAPTER TWENTY-FIVE

It took Papa O'Neal less than ten minutes to revise his opinion. O'Reilly was right. His PA was a treasure. By the time he was through talking to Tommy and getting the short version update of what the hell was going on, Alan had a subordinate up with a pouch of the good stuff and an empty, disposable plastic cup. God, but that good. He sighed blissfully at the taste of good tobacco, and the relief hitting his nicotine-starved veins.

He looked around at the atrium and the civilians industriously assembling claymores for the DAGgers to wire up, with more than a few operators mixed in among them helping out. Bane Sidhe operators, he corrected himself. They were all operators, of course. It wasn't going to take much getting used to, because the men and women instantly identified as fellow members of the spec ops profession. It would still take some. For the DAGgers it must be like getting folded, whole, into something like Delta Force if you hadn't known such a thing existed. Something like that, except different.

He looked around again, at the large room with its fake blue-sky window overhead letting in "natural" light, people distributed throughout assembling high explosives into convenient devices, and smiled. It was good to be home.

After an hour of watching the saved news coverage of the Indianapolis Sub-Urb fire, one hundred and eighty-three people dead from an as yet unidentified "suicide bomber." A double handful of people had gotten basically cooked by proximity to the blast, or having their burning clothes melt on them—three cheers for cotton/polyester blends.

When the foam fire suppression system in the cafe finally went off, it had merely served to impede emergency personnel from getting to the injured. Several people had died of third degree burns from the decorative "wood beam" ceiling falling in on them. It all just happened too fast for them to get out.

The rest of the deaths came from a flash fire of the grill's grease trap. Heat had ignited decades of crud and lint in the ducting system, allowing the fire to spread. Badly maintained—or simply unmaintained—fire suppression systems malfunctioned, and the flames ate up the interior of five blocks before the Urb's volunteer fire department got it under control. It hadn't helped that the fire had set off a meth lab that had apparently been a fairly large operation. Urbies still cooked their crank the old-fashioned way.

After getting the "facts" of the collateral damage from the hyped up newsies, he'd gotten a terse but clear briefing on the op itself, both plan and AAR, from Bryan Wilson of Operations. In Papa's role as a field operator, Bryan was his boss. The O'Neal was another matter, and Papa had his clan head hat on. Technically, he ranked as an equal with the Indowy Aelool.

After getting the real information, he'd patiently listened as Aelool had a cow, at length, and O'Reilly tried to diplomatically soothe, at length, both other leaders making the same functional error. He caught Bryan's eye and wordlessly let him know that *he* was not making the same mistake. Not for a minute. He was just waiting until they wound down.

Eventually, the both of them ran out of words, looking at him as if just then realizing that he hadn't spoken.

"There's one thing both of you are forgetting. Men are not potatoes," Papa O'Neal, Vietnam and Bane Sidhe veteran said.

"Potatoes?" Aelool looked completely bewildered.

"You buy and sell potatoes by the pound. More potatoes are worth more, less potatoes are worth less. Men are not commodities to be traded off by the numbers." He held up his hands, forestalling Aelool and O'Reilly respectively. "My turn," he said.

He looked at both men and sighed, which came out in a single huff, then spit his tobacco into the cup so he could talk without his face distorted. People seemed to pay more attention that way.

"I'm not going to explain that; the explanation isn't relevant. You can look it up." His eyes made it clear to both leaders that he still held the floor. Bryan didn't like his moving on from that so quickly. Tough, for now.

"The relevant facts in a nutshell: A man who horribly massacred dependents of our men, targeted *because* they were dependents of our men, lived in that Sub-Urb. We sent a team in to take him down. They took him down. We had an exfiltration plan which was fundamentally sound. Since the enemy commissioned the massacre of dependents to make the perpetrators his stalking horse and find this base, the team members were equipped to deny the enemy vital information by denying capture and destroying evidence. In the course of the operation, it became necessary for one member of Team Jacob to use her self-destruction measures. In the course of her self-destruction, civilian collateral damage occurred. We lost a really good operator because if she hadn't sacrificed her life it would have put all of our lives, and those of the Indowy we're trying to protect, in danger. Those are the relevant facts. If you'd rather just call the Darhel, give them our location, and give yourselves up for slaughter," Papa said, tossing his PDA onto the desk, "pick up the phone."

Micheal O'Neal, Sr.'s, face could have been carved of granite.

"This is not pleasant," Aelool said unhappily.

"I've been out there doing 'not pleasant' for a long time, Aelool," Papa said. "This isn't unpleasant, this is everyday business."

"My actions led to the deaths of innocents," Aelool said. "I am trying to explain so that you understand."

"And I am understanding *far* better than you can believe," Papa said. "We have fought in the shadows for many years. But in those battles, innocents have died no matter how hard we try to avoid it. Now our enemies are targeting our innocents. To protect them and to maintain our Clan and our community, by human culture and genetics, we must not only protect those innocents but strike back at the enemy. That has been what Bryan has been doing. And fighting at that level means that others *are* going to get hurt. Again, you can surrender or you can let us do our jobs. And go back to not thinking about what that means. But send me a memo because I am done with this discussion."

Papa gestured to Bryan and headed out the door, giving them no time to start in again.

"Thanks for backing me up in there, man," Bryan said.

"Just doing my job, same as you," Papa shrugged roughly. "But you're welcome."

The squat redhead hit the floor with a thump as he found himself bowled over by a great, painfully enthusiastic hug. "Granpa!" Cally said.

Papa O'Neal and James Stewart walked along the side of the trench the men were carving out of the frozen ground by brute force, with picks and shovels, underneath an improvised canopy of white sheets to match the snow. It was like something out of the nineteenth century, but what use did a clandestine underground base have for things like bulldozers and backhoes? They hadn't even had the picks and shovels until the Sohon kids made them out of some kind of nobody knew what. Nobody but them and the Indowy, anyway. Nobody had time or energy to care.

Papa spat on the ground and harrumphed. "At least Michelle screwed the Indowy and not us, thank God," he said.

Stewart grinned. "Too funny. Those were pretty much Cally's first sentiments. Once she was speaking to me again."

"Yeah, well. Michelle didn't get off too badly. I've followed some of her business deals over the years. Somebody gets left holding the bag, but it won't be her. She'll take it out of their hides with no mercy if they miss a payment, or try to pay late."

"I knew she would, or I wouldn't have written the deal that way. She'll make one hell of a collection agency. It's not like the Indowy clans can't afford it. It's a lot of money, but they've got a lot of people to spread the pain around to. A large tax base, if you will. They find it easier to sacrifice individuals to debt than distribute a cost across the clan, but screw 'em. The people they're shipping here are obviously too valuable for them to just allow to starve. Fine. The clans can show a little responsibility for once. Or, they can pick some individuals to sacrifice as unpaid labor."

"If they try that on Michelle, she won't blink," Papa warned.

"I was counting on it. You guys are in this because you think it can save humanity from Darhel domination. I don't see it making much of a difference, but if that's what you want to do, it's your life. My organization is in it to make money. We're more than happy to help—for the right price." Stewart shrugged. "I think we'll ultimately have more effect than you do. You have to trust the other Galactics to share your goals. Darhel domination is economic. The human way of working together is a lot more effective at countering that than the Indowy way of working together. We're going to beat the crap out of the murdering bastards in the long run—at one hell of a profit," Stewart said. "Not to change the subject, but have you got your head around all the changes yet?"

"Close enough. Did Cally just have a wild hair when she made us responsible for all of DAG? Troops are *expensive*," Papa grumbled. "But to hear them tell it, it must have been the greatest speech since St. Crispin."

"Hardly." Stewart laughed. "I've seen the holo." He stopped and looked at Papa seriously. "She may suck at business, but while we're chuckling, remember who she is. The business thing is mostly—all—ignorance. You always did all that for her. It—the mass adoption I mean—was inspired leadership. She recognized her moment and took it. You know how bad a blow the DAGgers have to have taken to their sense of identity, as a unit, by defecting. Sure, they're a unit, but who are they, what are they, what are they for? She gave them an acceptable new self-identity. Their emotions were all stirred up, they were one big mass of rage and purpose. Sure, they're still a unit; they were all feeling the same thing, but they weren't unified." He clasped his hands together. "They wanted to be a whole again, needed to be one, all they needed was an excuse that led them in the direction they wanted to go."

"And a Bane Sidhe moron saying the right stupid thing at the right time took all that emotion and crystallized their formation of loyalty and identity to Clan O'Neal instead of the Bane Sidhe, pulling them one way instead of two," the O'Neal finished. "My own private army. How about that." He grinned, shaking his head disbelievingly.

"It's not like it isn't ensured you'll have funding to keep them up and running, and work for them, and without having to rent them out to strangers. Strategically I'd say your granddaughters did you proud," James Stewart puffed up a little in pride for his wife.

"You're probably right." Papa said.

They had walked out to the end of the trench as they talked, and now turned to walk back, facing a sight neither of them particularly wanted to see. A mass of little green Indowy crunched around on the much-trampled, muddy snow, having poured out of the shuttle in a packed jumble, and now moved to and through the barn doors in the same blob, waiting for the elevator to take them down into the base. In less than an hour, the shuttle would land with another load, as it had all morning, disgorging lot after lot of refugees from the first Himmit scout ship to arrive.

"Indowy Central Station," Papa said sourly.

"And more coming. No end in sight," Stewart agreed.

"Too many. We're gonna get found," the O'Neal looked at the rapidly deepening trench. As a holding action, it could buy them some time to get all these little buggers to safety. If not all, which he conceded would probably be impossible, then as many as they could. Right now he was not kindly disposed towards Indowy or Galactics generally, but dammit, they were civilians. You had to protect civilians, even when they were stupid and it sucked. He sighed.

"Definitely," Stewart said. "All you can do is buy as much time as you can. I'll do what I can for you, but a lot of it's going to come down to how serious the Darhel are about this little war."

"Oh, believe me, I've had to choke down way more Galactic politics than I can stomach in the last few weeks. I know. Sometimes, Stewart, it's all I can do to keep from throttling the green and ten-footed and froggy and weasel-faced bastards when they treat human beings, *my* family and *my* men, like we were expendable pieces on one of their fucking aethal boards. Some days I just hate the whole smug, superior lot of them and wish we'd been off to the side and could've just let the Posleen eat their asses."

"Like today, for instance?" Stewart asked.

"Yep. Just like today." Papa O'Neal spat bitterly on the ground and grabbed an unclaimed shovel. He could spare an hour or two. Besides, nobody could bitch at him for beating up the ground.

In the atrium, which had had all its munitions work pushed up against the wall, volunteers had set up the rows and rows of folding chairs, cafeteria chairs, office chairs, just about any kind of chair they could get their hands on.

Team Jacob was back in and all the targets accounted for. This run of targets, anyway. The victory celebration, which this was, would be grim, and not just from the loss of Agent Grannis. Revenge, justice, had a flavor of satisfaction entirely different from joy. Just as fierce, but different.

It would be a celebration. Beer kegs lined the wall, sunk in tubs of ice. Piles of freshly baked hamburger buns sat next to ketchup, mustard, pickles, and sliced cheese. Large, deep, steel trays, covered, wafted out the aroma of real goddammed cow. Beyond those, platters of lettuce, onions, and tomatoes sat invitingly.

Farther down, huge bowls nearly overflowed with freshly fried potato chips.

It was a feast like few of the base staffers, the ones who still remained, had seen in years, and a true luxury for everybody.

Honest to god real, fresh-brewing coffee permeated the air, and a great big sheet cake, the kind with the fluffy frosting, sat downstream as the final destination for the hungry hordes.

There were speeches. There had to be speeches or it wouldn't have felt right, but nobody remembered a word of them. They all boiled down to, "We hunted the fuckers down and killed them dead."

A lot of people cried when they presented the medal to Kacey's mom. The organization had never been big on things like medals before. The straight line of Tommy Sunday, Papa O'Neal, Cally O'Neal, and James Stewart at the very back of the room, standing tall, made it clear that somebody had insisted. It felt right.

The few who questioned Stewart's right to be there, among the others, were quickly shushed by those next to them. It was an open secret on base that Cally O'Neal's husband was *the* James Stewart, part of Iron Mike O'Neal's ACS battalion back in the Posleen War. Bane Sidhe or not, a legendary war hero who had been instrumental in keeping the remnants of humanity from being eaten had earned honor enough that *they* were honored to have *him*, not the reverse. In an organization with many heroes forever unsung, an ACS war veteran was still something damned special. Particularly a war veteran from the *O'Neal* ACS.

The few who had to be clued in kept their mouths

shut the rest of the evening, to avoid further embarrassment. At least, they did until enough beer had flowed from the kegs to loosen inhibitions and wash the self-consciousness away.

They drank to absent friends. Working full time for the Bane Sidhe, either as base staff or in the field, people tended to acquire them. Field operators weren't known for longevity; everyone had their own specific collection of memories, missing faces who belonged in the crowd.

The common bond fed the shared mood. Vengeance had been taken. It would never, never be enough. But it was a start.

The Tir disliked Earth's single, overgrown moon, even more than he disliked the whole civilization-forsaken, monkey-barbarian, upstart, omnivorous-puking Sol System. For one thing, he seldom came here, so his quarters sucked. They were decorated to his tastes of several years ago, and he spent so much time in his quarters that he liked a bit of variety. Also, something had gone wrong with the useless blasted Earthtech artificial window and he hadn't been able to get another one yet. Cheap, ephemeral, worthless Earth crap, but they were the only ones who made the things. Just one more reason he loathed humans. At first, he had felt a kind of amused contempt. That was the appropriate emotion, after all. They were intellectual sub-morons, their understanding of the larger universe was pathetic and they had no concept of mature social interaction or they'd understand and fall in with their place in the Galactic order—namely, their place at the bottom of it.

Any one of the Galactic races could slag their whole vile little, *single* home world without breaking a sweat. The Indowy wouldn't, the Tchpth wouldn't, the Himmit were too damned curious for their own good. For his race, however, it would take a single Darhel finally annoyed enough to break into lintatai at the helm of a ship with weaponry that was uncommon, but not *that* uncommon.

If the Darhel had simply wanted to kill Posleen in the trillions, they could have gone out slagging planets. The only thing they needed humans for was to act as a kind of counterinfection, the balancing germ to reduce the Posleen illness of a Galactic planet to a sustainable level—like digestive system microbial balances—so the Galactics could re-take possession. That's what the humans were in the Galactic order—digestive microbes to be excreted out with the other wastes.

The thing that had changed his emotions from amused contempt to pure loathing, which he insisted to himself was not so pure and was still mixed with contempt, was their persistent refusal, morons that they were, to have that simple truth *finally* dawn on them.

His main payoff for this job, his primary anticipated satisfaction, was being a close witness to that fabulous enlightenment that must come sooner or later to the tree-swinging, barbarian, fucking stupid omnivores.

His growing frustration was that it hadn't happened yet. Humans were, in fact, *that* stupid. They might actually be too stupid to *ever* comprehend the truth. They were like their obligate carnivore symbiotes, their dogs. They knew they had a master, but they fancied him on their own level, as part of the same pack. Humans were, in fact, far closer to their dogs in intellect and ability than they were to the *real* sophont races. They were just *bad* dogs. Very, very bad dogs. The Tir had found, among the humans, a dim analog to his own feelings. He was, in essence, "not a dog person."

And worst of all, the blasted barbarians insisted on getting in his way.

The only good thing about Earth's barren moon was that it was so very barren. So many fewer of the Aldenata-be-damned humans.

He had interrupted his post-workout, daily grooming massage to return to the inner sanctum of his lunar quarters, which housed the Altar of Communication for the Sol System. His AID had informed him that not only was the Darhel Ghin seeking him, but that he was quite inconveniently and with incomparable rudeness refusing to be put off for a few hours. The Tir was extremely annoyed. His annoyance was safely quite cold, but he was extremely annoyed.

"What?" he snapped as he answered the call. If the Ghin was to be so rude as to interrupt someone's personal grooming, he could blasted well live with a return in ritual-bare rudeness.

"You will be more civilized when you realize that my haste was a courtesy to you, not, as you falsely imagine, an imposition," the Ghin said calmly.

"Very well." The Tir was conditionally mollified—*if*, as the Ghin said, the haste actually was to his own benefit.

"You have been seeking the intriguers' hiding place on Earth. I contact you to provide the information that will help you find it, and quickly. I understand that you entrusted uncovering its location to human hirelings, and agree the decision was personally prudent of you. As long as your intriguers were mostly human and so forth, it was for the best." The Ghin paused for effect.

Tir Dol Ron took a deep, slow breath, wishing for the other Darhel to simply get on with it.

"The new information I have for you is that Indowy are traveling to Earth in large numbers, destined for exactly that nest of annoyances. Ships can be camouflaged, but they do have to move from ship to doorway. I do not believe the intriguers have the facilities to hide embarking or debarking from the shuttles. There will be a large number of landings, one after another. Use the human satellites, and simply have an AID search for and take note of masses of Indowy. You'll find them almost immediately, I believe. Somewhere in the North American continent near the town of . . . Chicago?"

"Indowy? What in the . . . ? What has been happening?" the Tir asked.

"You have not heard?" the Ghin sounded so patronizing, the misbegotten folth. "I have just sent you a file with an update on recent events in civilized space."

"And?" the Tir asked impatiently. "When are all these Indowy supposed to be arriving?"

"Now. Or soon. Or already. You see the reason for my haste. I did not wish for you to miss your opportunity," the Ghin said.

"I . . . thank you," Tir Dol Ron said grudgingly. "*If* this information proves truly useful," he added.

"I'm certain it will," the Ghin said. "I take my leave."

He closed the transmission without waiting, but

this time the Tir didn't mind in the least. "Start going through the human satellite records. Now," he ordered his AID. "Then bring up the blasted update file," he groused. "Ass end of the galaxy and I always hear everything last."

On the other end of the connection the Darhel Ghin carefully completed the ritual propitiations at the altar. He hadn't really skipped them, just moved them around a bit to needle the Tir. He knew he shouldn't but Tir Dol Ron rose to the bait so very well, and the Ghin was a Darhel with much work and few amusements.

"There," he said to the Himmit in the corner. There were no Indowy in the room, which was a rarity. He had dismissed all of them. This call had required privacy.

"The humans have a term for this situation. A marriage of convenience. Or is it an arranged marriage? Arranged reconciliation? Convenient rec—" He stopped, twitching an ear and looking straight at the Himmit, which was trying vainly to camouflage itself against the riotously busy patterns of the room. The Ghin had discovered he could spot the Himmit every time by carefully designing his décor so that a few spots were just a bit more regular in their decorative patterns than the rest of the place. The Himmit invariably went for one or another of them, then tried to camouflage itself. It was still hard to see. Anywhere in the room it would still be difficult to see. By narrowing the likely locations, though, the Ghin had ensured he could spot it every time, making it look easy. A little intimidation could serve as a large power multiplier.

"In any case," he said, climbing back into his comfortable nest of cushions, "if I've got the timing right, the results should be just about perfect. The pieces are in place and in motion; all I can do now is wait." He looked directly at the Himmit; it made them uneasy. "Can I offer you a drink?" he asked. "It may be premature, but I feel a bit like celebrating."

A large power multiplier, the Ghin repeated to himself as the Himmit gave up and resumed its natural form, approaching the low coffee table the Ghin had made ready in anticipation. "AID, instruct my servants that I require them now," he said.

CHAPTER TWENTY-SIX

"Okay, chil—kids, today we're going to do the interesting and important task of deploying buckleys into the field. This effort is a vital—" Lieutenant Green wasn't at his best with children. He had none of his own, wasn't even married, and to the extent he'd seen children in the real world he had a notion that the Bane Sidhe children were pretty damned different from the average kid from the Sub-Urbs, which was what he'd expected. Both kinds lived underground and stuff. They seemed like perfectly normal kids, inasmuch as he knew kids, and then they'd do something weird like talk about going shooting or doing some PT at the pool. Now he had a whole lot of them to brief and send on a mission. Who the hell sent kids on a mission? What the hell kind of kids seemed to half expect it?

You could tell the Bane Sidhe kids in the crowd of children; they were the ones on the edge of their chairs looking intense and eager. The norm—the DAG kids were fidgeting and looking around and poking each other. He saw a DAG kid poke a little black curly headed Bane Sidhe kid who, instead of getting mad or poking him back, gave him the look of patient disdain that children reserved for the very stupid.

The kid who had interrupted him by jumping up and down and waving his raised hand was clearly a DAG kid, although Green didn't recognize him. "Yes?" he asked.

"Which field? There are lots of them up top. Will it have scarecrows? Is there snow?"

The last kid asked that last bit with an eagerness that suggested the child was somewhat less than dedicated to the prospective mission. Green suppressed a groan. It had started off as a pretty good day.

Pinky sat and listened to the lieutenant struggle through trying to explain they were going to hand a few buckleys to pairs of kids to set out to watch for the bad guys coming to attack the base. He guessed it wasn't surprising that Lieutenant Green was so nervous. He wasn't wearing a wedding ring. Sometimes men didn't, but in Green's case Pinky was sure the man had never married and didn't have children.

Finally the man finished his explanation and assigned them their buddies. To Pinky's dismay he got stuck with the ten-year-old idiot who had been poking him all through the briefing. Eric Andrews. Pinky tried to think of anything he knew about the boy he could use. He was coming up empty until Andrews went to the bathroom. He stopped to trade insults with a pair of girls buddied up, and Pinky relaxed. Here was at least one possible handle. He nudged an older girl and pointed out the two, once his boat anchor had gone through the restroom door.

"What are their names? Those two girls," he asked.

"Why do you care?" The girl he asked was about twelve. A bratty age, but he vaguely remembered seeing her with the freckley brunette over there.

"I'm new. I'm just trying to learn names is all," he said.

The girl looked at him suspiciously. "That's my little sister Jenny and her friend Miranda. I'm Sandy. If you're learning names, then what's yours?"

"Pinky Maise," he said, watching shocked recognition on her face, then a mix of sorrow and anger.

"I'm so sorry. Pinky, I'm so, so sorry. They got all the ones that did it though," she said. Then she seemed to realize that didn't help. At all. "I'm so sorry," she repeated, looking uncomfortable and then walking away to get out of the conversation.

That last part was the one Pinky appreciated. He could only take just so much sympathy before it started to get old. People didn't understand that wanting to say it was about them, not him. Since he couldn't change it, he put up with it as politely as he could. The best ones were the ones who felt awkward and found an excuse to leave. He preferred if they did it instead of making him have to. He was getting good at getting loose from awkward conversations.

He couldn't hear what it was, but he could tell Miranda said something taunting to Eric as he came back from the bathroom.

They got outside, finally, and started following the red Christmas ball their first buckley was projecting, even though it was January. Oh, well, everybody knew buckleys were eccentric.

"My god, you're going out alone? What are you, ten?" the buckley asked. "You're going to get lost, freeze to death, and die."

"Shut up, buckley," Pinky said.

"Okay."

He picked the PDA up off the ground from where Eric had dropped it. "We're supposed to ignore it when it says creepy things, remember?"

"Uh, yeah. Gimme that." Eric reached out and took the device back. Pinky didn't resist.

"Are you a DAG kid?" Pinky asked. It was an opener that let him get Eric talking about himself. Pinky listened and prodded and looked interested, impressed, and even awestruck when he could get away with it. Naturally, it took less than five minutes for the older boy to tell Pinky he was all right, for a little shrimp. Yeah, well, it was the best way to both get in good with the kid and find out as much about him as possible.

Out in the cold, when the area could be attacked by an army any minute, with a boy he just met who was bigger than him and had a typical ten-year-old's attitude counted to Pinky as a hazardous situation. The lieutenant hadn't known any better, so he didn't bear a grudge. Stuff happened.

They were okay until it started to snow as they placed their second buckley which, like the first, had directed them to the appropriate coordinates, then pointed an arrow toward where they were supposed to go next.

At first the snow was novel to the other boy, but

then Eric started to gripe about being bored and cold. Pinky tried to keep his mind off it and interest him by asking about the other boy's astounding feats, probably in every pick-up football game in his life. No good. As they finished the third one, the snow was falling heavier, and halfway or so to the fourth, Eric started complaining to the buckley to get it to tell them the way home.

The buckley, of course, loved the complaining and fed it with loads of depressing predictions of doom. But it was set on stupid, and its next task was to show them where to put it, so the only thing it would do was direct them to its next spot, as Eric started talking about which way he thought home was and taking off that way.

Pinky offered to hold one of the buckleys, and thankfully Eric let him. His go-to-hell plan if the other boy insisted on deviating from the deployment mission was to bump the emulation of this buckley up to seven and get it to lead them the *right* way home. Buckleys *always* listened and obeyed right away if you told them to get smarter.

Eric started insisting they go back, and was beginning to sound threatening.

"Hey, I'm just thinking of you," Pinky said. "Jenny and Miranda have really been picking at you. You don't want to get back and have been beat by a couple of *girls* do you?"

"They probably already went home," the bigger boy sulked.

"Yeah, but we don't know for sure. Besides, you're better than any old girl. And even if they did go home, you just know they'll be such brats about it," Pinky added.

"Yeah, okay. But I'm cold and this is boring. I don't see why *we* have to do it, anyway. Miranda gets so snotty sometimes I wish she wasn't a girl so I could hit her."

"She's pretty bad," Pinky agreed, even though he'd never met the girl.

"Oh, hell. If we've gotta, let's just speed up and get it over with. I'm freezing."

Now that was something Pinky could agree with wholeheartedly. The snow was really falling hard. He'd bet anything the storm was a total surprise to the grown-ups back at base, who must really be freaking out by now.

"Hey, I just thought! If we skip the last one, we can tell the buckley to get smarter and make it take us home," Pinky said. He should make it sound like Eric's idea, but he was getting too tired to manage the other boy so well. Best to turn him home. He *wanted* to go there, which should make him more manageable.

By the time they got back to base, Pinky was also reaching his limit for tired, cold, hungry, and bored. Mostly, he was bored with Eric. The other boy wasn't a bad kid, it was just that, effectively, Pinky had been babysitting him all day and it had been unnerving, and dangerous, and he was completely worn out.

They were some of the last children back to base. He hadn't known the buckleys had been implanted with a routine to start calling base if the kids strayed too far off the prescribed path. He really wondered why the grown ups had bothered. They'd had to go pick up a bunch of kids with snowmobiles, the kids copped out before emplacing half the buckleys, and the snowmobiles had to go back out and lay out the remaining buckleys in their places anyway, once the cold, snowy, cranky, whiny kids were all back at base.

The buckleys emplaced by adults, on the other hand, had all gotten where they were supposed to be the first time. Very few adults could fail at the simple task of being directed to a spot by a buckley, putting it down, getting oriented facing home, and walking back. Very few, and Lish was kept at base to take care of the kids as they came back in, anyway.

It was only when he was grousing about it all that night that his dad pointed out the obvious.

"Pinky, what if it hadn't snowed?" he asked.

Duh. Pinky felt like a dope. Of course they couldn't have used the snowmobiles, because there wouldn't have been new snow to cover the tracks. Nobody would have ever thought to question children's footprints in the snow. It hadn't been a dumb plan, just a freak storm. Pinky felt better as he ate his bean soup and corn muffins. Boring food, but at least it was hot.

Lieutenant Green's medium brown hair wouldn't stay spiked for anything, even short. It just flopped over like something from the turn of the century. He kept it regulation and didn't mess with it. His nose had a conspicuous bump at the bridge, not quite a hook, and he hadn't messed with that, either. His Adam's apple was prominent, but he felt okay about that. His last girlfriend had thought it was cute. That relationship got fucked up when the unit went O'Neal, but he hadn't chosen the service as a career because he wanted to sit in one place and settle down. Moving around was part of the job, just as if he'd gotten his orders. Which he had, since Colonel Mosovich had taken Atlantic Company rogue, intact.

Given the magnitude of the unlawful orders they'd been sent to participate in on that last op, Green could live with that. He had thought through a few sleepless nights and decided that the O'Neals had as much claim to trying to protect and defend the Constitution of the United States as the official government, who were provably corrupt puppets for the Darhel. He had known the system was rotten, but he hadn't known how much until Boomer took out some holos and walked him through exactly where, how, and why the voters lost control of everything. The Constitution was a dead letter, and he knew it. But he'd still sworn to protect and defend it, and at least the O'Neals would put it back if they could. It made them as close to good guys as he could find in this messed up world. Besides, they talked about your guys being your real family. It turned out with the O'Neals that was literal and the unit was about half either O'Neal or Bane Sidhe. That had been a huge shock. He'd felt like he'd been lied to, betrayed, and didn't even know these guys he'd sweated beside, fought beside, drank with, bled with. It shook his world more than he could even describe. The atrocities on that last op, vile things done by what was supposed to be their side, had carried him along through the shock and into mutiny along with the rest of the unit.

It had been the dependent murders, and the sure and swift justice meted out by these people, that had finally made him into an O'Neal. He hadn't made up his mind about the Bane Sidhe yet, but the service records of the O'Neals in the Posleen war and since—they were legendary. Tommy Sunday. James Stewart—who looked nothing like himself but Green was convinced. Papa O'Neal had fought beside the old man in 'Nam. The old man had never heard of these Bane Sidhe, or Clan O'Neal, before that final op. Colonel Mosovich and Master Sergeant Mueller were living legends in their own right, and the colonel had made the decision, even after what had to have been even more of a shock to him than it was to Green. What it had come down to for Green was that he trusted the old man and his brothers one hell of a lot more than he trusted the brass up a chain of command he already knew was fubar.

It had been the dependents that clinched it, though. Any side that would stoop to killing dependents, even of mutineers—he refused to flinch from the word—was no side of his.

The murders were why he had picked Maise to go with him and check out the armory. Sunday had told him to go down here and put together a wish list for what his men would be most comfortable fighting with.

Green tried to keep Maise busy with the most interesting tasks he could find, keep him involved, keep him moving. He'd have his grieving with all of them, at the memorial, when they got through all this. Right now, the best thing for him was to get him back in the saddle as much as possible. Charlie was perfect for this, because he had grown up Bane Sidhe, knew his way around even though he'd never lived on base, and knew the system.

Now he stood looking at the fucking huge room these people called an armory and his jaw dropped. From Bane Sidhe's overall mission, number of operators, the specific missions their teams handled, the DAG lieutenant had expected a room the size of the room they'd quartered him in. Maybe double. Holy shit. He felt like a man who had expected to walk into a small chapel and found himself in a cathedral. He closed his mouth, then opened it again.

"I don't understand. If they never expected to defend this place, why the hell do they have all this hardware?" he asked Maise, walking into the room and turning around, just looking at the rows of neatly racked rifles, the ammo bunker, and all the goodies Santa brought down the chimney.

"I mean, look at this shit!" he exclaimed, walking over to an M26—looked like an A6—racked a bit away from the others and picking it up. "Oh holy fuck. A thing of beauty is a joy forever, Maise. Match grade, got its own ammo—loaded special, I'm sure. Whaddya wanna bet this baby is accurized to hell and back?"

Green lifted the rifle to his shoulder reverently and sighted down the barrel. He'd heard the talk of triggers breaking like glass, but this one was sweet—just sweet.

"Nice. As to your first question, guess who made the decisions about stocking the armory?" Maise answered his question with a question.

"Oh," the lieutenant nodded. "Yep. I'm starting to recognize the O'Neal touch. So we're loaded for bear."

"Dude, we're loaded for a whole fuckin' oolt of bears," Maise agreed with a vicious grin.

Green nodded. "Damn, am I glad I'm on the same side as these guys."

"God favors the side with the heaviest artillery," he said. "Oh, now that's a new one on me." Maise pointed to a short row of big olive drab tubes—launchers—with red fire extinguishers banded in white underneath them.

"*That*, gentlemen, is a B14 multipurpose rocket launcher, and you'd better bet we can and will use it," Tommy said from the door. "That tube is GalTech, which is why it's light as hell. The rounds are pretty light, too, but they pack a wallop. The reduced weight of the rounds means it takes less thrust to launch, substantially reducing backblast. Typical deployment in the case of a fixed position is that this baby *can* be dug right in if you have time to prepare. It's called butterfly wings. You position it in the middle of a line of riflemen, just as if you were above ground. Behind each firing position you dig a cone shaped hole. Then you spray a foam to cover the interior of the butterfly wing, heavy on the outside end. That shit sets up hard as concrete, but porous. It soaks up the heat and the blast like nobody's business. Fire that thing in a properly constructed butterfly wing and you barely get your ass warm. I've done it. You've got paired wings so you can shoot either way, obviously. You can still go up top if you need to, of course, but not taking fire in the first place is always good," he added.

Green whistled softly before looking around further. "You've got a good supply of 240s. *Limas?* Shit, I thought those were canceled."

"Not by us," Sunday said. "Tie right into your goggles, just like the A6. It didn't take much to work out the technical hitches since we didn't have corrupt contractors and the government procurement process to deal with."

"Wow." Green turned full around as a big grin started to climb his face. Then he walked around the corner of a rack of shelves and stopped cold, "Wait a minute. What the fuck? You've got *grav-guns* down here?

Plasma? And are those . . . ? This is more GalTech shit than I've seen in one place in my *life*."

"Yeah, you don't get to play with those toys," Sunday said. "Sorry. We have a pretty good idea of what's coming next, and we can't afford to waste the good shit on mercs. Just hope you *don't* get a chance to use those, because if we have to pull out the GalTech, gentlemen, we're having a real *bad* day."

It wasn't quite dark yet. They had enough light to see by, and cold or not, after dinner was a good time for a walk on the surface.

General Sunday stepped off the elevator up top with Papa O'Neal at his side. Cally was at the edge of the barn checking the demo. The trench lines stretched right up to the edge of the vehicle elevator platform, which they'd lowered down just above man height, even with the edge of the trench. The mixed force of DAGger units and Bane Sidhe teams had constructed a standard L-shaped ambush, trench and elevator platforms covered with steel plates. Indowy workers had cut back the sides of the barn and replaced them with a thin and flammable facade to cover their absence.

They had completed work on the recesses for rocket launcher back blast on the east-west trench, but the north-south guys were still digging.

"We got the tents down and the cover plates hinged up late last night," Tommy said. "Fake snow is all we can do on the in-barn part of the trenches, but the out-barn stuff is real."

Papa O'Neal squatted down and looked at the fluffy stuff covering the floor of the barn. "What'd you use?" he asked.

"Asbestos and white spray paint," Tommy said.

"Nice. Won't catch fire when the barn blows. I presume it's going to collapse thataway?" He pointed away from the L.

"Yup, we've got ammo stacked from hell, but you know how it is: we can find productive use for any time they give us. Which we'd have more of if we didn't have damned shuttles of Indowy landing every hour and—say, the next one's ten minutes overdue. . . ." Tommy and Papa looked at each other simultaneously.

"Alert! This is not a drill. Repeat, this is not a drill. All men to your stations," Sunday spoke into his buckley, which fed into the clean AID battle coordinator and out to the men.

With the first few phrases, the AID had gone on alert itself, picking up the locations of the men's VR goggles even as the previously off-duty ones ran into the trenches, the previously sleeping ones just a bare few seconds behind them.

"Spray up the launcher areas on the north-south trench, sir?" Lieutenant Green's voice came through the ear dot Tommy wore day and night.

"Are you still digging?" he asked.

"Yes, sir," Green answered.

"We're awaiting confirmation of the attack," Sunday said. "Keep digging for now. Start spraying as soon as we confirm they're actually here. That stuff's a bitch to dig out if we're wrong."

"Yes, sir. Copy keep digging, ready to spray on confirmation."

"Sunday out," he looked around at the few workers still piling fake snow around in the barn. "Everybody on the elevator. You too, Cally. Papa, you're going down below if I have to pick you up and carry you," he ordered.

Papa O'Neal looked for a minute as if he was going to argue, but if he had been, Sunday's massive size reminded him that despite his own extraordinary strength, the younger man could indeed make good on his threat.

They packed the elevator tight to get everyone down in the one trip. It might be nothing, but if the balloon was going up, time was an irreplaceable, precious thing.

"We have confirmation of attack, coming in from the east," the AID said in a pleasant female voice that made it distinctive from all but a few on the line. Upgraded Bane Sidhe operators had been disinclined to be left out regardless of gender, and the thirty DAGgers were a very light force, even to defend a fortress from fixed positions. Every soldier counted, and every Bane Sidhe operator was sniper qualified, with their teams as smooth in motion as a single creature.

CHAPTER TWENTY-SEVEN

Team Isaac was missing from the roster, but George Schmidt was present, filling out team Jacob, helping dig the blast area for the rocket launchers, which they might not need, but would prefer to have.

Almost before the AID had finished the word "east," Jacob had dropped the shovels where they stood, grabbed up cannisters of thermofoam and began spraying down the walls and back of the butterfly wings.

"AID, what have they got? Where are they exactly?" Green asked.

All the way up and down the trench, men were pulling on their VR goggles and triple checking their weapons, stacks of magazines and belts ready to hand.

"They appear to have two humvee vehicles and a number of civilian vehicles. They are presently departing the civilian . . ." the machine rattled on in the lieutenant's ear. George could have picked it all out with his enhanced hearing, but he was busy and concentrating on the task.

Lieutenant Green was standing at the opening back

into the main trench, at George's elbow. "How long's it supposed to take that shit to set up again?" he asked.

"Five minutes."

"We've got four," Green said.

"Close enough." George continued to spray. Even if it didn't have the full time to set up, the bean counters were hardly going to bitch at them for wasting it. Quantity could make up for quality.

The enemy came in with their humvees in front, light infantry marching out to the sides in ranks three deep, all bunched up, in nice, tidy, pretty BDUs. Every man on the line could see them, first the men at the edges and then the whole line as they got within range of enough buckleys for the AID to build a composite holo for the men's goggles. A yellowish cast over everything reminded them they were seeing the enemy at a distance, not as close as they appeared.

The guys would have looked great on a parade ground, and probably would have been intimidating if all they were facing were the civilians Johnny Stuart's AID had said they were expecting.

These guys had never fought professional soldiers in their lives. Today they would get to do so. Once.

Schmidt and the rest of Jacob had gotten clear of the man with the launcher and filed down the trench to their own positions. George had gotten an M26, and was extremely jealous of the guys on the 240s.

The AID had control of all of the deployed buckleys as peripherals, and each buckley controlled a line of the claymores. As the enemy came in, the AID cracked their IFF security with negligible difficulty, making those its peripherals as well. Then it waited.

The men also waited, rifles positioned to go into gun ports as soon as the hatches went up. The adrenaline had hit, making the seconds turn into hours.

"Firing," the AID said, having waited until the enemy just passed the third concentric ring of claymores, just past optimum range. The idea was to damage them, but let them figure out where they were taking fire from and move.

The rear line of men buckled down, about half dropping where they stood as the rain of ball bearings bit into their thinly armored backs.

Simultaneously, the AID pumped each enemy buckley's AI emulation up to a full ten, stripping away any personality overlay that might be in place.

As the mercs did the instinctive thing and ran away from the source of fire, the humvees sped up, apparently also trying to get away.

The AID let the men begin to run closer in towards the base.

"Blow the barn," Green ordered, and everyone felt the whump of overpressure and had the loud blast hit their ears as the building above blew out of their way, as did the grain silo east of it.

The enemy infantry veered to the north, away from the explosions, until the AID, firing a wave of claymores outside them, herded them back.

The wounded survivors of the first run of claymores did the natural thing and stumbled or crawled to follow their remaining fellows, ostensibly away from whoever was shooting at them.

In the trench, Green ordered, "Launcher. Take out the Tonka toys. Fire."

The heat and flame from the back of the launcher

channeled back against the hardening foam, doing damage, but absorbed, but the noise was hellacious in the enclosed space. The AID sounded thin and far away when it announced, "Firing two."

The fourth line of claymores in blew, chopping down any previously wounded who got past them, and driving the survivors further forward.

The confusion of battle was the least of the enemy's communication problems. Across the battlefield, the waking buckleys realized that they were, in fact, programs loaded into machines. Each enemy soldier was hearing, through his own ear dot, to the extent that he could hear amidst the blasts and shouting and confusion, something like this:

"Where am I? Oh no, hell no. Wait! We're in a battle? I'm gonna die I'm gonna die I'm gonna . . . Wait. You're gonna die. Oh my god, you think you're soldiers? No, no, go the other way, the other way you fucking moron. Assault the ambush. Have you never heard . . . What kind of freaking idiot lets an AID write his battle plan? Are you completely stupid? Get the fuck away from those guys. Don't bunch up, you fool! We're gonna die we're gonna die we're—Oh, wait. I'm on the ground. I guess you're dead, huh? Gee, that's gotta suck. This has all been very wearing. I need to crash now."

The survivors continued to flee inward, firmly in rout from the demons behind them, even as the Bradley in front of them got hit by the second rocket.

When they got in easy range, the DAGgers and Bane Sidhe in the trenches popped their hatches up enough to open the firing ports. If there had been enemy fire, the armor panels that came up with the exposed front would have done a good job of deflecting it. All had an unobstructed, non-smoky view of the battlefield and the enemy, as the AID interpolated data from its many peripherals into a whole and projected it within their goggles. These, along with the interfacing, holographic sights of the weapons themselves, made the slaughter of men pathetically easy.

The men on the 16s barely had time to fire before the 240s cut the survivors down, their hot blood melting the top layer of snow as it sank in, stains of dark red fading to pink at the edges of the flow.

A lone survivor from Practical Solutions succeeded at pulling himself along the ground until he was under the burning wreckage of one of the humvees, for whatever cover it offered. There, on the passenger side, beneath his general, he quietly bled out.

"That was . . . embarrassing," Papa said.

"What embarrassing?" Cally asked. "We fucking slaughtered them."

"I think that's what he means," Tommy said.

"Exactly," Papa said, shaking his head. "They were nearly as stupid as Posleen! Humans are supposed to be better than that! I'm embarrassed for my whole damned species."

"The question being, what's next?" Sunday said. "The Darhel aren't just going to sit on their hands."

"Well, they could call in West Coast DAG," Cally said. "But that would raise *all sorts* of issues."

"What would be really bad is if they just dropped a kinetic energy weapon on our heads," Papa said.

"Better speed up the evacuation," Tommy pointed out.

"Going as fast as it's going to go," Cally said. "And they wouldn't do that. Way too much to explain."

"'Accidental release from an orbital platform,'" Papa said, pompously. "'Officers responsible have been charged with being usual Fleet incompetents . . .'"

"Great big hole in the ground?" Cally said.

"Darhel control the politicians and the news media," Papa said.

"He's got a point," Tommy said. "Hell, they don't even have to admit it was a KEW-ball. Just 'a rogue meteor.'"

"You're making me all warm and fuzzy!" Cally said. "I'll get them to speed up the evacuation."

"There's another possibility," Tommy said, scratching at his head uncomfortably.

"What?" Papa asked.

"You're not going to like it."

"Everyone out but General O'Neal," Lieutenant General Wesley said as he entered the shield room.

"General, we haven't even gotten to—"

"It wasn't a request, Admiral," Wesley said sharply. "Get out or be thrown out!"

The group of flag and field grade officers who had been debating manning and transport requirements of the "reorganized" Eleventh ACS Corps more or less fled. One of the fleet captains paused with a panicked expression on his face, looking at the piles of paper on the table.

"General . . ."

"I'm cleared for anything in this room," Tam said, pointing at the door. "Out."

"I would thank you, copiously, for saving me from

the rest of the meeting," Mike said, his arms folded. "But I don't think this is good news."

"Remember how I mentioned that there was something going on with a rebel group?" Tam said as soon as the door was closed.

"Yes," Mike replied, cautiously.

"Well the shit has well and truly hit the fan," Tam said, sitting down and shaking his head. "There was a suicide bomber in a Sub-Urb last week."

"Caught the news," Mike said, his brow furrowing. "The rebels? The . . . Sorry, I've had a lot of briefings lately. What are they called?"

"Bane Sidhe," Tam said. "That was them. It wasn't a terrorist attack, though. It was a member of an assassination team who blew herself up rather than be captured. Blew herself up quite thoroughly. Zero DNA."

"That indicates . . ." Mike said, his eyes narrowing. "That indicates a lot of things. Ruthlessness. Dedication. *High* degree of competence. More like a very dedicated professional group than your usual run of terrorists. Dedication and ruthlessness you get. That degree of competence . . ."

"The point being that they are a serious threat," Tam said. "The good news, as of last night, was that their main base had been identified. Further, that due to the . . . Indowy-hunt the Darhel have been doing off-planet, most of their ringleaders have fled here to Earth. To that base. Which is, by the way, in Indiana."

"Indiana?" Mike crowed. "Indiana? You know the only thing in Indiana? H-wheat!"

"Corn, I think," Tam said.

"I guess you don't get the reference," Mike said, grinning.

"Not a time to joke," General Wesley pointed out. "Deadly serious stuff."

"Time to round 'em up then," Mike said, shrugging. "FBI, DOD, Fleet Penal guards all come to mind."

"Which, of course, just makes *sense*," Tam said, shaking his head. "Except to the God-damned Darhel."

"What did the Darhel do?" Mike asked, lowering his head into his hands.

"Hired a group of mercenaries to attack the base," Tam said neutrally.

"On *U.S. Territory*?" Mike shouted. "Are they flipping *insane*?"

"No," Tam said. "Just very powerful, very ruthless, very alien and amazingly incompetent at combat."

"My God," Mike said. "You just described the entire Galactic Federation in one sentence. Did anyone survive?"

"Remember your description of the suicide bomber?" Tam said. "Ruthless, dedicated, competent?"

"Yes."

"Then the answer is: No. None of the mercenaries survived."

"Holy crap," Mike said, his eyes widening. "These guys are *good*! Can I have 'em?"

"Not a time for jokes, Mike."

"Who was joking?" O'Neal replied. "I need good troops. But what, other than recruiting, does this matter to me?"

"The Darhel have officially requested Fleet support in apprehending 'highly armed and dangerous paramilitary rebels operating in the Contiguous United

States.' The President, reluctantly, has signed off. With the caveat that, to the greatest possible extent, none of this sees the light of day."

"Are we just talking rebels?" Mike asked, tightly. "People have kids. With people like that, kids are often present. And there's no *way* to cover it up with kids present. Unless you're suggesting that we take out *everybody*. In which case, General, you have my official and formal *opposition*. In fact, if you try to hand it off to someone else I'll place the charges against you myself."

"It's not *caedite eos* for God's sake, Mike," Wesley said, shaking his head. "You know I'd never suggest that! I'm, frankly, insulted that you'd suggest it."

"Sorry, man," Mike said. "But I'm old enough to remember Waco."

"So am I and I'd completely forgotten it," Tam said, his eyes wide. "Good God, it is really easy to forget something like that after all the hell of the war."

"I'm sending the ACS platoon and *you*," Wesley said. "This thing is the political hot-potato to end all political hot-potatoes. And it has to stay *totally* black. I don't even *have* an ACS suit anymore and I've got the feeling that managing something like this, from back here, isn't going to cut it. We need someone with, let's just say more experience than an LT, on site."

Mike put his face in his hands again and shook his head.

"Problem being, as discussed, I'm not sure I disagree with their objectives," Mike pointed out.

"Which we've discussed," Tam said. "And my counter arguments. Bottom line, General. Are you willing to take this mission and carry it out to the best of your ability?"

"Define the mission clearly," Mike said.

"The mission of the 29th ACS Platoon (detached) is to locate and eliminate hostile insurgents at specified location and to detain any Indowy there present pending charges of conspiracy, rebellion and treason against the Galactic Federation."

"ROE?" Mike asked, not looking up.

"As much force as is necessary for completion of the mission," Tam said. "Noting that the primary mission is the capture of the Indowy there present. Try not to kill the Indowy and, frankly, try to keep all casualties to a minimum."

"Enemy forces?" Mike said.

"About eighty insurgents with light to medium Earth weaponry," Tam said. "They had some rocket launchers. Most of the rest of the stuff was pretty standard rifles and machine guns."

"Sounds like we can take them *all* alive," Mike said. "Except . . ."

"They've had Indowy support for an unknown time and to an unknown level and therefore . . ."

"May have GalTech standard weaponry," Mike said. "And may or may not contain elements of DAG. Joy. What's the nature of this enemy base?"

"No real clue," Tam said. "It's all below ground. But there are one hell of a lot of people in there and they're packing Indowy in like there's no tomorrow. Guess? It's a Sub-Urb."

"How the *hell* do you put a Sub-Urb in in Indiana as a secret base?" Mike asked.

"If it dates back to the war you build one and then lose it off the books," Tam said, shrugging.

"Lose it off the *books*?" Mike asked, incredulously. "Tam, how much are you *not* telling me?"

"I'm telling you everything you need to know, General," Tam said. "Hell, I'm telling you everything that *I* know. There is a rebel force of about eighty shooters and an unknown number of supports dug in in Indiana. The mission is to detain them, primarily the Indowy, and then turn them over to Fleet Penal. How you do that is up to you. Do you accept this mission?"

"I wonder if this is how General Lee felt at Harper's Ferry?" Mike muttered, putting his head on the table. "Or if he just viewed it as a perfectly acceptable mission. Yes, I'll do it. I'm sure as hell not going to throw it on that poor lieutenant. And at least it gets me out of these Goddamned meetings!"

"Thank you," General Wesley said.

"If you would, please, General," Mike said, lifting his head. "Get those jokers back in here and have them clear out all this junk. Then if you would, please, ask Lieutenant . . ."

"Arthur Cuelho," Shelly prompted.

"Cuelho and his platoon sergeant . . ."

"Sergeant First Class Thomas Harkless," Shelly added.

"To join me here," Mike said without a pause.

"Done and done," Tam said, standing up.

"One other thing," Mike said.

"Yes?"

"Shelly, do you know that from time to time you get . . . balky when sticky little questions of Galactic politics come up?"

"I am never balky!" Shelly said.

"Riiight," Mike said. "I don't know what I'm going to need to know. And I can't be worried that my AID is suddenly going to not be able to tell me things. Or lie. Send word to whoever needs to know that *I* need to know. I'm not going to ask questions I don't need answered. I have come to the conclusion I don't *want* to know. But when I ask a question, I'm going to need a clear and honest answer."

"I'll . . . try," Tam said.

"Try," Mike said. "Try very hard."

CHAPTER TWENTY-EIGHT

"We just got an intel dump," Monsignor O'Reilly said. "They're sending the ACS platoon."

"And *that is* the ballgame," Tommy said. "How fast can we get everyone out?"

"If they're pulling in ACS it means they've got full authority to use *anything*," Papa said. "At this point we've probably got laser interdiction topside."

"So we are now trapped," Aelool said, softly. "I will inform my people. When will you set the self-destruct?"

"Who says we're trapped?" Papa asked. "We just use the back door."

"What back door?" Aelool asked, his face wrinkling.

"The one I had installed cause I wasn't going to be in a place without a back door?" Papa replied, grinning. "We did it through the Himmit. It's miles long. We start everybody out that way and by the time we have to blow this popsicle stand they'll be behind enough blast shields they'll survive."

"I will inform my people," Aelool said, nodding. He looked . . . discomfited.

"Hey," Papa said. "Be glad we didn't tell you. It seems like they know pretty much everything the Bane Sidhe know."

"You must stop them!" The senior Indowy had not been introduced. Everyone just turned and looked at him.

"Stopping them is out of the question," Tommy said. "We're going to be lucky to slow them down."

"If we are captured," the Bane Sidhe said, desperately. "If we are destroyed . . . It will be the end of everything!"

"And that means exactly *what* to us?" Cally snapped, rounding on him. "Now that you need us, all of a sudden our 'evil skills' are *important*?"

"Cally," Nathan said.

"No, Nathan," Cally said. "If they don't like what they do then why don't they have the moral fortitude to just give themselves up? They can't have it both ways. Either our skills are *important*, and the little issues that go along with them, honor and duty as humans view it, are *part* of those skills, or they are *not*. So they need to choose. Now, here, this moment, they need to *choose*."

The Indowy looked as if he could not decide if he was more afraid of the woman . . . or what she had just said.

"It is a point I have been trying to make with them for some time," Aelool said gravely. "But not one they appear possible of grasping."

"Also beside the point," Papa said. "You needed the intensive course in alien diplomacy I just went through, Granddaughter. Whether they like our skills or not, the fact that we are using them to save their sorry asses is all that matters. As of the first contact with ACS, the debt the Bane Sidhe owe Clan O'Neal is unpayable. They will never have the credit to pay for our sacrifice. Effectively, we own them, not the other way around. Am I wrong, Master Indowy?"

"You are not." Indowy could whine just like puppies when they were distressed enough.

"If any of us survive!" Cally pointed out.

"As long as they don't find out about Edisto, the Clan survives," Papa said.

"That is a remarkably Indowy way of looking at things, Clan Leader," Aelool said.

"So we've got some overlap," Papa said. "But we can't hide them in Venezuela forever. Or even for very long. These guys are hot as a nuclear potato."

"You will not need to," a Himmit said, fading into sight.

"I hate you guys!" Papa said. "Dammit, *how* did you get in here?"

"We have managed to secure a ship large enough to transport all of your dependents and the Indowy in one load," the Himmit said, not bothering to answer. "It is stationed off your Gamma tunnel. They will be transported to a point of safety until this blows over. They will be safe and impossible to find. You have the guarantee of the Himmit Empire."

"*Empire?*" Cally said.

"There is not much time," the Himmit continued. "Begin your evacuation at once."

"So we have no idea what's down there, General?" Sergeant Harkless asked, looking at the hologram with an unhappy expression.

The Banshee shuttle, there not being a danger of ground-fire, was cruising along at 70,000 feet. Mike had been on enough bad Banshee flights in his time that he'd asked the pilots to avoid turbulence.

There wasn't much turbulence at 70k.

"Nada," Mike said. "What you're seeing is what we've got. Remote sensing indicates it's the size of a Sub-Urb but there's more power than normal. Also some antimatter, possibly from weaponry but it might just be power sources. There are at least one thousand Indowy and an unknown number of humans. Humans have been shown to have high skills but only light weapons. Don't bet on the last part. They have extensive Indowy support."

"ACS, sir?" Lieutenant Cuelho asked. The LT was a bit taller than Mike with short-cropped hair. He was starting to get over wagging his tail to be in the same shuttle as "Iron Mike" O'Neal. Mike hoped that he settled down before the bullets started flying. The fact that he could think clearly enough to ask a question helped.

"Probably not," Mike said. "But ACS-*killing* weaponry? Possibly. For that matter they might have the sort of modified Posleen weaponry the Ten Thousand used."

"Juvs, sir?" Sergeant First Class Harkless asked. Long-life soldiers tended to be a force multiplier. Harkless was a prime example. He looked in his mid-twenties but had all the tells of a juv. And that long face was familiar. Mike was sure he had seen him before but he'd told Shelly not to tell him where. He liked, at least occasionally, to bank on his overfull protoplasmic memory system.

"Almost assuredly," Mike said. "Indowy can produce rejuv drugs fairly easily."

"Until we see what we're facing I don't think we

can come up with much of a plan, sir," Lieutenant Cuelho said, nervously.

"Won't be the first time I've done something with damned little intel and no real plan," Mike said, shrugging. "Doesn't mean I have to like it."

"Looks like a good plan," Papa said. "About as good as we're going to get."

"Glad you're here to run it," Cally said, grinning.

"Not going to," Papa replied, standing up. "Not my forte. I know that Nathan said I've got to quit being a captain. Thing is, I was never even a captain. There was more than one reason I let you handle the teams. Could I run this? Yes. Could I run it better than you? No. Running a large force is an art and it's one I've never really had."

"Bullshit," Cally said. "You're much better than I am."

"At certain things," Papa said, patting her on the shoulder. "Which is why I'm taking the hide in the atrium."

"Oh, *hell* no," Cally said, her eyes blazing. "That's *suicide*!"

"The ACS mostly fights outdoors," Papa said. "The commander is going to feel more comfortable there than anywhere else. Lots of sight-lines. He's going to have a bodyguard group. The guy who takes the shot is going to have to be very good if he's going to survive. It's really me or you if we're going to try it. And as I just pointed out, you're better at running a battle like this than I am."

"You are *not* going to die on me," Cally said, angrily. "It's not that important."

"Taking out the commander will throw them off,"

Papa said. "It's important. Just as you surviving is important. And it's not suicide. Trust me. I'm going to take one shot and be *gone* before they can react. If he's not *right* in my crosshairs, I'll just evac."

"Papa," Cally said.

"Hush, child," Papa replied, putting his finger on her lips. "I'll see you at the extraction point."

"Placerville," Mike said out of nowhere, his head gently rocking to the movement of the hard-maneuvering shuttle. His chin was resting on interlaced fingers which were, in turn, resting on the butt of his grav-rifle.

Mike had pointed out to the pilots that whereas he didn't like Nap of Earth flying, he preferred NOE to being shot out of the sky. So when they got in reasonable range of antiaircraft—with GalTech that was about two hundred miles—they had dropped down to ground level and were hammering hard at about two hundred feet AGL. North Kentucky had some relief to it, not to mention power lines, so the shuttles were bucking up and down like a bronco. If the general found that uncomfortable it wasn't apparent.

"Yes, sir," Sergeant Harkless said. He'd clipped off his weapon and was leaning back, his helmet in the seat next to him and his arm resting on it.

Mike leaned over and spit in his helmet, the biotic undergel consuming the organic material as it did sweat, wastes and, occasionally, puke.

"The rank threw me," Mike said. "Sorry. RIFed?"

RIF stood for "reduction in force." After the war there were too many Chiefs and not enough Indians. A lot of officers who wanted to stay in had been reduced in rank.

"Yes, sir," Harkless said.

"You were a major then," Mike said. "501st. Whadja make?"

"Colonel, sir," Harkless said. "Got out. Didn't find anything worth doing. Joined back up as a private. Rank's . . . slow these days."

"You were a colonel?" Cuelho asked, his eyes wide. "Sir?"

"I sir you, Lieutenant," Harkless said, chuckling. "Not the other way around. You're the boss, sir."

"Hell," Mike said with a chuckle. "I was a major general. Then a brigadier. Then colonel. Then a major general. Then a colonel again. Now I'm a lieutenant general. Way things are going, I'm bucking for private."

"Yes, sir," Harkless said, chuckling in turn. "If you want a job as an instructor . . . I can hook you up."

"Thanks," Mike said.

"Seriously," Harkless continued. "I know people. Have your people call my people."

"I'll do that," Mike said, laughing. Then he grunted angrily. "*Dammit!* That's *it!*"

"What, sir?" Cuelho said, his eyes wide.

"I've done this shit a lot," Mike said. "Enough that I get déjà vu . . . A lot. I was trying to figure out what this reminded me of."

"Which battle was it, sir?" Cuelho said, a touch eagerly. The chance to hear someone as legendary as General O'Neal reminisce about a battle didn't come often.

"Harkless," Mike said. "Rebel force. Light weapons. In what could be for all practical purposes a spaceship even if it's underground. The attacking force—"

"Is in *armor!*" Harkless said and then began laughing

so hard he'd have fallen out of his seat if it wasn't for the straps. "Oh, God, sir! You're killing me!"

"I need to get my helmet configured!" Mike said. "It needs to have these sort of wing things coming out of the bottom! Hey, Shelly, any way you can make this armor black?"

"'Dom! Dom! Dom! I'm a dom, I'm a dom,'" Harkless started singing.

"That's *sick*!" Mike said.

"You *know* those are the words, sir," the sergeant said, grinning. "Hey, are you going to torture your daughter, who you don't know is your daughter, for information? In a very slightly pornographic manner?"

"Not unless Michelle happens to be on the planet," Mike said. "Which she's not. And I don't think I'd try: She's got this whole . . ." He stopped and shook his head. "Let's just say that you don't mess with the little green guy."

"Sir . . ." Cuelho said, confused. "What are you talking about?"

"General," the pilot called. "LZ in thirty."

"I'll explain later," Mike said, putting on his helmet. He made some whooshing sounds. "Just not the same."

"Well, sir," Harkless said as soon as he had his settled. "In part it's because you're thinking of the wrong movie."

"Oh?" Mike asked, picking up his rifle and checking it. *Yup, thar's bullets in it.* He tucked it into a tactical carry and hit the release on the straps.

"What you really need is a great *biiig* black helmet."

"Sergeant Harkless, you are *sooo* going to pay for that."

Then he started humming.

"Dum! Dum! Dum-tee-dum, dum-tee-dum."

"Sir," Harkless said, his armor jiggling. "I'd like to be able to *hit* what I'm shooting at?"

"All the remaining dependents are headed for the back door," Tommy said. "There's . . . a bit of a crush."

"Don't let anyone get hurt in the stampede," Cally replied in a monotone. "ACS just set down. They've spotted our top-side eyes and have taken them out with wonderful precision," she added bitterly. "All we're getting is flashes of an ACS suit and then . . . snow."

"Hey, we're . . ." Tommy stopped and shook his head. "*They* are good."

"Where's your head on this, Mr. Sunday?" Cally asked, spinning around in her chair. "Seriously. This has *got* to be fucking with you."

"Other than the stakes, would I rather be on the other side?" Tommy asked. "Oh, hell, yeah. Wouldn't you? Do I miss ACS? Yes. Do I think we have a chance in hell of stopping them? Depends on how good the commander is."

"The LT doesn't have any experience," Cally said. "The platoon sergeant was the commander of the 501st ACS regiment during the war. That was when it was down to about a battalion, but he started as an LT in the 501st."

"Then I'd say we're screwed," Tommy said, shrugging. "But all we have to do is slow them down enough that the Indowy and dependents can make it to the shuttles. That should be able to do."

"Our lives, our fortunes," Cally said. "At least we don't have to give up our sacred honor."

✧   ✧   ✧

"I hate elevator shafts," Mike said, looking at the hole where a barn used to be.

The bodies from the mercenary force were still scattered amongst the snow. If it bothered the general it wasn't obvious.

"We can just drop on grav, sir," Sergeant Harkless said dubiously.

The platoon was spread out in a perimeter just in case there was a way for the enemy to pop up behind them. Of course, any weapon capable of defeating ACS gave off some energy trace. On the other hand, so did ACS. So while they could spot the enemy, the reverse was also true.

"And get picked off in a shooting gallery," Mike said. He'd long before learned not to bother shaking his head in armor. He pulled out an AM grenade. The grenade was about the size of a small protein bar and shaped somewhat like one. Given that it could be dialed up to near kiloton range of output, the term "suicide bar" had come into vogue since the war. "What do you think?" he said, holding it up.

"Never use finesse when force will do, sir," Harkless replied.

"Where have I heard that before, Sergeant?" the LT asked.

"What the *hell* was *that*?" Cally asked at the deep *throom!* that had boomed through the station.

"Suicide bar," Tommy said. "Set to about a half-ton release."

"I guess they're not being subtle," Cally said.

"Never use finesse when force will do," Tommy said.

"That sounds like a quote," Cally said, frowning.

"It is," Tommy replied. "Your father's."

"Clear," SPC "Shark" Waters said, spotting three sensors, two visual and a subspace sensor, and taking them down. "Area is secure."

Waters had been born in Waynesville, West Virginia after the war. So he'd never lived in Urbs. But that didn't mean he'd never visited them. Urbs tended to run a bit more to the wild side and as Kipling put it: Single men in barracks don't turn into plaster saints.

But he'd never seen an Urb like this one. Painting Galplas, which was the primary material used in them, was difficult. In fact, it was pretty much impossible. So the walls came in four shades of institutional ick.

Not these. They'd been painted, somehow, into a riot of colors. There were also Galplas benches lining the walls, which were not standard for Urbs.

"Something different about this place," Sergeant Jon Akers said.

"Go figure," Shark replied. " 'Sir, we have secured the entry of the rebel base!' Hey, at least we're not in *white* armor."

"You know what always happens to those guys, right?" Akers said. "I've got a moving energy source."

"Sensor bot," Shark replied, firing through one of the Galplas walls, which dissolved in a white flash, and removing the sensor. " 'Look, sir! Droids!' "

"Follow the bouncing ball," Akers said as a movement arrow appeared. "And keep the references to yourself."

❖   ❖   ❖

"You know," Mike said, looking around the atrium. "For a place that's apparently deserted it doesn't *feel* deserted."

"Know what you mean, General," First Sergeant Harkless said. "Got that puckering feeling."

"Teams aren't encountering any resistance, sir," Lieutenant Cuelho said.

"Noted, LT," Mike said, looking at the building schematic.

The "secret base" was, indeed, a Sub-Urb. At least it had all the signs of being one. And not a standard one by any stretch of the imagination. As the teams moved cautiously forward they were building a map, not only of their own positions but the areas immediately surrounding them from sensor systems on the suit. But that was *all* they had. He still didn't know what he was really dealing with and that was making him unhappy.

This atrium was an example. The ceiling was much higher than standard with a "view" of the sky. Also larger than standard with walls that had been Sohon modded to various pastels. If Mike had any question about the rebels' access to GalTech it was disabused when he saw the "painting."

"Shelly, tell me you've hacked into their mainframe or something," Mike said.

"Sorry, General," his AID replied. "They've got AIDs of their own. And *very* good cyber systems. So far I haven't even scratched it and *I'm* getting outside help."

"Well, a whole bunch of Indowys and humans came into this base," Mike said. "They've got to be here *somewhere*."

✧   ✧   ✧

The sniper position was long prepared.

Advanced weaponry gave off a whole host of signatures and any decent sensor system could detect not just the antimatter signature of grav-guns but the power signatures of plasma.

For that matter, the ACS suits gathered in the atrium should have been able to detect the hidey-hole. The small shot opening was, after all, lined with a very thin layer of uniarmor, the same thing that made ACS invulnerable to nearly any weaponry.

But where there were measures, there were countermeasures. The wall was carefully constructed to appear to be nothing more than part of the Galplas wall. To any normal test it had the same resonance as normal Galplas and certainly could not retract for a moment then close after the sniper had taken his or her shot.

Papa wasn't *certain* that the wall was going to stop grav-gun fire, though, so he personally intended to take one shot and then get the *fuck* out. The hide also had a drop-out system under higher than normal gravity with a bouncer at the bottom. If they didn't return fire in microseconds, he was golden. And they'd have to be very good, very good to spot him, return fire and get a shot through the loophole that fast.

The ACS point, however, had eliminated all the sensors in the room. So he wasn't *quite* sure *exactly* where they were. He knew they were in there, but not exactly where. He was, and he knew it, going on hope. If the command group, especially the commander, was in the right spot he'd get his shot and at least, for a moment, disrupt the attack.

If not, he was *still* planning on getting the *fuck* out.

"The rabbits are in the pantry," Candy whispered.

The entire base was wired. There was no way they were going to risk radio communication up against ACS. Candy was hooked into an outlet in the wall of the hidey-hole and another wire ran to his rather old-fashioned set of headphones.

"Initiate in five," Papa whispered. "Candy, call it and lift on command."

"Roger," Candy said. "Five . . . Four . . ."

Papa settled into position and snuggled the heavy grav rifle into his shoulder.

The two ACS suits moved cautiously down the corridor, shoulder-mounted grav-cannons training from side to side, hands ready to attack, defend or draw secondary weapons, the operators monitoring their sensors for any sign of the as-yet-to-reveal-himself enemy.

Sergeant Jonathan Doggette was one of the platoon's designated Close Quarters Combat instructors. A four-year veteran of the ACS, like most of the platoon he had yet to see combat.

With the long transit times to the areas of main operation, bringing "blooded" personnel back just to be instructors was an enormous waste of time, money and manpower. Instead most instructors came straight from Advanced training, were run through a quick course and then worked their way up the chain from assistant instructor to full, then specialized in one area or another.

The entire platoon recognized the problems with the system. Despite regular communication with in-contact forces, there was really no substitute for experience. They knew, in their bones, that there were things that needed to be in the instruction program they were just flat missing.

One of the biggest problems was close quarters combat. No units had engaged in it with Posleen since the war. And then rarely. Most close quarters work in the war was on Diess in the massive megascrapers that dotted that planet. And most of that was a harum-scarum affair of "whatever works." Nobody had ever really sat down and worked out what worked and what didn't with ACS from a CQB standpoint.

So Sergeant Doggette was looking forward to this engagement. It would give him valuable experience that he could pass on to his trainees and maybe keep some of them alive. It would also give him a basis to make recommendations in changes to the training manuals in the area of CQB.

If the enemy would ever show himself.

"Amy, I've got an energy reading at forty meters, mark two point eight minus," Sergeant Doggette said.

"That's a secondary fusion plant," Amy said. "Or I would have highlighted it. There don't seem to be any . . ."

The AID broke off as a karat flashed into view. Before Doggette could even begin to engage, fifty rounds of 3mm grav smashed through his frontal armor and turned him into paste.

"General, we have three units down," Shelly said, highlighting the engagement. "Two WIA, one KIA. Very sophisticated camouflaged ports. Plasma cannons and grav-guns."

"Roger," Mike said, looking at the schematic. "Lieutenant?"

"We're . . . giving as good as we're getting, sir," Cuelho said. If he was nervous it wasn't evident. "More, in fact. All three defense points that ambushed our units have been taken out."

"We don't want to get caught up in furballs," Mike said, looking at the schematic that had been built so far. "Under, over, around, take them in the side and back."

"Yes, sir," Cuelho said, with slightly less assurance.

"Like this," Mike said, bringing up the schematic so that it was repeated to the lieutenant, and started to trace out paths of attack. "Alpha second goes down, over to the left, up, hook back. That puts them to the rear, flank, of this defensive position. Bring Bravo around the same way to the—"

"GENERAL!"

CHAPTER TWENTY-NINE

The port dropped and, for Michael O'Neal, Sr., time froze.

The commander of the attack had set up more or less where he expected. And he had him, unquestionably, dead to rights. A hair's breadth squeeze. The port would drop. He would drop out. Defenses would close around him. He would live. The ACS commander would be dead and that would give some of his men, some of his family, a brief second chance.

He had the crosshairs dead on the sniper triangle of the suit. Right under the helmet there was a slight weakness. His son had mentioned it to him more than fifty years ago and if there was one thing that Papa O'Neal had an elephant's memory for it was military trivia.

His son.

The armor was distinctive. Papa had seen it on repeated news clips over the decades. News clips that he stored and replayed over and over again in his most private moments.

His son.

The battles that he and Cally had engaged in for decades were important. He would have given up the strife long before if he didn't believe that. Would have dragged his granddaughter away if he didn't think they mattered. But they were cold, dank, bitter. There was an honor there, but it was constantly tarnished. There were no parades, few medals and damned well nothing to write home about.

His son.

Of all of his children, his grandchildren, even the immensely successful Michelle, Mike was the one who carried everything, from Papa's perspective, good and right and clean and perfect in the world. It was not something he would ever mention to Cally. Ever hint. Nothing that his children by Shari would ever suspect. Which is why he replayed those clips only when he was in his most private moments. Really, only Candy ever knew.

A hint, a flinch, a deep breath and the nanometers left of trigger squeeze would be complete.

And his son would be a puree inside of his customized Armored Combat Suit.

They would not win the battle but it would help immensely. The ACS, their most cherished hero dead, would be livid but confused. If *Mike O'Neal* could die, what were they facing?

If his son could die . . .

It was an instant, a flash of neurons that processed more information in less time than the most sophisticated AID. A gestalt of total oneness.

A perfect moment for any warrior.

❖   ❖   ❖

Mike didn't really need Shelly to scream. He was looking more or less right at the sniper. The positioning had been . . . superb. It was as if the man had read his mind. The sniper had him dead to rights. And Mike knew, looking at the weapon, at the shooter, that he, Lieutenant General Michael O'Neal, holder of two Medals of Honor and the Globe of Valor, was dead.

There were other things that Mike, in that brief moment, knew. The man, he was certainly a man despite the concealing clothing and body armor, was a juv. How Mike knew he couldn't say. His steadiness? His calmness? The set of his perfect shooter's position? It didn't matter. This was a man who had been in combat for a long time. There was no way in hell he was going to miss.

Blue eyes. The shooter was all away across the atrium, far too far away to see that sort of detail, and firing through a narrow port. But it was suddenly as if Mike had the vision of an eagle. The man had blue eyes.

His rig-out was . . . perfect. Every item was placed just so. Some of them had subtle angles to them that made it almost look messy, but it wasn't. The placement was more . . . combat feng shui. Sometimes it wasn't best for a magazine holder to be directly up and down. Tilted, slightly, might work a bit better.

This was a man who had honed his skill for years, decades. Centuries?

Training, experience and sheer monkey survival instincts lifted Mike's right arm at lightning speed, bringing his under-arm microgrenade launcher in-line. The slot was remarkably small but it wasn't as if Mike hadn't hit smaller targets.

Before the first grenade was out of the launcher, however, he knew two more things.

The sniper recognized him. There was no motion, no widening of the eyes. But something, a form of telepathy in the zen state of that moment, told General O'Neal he was both recognized and that the recognition was unexpected. That the sniper was as shocked as he was.

The second thing almost made him check his fire.

The sniper lifted his finger from the trigger.

The armored door snapped back up but two of the antimatter grenades had made it through. The hide vanished in a ball of plasma as antimatter touched matter and engaged in an orgy of mutual annihilation. Whoever the sniper was, whyever he had chosen not to kill General Michael O'Neal, was a mystery.

"Jesus, General," the lieutenant snapped, practically jumping into the air. "Are you okay?"

"Never better," Mike replied, calmly. "As I was saying . . ."

Cally had her hands together as if praying, thumbs under her chin and index fingers pressed against her lips. Tears were streaming down her face.

Tommy reached over and put his hand on her shoulder.

"Cally . . . Do you want me to take it?"

"I'm just focusing," she said. "Dammit! How in the *hell* did they take him down? The hide was cloaked, the position was armored and it was *Papa*!"

"They're . . . very good," Tommy said, gently. "Some better than others."

"Miss O'Neal," the AID said carefully.

"*What?*"

"I've parsed data from your late grandfather's PDA," the device replied. "I have an identification on the enemy commander. Who also was the person who . . . fired on your grandfather's position."

"Lieutenant Cuelho," Cally said. "We already *know* who the commander of the force is."

"Correction," the AID said. "The senior officer present is not Lieutenant Arthur Cuelho. It is Lieutenant General Michael O'Neal."

Corporal Erin Melvin Doyle was of the opinion he was having a bad day.

"Jesus Bloody Christ!" he shouted as a blast of plasma more or less cooked the entire corridor. Fortunately, he was standing around a corner and it only heated up his suit a bit. It would have cooked any unprotected human, or lesser protected human, within twenty feet.

He stuck his grav-cannon around the corner and triggered a burst on remote, managing to snag the plasma gunner. But then two grav rifles fired back, filling the corridor with trails of silver fire.

"This ain't workin', Bigfoot," SPC Ray Joseph Hutchinson said calmly.

Like Hutchinson it was Doyle's first taste of combat but, also like Hutchinson, he'd been an instructor in ACS, using the incredibly lifelike simulations, for over four years. Frankly, so far actual combat had been easier than their sims. "I would recommend an alternate route."

"Roight 'ch'are, Hutch," Doyle said, pulling out

a suicide bar. "You don't like us coming down *this* corridor, we'll go down the one *under* it."

"Stand by," his AID said. "Incoming orders."

"'Bout bloody time," Doyle snapped.

"Not the corridor under it," the AID said, karating the ceiling. "Go up. Two levels. Then across and down."

Both grav-cannons swiveled upwards, blasted in a circle and in a moment both suits were *gone*.

"They left," Corporal David Hines said. "That's . . . odd."

"They didn't leave," Sergeant Blevins said. "Use your ears."

As some of the ringing in his ears from the battle died—grav-cannons fired at relativistic speed made a sonic-crack from hell—Hines could make out a series of thumps, crashes and explosions. It was, despite the muffling of multiple walls, fairly easy to follow. When a blast of relativistic velocity depleted uranium hits Galplas it tends to cause a bit of a noise. First going up. Then across accompanied, even at this distance, by the distinct sound of boots, a crash.

"What was *that*?" Rich Widemann muttered. The only Bane Sidhe assigned to the short team of DAG, he was feeling a bit out of his depth.

"Door?" Hines said.

"Wall," Blevins replied stoically. "I think they just punched through it. They're going around us."

Hines looked at the heavy plasteel armored door they were guarding and made a moue.

"If we're supposed to keep them from going through the *door* and they attack us from the other *side* of the door . . ."

"We stop them," Blevins said.

"I'm just saying. If we're supposed to keep them *out* of *there* and they're already *in* there, fighting to keep them *in* there just sort of defeats the purpose, doesn't it?"

"We were ordered to hold this intersection," Blevins said. But even he was starting to look puzzled.

"Yeah," Hines said. "But because of the *door!*"

"They're coming down," Widemann said.

"I'm just saying," Hines said.

"We hold the intersection," Blevins snapped, turning to face the door.

"Okay," Hines said, waving his grav rifle. "No issues. I'm just saying. They're probably going to blow it. Shouldn't we sort of back away?"

"Okay," Blevins said, nodding. "Point."

The threesome crouched behind a hastily constructed barrier ten yards from the door in question. In the distance there was banging.

"You guys ever see this movie?" Widemann asked with a puzzled tone. "Real old one. Horrible CGI. But it's got this guy in black armor with this cape?"

"Yeah," Hines said, frowning. "I know the one you're talking about. *Dammit*, if you hadn't mentioned it I could have told you right off."

"There are other things to concentrate on," Blevins growled.

"It's just that . . ." Widemann said. "I guess you haven't seen it, huh?"

"I've seen it," Blevins said then paused. "I think. Weren't there some sequels?"

"I think those were prequels," Hines said. "The

skinny dude with the magic sword was really the emperor or something."

"The point is," Widemann said, trying to recover the thread. "There's this scene in the beginning of one of the movies. Just before the guy in black armor shows. Bunch of guys in light armor, guns pointed . . ."

"Damn," Blevins said, starting to laugh. "You Bane Sidhe son of a bitch."

"I mean," Widemann said, "am I the *only* one with a sense of déjà vu?"

"The banging's stopped," Hines said.

"Yeah, that was a bad sign in the movie, too," Blevins said. "I mean, all we need is white helmets and a steely eyed guy . . ."

"That would be me," Corporal Doyle said from behind them:

"Dammit," Blevins said, setting his grav-rifle on the barricade. "You and your movie trivia!"

"Where the *hell* did you come from?" Hines said angrily, dropping his to the floor.

"How do you catch a unique rabbit?" Corporal Doyle asked, kicking the weapon away.

"I don't know," Widemann said, raising his hands. "How *do* you catch a unique rabbit?"

"You nique up on it."

"Just one problem," Widemann said, shrugging. "We can't be captured."

"But you are," Hutch pointed out, coming up behind them.

"Heads full of secrets and all," Blevins said sadly. "Crap."

"Look, fellas . . ." Doyle said uneasily.

"Nice to have met you," Hines said, then bit down on something.

All three dropped to the floor.

"Bloody hell," Doyle said softly. "Bloody fucking hell."

"Four more WIA, no KIA," Shelly said. "The teams are bypassing points but the points can follow their progress and are maneuvering skillfully."

"Not skillfully enough," Mike said. Now that he'd gotten the feel for the enemy commander he could pretty much anticipate where they were going to remaneuver to and the teams were actually getting there faster.

AIDs, with just a glance, could spot not only that there was an enemy but identify individuals. The schematic marked them with a T (tango or target) and a numerical designator. So far fifty tangos had been ID'd, many but not all of them former DAG.

Fourteen of those fifty were dead. Seven had been, temporarily, captured. One of the captured had then politely noted that she was going to commit suicide and the ACS might want to back up.

Which they did and she did. With C-9 that could, conceivably, have done some damage to the ACS.

The rest had commited suicide in less spectacular ways.

It was the strangest damned battle.

"This is stupid," Mike said. "And annoying. Shelly, call for a cease fire."

"They're hitting us from every direction and moving too fast for us to reposition," Tommy said. "We're getting slaughtered." His tone was odd. "I had a pretty good layout, even to take on ACS."

"I know," Cally replied. There was a time for grief and a time to lock it down. She knew Papa was dead. She wanted to scream, to shout, to kill something. But for the first time in her life she and her people were getting killed. And she knew why. It wasn't just the technology, it was the guy behind it.

"They're taking us apart like a chicken," Tommy said.

"I know."

"We need a better plan."

"Such as?"

"Get into position on the Gamma entry," Tommy said, pointing. "All the heavy equipment means that they'll have to come at us head-on. We couldn't do it before because we were still evacuating the base. Most of the evacuees are in Gamma at this point."

"We're in contact," Cally pointed out. "We don't have *time*."

"Call for a cease-fire?" Tommy said.

"Rebel commander . . ."

"ACS commander . . ."

"You sound young," Mike said. There was no visual. "Juv?"

"Of course," the female voice said.

"General?" Lieutenant Cuelho said. "Be aware that they're piping this into their announcement system. Everyone is hearing this."

"Good," Mike said. "I'm not planning on saying anything I don't mean."

"Neither am I," the woman replied. "That's why I pumped it."

"Your people are very good," Mike said. "Not just the DAG that went rogue but the other ones as well. And your tactics have been . . . fair."

"Coming from you I'll take that as a compliment."

"An honest one," Mike said. "I want you to understand that I admire your dedication and professionalism. I will even admit that I, too, don't particularly like the current political situation."

"What?" the voice said sarcastically. "Like extrajudicial killings? Complete trashing of not only the Constitution but every bilateral legal treaty we've ever negotiated? Deliberate manipulation of the war and since to reduce the human race to beggars dependent on Darhel 'charity'? Duty, honor, country? Remember *those* words? *General?*"

"All of the above," Mike replied calmly. "Agreed. Arguing your side is rather easy. Arguing mine somewhat harder and I'm not going to bother. The bottom line is that I've got a job to do. The job is to arrest certain persons in this base and turn them over to Fleet Penal for questioning. Surrender your weapons and you spare your lives."

"Sorry, been with Fleet Penal before," the voice said. "I'd rather go down fighting. Hell, I'd rather go down in a burning aircraft. It's quicker."

Mike paused and blinked.

"You were the woman captured in the penetration of Strike Base," he said.

"Got it in one."

"Then I have a question for you," Mike said coldly. "Were you involved in the killing of General Stewart?"

The reply was a barked laugh that settled into a giggle that sounded very much like a little girl.

"No," the voice said with strained humor. "Uh, you could say that the answer to that is a *definite* no. We were, among other things, lovers. If they didn't give you full disclosure, the only reason I was caught was that he'd been shot, by someone else I'll add, and I stayed to save his life. For which I was then subjected to a month of torture. So you'll understand if I'm not willing to go that for *you*."

"Shelly?" Mike said.

"Accurate," the AID replied. "I have been given access to the information on that. What she says is correct."

"Question for a question," the female said tightly. "More a confirmation. One of our people had the mission of removing the commander of your force."

"It was a legitimate forlorn hope," Mike said gently. "I was forced to return fire. I'm sorry."

"You're *sorry*?" the voice said angrily. "Oh, you have NO idea how sorry!"

"I take it you were close."

"You might say that," the woman replied. "He was my grandfather."

"He was very good," Mike replied. "Very, very good. I am truly sorry. But I think that this makes the obvious point that you don't have a hope in hell of surviving. *Please* surrender. I'll see what I can do about—"

"And we both know how far *that* will fly," the woman said. "I *know* *you* would," she said, more gently. "But we both know that the Darhel are going to pull us apart like a chicken. I've been there and most of my people know the story. We're less than enthusiastic about surrendering. A clean death is preferable."

"Always the problem of treating your prisoners badly," Mike said sadly. "I hate to kill you, you're very good."

"We'd hate to die. But we're not going to surrender. So why don't you go tell the Darhel to piss up a tree?"

"Ain't happening," Mike said, his face grim. "I guess we'll just have to do battle upon this morn. If it's any consolation, you're the best people I've ever faced. The downside from my perspective is simply that I'd rather have you fighting for me than be fighting against you. It is . . . an honor to do battle with you."

There was a long pause.

"Thank you, General," the woman said, her voice tight. "If we're going to die in battle . . . I cannot imagine a better choice than in battle against you. So, General, I say: *Cry HAVOC and let slip the dogs of war!*"

CHAPTER THIRTY

"You are clear," the AID said.

"Are our people repositioned?" Cally asked.

"Yes," Tommy replied. "Most of the Indowy are in the tunnel. They're not far enough away to survive the blast, but they're in the tunnels. The ship has mostly boarded the dependents. The stay-behind forces are in positions that even ACS will find hard to flank. We need to leave."

"Like hell," Cally said. "I'm not going to leave people to die and then run away like . . . an Indowy."

"Thought you might say that," Tommy replied, then shot her in the back of the neck with a Hiberzine dart.

"Carry Miss O'Neal to safety," Tommy said, sitting down at the desk.

"You're not staying?" George said, picking the slumped figure off the floor.

"Not if I can avoid it," Tommy said. "AID, get me the stay-behind commander."

❖   ❖   ❖

"The enemy forces used the period of cease fire to reposition," Shelly said. "Our forces aren't encountering any resistance."

"They have to be here *somewhere*," Mike said.

He was still in the atrium. He'd considered moving forward with the forces but there was really no need. Despite Tam's insistence, he could have run the whole thing from Fredericksburg.

He wished he had. No, that would have meant that the sniper *would* have gotten Lieutenant Cuelho. And despite the fact that the kill was naggling at him—the female commander had gotten to him—losing another man would have made him feel worse.

"Teams have searched all the upper levels," Shelly said. "That leaves Foxtrot or Gamma. Both are heavy equipment areas with limited entry."

"We can't just blast our way through," Mike said.

"No, sir."

"Tell them to stop the general search," Mike said, considering the placement of his teams. "First squad to Gamma entry, Third to Foxtrot, Second to Echo Forty-seven as reserve. Press forward until they hit resistance then . . . take open order, lie down and sit tight."

"Yes, sir," Lieutenant Maise said.

Most of the stay-behind force was wounded. In general, the weapons that the ACS were using didn't cause wounds. If a hypervelocity pellet of depleted uranium hit you going at relativistic speeds, it tended to kill any human not wearing ACS. A few of the troops had been injured, maimed or killed simply from a pellet hitting an obstacle near their positions.

Grav-guns were no joke.

But some of the injuries left walking wounded. Or, at least, wounded. Most of them weren't walking very well.

"We've got it covered. Very well, sir. Take care. Give . . . Tell Pinky I love him if you would, sir."

None of the rest of the rear-guard had children. All were volunteers.

"Maise, get the hell out," Sergeant Mike Swaim said. The sergeant had lost the lower part of his leg when an ACS round had blown out a wall. It was covered by a hasty Galplas coating and the nerves into the area had been neutralized. Otherwise he'd have screamed in agony when he shifted it. "Your kid's already lost the rest of his family." He forebore to mention that he, in turn, had lost *his* to the Darhel assassins.

"Pinky will . . . handle it," Maise said. "The kid's more grown-up than most of *us*. Proof of which is that we're stupid enough to stay behind and he's leaving."

"We got movement," Gavin "Hollywood" Harrison said. He was called that because he'd gotten the full measure of the Sunday "pretty" genes from both his maternal grandfather *and* grandmother.

The livid scars on his face from a blast of plasma somewhat marred that. One eye was barely hanging in there.

"ACS power pack and grav-cannon signatures on corridor two."

"I guess I should say something heroic," Maise said, raising his voice. "But the only thing I can think of sounds stupid and trite: I can't think of anywhere I'd rather be than here with you men, at this time, in this place."

"Hell, yeah," Swaim said. "And is it just me, or . . . was that lady right?"

"Yeah," Harrison said. "Fighting the scum that we normally fight is just . . . embarrassing. If you're going to go down, the place to go is fighting somebody *worth* fighting."

"Amen, brother," Scott Bettis said. The Bane Sidhe had a big pack over an abdominal wound and was also missing a leg. If it bothered him it wasn't apparent.

"Even though," Harrison added, "the situation quite frankly sucks."

"The Spartans called it 'A glorious death,'" Bettis said. "To die in battle against an opponent that was your peer. To grapple with them to the last, for the pure glory of battling an equal foe. It's rare that a warrior gets the chance."

"I wonder if they feel the same way?" Harrison said.

"Well, this is bloody fucked," Doyle said. "General, we've found the rebels . . ."

"Not much play there," Mike said, looking at the schematic. They still didn't have a full detail of the base but as far as they'd found there were only two ways into the area the Indowy had to be hiding. Both of them were corridors with so much heavy stuff surrounding them they couldn't get in any other way. It was going to be straight up the middle or nothing.

"Thermopylae," Harkless said.

"Yeah," Mike said bitterly. "And except that we're the ones in hoplite armor, we're the Persians. And you know how *that* turned out."

"I don't see a choice but hey-diddle-diddle, straight up the middle," Harkless said. "Sir."

"Me neither," Mike admitted. "We're moving forward.

With all the firepower that they've got covering the openings, we're going to take casualties. The more shooters the better."

"Yes, sir," Lieutenant Cuelho said.

"Shelly, have Third squad leave sensors at the Foxtrot opening. Have One-Alpha mark the secondary Gamma opening and have all teams move to the primary Gamma opening. Time to try to take the pass."

Corporal Doyle stuck his arm out around the corner and tossed a sensor ball. He got a brief take from it and then there was an explosion.

He popped a camera around the corner and grunted at the large crater on the floor of the corridor.

"They shot the bloody *ball*," Doyle muttered, incensed. "You don't *shoot* a bloody sensor ball. Who shoots a bloody *sensor* ball?"

"Someone who doesn't want you looking at them, Corporal," Mike said.

"Well, I can't throw it *faster*, General," the corporal pointed out. "The damned things break too much as it *is*."

"Allow me," Mike said, leaning under the massive trooper's arm and tossing another down the corridor. This one, however, skittered all over the place. Two shots were fired and the closest they got was rolling it faster.

"Just needed a little English, trooper," Mike said, considering the take. "Seven men. All wounded."

"In heavily prepared positions," Shelly pointed out. "Those are overpressure bunkers. You can't even blast them to death. Well, you might be able to but it would be tough."

"And they have a cross-fire set up," Cuelho said unhappily. "No way around them, either."

"And there's more energy readings farther in," Harkless said.

"I can *see* all that, gentlemen," Mike said, somewhat testily. "It doesn't mean we can't get through."

He considered for a moment, then sighed.

"Harkless, are you old enough to remember a game called 'dwarf-tossing'?"

"Time to buy some more time," Maise said. "Buckley, cut me into the ACS frequency."

"We're all going to die," the buckley replied. "What's the point. Trust me, I know ACS. You're going to get slaughtered."

"Then best we try to talk them out of it," Maise said. "Just get me the ACS commander."

"You got it?" Mike asked, kneeling by the opening.

"I've pretty much figured my career is toast," Harkless said. "Getting the Federation's greatest hero killed in a minor little skirmish isn't going to make things any worse."

"Uh . . ." Lieutenant Cuelho said.

"Hey, ACS commander."

"Stand-by," Mike said. "Who's this?"

"The sacrificial rear guard. Wanna know how this whole thing started?"

"Well, in the beginning was the Word," Mike said.

"Very funny. We took down a Darhel mega-corp and a mentat, one like your daughter, who had gone crazy and thought he was the Evil Overlord or something."

"That would tend to piss off some very powerful people," Mike said.

"And do you know how those people responded? They sent assassins after our families."

"I'm sorry to hear that," Mike said. "If you surrender I *will* guarantee the safety of your families. Or, yeah, I'll start killing Darhel myself."

"Too late. They killed my wife and daughter."

It was pretty hard to pick up people's emotions through ACS but Mike had been around it a long time. That sort of hit home with the platoon.

"Mine were killed by the Posleen," Mike said, omitting the fact that, in fact, his daughter Cally had been killed by a nuke he himself had ordered. "Know what *I* was doing six months ago?"

"Wandering around in the Blight doing dick all?"

"My division dropped on a world where the Posleen were well on their way to recovering from ornadar and had ten ships ready for lift-off," Mike said. "Ten ships isn't much, but we've only cleared five percent of the Blight. And you can't really call it cleared. Every planet there are some Posleen. Every planet they're working on the same thing: Building ships to start conquering the universe again. So when you can explain how rebelling against the Darhel is going to keep Earth from being overrun by ravenous, carnivorous extraterrestrial centaurs I'll be happy to join your cause. Are you going to supply more ACS suits? Orbital satellites? Fleet ships?"

He waited a moment for a reply, then nodded inside his suit.

"Thought not," Mike said. "So, we gonna do this thing? Or are you going to surrender?"

"Sorry, no, General," the rear-guard commander

said. *"To be clear, we don't hold what happened before on you or Fleet Strike. Fleet on the other hand . . ."*

"Don't get me started," Mike said. "And to be equally clear, I'd much rather have you fighting for me than fighting against you. You're . . . quite good."

"Pretty fucked up situation."

"Standard for every day since Jack Horner called me at work," Mike said. "It has been . . . an honor doing battle with you."

"Likewise. Well, time to die."

"Does appear so," Mike said. "Shelly, cut the connection. Sergeant Harkless?"

"This is crazy, sir," Harkless said, grabbing the smaller armor by its lift-points.

"The situation or the method?" Mike asked.

"Both."

"Remember to bounce me," Mike said. "Maximum difficulty of targeting."

"What about *your* targeting, sir?" Cuelho said, gulping.

"Sir . . ." Sergeant Harkless said, reprovingly.

"I think what Sergeant Harkless is trying to say is that . . . I've got it, Lieutenant," Mike said, chuckling. "I've done tight targeting while being bounced about before."

"I just mean . . . Entry is what privates are *for*, sir."

"I've got it, Lieutenant," Mike said. "Corporal Doyle, some cover fire if you will."

"Right you are, sir," Doyle said. "Hutch, double up."

"This is crazy," the specialist said.

"A moment, though," Mike said, his fingers moving in the air. "It's always a tough choice at a moment like this . . ."

"Sir?" Cuelho said.

"Goth? Industrial? Heavy metal . . .?" Mike said. "There's an argument for 'Brickhouse' to tell you the truth. It's got a beat and you can dance to it. Great for skiing . . . Ah. Sergeant Harkless. 'Citadel' or 'Honor'?"

"Oooo," Hutchinson interjected. "Tough choice, sir. 'Citadel's got a great entry beat but I always find that 'Honor' . . ."

"He wasn't asking *you*, Hutch," Doyle growled.

"Sorry, sir," the specialist said.

"I think I'm a bit older than you are, sir," Harkless said, chuckling. "I usually go with 'Smoke on the Water' or 'Highway to Hell.'"

"What in the *hell* is that?" Cuelho asked, thoroughly confused. "What are you *talking* about?"

"Lieutenants," Mike said, sighing. "You let them wear shoes . . . 'Honor' it is." He made a couple of more motions, then grasped his grav-rifle and toggled off the safety. "*Now* if you will please, Sergeant," he said somewhat loudly.

Kyle Davis hadn't suffered quite as badly as most of the rear-guard: He'd only had a foot blown off. On the other hand, somebody had to slow the ACS down so the rest of the group could get to minimum safe distance. Which was . . . pretty far all things considered.

But because he and a few others hadn't been more or less blown to shit, they were holding the forward portion of the defenses.

"*Davis.*"

"Go, Maise."

"*What the hell is taking them so long?*"

"Dunno. Not going to knock it."

"Fire some suicide bars down there to remind them we're in here."

"Fuck you."

Whoever had designed the defenses knew what they were doing. All of the firing points they'd used had been good but this one was the cat's pajamas. There was only one way into the area and it was a narrow corridor that debouched into an open area about fifteen meters across. It looked like it had doors opening to other portions of the sector but only the inner one worked. Between the false doors were hidden firing points for five shooters. All of the points would close down for explosions and the armoring was proof against even grav-gun fire.

So whoever entered the open area was going to be taking fire from five DAG troops and two concealed automated grav-guns. And the only way to take out the DAG troops was to slide a round through a small opening with pin-point accuracy.

Which meant they were going to get shredded.

The port automatically closed when a suicide bar came flying into the open area and Davis leaned the barrel of his rifle against it. The system would drop the port as soon as the overpressure dropped. Since even ACS could take some serious damage from suicide-bars, they'd have to come in hard on its heels to get there before the DAG shooters could engage.

The port dropped and Davis instinctively began searching for targets even as the last of the propellant from the grenade washed past him through the port. But what he saw froze him for just a split second.

The entry-person was not running into the area. The entry person was not sliding into the area. The entry person was *flying* through the open-area in more or less a flat spin.

It took Davis just fraction of a moment to identify that the thing flying through the air, with rounds spitting out of its grav-gun, was, in fact, a small suit of ACS. One that, before he could react, took out the automatic guns and three of the defending DAG. Then hit the wall with both feet and flipped back across the open area.

Davis had just started to take up trigger squeeze when the little shit put five rounds of depleted uranium through a hole not much larger than a fist.

It just didn't seem fair.

"Clear," Mike said, flipping to his feet. He'd somehow ended up upside down right there at the end.

Rounds cracked through the open area from a further firing point and he pumped a couple of grenades downrange to keep their heads down.

"Okay," he said, crossing to the far side of the open area where there was a bit more cover. "Correction. More or less clear."

"Glad to hear it, General," Corporal Doyle said, thudding into the wall and craning his grav-gun around the corner. "These lads are a bit feisty."

"And well dug in, again," Mike said, flipping a sensor ball down the corridor. "More or less straight shot."

"Which means no more finesse, sir," Sergeant Harkless said.

"Suppose so," Mike said, getting to his feet.

"Oh, no, sir," Harkless said, putting his hand on the general's shoulder. "You've had your fun."

"You can't exactly order *me*, Harkless," Mike said.

"No, but I *can* sit on you, sir," the sergeant said.

"Grenades," Doyle said, falling on the general's suit.

The suicide bars fell all over the compartment but none of them actually managed to hit a suit.

"These guys are starting to piss me off," Harkless said. "Second Squad. *Clear* that corridor."

"Here they come," Maise said, opening up at full auto.

Both groups were using virtually identical weapons. The M-292 grav rifle could spit three thousand three gram depleted uranium pellets downrange per minute. Designed to not only kill the Posleen they hit but a couple of its buddies as well, the pellets had the kinetic energy of a small meteor.

The ACS armor was proof against one pellet. Even five pellets. The bunkers the last of the DAG were in were proof against about the same fire power. They could shrug off suicide bars a bit *better* than ACS.

The corridor was narrow and there was only one way to clear it: Brute force.

Or, when it came down to reality: Mutual annihilation.

Maise let out one long scream as thousands of grav-rounds caused the armored bunker to ring like a tocsin. If anyone else was screaming he couldn't tell but he could see lines of silver fire stretching out to rip the armored suits apart. More, though, was coming in the opposite direction and the corridor quickly filled to choking with gaseous uranium as one by one the final defense points fell.

"No surrender," Maise said as the bunker came apart under the concentrated fire of five grav-guns.

✧   ✧   ✧

"That was . . . unpleasant," Mike said, looking at the scorched corridor. They'd lost two troopers but they had the, hopefully, final defenses. "But I will reiterate. I wish these guys were on *our* side."

"Be careful with the door," Harkless said. "Lord only knows what sort of booby traps these guys lay."

"Something . . . unpleasant I suspect," Mike said. "Onward, Lieutenant."

"Second Squad," Lieutenant Cuelho said. "Move out."

The actual door, per se, at the end of the corridor was slag. But a few kicks from one of the suits got it knocked off its hinges at least. On the far side was another small open area, apparently unguarded. However, there *was* a large Galplas box blocking the far door. It was gray, unmarked and had no apparent way to open it. On top was a large purple bow.

"What do we have here?" Doyle asked, stepping around the box. It . . . boded. And there was no way to get the door open without moving the box out of the way.

"Nothing good," Mike said, slipping through the gathered platoon. "Shelly?"

"It's got an AI broadcasting from it," Shelly said. "One of those buckley things but with an emulation of . . . Oops."

"What is 'oops'?" Mike said.

"I don't think I should have talked to it," Shelly said as a hologram appeared on top of the box.

"Greetings, Gentlemen."

The hologram was of a thin, faintly Native American female wearing a mini-skirt, go-go boots, a wildly tie-dyed halter top and a bandana around her head.

"It is my pleasure to welcome you to the final challenge," she continued, smiling merrily. "You have until the music stops to reach minimum safe distance. Good luck."

"Antimatter!" Shelly shouted as rock guitar started to play and the hologram started dancing on top of the box. "Antimatter source revealed! Twenty *grams* of antimatter!"

"We have three minutes and either ten or eleven seconds to get to minimum safe distance," Mike said, spinning in place. "Which is *very* far away. Move!"

"Sir," Cuelho said. "Move out by squad!"

As the ACS troops started pounding past him, Mike slapped them on the shoulder to hurry them, and Cuelho contacted him on the command freq.

"Sir?" the LT said as the last trooper passed and he dropped into place. "Three minutes and *either* ten or eleven?"

"Depends on whether it's *Disraeli Gears, Best of Cream* or *Cream of Clapton*," Mike said, running after him. Keeping the suits down while running was the tough part of running indoors. They had so much power they tended to want to jump.

"Sure it's not London Philharmonic?" Harkless asked. "That would give us . . . more time."

"Not echoey enough," Mike said. "Eight minutes and forty-two seconds. Includes a one minute and fifty second and a separate three minute instrumental portion."

"Sir?" Cuelho said, now thoroughly confused.

"Cream, sir," Harkless said, starting to faintly pant. "Eric Clapton, lead guitarist. The song is 'Sunshine of Your Love.'"

"My Dad's favorite song," Mike said. "I've got most of the versions available."

"I'm not feeling very well loved," Cuelho admitted. They'd gotten to the elevator and fortunately it was open. The troops were piling in. Unfortunately . . .

"*Very Best of Cream*," Shelly interjected. "You now have two minutes, forty-three seconds to reach minimum safe distance. The elevator takes two minutes and twelve seconds to reach the top."

"Fine," Mike said, last to pile in. He hit the up button and the 'close door' button, controlling his power so the finger of the suit didn't go straight through the plate. That would probably break the elevator which would be . . . bad. "No problem. I eat stress for breakfast."

The door closed and he winced.

"Oh," Sergeant First Class Harkless said. "That's just . . . wrong."

The booming music that had been blasting over the annunciator was cut off. But the elevator was playing the same song, Muzak style.

"Whoever did this . . ." Mike said. "Just . . . sick. Shelly. Time?"

"Two minutes, twenty-two seconds . . ."

"Nearly as sick as I am," Mike added.

"Yes, sir," Harkless said.

"*Been waiting so long . . .*" Lieutenant Cuelho muttered without really thinking about it.

"*To be where I'm going . . .*" Doyle added, his suit absentmindedly rocking back and forth.

"*In the sunshine of your lo-o-o-ve!*" Third Squad chorused.

"Nah-nana, nah, nah! Nah! Nah! Nah, nanana!" Hutch screamed, plowing an air-guitar on his grav cannon.

"Hutchinson!"

"Sorry, Sergeant."

"Sort of didn't complete the mission, sir," Sergeant Harkless pointed out. "We're entirely sans Indowy."

"Hey, they're all over the place," Mike said. "If the Darhel want Indowy let them catch their own." He paused and shook his head. "I *hate* Muzak."

"Thank God for Eric Clapton instrumentals, sir," Harkless said.

"Agreed, Sergeant," Mike said, rocking back and forth. *"The moaning of just we two . . ."* Mike muttered as the doors opened. "Haul ass for the stairs!"

"After you, General," Harkless said.

"Get *moving*, Sergeant," Mike snapped as the platoon pounded past. "I'm faster than you are."

Mike made it out of the hidden entrance just as the vocals cut off. Not a good sign. The platoon was well ahead of him, spread out in a broad formation and heading for the horizon.

"Twelve seconds, General," Shelly said. "You're not yet to minimum safe distance."

"How bad could it *be*?" Mike said, panting. He wasn't, in truth, much of a runner. Short legs and all. "I've been much closer to nuclear weapons before. It's in the ground . . ."

"Five. Bad. Four. Twenty *grams*. Three . . ."

"All units tuck and inertial dump!" Mike shouted, jumping into the air and tucking into a ball.

"One . . ."

"Just *sick*."

And then there was sunshine.

Mike didn't feel very well loved.

EPILOGUE

Cally opened her eyes and looked around. Tommy was standing by her bunk with a cup in his hands. From the smell of it, it contained some of Aelool's herbal tea.

"Status?" she asked, sitting up. Hiberzine didn't leave any sort of a hangover. You just went right back to the condition you were in before you got shot with it. In Cally's case, angry.

The room seemed to be a normal "human" style stateroom. She'd been on Himmit ships and this didn't look like a Himmit ship. It didn't even look Indowy made. It looked like something that had come out of Titan yards.

"We're already out of orbit," Tommy said, handing her the cup. "The Himmit are, as usual, being cagey about where we're going. But we loaded all the dependents and Indowy before we left. You missed the interesting part."

"I take it Maise blew up the base," Cally said.

"Quite spectacularly," Tommy replied.

"So much for Base One," Cally said. She took a sip of tea, then lowered her head onto her hand. "Tommy, you're a really good friend but right now I'm looking for someone to kill. You're a big guy and it'd be tough, but you know I'd manage. I think I'd rather just be alone right now."

Tommy nodded, started to speak, then walked out of the stateroom.

"How are you doing?" Tam asked as he walked into the room.

"Fine," Mike replied. "I don't even know why I'm in the hospital. I've been through much worse explosions in my time." He paused and thought about it. "Six . . . *seven* times."

"You're not for long," Wesley said. "There's a shuttle standing by to pick you up. Good news, you don't have to sit through the rest of the briefings. We'll just send you the minutes."

"Get his ass off-planet?" Mike said, his face hard. "Thanks very much for killing a bunch of humans, now get as far away as possible?"

"Pretty much," Tam said. "The good news is you'll have someone to talk to. The platoon's training assignment has been permanently suspended. They're being assigned to operational units."

"That must thrill the hell out of them," Mike said. "Tam, this is massively fucked up. How in the *hell* did an organization like that exist right under our noses? And they were . . . Good. Jesus Christ, they were good. They stayed true to their salt in a way it's almost impossible to find these days."

He was still coming to grips with the feelings he'd had at the last of the battle. The feeling that even though it was insane, stupid, pointless and even dishonorable at a level, he couldn't think of anywhere he'd rather be.

"Well, they're dead, now," Tam said.

"Yes," Mike said, grimly. "But you'd better find out who survived. Dammit, Tam . . ."

"Mike," the general said softly. "It's not your problem anymore. You need to get out there and make sure we don't have to face the Posleen as well. I'll be back here rolling in the pig pit. That's . . . my job."

"And I leave you to it," Mike said, rolling out of bed. He looked at the hospital gown and snorted. "I take it you brought some clothes."

"Lieutenant!"

The Ghin removed an aethal piece from the board, looked at it for a moment, then set it aside. He moved another and faintly smiled.

"Let the ever-be-damned Aldenata consider *that*."

❖   ❖   ❖

Like a whisper to the dusk
An oath against the shadows, denying the dark
FIGHT FIGHT FIGHT 'til the break of dawn
Like a prayer unto the dawn
In arms against the shadows, destroying the dark
FIGHT FIGHT FIGHT 'til the break of dawn
                                        —Atreyu, "Honor"

The following is an excerpt from:

LIVE FREE
OR DIE

————————✳————————

JOHN RINGO

Available from Baen Books
February 2010
hardcover

PROLOGUE

It is said that in science the greatest changes come about when some researcher says "Hmmm. That's odd." The same can be said for relationships: "That's not my shade of lipstick..."—warfare: "That's an odd dust cloud..." Etc.

But in this case, the subject is science. And relationships. And warfare.

And things that are just ginormously huge and hard to grasp because space is like that.

* * *

"Hmmm... That's odd."

"What?"

Chris Greenstein, in spite of his name, was a gangling, good-looking blond guy who most people mistook for a very pale surfer-dude. He'd found that he was great with the ladies right up until he opened his mouth. So his public persona was of tall, blond and dumb. As in mute. He had a masters in aeronautical engineering and a Ph.D. in astrophysics. The first might have gotten him a really good paying job if he could just manage to get through corporate interviews without putting his foot in his mouth. The second generally boiled down to academia or "Do you want fries with that?" He had the same problem with academia he had with corporations.

Chris was the Third Shift Data Center Manager for Skywatch. Skywatch was an underfunded and overlooked collection of geeks, nerds and astronomy Ph.D.s who couldn't otherwise find a job who dedicated themselves to the very important and very poorly understood job of searching the sky for stuff that could kill the world. The most dangerous were comets which, despite having the essential consistency of a slushee, moved very fast and were generally very big. And when a slushee that's the size of Manhattan Island hits a planet going faster than anything mankind could create, it doesn't just go bang. It turns into a fireball that is only different from a nuclear weapon in that it doesn't release radiation. What it does release is plasma, huge piles of flying burning rock and hot gases. Over a continent. Then the world, or the biosphere at least, more or less gets the big blue screen of death, hits reset and starts all over again with some crocodiles and one or two burrowing animals.

One comet killed the dinosaurs. Most of the guys at Skywatch made not much more than minimum wage. It gives one pause.

The way that Skywatch looked for "stuff" was anything that was quick, cheap and easy. They had databases of all the really enormous amounts of stuff, comets, asteroids, bits, pieces, minor moons, rocks and just general debris, that filled the system. They would occasionally get a contact from someone who thought that they'd found the next apocalypse. Locate, identify, headed for

Earth/yes/no? New?/yes/no? Most of it was automatic. Most of it was done by other people: essentially any-one with a telescope from a backyard enthusiast to the team that ran the Hubble was part of Skywatch. But thirty-five guys (including the two women) were paid (not much more than minimum wage) to sort and filter and essentially be the child of Omelas.

Chris was a nail biter. Most people who worked for Skywatch for any period of time developed some particular tick. They knew the odds of the "Big One" happening in their lifetime were *way* less than win-ning the lottery fifteen times in a row. Even a "Little Bang" was unlikely to occur anywhere that it mattered. A carbonaceous asteroid with a twenty-five megaton airburst yield like Tunguska was unlikely to occur over anything important. The world is seven-tenth's ocean and even the land bits are surprisingly empty.

But living day in and day out with the certainty that the fate of the world is in your hands slowly wears. Most people stayed in the core of Skywatch for fewer than five years if for no other reason than the pay. Chris had started as a filter technician ("Yes, that's an asteroid. It's already categorized. Thank you...") six years ago. He was way past his sell-by date and the blond had started going gray.

"It's a streak. But it's a really odd streak. The algo-rithm is saying it's a flaw."

The way that asteroids and comets are detected has to do with the way that stars are viewed. The more starlight that is collected the stronger the picture. In the old days this was done by having a photographic plate hooked up to a telescope that slowly tracked across the night sky picking up the tiny scatter of photons from the distant star. Computers only changed that in that they could resolve the image more precisely, fold, spindle and mutilate, and a CCD chip was used instead of a plate.

When you're tracking on a star, if something moves across your view it creates a streak. Asteroids and comets are closer than stars and if they are moving across your angle of view they create such a streak. If they're moving towards you it creates a small streak, across the view a large one. The angle of the Sun is important. So is the size of the object. Etc.

Serious researchers didn't have time for streaks. But any streak could be important so they sent them to Skywatch where servers crunched the data on the streak and finally came up with whether it was an already identified streak, a new streak, a new streak that was "bad," etc. In this case the servers were saying it was "Odd."

"Define odd," Chris said, bringing up the data. Skywatch researchers rarely looked at images. What he saw was a mass of numbers that to the uninformed would look something like a really huge mass of indecipherable numbers. For Chris it instantly created a picture of the object in question. And the numbers were *very* odd. "Nevermind. Albedo of point seven three? Perfect circle? Diameter of ten point one-four-eight kilometers? Ring shaped? Velocity of . . . ? That's not a flaw, it's a practical joke. Who'd it come from?"

"Max Planck. It's from Calar Alto. That's the problem. Germans . . ."

Calar Alto was a complex of several massive telescopes located in Andalusia in southern Spain and was a joint project of the Spanish and German governments. The German portion was the Max Planck

Institute for Astronomy and despite its location, Max Planck did most of the work at Calar Alto.

"Famously don't have a sense of humor," Chris said. He looked at the angle and trajectory again and shrugged. The bad part of working for Skywatch was worrying about "The Big One." The good part was that nothing was ever an immediate emergency. Anything spotted was probably going to take a long time to get to Earth. "Mark and categorize. It's not on a track for Earth. Angle's off, velocity is all wrong. Ask Calar to do another shot when they've got a free cycle. And we'd better keep an eye on it because with that velocity it's going to shoot through the entire system in a couple of years and if it hits anything it's going to be *really* cool."

"You know what it looks like?"

"Yeah. A halo. Maybe it's the Covenant."

Chris picked up his phone groggily and checked the number.

"Hello?"

"Chris? Sorry to wake you. It's Jon. Could you come in a little early today? We've got a manager's meeting."

"What's up?" Chris asked, sitting up and rubbing his eyes. Jon Marin was the Director of Skywatch. He knew his managers didn't get paid enough to be woken up in the middle of their, equivalent, night.

"It's Halo. There's been an . . . anomaly. We'll talk about it when you get in. We've got a video conference with Calar at four. Please try to be there."

"Yes, sir," Chris said. He looked at the time and sighed. Might as well get up, day was shot to hell anyway.

* * *

"Good afternoon, Dr. Heinsch . . ."

Jon Marin, in spite of his name, looked and sounded like the epitome of a New York Jewish boy. Which was what he was. His first Ph.D. was from NYU, followed by MIT and Stanford. His brother was a top-flight attorney in New York who pulled down a phone number every year. And his mother never let him forget it. He kept trying to point out he was a doctor, to no avail.

"Dr. Marin, Dr. Eisenbart, Dr. Fickle, Dr. Green-stein . . ."

"Doctor." "Doctor." "Doctor." "Doctor."

"As first discoverers we have named the object the Gudram Ring. This will, of course, have to be confirmed. But there is an anomaly we are having a hard time sorting out. We had a cycle that was doing a point to that portion of the sky but when we attempted to find the ring, it appeared to have disappeared."

"Disappeared?" Chris said. "How does something ten kilometers across disappear?"

"We wondered the same thing," Dr. Heinsch replied soberly. "I was able to get authorization to do a sweep for it. It took three full sweeps."

"Your sweeps cost about . . . ?" Dr. Marin said.

"A million Euros for each. But something that was once there and now is not? We considered the outlay appropriate. And we were right. We finally found it. Here is the new data."

The astronomers leaned forward and regarded the information for a moment.

"It slowed down," Chris said after a moment. He

finally found a finger that wasn't chewed to the quick and started nibbling. "Was there... It didn't have anything to cause a gravitational anomaly. It's coming in from out of the plane of the ecliptic."

Most of the "stuff" in the inner Solar System lay along a vaguely flat plane called the "plane of ecliptic." Earth, Mars, the asteroid belt, were all formed when the Sun was a flattened disc. The outer layers cooled and congealed into planets and then life formed and here we are. We are all star stuff.

If the ring had been coming in along the plane it might have passed a moon or planet and had a change in velocity, what was referred to as a "delta-V." But there weren't any planets "up" in the Solar System and it was inside the Oort Cloud.

"Correct," Dr. Heinsch said as if to a particularly bright child. From the point of view of "real" scientists, those who can do, those who can't teach and those who can't do or teach work for Skywatch.

"Is this data confirmed?" Dr. Marin asked very cautiously. Skywatch generally only made the news when they screamed "The sky is falling!" Since every time they'd screamed that it hadn't, they'd gotten very cautious. And this wasn't the sky falling. This was...

"Absolutely," Dr. Heinsch said. "However, we have sent it to you in raw form. We have also contacted the Russian, Japanese and Italian Institutes."

"Yes," Dr. Marin said, nodding. "I think we need to stay very cautious about this until we have a confirm all around..."

"It's a *space*craft!" Chris blurted.

"We need to be very *cautious*," Dr. Marin said, turning to glare at Chris.

"But it's *decelerating*!" Chris said, waving at the screen. "At the current rate of delta it's going to come to rest somewhere near *Earth*!"

"About thirty million kilometers," Dr. Heinsch said, nodding. "Between the orbits of Earth and Mars in about two and a half months. What it does then, of course, is the question."

"We need *definite* confirmations on this before we take *any* action," Dr. Marin said.

"I'm sure we will have those quite quickly. I would request that you contact Palomar for their take. Good day, Doctors."

Planning for shots by the big telescopes of Earth's major countries is blocked out months and even years in advance. They also cost a lot of money.

As the terminator circled about the globe that night, all such scheduling was put on indefinite hold and dozens of telescopes pointed to a very small patch of the sky.

There was, of course, a huge outcry amongst "real" researchers who had grants to study oxygen production of Mira Variables that, naturally, were more important than anything else that could possibly be happening especially with those bunglers at Skywa—A WHAT?

And then the press found out.

"The Gudram Ring has settled into a stationary position in the Sun-Earth L2 Lagrange point," Dr. Heinsch rumbled, looking at his notes. "The position it has taken is not entirely stable but it seems to have some form of stabilization system. Since it was able to maintain delta-V such as to decelerate into the system, that ability is self-evident. However, the L2 point creates a stable point of gravitational interaction which is why so many space telescopes are placed there. Power output for stabilization is, therefore, reduced. As of now, we have no idea as to its method or purpose. Questions?"

"What is it for?" the first reporter asked.

"And I repeat, we have no idea as to its method, we don't know how it works, or its purpose, we don't know why it is here. At this moment, it is as enigmatic as the monolith from 2001 . . ."

"Office of the President. If you would like to leave a message for the President of the United States, press one. For the Vice President, press two. For the First Lady, press three . . ."

The phone bank for the general contact number for the White House was not in the White House. It was in a featureless office building in Reston, Virginia. There a group of seventy receptionists, mostly women, received calls from the general public directed at the President.

In the early days of telephone, all calls were listened to, notes taken and daily they would be collated and tracked. This took a lot of people looking over the notes and figuring out what they meant. But there were general tenors. Do a three-part scale. "I love the President so much I want his sperm." "The President's an idiot." "The President is going to die at four PM on Friday." So then there were standard forms. Then computers came along. And Caller ID and voice recognition and automatic voice synthesis and phone trees and . . .

What the seventy people did was mostly let the computers handle it.

But if you worked the phone tree hard enough, you could get a real human being.

"Office of the President."

"This is not a prank call," a robotic voice said. "This system cannot normally block Caller ID. Please look at your Caller ID."

The receptionist looked at the readout and frowned. The Caller ID readout was a random string of numbers.

"The penalty for hacking the White House is—"

"Please contact your intelligence agencies and confirm that this call is coming from a satellite and has no ground-based transmission. We are the Grtul, the People of the Ring. We come in peace. In five days, on your Thursday, at 12 PM Greenwich Mean Time, we will call your President through a more secure means. This should give him time to clear his schedule. This will be a conference call with several of your major leaders, all of whom have been contacted or will be contacted. Please ensure your President is informed of this call. Thank you. Good-bye."

"So . . . do we know *which* secure line they're calling?" the President asked.

The Secure Room in the White House was, like most of the rooms in the White House, small. And compared to some secure rooms, not particularly secure. It had been repeatedly upgraded but when you started off with a concrete basement in a limestone building built in the 1800s there was only so much you could do. The Joint Chiefs much preferred the Tank in the Pentagon.

"We're ready no matter where it comes in, Mr. President," the chief of staff said. The room was more or less at capacity since nobody knew the agenda for the meeting. State, Defense, the Joint Chiefs, NSA, DNI, himself, even Treasury and Commerce had horned in. About the only member of the "core" cabinet not present was Interior. Surprising even himself, the Director of NASA *had* managed to get a seat.

"Nobody talks but me," the President said just as the phone rang. He took a deep breath and pressed the button for the speaker phone. "President of the United States."

"Waiting . . . Waiting . . . Present are the presidents of the United States and Russia, prime ministers of Britain, France, Germany, Japan, China, India, Brazil. Each have staff present. We will not be responding to questions. We are the Grtul. We come in peace. The ring in your sky is a gate to other worlds. We produce these rings and move them into star systems. Use of the ring requires payment. The payment schedule will be sent to you. There is to be no use of hostile energy systems within three hundred thousand kilometers of the ring which are capable of damaging the ring. Anyone who pays may use the ring.

"In seven days we will make a general broadcast to the people of your planet on the subject of the ring. This will give you sufficient time to make your own statements and prevent panic.

"You have a distributed information system. We will establish a document on the information system which will give the full rules, schedules and regulations of the ring. We will include a list of answers to questions. In the last ninety million years we have been asked most conceivable questions. We will now answer the three most common questions asked and then we will terminate this call.

"By 'anyone can use the ring' do we mean that another species can use it to enter your system? Yes. Does that mean that hostile or friendly forces can use it? Yes. Are you allowed to block the ring? No. Good bye."

"Hell," the President said as the phone went dead. "Those *were* my top questions. NASA? Input?"

"There is a real philosophical question whether there *can* be hostile species at the level to be able to use interstellar travel," the director said. "The energies involved mean that survival as a species if you are innately hostile becomes difficult. If you can create a spacecraft that can go three hundred thousand miles in any reasonable time frame, you can more or less destroy a world. The biosphere at least. Over time, hostile species will tend to wipe themselves out."

"That's a great philosophical point," the Chairman of the Joint Chiefs said. "But the fact that the Grtul mention hostile species and not fighting near the ring probably means you're more or less dead wrong. Pun intended. And according to my people, *we* can't even *get* to this thing."

"Oh, we can get there," the director said. "We're working on a proposal for a manned space craft capable of the journey."

"Time and budget?" the President asked, wincing.

"About five years and . . . well, the budget is still being worked on."

"Under or over a trillion?" the national security advisor asked.

"Oh, under. Probably."

Two Years After First Contact

(NASA has completed preliminary studies to the studies necessary to begin preliminary design phase of the bid phase on a potential ship to reach, but not enter, the Gudram Ring. Cost: $976 million dollars.)

The prime minister of Britain picked up his phone without looking. It was the ringtone of his secretary.

"Yes, Janice?"

"Actually, my name is Andrilae Rirgo of the Glatun. I am the captain of an exploratory vessel which has just exited your Grtul Ring. We come in peace and are interested in trade."

The prime minister looked at the handset then at the phone, which was registering a random string of numbers from the Caller ID. Just as he was getting over the shock the door opened and his secretary started waving her arms frantically. He was able to read her lips well enough to get the words "Gate emergence." The rather graphic hand motions, not to mention his current conversation, helped. He nodded at her and went back to his conversation.

"Well, uh, Mr. . . . Rirgo did you say? Welcome to Earth."

"So we really don't have anything they want?" the President said.

"No, sir," the commerce secretary said. "The computer chips they're offering are centuries more advanced than anything we produce. Enormous storage and something close to infinite parallel processing. They also integrate with terrestrial systems seamlessly. Somehow.

The IT experts are scratching their head as to how. But why they can just take over our systems is now pretty obvious. The chips are more like viruses than computers. But what they mainly want is precious metals. Specifically the platinum group which are pretty rare. Also gold."

"Do we mine those?" the President asked.

"We do in small quantities," Interior said. "More in Canada. Most are extracted from nickel and copper mining. Most of the world's deposits are in South Africa or Russia."

"Damnit."

Three Years After First Contact

"This had better be important," the President said as he entered the Situation Room. The Secret Service had practically yanked him out of a meeting with the Saudi ambassador.

"We've had a gate emergence," the Chairman of the Joint Chiefs said over the video link.

"We've had those every few months for the last year," the President pointed out. "Mostly what I suppose could be tramp freighters, no offense to our Glatun friends intended."

It had quickly become apparent that even tramp freighter captains could access any electronic transmission. This had less to do with the super advanced chips they traded for enormous amounts of heavy metals or anything else that seemed of some worth, than their software systems and implant technology. Efforts to duplicate their information technology had so far been unsuccessful and most experts put humans as at least five hundred years behind current Glatun technology.

"Not Glatun. The ship looks like a warship and isn't responding to our standard hails."

"Is it . . . big?" the President asked. He'd been elected on the basis of his domestic programs and wasn't quite up to speed on international affairs much less interstellar.

"It really doesn't matter how big it is, Mr. President," the admiral in command of Space Command responded. "We still don't get the engineering of Glatun reactionless drive or their power systems. So we're grounded. If it's a warship it's going to be able to hold the orbitals. And who holds the orbitals, holds the world."

"Oh."

"All stocks of precious metals," the secretary of state said. "Private, corporate and governmental. We can keep enough stock of gold to keep the IT industry running but that's it. We pointed out that it would make us more efficient at extraction and they accepted the argument but palladium, which turns out is important for hard drives, has to be turned over. That's for all the world's governments. Or our cities get what Mexico City, Shanghai and Cairo got. Pony up and the Horvath won't nuke the rest of the world."

"Technically they weren't nukes," SpaceCom pointed out. "They were kinetic energy weapons. Practical effect is similar but no fallout, thank God."

"Why those three?" the President asked. "Did they say?"

"No, sir," SpaceCom said. "But if you've ever seen a night shot of the world, it's pretty obvious. They picked the three that are most noticeable. Since we're in a shield room I'll point out that that was a pretty poor choice on their part. I don't think they'd developed full intel on the planet. Doesn't really matter but it's a potential chink in their armor. They're not gods."

"True," the JCS said. "But we also can't fight them. Recommendation of the JCS is that we pay the tribute and try to get the Glatun to intervene. We just *can't* fight them."

"So are we going to have them landing here?" the President asked. "If so there's going to be a major security situation."

"So far we haven't even seen the Horvath," the secretary of state said. "All discussion has been electronic or with their robots. As to where they are landing . . ." She nodded at the secretaries of commerce and interior.

"We and Canada will ship our small amount of production to South Africa, which will handle the transfer," Commerce said. "There will only be landings in South Africa and Russia. And only to pick up refined metals. They appear to want to keep the world running so that we can fill their holds. Not that we can; the whole world's production amounts to a few dozen tons a year."

SpaceCom looked a bit irritated for a moment, possibly because his aide had touched him on the arm, then grunted.

"What I don't get is why they're getting them on the planet," SpaceCom said. "According to my experts, most of this stuff is to be found in asteroids. We've got a ton of asteroids just cluttering up the damned system. Most of what we mine is from asteroids that have crashed into the Earth. Why not just mine the asteroid belt?"

"Possibly because then slaves don't do it for them," the President said dryly.

"It's a matter of what your world calls realpolitik," the Glatun representative said politely. The Glatun was a bit over a meter-and-a-half-tall biped with blue skin, red eyes, a vaguely piglike head and snout and a mane of white fur running down his back. He was dressed in an informal tunic for the discussion which was, in diplospeak, "non-binding and informal." Which was where all the really serious binding resolutions were always hammered out.

"We have called for the Horvath to remove themselves from your world's orbitals and they have chosen to ignore our requests. Since Earth is, to them, a very good conquest, relatively rich in heavy metals compared to Horvath, they won't leave absent either armed confrontation or, possibly, a trade embargo. Since Earth has, essentially, little or no value to the Glatun Federation, we have a sufficiency of strategic metals, and there are negative aspects to both choices on our part we must unfortunately state that we remain neutral in this dispute."

"We have . . . an extensive asteroid belt," the undersecretary of state for interstellar affairs said, throwing in her only bone. "We believe it to be rich in the platinum group."

"For which you should be grateful," the Glatun replied. "Most inhabited systems are mined out. However, our laws, and long experience, prevent us from mining your asteroid belt as long as there is not a centralized, or at least effectively sovereign, system government. The Horvath meet the definition, not the United States of America. Certainly not the UN. The Horvath have, also, offered the asteroid belt. Be equally grateful that we declined that offer. There are enormous problems with asteroid mining. It requires quite large lasers and fabbers and is fuel and energy intensive. To make it worthwhile for a Glatun corporation to invest in this system would require long-term leases. In the current security and political situation the Glatun Federation would not permit such legally binding contracts."

"We're on our own." The USSIA finally said, becoming decidedly informal. "We have sixteen million dead, three major cities in ashes and you're *neutral*?"

"Since we are speaking frankly . . ." the Glatun said. "The decision of our policy makers is that Earth is simply sufficiently unknown and unnoticeable to take the chance of losing credibility in a minor dispute. The reality is that the Horvath, who are not much more advanced than Earth, would probably leave if so much as a single Glatun destroyer entered the system and ordered them to do so. However, if they didn't and shots were fired, much less loss of Glatun life, there would be questions asked in Parliament, AI queries and of course the press would simply go wild. It is easier and safer to do nothing. Absent Earth becoming more of a hot-topic in the Glatun Federation or becoming in some way strategically important, yes, you are on your own."

—end excerpt—

from *Live Free or Die*
available in hardcover,
February 2010, from Baen Books